Split the Party

By Drew Hayes

Acknowledgements

This one goes out to all the GMs out there, putting up with rules lawyers, unpredictable groups, and more diplomacy checks than anyone should ever have to deal with. Without you, there would be no game, so thanks for making them happen.

Also big thanks to my beta readers. To Bill Hammond, Antoine, Priscilla Yuen, and E Ramos E. You all gave me +5 Competence and Confidence when tackling this CR 20 project.

Prologue

Moonlight glowed on the shovel's silver surface as it dropped the last load of dirt. Careful hands reached down and smoothed the pile, tenderly blending the corners so that it looked like no more than a misshapen lump of earth amidst hundreds of its brethren. He rose from his crouch and surveyed his work, making certain to note every detail of the surroundings.

There was nothing to mark the hole he'd dug, no telltale sign hinting at the treasure buried below the soft bump in the earth's surface. This, they had all agreed, was the best way. Build a treacherous dungeon or hire an unassailable guard and it was just a matter of time before the adventurers were drawn in, seeking a prize despite knowing nothing about what it was. Anonymity was the greatest defense they possessed. This spot would have no treasure map, no legends surrounding it, no indication at all that one of the most powerful artifacts in the known world was carefully tucked several feet down in the soil. Taking it a step further, only one of them would know of the spot where it was buried. If he should pass, then the secret would go with him.

Brushing his hands clean, he stowed the shovel atop his backpack and slung it heavily over his shoulder. It would take him half a day to rejoin his group, and he was eager to begin the journey. Despite all assurances that these woods were as safe as one could find, he still felt ill-at-ease without the others to watch his back. The only true weapons he had were a short sword, slightly enchanted armor, and his natural stealth.

He hurried across the grass, quickly vanishing into the trees. For the first several miles, he could still feel the artifact calling to him, beckoning for him to come retrieve it and keep it close. The temptation was real, but far from overpowering. Anything that could reach into his head and speak directly to him was an item he preferred to have at a distance, even if circumstances hadn't demanded they hide it.

In the grove behind him, moonlight continued to fall upon the recently turned earth. No sudden tremors signified a rising of the object, nor did a mysterious shadow fall across the mound. It sat, undisturbed, as the sky eventually lightened and the sun broke into dawn. There it would sit for a very long time, just as had been intended.

But, of course, nothing ever stayed buried forever. It just wasn't how the world was designed.

Chapter 1

"There's no beer in the fridge!"

Everyone at the table heard a door slam shut. Stomping filled the air as a tall woman with a nose ring and dyed purple hair entered the kitchen. She scanned the room quickly, locking her eyes on a young man who already looked exasperated as he set up the cardboard screen in front of his books and dice.

"Russell! What the hell? How is there no beer at a *Spells, Swords, and Stealth* game?"

Adjusting his glasses carefully and already regretting certain decisions he'd made, Russell responded in the measured tone of a man who knows he will have to ration his patience carefully throughout the day. "There's no beer because none of the rest of us are twenty-one yet."

"So? That never stopped my old group from scrounging up some authentic refreshments."

"Light beer is hardly what I'd call 'authentic,' and besides, we aren't playing with your old group," Russell told her. "Cheri, you're the one who wanted to play while home from college, and that's fine, but we are playing my kind of game. One that involves cordialness and sobriety."

"For the record, I actually am twenty-one." A tall, broad-shouldered man raised his hand gently, careful not to hit the table and upset all the dice he'd laid out in front of him. "I didn't bring any beer, though. Alexis said chips and soda would be fine."

"You didn't even need to do that, Bert, though we appreciate the hospitality," Russell replied.

"At least I'm not the only one over the drinking age," Cheri grumbled, sliding into her seat next to the sole other person she knew, Russell's friend Tim. He was hunched over his character sheet, poring

3

through each detail with exceptional scrutiny. Cheri remembered when she'd obsessed about every aspect of her characters like that, but after five years of playing, her "technique" had mostly become a system of rolling her stats and then finding the best assortment of features to maximize her usefulness.

"Russell didn't say it was a requirement when he asked us to play." This came from the other woman at the table, whose wispy brown hair hung down in front of her eyes, blocking most of her expression from view. Her voice was quiet, so soft it was easy to miss if she spoke when others were talking.

"Nothing to worry about, Alexis; drinking is neither demanded nor encouraged at my gaming sessions. I do not want a repeat of dealing with my last group's shenanigans."

"Aw, did my widdle brother forget how to properly corral his party?" Cheri asked. "I can still take over and run the game, if you like."

"I'd prefer if you just focused on getting your character made," Russell replied, resisting the powerful urge to remind Cheri that she'd kept her party "corralled" by all but forcing them onto the paths she wanted them to take.

"Psh, I finished that in five minutes." Cheri held up a character sheet for the table to see, which did indeed have every section and slot filled out appropriately. "Chalara the sorceress. Give me a little credit here, I'm not rolling elves."

"I'm sorry, rolling elves?" Bert looked confused and flipped through the book in front of him, clearly trying to find source material for the term. As the only one at the table with zero experience playing an RPG, Bert had spent the night before studying as much as possible and was perturbed to think there was something he'd missed.

"It's slang for being a new player," Russell explained. "Most first-time players try to create, or 'roll up,' an elf, regardless of whether it fits their character or not. They're sort of the default iconic race of fantasy. There's nothing wrong with them, by the way, if that's what you were thinking of making."

"I'm an elf," Alexis said softly. "Her name is Gelthorn, and she's a forest warrior."

"I getcha." Bert closed the book in his hand and smiled, relief evident on his face. "They are pretty cool characters, but I actually went with a gnome. Her name is Wimberly, and she's a gadgeteer."

Cheri snorted loudly and then looked around, waiting for others to join her mirth. "Oh, come on, that's funny. This guy looks like he could squat my car and he's playing a female gnome who uses traps and gizmos?"

"It's a role-playing game. The whole point is that you can be anyone or thing you want to be," Russell shot back, his veneer of patience beginning to wear thin. If not for the fact that Cheri had let him play in her groups when he was still learning, he likely would have refused her entrance. But she had, so he owed her. Plus, everything in his new module was designed for a four-person party. "Personally, I commend Bert for such an interesting choice."

"Truthfully, I didn't do it because it was interesting as much as because the gnomes can—"

"Done!" Tim slammed down his mechanical pencil so hard that the table, and many of the dice sitting on it, shook in response. He looked around, suddenly sheepish as he realized what a spectacle he'd made of himself. "Whoops. Sorry, everyone. I was just a little excited."

"I take it from your outburst that Timanuel the paladin has finally been completed?" Russell asked.

"He has indeed. Sorry it took so long; I really wanted to find the right god for him to serve. After a lot of research, I decided that would be Longinus: god of valor and heroics."

5

"Also known as the default paladin god everyone picks," Cheri said in a mock-whisper.

"I'm sure it's a good fit for a lot of other players, too." Tim patted his sheet gleefully, refusing to let Russell's sister bring him down. After months of trying to find new players, they finally had a group again, and at long last he was going to get to try his hand at playing paladin. Not even Cheri's trademark snark could tarnish his joy in that moment.

"Well then, since all of you now have characters, I guess it's time to decide which interesting rumor your party decides to pursue." The sound of pages rustling filled the air as Russell rifled through his new module for the kingdom of Alcatham. He'd spent weeks trying to get his hands on one of the limited edition copies produced by a small company, coming up fruitless for attempt after attempt. Then, two weeks prior—just before they met Alexis at the comic shop and got her to join, along with her friend Bert—a copy had shown up at Russell's door. It cited a pre-order number that turned up gibberish on the internet, but he figured he must have signed up for it when he got the first module. That was the only explanation that made sense, anyway.

"As your party journeys across the borders from the neighboring kingdom of Thatchshire, you hear tales of magical and unnatural happenings across the land of Alcatham. To the north, it is said a mighty dragon is amassing many magical items in its hoard, leading some to speculate that it has a greater plan than merely gathering wealth. To the east, there are tales of a town that uncovered a strange, mystical artifact which is causing many to fall ill. And to the west, there are stories of a wizard's tower that has sprung up next to the city of Everend, along with an influx of monsters not native to the area suddenly populating its woods."

"Dragon, has to be the dragon, dragon all day, let's kill a damn dragon!" Cheri thrust her finger into the air like the tip of a spear, already bent on an imaginary charge for her dragon foe.

"No way, he's not a big threat right now," Tim countered. "The town full of sick people seems a lot more pressing. We need to help them."

"Sick people have rags and phlegm. Dragons have mountains of treasure, magical items, and possibly even an ultra-rare trinket or two."

"I'm actually going to vote that we go for the wizard's tower," Bert said. "It's bound to have lots of loot, plus it poses an imminent danger to the population of the nearby city, which I'm assuming is bigger than a town."

"Your assumption is correct," Russell confirmed.

"So, we save more people, still get loot, and are dealing with a complex situation that will allow for various tactics. It's a win all around," Bert concluded.

"Which of the three is nearest to a forest?" Alexis asked.

"Roll a Geographic Awareness check," Russell instructed.

Alexis complied, revealing an eighteen on the dice. Russell knew that was plenty high enough, even before she looked up her modifier.

"The wizard's tower sits on a cliff above the town and next to a massive, sprawling forest."

"Then I vote tower."

"That's two for tower, one for dragon, and one for sick town," Russell announced, tallying the votes by ticking off fingers. "Anyone want to change their votes?"

"Tower works fine, as long as there's a fat reward at the end," Cheri muttered.

"I guess, as long as I'm helping people in need, Longinus will probably be okay with my actions," Tim said.

"All right then, your party heads west, leaving the dragon unchecked and the town of sick people on their own."

Russell was right about his party's direction, and it was true that the dragon would continue its amassing of wealth freely for some time to come. However, he was wrong about the town of sick villagers: there was another party already en route to their location.

Though, calling them "helpful" might have been a stretch.

*   *   *

"Can someone please explain to me why we're heading to a place where people are suffering from a magical sickness when none of us has any protection from getting magically sick?" Gabrielle shifted in her saddle, trying to get more command of the old, apathetic horse they'd bought at the last trading post the group went through.

"I can come at it from a variety of angles, if you'd so like." Thistle was riding with Grumph, who was the only one to purchase a steed still in semi-peak condition. It had been necessary in order to find one capable of supporting his sizable frame, and adding Thistle's weight to the mount had been no more than the equivalent of tacking on an extra saddlebag.

"From an exploratory perspective, we're searching for magical items with ill-defined properties, and whatever the town of Briarwillow uncovered fits that bill, at least based on rumors. From a safety perspective, we're hiding from the mad king of Solium, and riding toward a plague is a move even he is unlikely to anticipate. From a moral perspective, I am a paladin, and there is some chance that my healing could offer aid. And lastly, but far from leastly, there's the basic sanity perspective. Based on the rumors we've picked up from various traders, going north takes us to a greedy dragon, which is probable death. Northwest is a wizard's tower and heaps of monsters, which is even more probable death. South would take us back to Solium, and that's certain death, so that only leaves us going northeast, which is only a semi-probable death."

8

"You left out staying still," Eric reminded him. His horse was also old and slow, though that didn't bother Eric as much as it did Gabrielle. He saw the value in caution, especially when riding a road of which they had no knowledge. His dark eyes were constantly scanning the road, searching for any signs of a trap or ambush lying in wait. After several peaceful weeks, he could feel the itch of paranoia pecking at his brain.

"Ah yes, staying still; the course in which the forces of King Liadon are certain to find us, and we once again arrive at certain death," Thistle added. "All in all, not a great array of options lay before us."

Gabrielle adjusted her grip on the saddle once more, shifting the weight of the hefty axe strapped to her back. "There's also the option of fighting, you know. We're not exactly helpless. We can send Liadon's men back in pieces."

"Killing men in Liadon's employ would just tell him where you were, which means he would send more. Not to mention it would place whatever town you were staying at in danger, and wasn't that what you started all this to avoid?" Timuscor's voice was hesitant as he plodded along slightly behind. Despite his handsome face and powerful frame, he was the least confident of any of them. Perhaps it was because he was still coming to terms with the insanity they had told him about the world, or it was due to not having tested himself in battle as they had. Regardless, the party had learned that when Timuscor did find the courage to speak, it was worthwhile to listen.

"Well put," Grumph grunted with his usual loquaciousness. Between him and Timuscor, it was possible for whole days to pass with nary a single word uttered. No one was certain if that made them the best of friends or utter strangers, but it did mean that when they took the night-watch shifts, everyone else slept a lot more soundly.

"And that ignores the fact that right now, one of the few things in our favor is Liadon having scarce resources, since he sent so many adventurers to their death in that dungeon. While his agents are few, we have to get as far away as possible. If we can find a safe place to hole up,

9

all the better, but the longer we stay close to Solium, the greater our danger," Thistle said.

"Fine, I get it: we're going to the sick town. What are we really hoping for, though? That Thistle can cure everyone with a clap of his hands and, oh yeah, that they're also holding a piece of . . . well, you know." Gabrielle, like the rest of her group, avoided saying the name of the artifact out loud whenever possible. There was always the chance that someone with real power was listening for just such an utterance, and the last thing they wanted was to bring that person's attention down on their group.

"It would be nice; however, I should point out that I don't really heal them. I am merely a conduit for Grumble's power," Thistle told her. "But no, most likely we'll find some cursed object making everyone sick, at which point we'll either try and break it or get as far away as possible. So long as we all survive and don't leave a trail for the mad king to follow, I'll call either scenario a win."

Eric sighed and scanned the road once more, trying not to dwell on Thistle's statement. What bothered him wasn't the bleakness of such a meager goal, or the unknown elements waiting for them further down the Alcatham roads.

It was that, deep down, he knew Thistle was actually being overly optimistic.

Chapter 2

Briarwillow had started out as a simple trading post, not unlike many of the ones the party had already passed through in their fleeing of Solium. Those who settled down there quickly discovered that the soil was of exceptional quality, though. Once they also factored in proximity to the nearby stream, the mild climate, and the nearby mountains providing moderate protection from monster attacks, it became clear that Briarwillow was actually quite the prime location. Within two generations it had swollen exponentially, surpassing trading post, skipping right over village, and finally reaching the status of a reasonable town.

Like most such places not filled with those who fought magical beasts for a living, farming was the primary occupation of most of the town's inhabitants. It was for this reason that the party's weary horses set foot on land technically considered to be part of Briarwillow a full half-day's plodding ride before they ever laid eyes on the town proper.

Winding roads ran between fields dotted with half-grown wheat and corn. At first, it was an almost beautiful, homey view, but after the second hour every member of the group except Timuscor remembered why they'd never gone riding in the fields around Maplebark: the view got very monotonous very quickly.

Despite not being farmers themselves, the adventurers did notice a few things that seemed out of place. Birds were gorging themselves unchecked, and masses of weeds were springing up in the fields at irregular intervals. It wasn't exactly a dragon's shadow flying overhead in terms of omens, but everyone did move their hands just a few inches closer to their weapons as they rode. Sick, weakened townsfolk made easy pickings for monsters and bandits. And given how far the rumors of Briarwillow's struggles had traveled, it would have been folly to trust they were the first to ride its weakened roads.

By the time the town finally came into Eric's sight, his sharp eyes spotting the familiar outline of buildings as they crested a hill, he felt like his whole back was going to snap under the amount of tension he was carrying in it. Always braced for the attack that never came, always on the edge of a cliff that never fell out from under him, Eric realized he was either going to have to find a way to internalize his stress or buy a far more comfortable saddle; otherwise, he'd be hunched over like a broken tree in under a year's time.

"That strikes me as a bit odd." Thistle had wormed his way around to the side, where he could gaze past Grumph's back and get a view of the town they were heading toward. "Given how much neglect we saw in the fields, I'd expected to come upon a near ghost town. That place seems to be positively bustling."

Eric saw that Thistle was right in one quick glance. Dozens of people appeared to be milling about in the town square, with even more rushing about between buildings at irregular intervals. He strained his ears and could pick out the strangest selection of notes fluttering through the air.

"Does anyone else hear music?" Eric asked.

"Aye, picked that up a few moments ago." Thistle might have the smallest, most misshapen body of the lot, but his awareness was second only to Eric's. Unlike the human, though, it was a learned skill rather than a natural gift. Being a gnome with a crooked body and no talent for magic had necessitated that Thistle either stay constantly abreast of his surroundings or find himself in a deadly situation.

"I kind of hear it now." Gabrielle tilted her head slightly, golden hair falling down past her ears. "It's . . . familiar. Sort of like the songs we played during the harvest celebrations."

"I do believe you're correct," Thistle said. "Which is all the more perplexing, as harvesting seems to be the furthest thing from what they're doing in those fields."

"Maybe they're celebrating people feeling better," Timuscor proposed.

"Maybe." Grumph's voice didn't carry much hope, or if it did, it was the half-orc sort of hope that mostly centered on quick deaths and full stomachs.

"You know, it is always possible that other adventurers came through here before us and fixed the problem," Eric said. "We know better than most how many of them are out there. This could be the town celebrating being saved."

Thistle nodded, albeit slowly. "If that's the case, then we best resupply, grab some quick rest, and get back on the road. Crowds are bad for fugitives, and I'm never one to trust the good mood after a curse is beaten. Seen one too many of them toss out an aftereffect as a parting gift."

"We could always just ride through the town entirely," Gabrielle suggested.

"Sadly, I fear our foodstuffs are a bit lean, and by all accounts it's another week's ride north to the next trading post. Unlike Solium and its density, Alcatham is a sprawling kingdom. We could turn west toward Cadence Hollow if we had to, though a city that size is something fugitives are best off avoiding." No one asked why Thistle was familiar with this kingdom's terrain. All but Timuscor knew the gnome had once traveled with a party of adventurers, so his curiously broad knowledge was simply dismissed as one of his peculiarities.

"Perhaps we'll get lucky and it's just an honest-to-goodness celebration," Eric said. "We had those all the time back in Maplebark."

"Aye, we did indeed." Thistle said nothing more as he slid back into the saddle behind Grumph. It would take Eric—all of them, really—time to understand that more came with being an adventurer than mere danger and treasure. The very world seemed to react to the presence of adventurers differently, filling their paths with coincidence, plot, and potential death. Were they still simply Maplebark denizens playing at their roles, they might very well have happened upon a village's earnest celebrations. But since they had accepted the mantles of their once-lies as truths, he strongly doubted they would have such fortune.

Adventurers simply didn't possess that sort of luck.

*   *   *

While Briarwillow wasn't having a full-blown festival, there could be no doubt that a celebration was certainly under way. The town square was dotted with tables laden down by food and mugs of ale. A makeshift company of farmers who'd once dreamed of traveling as bards were gathered in the center, playing their formerly-stowed instruments with the fervor of those who are drunk on the joy of creating art. Shops had their doors wide open as people came and went, laughing with friends and strangers alike as the mood of the town seemed to virtually bubble with exuberance.

"I don't trust it," Thistle muttered softly, words quiet enough that only Grumph could hear him. The others were smart, strong, and brave, but they lacked experience in playing things close to the vest. Until he knew the situation, Thistle was determined to keep his suspicions to himself. No sense in wrongly worrying the others, or in making them so nervous that they started trouble on their own.

"Oh my gods . . . do you all smell that?" Eric was leaning so far forward that his ancient horse was bending slightly, its weary legs not ready for the shift in weight. "That's food. Real, cooked food. Does anyone even remember the last time we ate something that wasn't dried or hastily roasted above a fire?"

"Grumph managed to make a stew about . . . let's see . . . three weeks ago," Gabrielle reminded him.

"And delectable as that was, I think we can all agree it wasn't a substitute for real, delicious cooking." Eric pulled himself back into his saddle through sheer force of will alone. His senses buzzed with all the

14

activity and his mind whirred as it calculated different places they might be attacked from. As much as he wanted, *needed*, to unwind and enjoy some real cooking, it was a luxury they couldn't afford.

"Seems to me there's only one thing to do," Thistle said. "Let's stable the horses and see if we can trade these lovely people a few coins for some of that food."

"Shouldn't we be more careful than that?" Timuscor asked.

"Seeing as we have to buy supplies here anyway, we're already working off the assumption that the food won't be poisoned. Plus, everyone else seems to be eating it just fine. There is always the chance that they're either all immune to an ingredient or too far gone to care, but trying to get past here without stocking up is going to have us risking starvation in the woods. If I have to court death, I'll take the quick one over a lingering, painful experience."

"Only Thistle could make eating at a town we know was recently plagued by magical sickness seem like the rational choice," Gabrielle sighed. They were quickly drawing near to the town's actual streets; already, heads were turning and children were pointing at their approach. Whatever plan they decided on needed to be set before arrival. Since she trusted Thistle's judgment, and had no better ideas to offer, Gabrielle decided to follow the gnome's instructions.

"I see plenty of places to post the horses while we find out where the stables are. Should we split up and investigate?"

"Much as I am loath to do so in an unfamiliar environment, I fear it may be the only way," Thistle said. "Gathering information and supplies are our highest priorities, and handling them independently of one another will allow us to exit the town quickly, should the need arise."

"Grumph and I can handle getting the supplies," Eric volunteered. One might have assumed that he was bringing the half-orc along as the designated pack mule, but nothing could be further from the truth. As the only one of them to have actually run a business, Grumph possessed the best knowledge of what items were actually worth and how to haggle the seller down to that number.

"I can help carry things as well," Timuscor volunteered. Although he had bravery enough to face a hoard of veilpanthers or a small dragon, Timuscor balked at the idea of having to talk with lots of people. His social skills had never been particularly well-developed, as his training had always centered on how to dispatch an opponent before they could kill him.

"Which leaves Gabrielle and I to schmooze the townsfolk and uncover exactly what is going on," Thistle said. He'd have preferred Grumph for a situation like this one, but Gabrielle made a solid backup choice. Her skill with the axe was growing every day, and years of pretending to be a polite, proper young lady of society had taught her the art of selling a lie.

"Do we have a plan for if something is secretly amiss?" Eric asked.

"I guess if we can run from it, we do, and if we can't, we try to kill it," Gabrielle replied. "You know, our usual."

"If that's our usual, then we should really work on that first part. By my recollection, we seem to get drawn into the fighting more than we escape from it," Eric pointed out.

"Well, we are all relatively new at this," Thistle said. "Now, everyone put on big smiles and act friendly. Whatever may be going on here, we're far more likely to get answers as jovial travelers than suspicious adventurers." To sell the point, Thistle leaned out from Grumph's side and gave a merry wave to the children who were staring unabashedly at the approaching party. The adults were also watching, but they at least had the politeness to pretend they weren't.

The others followed his lead, donning large grins and greeting the villagers as they approached. Grumph was the only exception, as he'd long ago learned that a smiling half-orc looked more like it was baring teeth in preparation for attack rather than conveying joy. Instead, he pulled in on himself, doing the best he could to seem less physically imposing. It was a trick he'd all but mastered throughout his younger years, though he was a bit out of practice.

Grumph had just about gotten it right as the horses' hooves clacked off the worn stones of the town's streets, signaling their true arrival in Briarwillow.

*   *   *

Stabling the horses proved to be a quick affair, as the rosy-cheeked young boy who took them cheerfully informed them that travelers had become all but nonexistent in recent weeks. The stories of a whole town driven ill by a mystical plague had sent those who were wiser and less desperate than Eric and his friends in alternate directions. There was no sign of illness in the lad as he leapt about, moving with an energy that almost bordered on manic. Within moments, he'd collected a few coins for his service and was leading the horses into a sturdy, well cared for barn.

"Maybe it's just me, but that did not seem like someone who'd been recently ill," Timuscor muttered. He unconsciously adjusted his armor, along with the shield strapped to his back. As the only member of the party with formal training, Timuscor had ingrained habits that made certain his shield was always ready to grab and his sword was always in easy reach.

"It's not just you." Eric glanced around the town, noting the bustling array of villagers. They were darting about hurriedly, wide— almost too-wide—grins plastered to their faces. It reminded him of something, but he couldn't quite put his finger on it. "Still, I suppose this is better than a whole town of people at death's door."

"Death has many doors." Grumph began walking down the street slowly, making sure his movements couldn't be interpreted by anyone as

17

threatening. Eric and Timuscor followed behind, noting the exuberance that seemed to have infected every person they saw.

The walk from the stables to a large shop that sold smoked meats was a short one, made a touch longer by the pains in their bellies that the drifting smells caused. Thistle had not exaggerated the shortness of their supplies, and the last few days' meals had been little more than a few bites of stale bread and dried meat. Monsters and animals alike had grown scarcer as they drew near Briarwillow, a fact that everyone had noticed and no one had commented on.

Eric took the lead, entering the shop and barely stepping aside in time as a gaggle of bright-faced children darted past him, hands filled with various meat treats. He then quickly found the shop's proprietor, a wide man with the standard Briarwillow grin. The owner waved them over toward the counter with large, exaggerated motions that sent small droplets of sweat cascading off his arm. Eric was momentarily perplexed by the sweat, until he remembered the man worked around fire all day. That would drive anyone to shed moisture.

"Good afternoon, sir," Eric greeted, for the sun was indeed on its downward slope through the sky. "We've come to see about purchasing some of your wares for the journey ahead." Through trial and error, they had learned that having Grumph speak first could take people off guard, and be interpreted as unintentionally intimidating. Haggling worked better if they let someone else open the dialogue, see if the merchant charged a fair price. If they didn't, then Grumph got involved, and there was nothing unintentional about his intimidation when he haggled.

"Travelers, eh? We haven't gotten any of your ilk for some time. Of course, that was when the plague beset us, so I can hardly blame you all for keeping a distance." The man laid his sweaty palms on the thick wooden board that ran the length of his countertop. His face was slightly flushed, just like the stable boy. Just like almost all of the town's folk, Eric was realizing.

"You've got a touch of luck traveling with you, though. If you'd come three days ago, I'd have had almost nothing to sell. But then a miracle hit our humble hamlet. The plague broke, all at once; no doubt thanks to the intervention of the gods themselves. After we decided to celebrate with the festival, I started cooking up every scrap of meat I could find. Let me get you a few samples so you can see what you like best." The man turned and began lumbering into the back, droplets of sweat falling down the back of his bald head.

Something wasn't right. Eric could feel heat coming from the back, but the man was sweating like he was standing over a campfire. And his skin . . . a flushed complexion made sense on a stable boy who worked in the sun. On a man who spent his life indoors, though, it was peculiar. Then there was the way everyone was acting. Too energetic, too cheerful. It was like the time his mother had taken ill and he'd caught her outside trying to box one of the sheep. In fact, they looked exactly like his mother had that day.

"It's a fever," Eric said, quiet enough that he hoped only Grumph and Timuscor would hear. "That sickness didn't lift at all. It just turned into a fever. And it seems like it's infecting every single person in this town."

"I'm not a physician, nor a cleric, nor any kind of healer," Timuscor said. "But I have to imagine that can't be a good thing."

Grumph nodded slowly, letting the idea sink in. "Definitely not good. For them, or us."

Chapter 3

Thistle had a bad feeling in his stomach. It wasn't some strange pang of intuition making itself known through discomfort; there was no need for anything as subtle as that. He was keenly aware something was amiss, and after a few moments of gazing into glassy-eyes, too-wide smiles, and flushed faces, he'd quickly put together that the "miracle" everyone seemed to celebrating was in fact little more than a new type of sickness.

The bad feeling certainly wasn't hunger either, as he had already helped himself to an array of dishes that were set out for the townspeople to enjoy, and had gone back multiple times for meat pies from a woman with great culinary talent. If he was going to get ill here, Thistle was determined to at least gain some pleasure from the manner of his infection. He was also reasonably certain that being a chosen servant of Grumble offered him a hardier constitution than most. At the very least, he'd been the only one not to get stomach pains after they let Timuscor try his hand at trail cooking during their travels. Then again, that could have been mere coincidence. Being a paladin didn't exactly come with a handbook.

Gabrielle seemed to be aware of the strangeness too, her hand twitching involuntarily whenever one of the grinning, slightly sweaty townsfolk drew too near. He knew she was resisting the urge to rest her hand on the axe strapped carefully to her back. In truth, Thistle had been holding out a slim hope that this town might have a still-functioning blacksmith, as the axe Gabrielle had lifted from the dead adventurer in Grumph's tavern had taken quite a beating during their travels. Between the scales of the demons and the rough hide of a transformed wizard, Gabrielle's axe bore many nicks and dings. She was the only one still wielding a pilfered weapon, although if it wasn't repaired soon, Thistle doubted that would be the case for many more weeks. Sadly, it seemed her equipment issue would have to wait, as, at the moment, information trumped finding a smith.

Weaving through the celebrating citizens, Thistle found his way to a small alcove in front of one of the shops, where chairs had been set beneath an awning for the older members of the town to rest in. They would be the true font of information in Briarwillow, if one existed. Thistle had always been perplexed over why roaming adventurers stopping in Maplebark invariably came to Grumph or the local guard captain to ask about rumors in the surrounding area. Grumph had a bar to run, and the guard captain had men to command. The elderly had no such responsibilities. All they did, and all they wanted to do, was gossip.

"Afternoon, my fine gentlemen." Thistle resisted the urge to try and climb into one of the free chairs beside the two older men. This was done in part out of deference to the fact that one of their number may yet come to occupy the seat, but also because he had no desire to put on the show of a gnome struggling to pull himself up into a human chair. He was here to probe, not entertain.

"That's the time of day all right," muttered one of the men, wisps of white hair protruding from his scalp in all directions. Despite the fact that he too wore rosy cheeks and a sheen of sweat, the persistent good humor of Briarwillow seemed to have passed over his scowling countenance.

"Ignore Kendal," said the other old man, whose bald head would have gleamed brightly were it not covered by the awning's shadow. "He's always like this. I'm Gurt, and it's my pleasure to welcome you to Briarwillow, fair travelers. You've come at the best possible time, you know."

"So I can see," Thistle said. He shuffled himself over slightly, moving a touch closer to Kendal and Gurt without seeming to. This act both pulled him in for easier discussion and hopefully made him seem friendlier. People liked feeling as though they were drawing others in, after all. "I am Thistle, and this is my friend Gabrielle. We're making our way through your kingdom, and must say we were quite surprised to find your town in this state. Can you tell us what's actually gone on here?

21

There are rumors running up and down the Alcatham road, but it seems none of what we've heard is accurate."

"The rumors ain't the thing that's wrong," Kendal spat.

"Well, that would depend on which rumors you heard," Gurt added quickly. "Please, enlighten us to the story you were told, and I can correct you as inconsistencies come up."

"Certainly." Thistle glanced up at Gabrielle, who gave a gentle nod. He wanted her to jump in if she had a thought, but Thistle had been chosen to act as the group's voice on most occasions. It was his duty to spin the yarns, even if they were composed from threads of truth.

"As it was told to us, some of your neighbors were excavating a small cave at the foot of the mountains when they came across a mysterious object. Within a day of their bringing it back to town, much of the populace had fallen ill. No alchemist or herb was found that could break the sickness, which left its victims confined to their beds, sick with pain and exhaustion. Thus, it was determined to be magical and likely caused by the object your people found."

Kendal snorted. "Makes it seem so pretty and simple to hear it put like that. Skims over how many we had to bury, how much that damned skull took from us."

"Excuse me, did you say skull?" Gabrielle asked.

"Your story is fairly accurate," Gurt said, meeting Gabrielle's eyes so she knew he'd heard her question. "But there were several details lost in the passing of the tale. For one thing, yes, the object uncovered was indeed a skull. It was pitch black, with runes etched up and down every inch of its bony exterior. The other mistake is that the people who found it were not our townsfolk. They were travelers, seeking rare minerals they hoped to find in the mountain's foothills. We gave them lodging, because that is what a town with an inn does, after all." Gurt's cheerful, feverish face clouded over slightly. "Had they told us what they found that day, had they shown us what they unearthed, we would never have allowed them to set foot in Briarwillow with such an object."

"I see. So they brought this plague upon you without your knowledge. May I ask what became of these people?"

"Dead, all three of them." This time, Kendal actually did spit after he spoke, as if trying to hack the taste of the words out of his mouth. "Along with anyone else who touched that damn skull. Thing was cursed beyond cursed. We found them, and it, dead the morning after they brought it into our town."

"You said it 'was' cursed," Gabrielle noted. "Did you manage to destroy it?"

"Sadly, no," Gurt told her. "We originally planned to call a priest from Alcatham's capital to come look at it, hoping they might find a way to break the curse and cure us. But on the third day of the plague, when our mayor opened the chest he'd locked the skull in—to draft a thorough description—it had vanished. None of the guards saw a thing, and the chest was undamaged. As near as we could figure, it simply didn't want to be locked away. At first, we thought its leaving would weaken the hold it had over our town. The coming weeks dispelled us of that optimistic notion."

"Yet you all seem to have reason to celebrate now," Thistle pointed out.

Gurt's feverish face brightened once again. "That's right! A priest of Longinus came through several days ago, leading us in endless hours of prayer and ritual to cleanse our town of the taint that was destroying us. That night, a green light shone down from the stars, and when morning broke, the plague had lifted. We could move and laugh and live once more."

"A priest of Longinus? That may be our good fortune as well; we could certainly benefit from counsel with one powerful enough to break such a curse." Thistle didn't consider this to be a lie, as anyone swinging that kind of magic around really would be beneficial to talk with.

"Skipped town after the deed was done." Kendal scratched absentmindedly at the wooden armrest of his chair. Shallow grooves were already there, a testament to how many times he'd indulged in this strange action.

"Yes, when the priest saw that we were healed, he returned to the road once more, saying there were more in need of his service," Gurt confirmed. "He was heading west and left around this time two days ago, so if you ride hard, you may be able to catch up with him, should your need be dire."

"While I appreciate it, I'm afraid my friends and I are going in another direction. Perhaps you could tell me, though, what name did this priest have? I shall keep an ear to the ground for him in our travels." Thistle indeed planned to listen quite hard for this mysterious traveling priest, though whether he would run toward or away from the man would depend on what happened to this town once the fever had done its work.

Gurt shook his bald head, nearly putting the would-be-gleaming dome in the sunlight's path. "I'm afraid the priest gave us no name. He said that the truly dedicated servants of the gods wore no names of their own; they existed only as tools for their gods to use. Said we could think of him as Longinus's finger, reaching down from the heavens to bless us with salvation."

As Gurt spoke, Thistle felt his entire body try to seize up. He did his best to hide it, but there was no doubt in his mind Gabrielle had noticed the tension wracking his bones. Kendal also seemed to be paying him more attention than before, studying the gnome with sudden interest. If there was one thing Thistle knew well, it was when to retreat, and that moment had come for him. Plus, the pain in his stomach was growing worse by the second, and he was beginning to harbor a few suspicions about what that might mean.

"Well, gentlemen, we thank you for your time and story. We must regroup with our friends and see about getting supplies. Congratulations on the miraculous recovery, and I wish you and your town only the best from here on." Thistle turned without waiting for them to return his goodbye, or even to see if Gabrielle was following. He was just off, walking as quickly as his crooked gnome legs would permit him to without breaking into a full run.

Gabrielle caught up to him in a few strides, saying nothing, but shooting an expression of curiosity that was impossible to mistake.

"Later," Thistle whispered. "When we're back with the others and somewhere safe. If my suspicions are right, I do not want prying ears to overhear this conversation."

With a quick nod, Gabrielle accepted his explanation and the two headed off toward more of the shops. The information gathering was done, so far as Thistle was concerned. He knew all too well about the order of priests that sacrificed their names.

And they did not serve the god of heroics.

*   *   *

Timuscor, Grumph, and Eric were all weighed down by the amount of supplies they'd ended up purchasing. While the townsfolk were unaware of their own fevers, they were certainly exuberant at the appearance of travelers, especially when those travelers were looking to spend some coins. After getting a generous supply of smoked meats for a fair price, they'd stocked up on tack, grabbed a few fruits and vegetables for early in their traveling, replaced some worn out water skins, and restocked emergency feed for the horses. Timuscor was hefting the bulk of the supplies, with Grumph taking a fair share and Eric carrying as much as his slender body could handle.

Grumph was thankful they'd managed to get so much. The longer he walked through the town, the more he saw of the people's ruddy complexions and glassy eyes, and the greater he began to fear the

25

danger might be. If the cause of the illness were still around, or if it could be spread from person to person, then the entire party might very well be lost already. It was possible Thistle could use Grumble's gift of healing to restore them, but they'd learned early on that he could only call up so much of that divine favor in a given day. There was no guaranteeing it would be enough to cure even one of them, let alone all five.

That was all conjecture, of course. It was equally possible that the underlying cause of the disease had come and gone, leaving only slowly recovering victims in its wake. Even before he learned the basics of spell casting, Grumph had known better than to try and apply realistic logic to the way magical things functioned. A regular plague had ways of being avoided and controlled. With a magical one, the best he could do was hope they didn't catch it and keep pushing forward to get out of harm's way.

"Should we look into getting a room?" Eric asked. He pointed up at the sky, as he was the only one of them with a hand not weighed down by supplies. The sun was dipping quickly downward, heading for the horizon at an unyielding pace. They had some time left, perhaps an hour or so, before dusk would be upon them, but there was much to do if they wanted to be saddled up and heading out onto the road before night fell.

Generally speaking, Grumph favored known dangers over unknown ones. When one knew what the threat was, they could make careful, informed choices that maximized the chances of survival. Unfortunately, being on the road was inherently an unknown danger. Monsters had been scarce as they came toward Briarwillow, but so had the Alcatham kingdom's patrols. If the townsfolk were recovering from their illness, then any infected monsters might be as well, and with few patrols coming near the formerly plague-ridden area, such beasts would be running unchecked. Going onto the road, at night, as adventurers . . . they could very well be serenading death.

On the other hand, the town was still under the spell of a magical sickness they knew nothing about. Perhaps it was harmless, or perhaps they were already infected. Perhaps the people of Briarwillow would grow horns and try to devour the street's stones; nothing could be predicted with certainty where magic was concerned. Staying may very well increase their chances of infection, but leaving now could leave them ill and helpless on a road often threatened by wild dangers.

All of this ran through Grumph's mind in the span of three footsteps. When he answered Eric's question, it was with the same stoicism and calm he worked hard to convey constantly. "Maybe. We should find the others first."

He noticed a few nearby people start at the unexpected sound of his rough, half-orc voice, but he paid them no mind. Honestly, hearing a half-orc suddenly speak was enough to rattle his nerves too; Grumph was just better at not showing it. As with most elements in life, practice helped.

"That may not be an issue." Timuscor swept his head away from the setting sun; those following his gaze noticed Thistle and Gabrielle moving briskly down the path. Neither seemed particularly hurried, unless one had known Thistle as long as Grumph had: then they could take in the steady, determined speed he was using rather than his usual unassuming gait. The gnome was doing his best to stay inconspicuous while still moving as quickly as possible.

No sooner had they spotted the two missing members of their party than Gabrielle and Thistle spied them right back. The two bustled over quickly, with Thistle reaching up and grabbing Grumph firmly on his thick forearm.

"We need to take a room," Thistle said. His breath was shallow, and under the gleaming armor he wore, Grumph could see the rapid movements of his chest. Either fear, effort, or a combination of the two had stolen his breath. "There's much to discuss and decisions to be made. Gabrielle and I found an inn; bring the supplies and let's get upstairs."

Grumph held his friend's gaze while Gabrielle gave a similar version of the speech to Eric and Timuscor. Thistle knew something, and while he would certainly be telling the rest of the group much of it, now might be the only opportunity for him to give Grumph any additional details the others might need to be left unaware of.

Sure enough, Thistle beckoned Grumph down, and he obliged under the guise of shoring up his grip on one of his bulging leather bags. When he was within whispering distance, the gnome's voice filled his ear, and Grumph found himself wishing he'd allowed himself the luxury of staying ignorant.

"It seems this town was visited by a priest who bore no name."

Then the two were parted and the group was heading for the inn. Thistle hadn't said who those priests served, and it had been a wise decision not to do so. Unless one was in a safe, private place, there was no sense in tempting fate by saying the name of the god of darkness out loud.

After all, there was always a chance that Kalzidar might be listening.

Chapter 4

"—and watch over us, protecting us from prying ears and eyes. This I ask as your paladin and servant."

Thistle rose from his knees, a short journey given the length of his legs, and unclasped his hands. Around him, the others looked on silently, taking up nearly all the space the single room was able to offer them. Despite having the gold to sleep separately, no one felt quite safe enough to split apart from the others again. Especially not with the way Thistle was acting. Something was up with this town, and until they knew what it was, everyone would feel safer knowing the others were nearby. If they were to perish, they would at least perish as a party.

"And with that, hopefully Grumble will shield our conversation," Thistle announced. "I'd feel better if Grumph knew some spells to the same effect, but as it stands, all we can do is bar the door, say a prayer, and hope dearly that no one of importance overhears what I'm about to tell you. Gabrielle, I heard talking during my prayer. I assume you brought the others up to speed?"

"Told them about the skull, the priest, and the day of praying and rituals," Gabrielle confirmed.

"Thank you, that will make this go more quickly." Thistle walked over to the small, thin bed and hopped carefully up onto its corner. "What I am about to tell you should not leave this room, nor be spoken of to people outside of it. I would also ask that you not question how I came upon the knowledge I am going to share with you. Those of you who knew me in Maplebark were aware that I took some odd jobs working as a minion for various would-be evil wizards and conquerors. Generally, I was good about selecting those who were not a real threat, but occasionally I made . . . misjudgments."

"It was just a job, Thistle," Eric assured him. "We know you aren't evil. Heck, you're a paladin for goodness' sake. I mean that literally: paladins only exist for the sake of goodness."

"No, we exist for the sake of godness," Thistle corrected. "A paladin is one who pledges themselves to their just god's service. There are wicked gods as much as there are kind ones, although their devoted wear a different name than 'paladin.' Which is, in a roundabout way, what I wish to talk with you all about. The priest who came to this town said he had no name, that he was merely an appendage of his god's will. Longinus does not ask his servants to forsake their identities, however. In fact, his teachings require a certain amount of individuality. There is only one god in the known pantheon who demands his most devoted sacrifice their names and sense of selves: Kalzidar, god of darkness and hex magic."

Gabrielle's eyes widened and her hand brushed against the base of her axe. Eric swallowed hard, his eyes darting about the room. Timuscor looked as though he were considering being sick in the corner, which might have had more to do with dragging heavy supplies through town all day than Thistle's revelation. Only Grumph appeared composed, which was both how he normally looked and unsurprising since he'd been forewarned.

"How? I mean, just in so many ways. How could a priest of Kalzidar, one of the wicked gods, pretend to serve Longinus without anyone noticing? How did he change the curse, since we all know it isn't lifted? How did he even know to come here in the first place?" Gabrielle paused for a moment in her rapid-fire questioning, forcing herself to calm down and think with strategy. "And most important of all, isn't the hows, it's the what. As in, what does all of this mean for Briarwillow, and for us?"

"If a priest of the god of darkness has come here and worked magic, then I fear it can be nothing good," Timuscor said.

"Worse than that, I'm afraid," Thistle pointed out. "He had the people help, making them weave the spells on themselves. That complicates all of this to a level that I fear even a properly educated wizard—sorry, Grumph—would have trouble unraveling."

Grumph gave a snort that either indicated he took no offense or that he'd roast Thistle's head on a dagger. The nonverbal language of his people was intentionally difficult to interpret, as it led to more misunderstandings and therefore more opportunities for violence.

"As for the 'how' questions," Thistle continued, "those who serve Kalzidar faithfully are given powers of their own, not unlike the way I wield Grumble's gifts. Theirs, however, focus on magic and deception. So long as his name is unknown, one of Kalzidar's priests can deceive all but the most willful and stubborn of minds. That is how he was able to fool the town about the god he serves, his purpose for coming, likely even what rituals they were performing. The only thing we can be certain of is this: whatever that priest did, it was not meant to make these people's situation better."

"Three days ago." Grumph said these words not to any person in the room in particular, more just out loud to the world as a whole. He was turning that fact over in his head, circling it carefully. In terms of wizardry, Grumph was about as inexperienced as one could be. He knew a total of five spells, and it had taken the intervention of a legendary artifact to help him grasp the last of those five. But Grumph was dedicated in his studies, and he'd grabbed every meager piece of information he could on their travels so far, as well as poring through his spell book day after day. In that time, he'd noticed that a lot of magical practices ran on certain numbers. Three, seven, and thirteen were the ones he'd noticed most frequently.

"Three days, as of today." Grumph glanced out the small, barely noticeable window. What precious time they'd possessed had dwindled as they got a room and Thistle prayed. Dusk was nearly upon them, and the night would quickly follow. "As of tonight," Grumph amended. "This may be trouble."

"Unfortunately, I'm forced to agree, though perhaps not for the same reasons as Grumph," Thistle told them. "Fate seems to have handed us what most adventurers would consider an incredible experience. For us to have arrived at just this moment, when the situation is so evidently

31

perilous and fraught with danger . . . it would be folly to assume we won't bear witness to the tipping point when this all goes south."

"How can you be so sure of that?" Timuscor asked.

"Because that is the way the world works for adventurers," Thistle replied. "I spent years seeing it firsthand, and while I can't say I fully understand the reasoning for it even now, I do accept the inevitability to a certain extent. There's always the chance that I'm wrong, that perhaps it will be the seventh day when things go amiss and some other group of travelers will deal with the fallout, but I'd advise that we all brace for the worst rather than allow ourselves to succumb to optimism's siren song."

"Why don't we get out of here?" Eric pointed out the tiny window, where the dwindling light of day was streaming in. "There's still time to get on the horses and be clear of this town by nightfall."

"Maybe the town itself, but we'd still be in Briarwillow," Gabrielle said. "Remember how long it took us from seeing the first farm to getting here? That's a lot of space to cross with places for people and things to hide in."

"Additionally, if Kalzidar's servant has put something to work here, then he may well have stayed in secret to see it through." Thistle gently set his armored hands against one another, making a small *ting* that rang clear through the air. "Trying to escape from one who serves the god of darkness under the cover of night could prove to be quite perilous."

"So we should wait here to die?" Eric stood from his seat, moving almost soundlessly, even in heated impulse.

"I don't know." Thistle shrugged, rattling his armor as he met the uncertain eyes of every one of his friends. "Stay or go, either is risky. Not every situation has a perfect solution; often, you just have to take your pick from the array of poor choices spread out before you. Far as I can tell, it's a bit of a toss-up on this one."

32

"Right now, we have a room to barricade ourselves in, offering at least a little protection," Timuscor said. "Perhaps it's not much, but after weeks of sleeping out in the open, it feels like a fortress. If we flee, there's also the chance that we might run into monsters on the road."

"Or get sick," Grumph tacked on. The threat of infection was very real and needed to be kept prevalent in the others' minds.

"Dragonshit, that part slipped my mind." Gabrielle pressed her fingers to her forehead, checking for any signs of fever. "I was going to say we should run, but from what the people around here were saying, it seemed like the first stage of the plague was a death-like state. Being out in the open like that . . . we'd be food for the first monster that wandered in our direction."

"Maybe we should give it a night," Eric suggested. "If we're going to get sick, then let's assume it will happen soon. Come tomorrow morning, we ride out of here with dawn's light, gods willing. Should something go wrong before then . . . well, Timuscor was right, it's nice to have four walls and a roof as protection for a change."

"Wood and nails will offer us very little fortification against the power of magic, but I find myself inclined to agree nonetheless." Thistle nodded his head, though one of his hands went to his stomach and tried to rub it through the armor. "Little though it is, I'll take any amount of shielding I can get. Besides, I think we would all do well with a hot meal and a decent night's rest. Living on the run takes a toll over time."

No one disputed that fact, as the smells from the downstairs kitchen had been wafting up through the floorboards, tempting every adventurer with thoughts of fresh, warm food. Dire as the danger in staying might be, it offered some elements of comfort, and if they were going to die anyway, it seemed logical to at least go out with full stomachs and happy smiles.

"That's it then, we stay?" Eric asked.

33

"Aye, that would be the choice our group seems to be leaning toward," Thistle agreed. "We'll be cautious about it, barring the door and sleeping in shifts just to stay safe, but in the end, I doubt that we'll anticipate whatever the priest of Ḱalzidar is up to. Maybe if there were some servants or minions about Grumble would give me a bit of a clue, but as it stands, I think we are likely on our own."

"Well, if we're going to be waiting around for possible death all night, I'm at least going to have a buzz when it shows up." Gabrielle pulled herself away from the wall on which she'd been leaning and headed to the door. "Ale and food seem like the perfect ways to pass the time until bed. Anyone else want to join me?"

It took no more prompting than that to get everyone out the door and heading downstairs to the inn's kitchen. While the ale they found was somewhat lacking compared to the elixir Grumph had once produced, the food was hearty and delicious, made even more so by the elusive spice known as ravenous hunger. It was a night of comfort, warmth, and ease that the party had needed even more than they'd realized, a bright spot on the dingy path they'd been walking.

In the hellish nightmare of the next few days, this evening would be looked upon fondly, a shining reminder of the life they were desperately trying to get back to.

*   *   *

As the moon shone down on the untended crops, a single, svelte figure stepped lightly amidst the weeds and wheat. He was here for a harvest, though he had come for nothing so mundane as corn or grains. From his belt dangled a black velvet sack, bulging from the size of the item contained within. It bounced against the twisted symbol of his god, which was enchanted to appear as whatever false priest he was pretending to be. A useful tool, as were all the pieces of equipment he employed. He'd needed precious few of them to complete this mission; the desperation of Briarwillow's citizens had done most of the work for him.

How they'd gazed at him when he promised to save their town. Such longing, hope, and reverence all condensed into teary-eyed stares. It was almost enough to understand why some went into the work of heroing. That level of admiration was intoxicating, albeit misplaced when directed at him. He hadn't lied though, not as he saw it. He'd offered them salvation, and that was what he intended to deliver. If it was not the salvation they'd expected, well, that was their fault for not asking more questions.

His eyes charted the moon's movement through the sky, waiting patiently for the appointed time to arrive. Kalzidar had been very specific in the visions he sent to his servant. Divine guidance had told this priest to come to Briarwillow, retrieve the skull, and how to make use of it. Tricking the citizens into pledging themselves to the ancient totem's power had been simple enough, but it would all be for naught if the final piece of the ceremony wasn't handled perfectly. Even then, the task would be far from over; however, the priest did not dwell on such a fact. One did not slay a kingdom in a single blow, as the saying went. One did it by taking a single life at a time.

As the fat white sphere rose higher through the night sky, his pale hand plunged into the velvet sack, retrieving its contents with careful motion. The skull did not gleam in the night sky's pale light. Rather, it seemed to darken, causing the carefully prepared altar the priest had set up to become bathed in shadow. It was no matter to the man holding the skull; sight in even the darkest of pits was one of the first gifts Kalzidar bestowed upon his faithful. Power coursed up his slender fingers where he gripped the ancient totem, trying to worm its way in to work destruction on his mortal body. With a minor effort of will, the priest pushed the energy back to its source. He was no simple farmer or miner stumbling across power he couldn't hope to understand. Such petty tricks would not work on him.

The altar was a simple one, constructed from stones and magic over the three days he'd stayed hidden in the field. Three days to let the magic ripen, readying it for the harvest to come. Gingerly, he set the skull down in the center of a circle of runes that were the color of dried blood. It rested there quietly, as though there were nothing at all malicious about the power contained in the prison of bone.

He looked up the sky once more, certain that the time was drawing near. It wasn't a short window of opportunity, but he preferred to get things going as soon as possible. There was always the potential for interference, and he could not allow himself to fail on a mission directly from Kalzidar himself. The wicked god of darkness was, as one might expect, not known for his patience or mercy.

Raising his pale hands into the night air, the priest began to chant. His words hung on the moon's beams as they swirled about the makeshift altar. From within the skull, a new power began to pulse. Old, nearly forgotten by most, this magic had been sealed in earth and stone for countless years. Now, it yearned to stretch and move and exist. The power bucked against its prison, even as the priest's words weakened the seals binding it.

Very soon, it would run free, and death would follow at its heels.

Chapter 5

"Okay, Wimberly has two alchemist fires suspended in the trees overhead, a halberd trap ready to spring in the bushes, and two of her crafted, magical remote crossbows pointed at the clearing's entrance." Bert scanned the map carefully, focusing only on the part his character could see. "She raises her flare wand and shoots it over the tops of the trees, letting the others know that the battleground is ready."

"Vision checks, all around," Russell instructed. The difficultly of the check was supremely low, since they'd all been watching for the signal. He was essentially just checking for critical failures (rolling a natural one on the twenty-sided die). Those rolls resulted in automatic failure, and too many could even kill a character off entirely. That almost never happened, though; "almost" being the key phrase. After what had gone down with his last group, Russell didn't dismiss the possibility of anything going awry anymore.

"Woo! Twenty-five with my new goggles' bonus. Chalara sees the ever-loving shit out of that flare." Cheri took a sip of the soda she'd covertly slipped rum into before coming down for the day's game. She'd been drinking it less than expected, as the gaming group was actually turning out to be more fun than anticipated. Cheri had really just wanted a way to kill time and not think about the pile of shit she had waiting for her back at school, but after a few sessions, she'd fallen into the old groove and started digging the game.

It certainly helped that the players were actually pretty cool. Once Bert had seen how battle worked, Wimberly had become a damn savant in terms of strategy and field position. Even now, the little gnome was setting up a clearing for them to herd the barghests into, where they'd walk into all manner of gadgeteer death.

"With a fifteen, I trust Gelthorn is able to see the flare?" Alexis asked softly. Russell nodded, then braced, as did the rest of the table. They'd all quickly learned that while Alexis was quiet and meek, she was also *very* into roleplaying her character. And Gelthorn was . . . less gentle in manner and speech, to put it kindly.

"TO ME!" Alexis shouted, her voice suddenly as forceful as a speeding truck. "We drive them to the arms of Hell!" With that, she rolled an attack to draw the barghests' attention—as if the yell hadn't been enough—and the chase was on.

"I got a twelve, is that enough?" Tim asked, a bit of worry apparent in his voice. The plan relied heavily on him being ready to cut off the barghests' escape from the clearing, so if he missed the signal, things would get rough. Cheri could actually see him sweating a bit with nerves. It amazed her how seriously he took his role as the team's paladin, acting as though it were truly matters of life and death on the line with every battle. The kid was either nuts or a born role-player; either way, it made him more enjoyable to have in the game.

"That's plenty," Russell told him. "You can move to get into position on your turn."

"Chalara is going to climb up the ladder Wimberly readied and prepare to start blasting barghests." Cheri had been through many a character in her years of playing, but she always seemed to find the most joy in wielding the glass cannons that were mages. The ability to call down fiery magical wrath was something she might have enjoyed having in her real life—though even she would admit it would be utterly foolish for anyone to give her such power.

"Let's just hope we don't attract any other roaming monsters again," Bert said, still carefully studying the board. "This whole forest is thick with the things."

"Yeah, and we're tearing through them, grabbing gold and experience from every encounter," Cheri pointed out. "This has got to be the best campaign in the module. Imagine if we'd picked the one about sick people. We'd be fighting a case of the sniffles, or maybe a spooky bandage monster."

"We could always go investigate that once the tower is saved," Tim suggested.

"Please, with how hard Russell has been emphasizing time passage and reality? No way that quest option will still be there," Cheri told him. "Trust me; those people are probably long dead by now."

*   *   *

Thistle didn't know if it was the pain or the wailing that tore him from his sleep, nor did he have the presence of mind to figure it out amidst the twin distractions. Around him, the others bolted up from their mats on the room's floor as a symphony of screams echoed through the town. It was a horrid, soul-wrenching sound. These were not yells of anger, or hatred, or even terror. They were the sound of pure, unmitigated anguish. And yet, as awful as they were, they paled in comparison to what Thistle could feel in his gut.

It was as though a phantom blade had been slammed through his stomach and was somehow twisting about in his stomach lining. As soon as Thistle became aware of it, the pain vanished, and yet the sensation somehow remained. He was torn between the desire to groan, cry, and throw up. Instead, he slowly pulled himself up from the ground and grabbed his belt. On it hung a pair of sheathes made for him by Sierva, ones that let him call his daggers back after they'd been thrown. Generally, this was worn on top of his fitted armor; however, since he'd been trying to sleep, he was adorned only in simple clothing.

Gabrielle and Timuscor were similarly unprotected; only Eric was bothering to slip his veilpanther leather over his clothes. Since it was closer to cloth than armor, he was able to do so quickly, even as he pulled his father's short sword free from its sheath. Grumph had yanked free his own blade—made from the tail of a demon—while Gabrielle was unwrapping her axe. Timuscor, as the one who'd actually been keeping watch over the door, already had his sword and shield at the ready.

The five adventurers stared at the door, waiting for the first attack to come. If they were lucky, the small bar keeping it shut would hold and they'd have some warning of the impending assault. If they were unlucky, which certainly seemed to be the way things were going at the moment, then it would get knocked clear off and they'd be in a fray.

As they waited, the wailing slowly died away, leaving the town of Briarwillow unnaturally silent. Ears strained as they listened for the slightest sound of steps ascending stairs or creeping down the inn's wooden hall. They stared at the door, weapons ready, bodies tense and waiting for the signal to act.

After roughly five minutes had passed, Eric finally broke the silence that had descended over them. "Is it possible no one is coming for us?"

"Does sort of seem like they would have made a move by now," Gabrielle agreed. "Should . . . should we be going out there to do something?"

"Aye, seems that would be what any good party of violence-hungry adventurers would do," Thistle admitted. The twisting in his stomach was beginning to fade, albeit very slowly. Had he known for certain what it signified, he suspected there would have been obligations laid upon him by his service to Grumble. As it was yet in doubt, however, he was erring on the side of keeping the people he cared for safe. "But I can't say I think it's a good idea to leave here unarmored, especially with an entire town of potentially fever-mad citizens who may no longer be quite as friendly."

"Then I'll go." Eric slipped the belt with his sheath around his waist and put his blade away.

"You can't go out there by yourself," Timuscor said.

"Better me than anyone else. I'm easily the quietest of us all, as I neither have Grumph's weight nor your heavy armor. Plus, I made sure to memorize the layout of the town, and noted a few places in this building I could use to slip onto the roof." Eric realized how crazy that last part made him sound, only to conclude seconds later that it would have only seemed crazy if they weren't currently in need of exactly such information. Paranoia was only a hindrance where it didn't pay off.

"Eric is good at what he does," Gabrielle said, eyeing her oldest friend carefully. Once, there had been a time when no one could have uttered such words, but Eric was proving to be far more adept as a rogue than he ever was a guard. While she still didn't like the idea of him heading out into the unknown by himself, Gabrielle also knew Eric well enough to recognize when he was stuck on an idea. If he was beyond dissuading, then better he go out there with encouraging words in his ears rather than doubt in his heart.

"This is something Eric can do that the rest of us cannot," Thistle told Timuscor, leaning down and picking up the first pieces of his armor to begin the process of getting equipped. "Just as Grumph can call magic and I can heal, Eric can move with speed and silence. Both of which he will certainly need once he leaves this room." That last bit was said more to Eric than Timuscor, and the dark-haired human took the hint well. Once he was outside, they'd have to bolt the door behind him and start getting ready, which meant retreating back to the room was out of the question. Anyone who noticed him would have to be lost or . . . handled.

"I'll be quick," Eric promised. "If anyone comes to the door and you don't hear my voice, assume it's not me."

"That will have to do." Thistle knew too well how easy it was to duplicate something as simple as a voice, even without magic, but in the absence of options, he saw no other way to let Eric hurry on his way. When things calmed down, he would have to make a point of creating and teaching them all a non-verbal code of knocks and gestures to avoid situations like these.

Grumph was at the door, and as Eric drew close, the half-orc lifted the moderately sized bar that swung into place to keep them secure. Pulling the worn piece of wood slowly ajar, Eric quietly passed through the opening and eased the door shut behind him.

41

With the soft thud of the bar slipping back into place, Eric was officially on his own.

*   *   *

Briarwillow was a town with some means, though it was far from being as resplendent as one of the kingdom capitals. This meant that while it didn't have magical lighting hewn into the stones—as capitals often did—the town did spring for hanging lanterns positioned every few feet. These were put up carefully, far enough from the buildings so that an accident wouldn't start a fire, but near enough to cast light on many doorways. This meant that the streets were soaked in shadows as the dim light of the lanterns cascaded through the night, catching various objects in their gentle glow. In a sense, the strange, barely-lit landscape was a blessing to the cautious human creeping along the inn's rooftop: it made movement almost impossible to miss, as the slightest step would cause a swirling of shadows.

That was why Eric easily noticed the mouse skitter across the stones from a stack of hay to a hole in the shop where they'd purchased their smoked meats. He also caught sight of a bird flying overhead, perhaps intrigued by the sounds of the moving mouse. These two creatures' motions, subtle though they were, were worrying to pick up for a very key reason: there was no other sound or movement coming from anywhere else in the town.

Eric perched for no fewer than ten minutes, waiting to see something, hear a muffled cry or the sounds of battle, gain *any* sort of clue as to what was going on. Only silence and shadows greeted him. With quick, careful motions, he shimmied down the side of the inn, using the same tricks he'd used to sneak into the mayor's house when he was showing up late for a guard shift. It took deft hands and sure feet, both of which Eric possessed. He landed with only the slightest of sounds and began moving through the town.

The soft scuff of his boots against the road's stones seemed to echo in all directions, causing Eric to freeze each time he made such a noise. When no one came to investigate, Eric would continue forward,

42

determined to be more careful. He was quieter than the others, but that wasn't the same as being completely silent. Still, as his steps turned into strides and still not a single spot of movement caught his eye, Eric began to wonder if he was going through all this effort for no reason. Briarwillow seemed more or less deserted. If not for the hanging lanterns and the town-wide scream, he would have thought everyone had run off to some after-festival event in the fields.

The others would be in their armor soon, if not already, and there was only so long anyone would be able to talk Gabrielle out of coming to make sure he was alive. Eric decided it was time to take some real risks in the hopes of finding answers. Walking up to the nearest shop—a pleasant-smelling building that had been full of baking bread all through the day—Eric pressed his hand against the door. All he wanted to do was feel if there was a bar in place on top of the lock, as he couldn't very well unlock a wooden beam, but to his total surprise the door swung open freely.

Flickering lantern light from the street and a few errant moonbeams streamed through the window, illuminating a bakery that had been left utterly unattended. Eric stepped in carefully, mostly shutting the door behind him just to be safe. He might need to make a hasty exit, but he didn't want to lock himself in an unfamiliar location unless it was absolutely necessary. It was certainly strange that the door was unlocked, but this was just a bakery, and in a town that hadn't seen travelers in weeks. Perhaps they'd not felt the need to lock it. Eric held on to that thought as he quietly made his way through the dimly-lit front of the bakery, maneuvering past the counter and into the back.

There, he found what he'd expected: a sizable oven next to a kitchen area, with several bowls of dough proofing on a rear counter. There was also a bed, a cupboard, and a table big enough to seat two people at most. Resting on the table was a single cup, chipped and dented from what he estimated to be years of use. Eric dipped a pinky into the brown liquid resting inside the cup's depths. It was surprisingly warm, almost hot to the touch. Bringing his finger to his mouth, Eric delicately licked off a single drop, tasting the liquid.

"Tea?" He glanced at the oven and noticed a small teapot resting to the side, probably warmed by the glowing coals inside the iron beast. For the tea to still be warm, it would have had to have been made fairly recently, probably around the time they first heard the screams. A terrible idea wormed its way into Eric's brain, and he tried to push it away. Jumping to conclusions would color his perspective, and there was still more to see before he could be certain of what was happening.

All the same, he didn't put quite as much care into moving silently as he walked back through the bakery and out the front door. Even if Eric's mind wasn't yet ready to face the truth, somewhere in his heart he already knew what was waiting for him behind the rest of the town's doors.

*   *   *

"I'm going after him." Gabrielle didn't actually gesture with her axe when she spoke, but it was off her back and gripped forcefully in her hands all the same, adding an unwelcome amount of danger to her declaration.

"We're all going after him, and soon," Thistle told her. "But not quite yet. We need to give him enough time to work, otherwise we risk undoing all his efforts by blundering about and alerting others to our presence. Just a little longer."

"You keep saying that, then when I want to go, you say the time isn't here yet. What exactly are you waiting for?"

"Enough time that we're sure he's in trouble," Thistle said.

"And by that point, he might very well be dead." Gabrielle took a step toward the door, her eyes beginning to flash as the fury she kept sealed away for battles scratched at the inside of her brain, begging like a wild dog to be let loose. "We're done talking about this. I'm going after my friend. *Now.*"

"Then I suppose we're coming along." Thistle had known enough barbarians in his time to understand there was a point at which diplomacy failed to be a word they could even understand, let alone an effective strategy. Besides, the truth was he was getting worried as well. While the weird, twisting feeling in his stomach had faded a great deal, it was still there, constantly telling him that something was amiss. Much as he trusted Eric to do the reconnaissance quietly, none of them were incapable of failure, and he had no desire to bury any more of his friends. Thistle had gotten a lifetime's fill of that activity already.

A crisp, loud knock from the door immediately drew all their attention, as well as some of the weapons from their sheaths. Eric's voice followed the knocking, putting them at ease while simultaneously filling them with confusion. "You can all come out now. There's nothing here."

Grumph pulled up the bar and yanked open the door, revealing an unharmed Eric. Thistle quickly motioned for him to come in so they could close the door again. Eric obliged, albeit with an almost lazy gait to his steps.

"While I'm glad to hear there isn't any danger, perhaps you should still be quiet, lest we call some upon ourselves," Thistle said.

"I highly doubt that's going to happen," Eric replied. "When I said there was nothing here, that's what I meant. Not just that there isn't any danger, but that every single person in the entire town appears to have up and vanished."

"Wait." Timuscor's forehead scrunched as he tried to wrap his mind around what Eric was saying. "You mean there's no one in the streets?"

"Or the shops, or the homes, or any of the other buildings I had time to check. It's just us." Eric gestured over his shoulder, pointing back to the town at large.

"As far as I can tell, Briarwillow has become a complete ghost town."

Chapter 6

As dawn crested the horizon, casting long rays of morning sunlight through the fields and up to the base of the nearby mountain, it found Briarwillow almost entirely evacuated, as the few remaining people had spent most of the night verifying.

The search had begun carefully, moving in specific teams and keeping watch in all possible directions as they hunted. After the first hour of abandoned shops and homes, however, the party grew somewhat more concerned with speed rather than care, splintering off in all directions, hoping to turn up some clue as to where the people of Briarwillow had gone. With the sun's rise, they reconvened outside the inn to share their progress, or, rather, the lack thereof.

"I hope one of you found something, because I came up with jack," Gabrielle announced. "Just a bunch of empty houses and half-made beds. Not even any blood."

"Same here," Eric told them. "None of the doors were locked and nothing was out of place. Near as I can tell, it seems like everyone just got out of bed and left town."

"Aye, that would be my guess as to exactly what occurred." Thistle moved more slowly than the others thanks to the cruel prank the gods had played on his limbs, so his search had been shorter than theirs. At the same time, it had given him a chance to reflect on the events as he'd experienced them, as well as consider that ceaseless twisting sensation that persisted in his stomach. It had all come together to give him a theory, albeit a flimsy one. "I'd say that the fever we saw them in the grips of yesterday reached its next stage, one that involved some sort of town-wide migration."

"That doesn't make much . . . oh, magic." Eric answered his own budding question and sighed, trying to bite back the sense of frustration bubbling inside him. That damned unknowable source of power made life so much more complicated than it needed to be. He wondered how he'd ever managed to get through so much of his life without noticing the trouble that magic caused.

Timuscor set down his shield gently, taking the opportunity to stretch as best he could inside the heavy-plated armor strapped across his body. "What sort of magic could make sick people vanish? We only stayed inside for a few minutes, at most. That's not much time for the entire town to just walk off."

"There are a few spells I know of that could accomplish it, and certainly dozens more I've never heard of that could get the job done." Thistle turned to Grumph, who looked as though he'd been expecting to be consulted sooner or later. "Do you know of any from your studies that seem to be at work?"

Grumph shook his head, which was hardly surprising to the others. Adept as he was at wielding a wizard's stolen spell book, it was a far cry from an actual education in the use of magic. Then again, none of them actually knew if a real wizard would have had a clue about what was happening either. It wasn't as though they'd been through the training themselves.

"However they did it, someone definitely magicked away the town. Which brings us to the real question we should be asking: what are we supposed to do now?" Gabrielle had sheathed her axe and her anger as the search wore on, but her eyes continued to dart about as if waiting for an attack to materialize from nothing. She'd primed herself for battle and was finding it hard to adjust to the idea that bloodshed wasn't imminent.

"I found a few tracks on the road, I think," Eric said. "It's possible we could try to follow those and see if we can find where everyone went. Gabby, you're pretty good at tracking stuff."

It was true that her time with the goblins had given Gabrielle many skills, amongst them the ability to follow prey through the foliage and brush. Still, she shook her head slowly at Eric's suggestion.

"That's in a forest, not across stone streets and kingdom roads. Plus, I'm not so sure I want to track everyone down. Call me a coward or a bugbear-headed fool, but it seems to me these people may be well beyond saving. They've been sick for weeks, and whatever is happening to them is only getting worse. Sure, maybe we can track them down and see what happened, but then what? None of us even know what's going on, let alone how to fix it."

"There is nothing foolish about honestly assessing our capabilities of success," Thistle replied. "And you bring up many fair points. We do not yet grasp what is happening around us, and once we do, even if we can determine the solution, there is no guarantee we'll be able to execute it."

"It seems wrong to walk away, though. This could have been our town just as easily." Eric ran his boot across the stone road of Briarwillow. It was bigger than Maplebark, and certainly had more industry, but the overall feel of the place was the same: homey, cared for, and filled with the love of its citizens. Eric would never see his home again; Grumble's bargain had made sure of that, even if the king of Solium weren't hunting them down. He wasn't sure he had it in him to leave another such place in ruins.

"Right then, so going after them is unnecessarily dangerous, and abandoning the town feels morally repugnant," Thistle said. "Since neither of our two options is appealing, there's only one thing to do."

"Take the third." Grumph tilted his head back toward the part of town where they'd stabled the horses. Their mounts had thankfully been left untouched when last Grumph checked on them, and in a deserted town, he had no reason to believe that had changed. "We get help."

"My thoughts precisely." Thistle turned to the group and pointed down the western road that led out of Briarwillow. "Cadence Hollow is roughly three days' ride away from here. It backtracks us a bit, but in that sprawling city is a small outpost for the guild of mages. We can head there, tell them what happened, and allow them to find a proper solution. If we cannot save this town ourselves, nor bear to let it be abandoned, then the best path forward is to seek the aid of those who can get the job done. That's why kingdoms have soldiers and mages in their employ, after all."

"Huh." Timuscor scratched his head absentmindedly, staring at Thistle with renewed admiration. "That never occurred to me. I just assumed that since we found this problem, it was ours to try and solve."

"Don't feel too bad. Thinking around the way this stuff always seems to happen takes getting used to," Gabrielle assured him. "Hell, Eric and I didn't think of that either."

"It's a good idea, but will the town be able to even last that long?" Eric asked. "It's a long way to ride just on the off chance they can help."

Thistle nodded, his small face solemn. "It's possible that taking this route will mean we're too late to save the town, but it's also possible that this town is already beyond saving. As it stands now, we have no solid idea where everyone went, and the only one amongst us that might have a chance of tracking them down is Gabby, who has made her desire not to do exactly that abundantly clear."

"Especially now that Thistle has pitched a good counterplan," Gabrielle added.

"Right. So there is some risk to the town, I won't lie to you about that, but that risk exists no matter which path we try to go down. At least in this one, we bring Briarwillow people who are actually qualified to help."

Eric pondered the proposal for a few moments, sweeping his eyes about the abandoned landscape as he tried to contemplate what he'd want done if this were Maplebark. In the end, he supposed he'd rather have a chance at being saved than see a group of adventurers throw their lives away for nothing. If helping the town was really their top priority, then their best bet was in talking to the mages at Cadence Hollow.

"All right," Eric said at last. "I'm on board. Grumph, Timuscor, what about you two?"

"It was my idea," Grumph reminded him, causing Eric to go slightly red at the ears. Timuscor was less glib with his reply, merely bowing his head until his chin rested against the cool metal surface of his armor.

"You four spared me when you had no reason to, and freed me from the strange workings that wove through my mind. My life is yours, and I will follow wherever you command."

Gabrielle coughed into her hand, while the others merely tried to avoid making eye contact with Timuscor. Much as they'd tried to tell him that he didn't owe them a thing, he still seemed set on settling the debt he felt he'd incurred. They were also relatively certain he still didn't entirely understand the "puppet being controlled by beings from another world" part of his being freed, though none of them were entirely certain they had a good grasp on it either. Eric seemed the most clued in, and he rarely spoke of what he'd seen when holding The Bridge.

"You have no debt here," Thistle said at last. "But I'll take that as agreement with the plan, so that we can move things along. I suppose the only thing to do now is go get our supplies and horses, and then put ourselves on the road well before sundown."

"Are we not worried about getting sick anymore?" Eric asked.

"Personally, I'm more worried about what happens if all the people from town suddenly come back," Gabrielle replied.

"It is still possible we might take ill, but Gabby is right. At this point, I think the scales of danger have firmly tipped to the side of our leaving town. For Briarwillow's citizens, as much as for ourselves." Thistle tilted his head back to check the sun, which still hung low in the morning sky. "If there's any more to discuss, let's talk on the way. I'd like to be clear of Briarwillow's lands before dusk, just to be on the safe side."

50

Everyone began heading down the street, moving swiftly as they walked toward the stable where they could fetch the horses. It was only after they were about to round a corner that Eric noticed Thistle hadn't come with them. He turned around to find the gnome standing in the exact spot where they'd left him, a few feet from the inn's front door. Thistle seemed to be waving and gesticulating, though Eric wasn't quite sure what his friend was trying to say.

"Everyone, hang on. Thistle's still back there."

The others turned, and then followed Eric's lead as he moved carefully across the stone road. Whatever was going on, Thistle never acted without reason. If he'd refused to leave after telling them to go, perhaps he'd spotted an unseen danger and was waving to try and warn them. As Eric drew near, he realized that Thistle wasn't actually waving to them at all. Instead, he was reaching down, grabbing his armored boots, and tugging on them with all his might, only to end up wind-milling in an effort to keep his balance when his grip inevitably broke.

"Thistle," Eric said, realizing that perhaps they were not the ones in danger after all. "Are you okay?"

"Physically? Fit as a fiddle and spry as a fox. Mentally? I'd say I'm easily one of the quicker wits, in at least my arm's length. But spiritually, it seems, I may have stepped into something of a quagmire." Thistle reached down and grabbed his boots once more, tugging until his face was red and small tears slipped out from the corners of his eyes.

"What's going on?" Eric moved closer to try and help, stopping only when Thistle held up a hand.

"My attempt at self-denial proved insufficient, it seems. By what I can only imagine to be Grumble's will, I am unable to move so much as a single inch from this spot." Thistle banged the armor on his legs and tried to will the appendages to take a step, only to finally lose his balance and topple backward onto the ground. He stared up at Eric, who was looking down with unmasked concern.

"I fear we may have to slightly adjust our plans."

*   *   *

"Tactically speaking, we should definitely retreat." Bert was hunched over the game map, staring at the scene spread before them. All of his calculations had been spot on going into the fight, and the acid-splashing devices paired with blinding stunners had largely hobbled the bandit camps, allowing them to take the enemy by surprise. What they hadn't known was how many other bandits had concealed themselves in the trees and underground. With unexpected allies pouring in, what should have been an easy victory was quickly turning into a potentially deadly situation. "Wimberly is almost out of premade tricks, Timanuel has half a dozen bandits on him, Chalara is getting peppered by archers, and Gelthorn has been seriously injured."

"Can't do it." Tim had a look on his face that was somewhere between stoic and ill, but his hands were steady as he picked up the dice in preparation for his next, possibly final, turn.

"I know you're pinned down, but Wimberly has one more blinding stunner. She's near enough that she can toss it out and give you the chance to run," Bert replied.

"He meant that he literally can't run away," Cheri interjected. This was the risk one took with having a paladin in the party. All that power came with a few serious drawbacks, and they were about the deal with the one Cheri liked the least. "Remember how we had him use Sense Evil to tell where the bandits were hiding out?"

"Of course," Bert said. "That's how we were able to send Gelthorn to do recon and get the ambush on them."

"Right, well, the problem is that he did sense that there were evil people here. So he knows that in this camp, there is evil dwelling," Cheri explained. "And that's why he can't run away."

"Paladins don't ever back down from evil," Tim said. He checked his character sheet once more, as if health points or fresh mana would appear out of nowhere. "We're the wall that doesn't yield, the light that can't be extinguished. Even if it costs us our lives to do it, a paladin must do all they can to stop evil once they've sensed it."

"Oh." Bert reexamined the board with this new information in mind. A retreat was still their best chance at living, by far. If one of them couldn't go, then they were presented with the choice to save three out of four characters or risk the entire party to one very dicey battle. Personally, Bert favored the solution that would keep the most people alive, but it wasn't really his call to make. It was Wimberly's, and she'd been saved by Timanuel more than once already, in their fights throughout the forest.

"Do your best to survive the next round," Bert said at last. "By the time we come up in battle again, we'll have thought of something."

Tim nodded solemnly, and then threw his meager handful of dice.

Chapter 7

After everyone had taken a turn trying to tug Thistle from the ground, it was finally agreed upon that the gnome was good and rightly stuck to the road. They brought out some food and water, as the inn had plenty and a night of exploration had worked up quite an appetite, and then gathered around Thistle to discuss what they should do next.

"You have to go on without me." Thistle might have seemed more heroic in delivering this order were he not still lying sprawled out on the ground, limbs somehow bonded to where they'd struck the stones.

"Very sweet, very noble, and very not happening," Gabrielle replied. She tore off a piece of bread from the loaf she'd been working on and lowered it into Thistle's mouth carefully. "After everything that's gone on, we're not leaving you stuck like this all alone."

"Who said anything about leaving me stuck and alone?" Thistle quickly chewed through the fresh bread without even bothering to savor it and spat out the reply. "I only meant that some of you should go. We do still need the help of the mages, perhaps now more than ever. It won't take everyone, though, only two or three to be safe."

"Leaving one of us to stand guard over you night and day while you lie in the road?" Eric pointed out.

"I will gladly undertake such a service." Timuscor rose from the ground and grabbed his weapon, clearly ready to start before breakfast was even properly concluded.

"Thank you, Timuscor, but no one will have to stand guard over me. I have a hunch that, sooner or later, I'll be able to move again. This was Grumble's way of sending me a message, since I'd been ignoring his other, more subtle, hints."

"Paladin stuff?" Gabrielle asked.

"Paladin stuff," Grumph confirmed.

"I must confess, I know more than some about the lore of those blessed with the mantle of divine warriorship, but I have never heard of a god forcibly hobbling one of his own servants in such a way." Timuscor sat down slowly and picked up his bowl of stew. It was leftover from the night prior, yet still held more flavor than the leaves and berries they were likely to find on the road.

"Those who serve the just gods are obligated to uphold certain aspects of their tenants. One such example is that paladins are generally not allowed to flee when the weak and innocent are in danger, or when in the presence of undeniable evil. I thought Grumble might give me a bit of leeway in the latter department, seeing as he rules over minions and we are not known for our courage, but it seems I was wrong. Since we first arrived, I've had a strange, almost painful gut feeling. At first, I thought it was gas from an improper diet; however, I've begun to suspect I'm slowly developing the paladin's mythical ability to sense the very presence of evil."

"Truly, the gifts of the gods are incredible," Timuscor marveled.

"Yeah, that's a real neat trick. Give you the power to tell if there's evil around, and then demand you never run away from any sort of it. Sort of seems like more of a curse than a gift, if you ask me." Gabrielle offered Thistle another piece of bread, which he gratefully accepted.

"Curse or gift, it's still something we're going to have to deal with," Eric said. "Thistle apparently can't leave until the people are saved or the skull is destroyed or some arbitrary goal that satisfies his god is fulfilled. If we really want to pull that off, we'll need the mages' help, which would mean abandoning him in a town where we don't know exactly what's going on, but we basically have divine confirmation that it's evil."

"We have to split up," Grumph said. It was clear that was their only real way out of this situation; better to acknowledge that fact and start working on the real question—who went and who stayed.

"As the only one of you lot worth two shits at navigating a forest, I think we can all agree I'm on the Cadence Hollow team," Gabrielle said, keeping the momentum of Grumph's declaration moving before they could backtrack. Daylight was both precious and burning.

"Don't we just follow the road?" Eric pointed out.

"Sure, and as long as no monsters, or bandits, or natural obstacles force you off that road, you'd never need someone who can find her way around a forest." Gabrielle crossed her arms and waited for Eric to reflect on how many times they'd already had to leave the kingdom's road and trust in her navigation. He bit his lip, and then made a slight bow of his head to apologize. With how long they'd known each other, there was no need for words.

"Gabrielle and Eric go. Timuscor and I will guard Thistle," Grumph told them.

"Actually, I'm going to have to disagree with you, old friend." Thistle turned his head as best he could to meet Grumph's dark-eyed gaze. "Going to Cadence Hollow was too risky before, but if we've got to make a trip there anyway, then you should be one of those to head over. Short of a kingdom's capital, there's nowhere better than a mage guild to learn about magic and acquire more spells. Even an outpost will surely have some books and wares you can purchase. We may as well make this rotten fruit into wine, if the gods are going to force our hand."

Eric dropped his cleaned out bowl onto the stone below, causing a rattling sound that bounced off the empty shops surrounding them. "I'm with Thistle on that. Who knows when you'll get the next chance to learn more about magic? We're actively trying to avoid most of the places where you'd be able to get that sort of knowledge."

Grumph nodded slowly, though his eyes never left the small man who was stuck to the road. He trusted Thistle, and the point was a valid one, but all the same, he couldn't shake the feeling that his friend's crooked little mind was trying to coax as many of them into heading for safety as possible. His suspicions were all but confirmed at Thistle's next words.

"You might want to go as well, Eric. Between my paladin abilities, Timuscor's fighting prowess, and a whole town of places to hole up, there's very little chance of us actually facing any real danger here. The trip to Cadence Hollow is going to be the riskiest part of our plan, and having your eyes along may just make the difference in everyone arriving safely."

"Nice effort," Eric told him, a slight smirk betraying that he knew exactly what the gnome was trying to pull. "But anything that can get through Gabby and Grumph is more than my short sword will make a dent in. I'm better off sticking around here, trying to see if I can figure out where everyone ran off to."

"You don't know how to track very well," Thistle said.

"True, but I've got plenty of time to practice. Three days' worth, maybe six depending on whether or not they can use magic to get back here." Eric leaned down and patted his friend carefully on the helm that obscured part of Thistle's weathered face. "Besides, now that we all know you have certain compulsions when it comes to dealing with evil, do you really expect us to leave you with someone you might be able to give the slip?"

Timuscor looked around, wearing his confusion like a princess wore ribbons in her hair. "Why would Thistle try to get away from me?"

"So that he could do something idiotic, like confront the source of the evil by himself, get killed, and do what he thinks of as setting us free to go on without him," Gabrielle explained. "Completely ignoring the fact that if something killed one of us, we'd all damn sure try to get revenge, even if we died in the process."

"Your dedication and loyalty is both touching and highly inconvenient for keeping you out of harm's way," Thistle said. "But very well; Eric and Timuscor will stay with me, while Gabrielle and Grumph will ride with all haste to Cadence Hollow. If the mages are unwilling to help, then pay them to send word to Alcatham's capital. I cannot imagine the king wants a magical, mind-possessing plague to run about unchecked. Good or bad, they'll certainly do something about it, and hopefully it will work to our advantage. Now then, with that settled, it has been officially decided that I am staying in Briarwillow to investigate the source of the evil magic."

Thistle struggled against the ground, his armor rattling as he worked in vain to pull himself free. After a few moments, he tilted his head skyward and called out to the heavens with a raised voice.

"Ahem. I said, I AM STAYING IN BRIARWILLOW!"

A soft popping sound, like a leg pulling free of mud, filled their ears, and Thistle's right arm rose from the ground. He tried the other limbs and found them slightly more mobile, yet undeniably still stuck to the road.

"A dozen gods in the pantheon, and I had to worship the one who enjoys being glib."

*   *   *

By the time the horses were unstabled and loaded up with supplies, Thistle had regained full movement of all his limbs and pulled himself free from the road's grasp. Despite the returned mobility, he was under no illusions about what would happen if he tried to mount one of their steeds and ride out of town. This was one of the obligations that came with wielding the power of a god, and was exactly why he'd tried to turn Grumble down in the first place. There was no use standing around complaining, though; Thistle preferred to spend his mental energy attempting to find some method for escaping the predicament.

As he watched Gabrielle and Grumph ride quickly out of sight, Thistle reviewed the facts as he knew them. They were in a town that had unearthed a skull that killed any who touched it and had cursed the whole town with a sickness. That same skull had vanished from a locked chest that was under constant guard. A priest of Kalzidar came to town some time later and tricked the townspeople into performing unknown rituals, which transformed their death-like sickness into a maddening fever. Then the screaming came three days later, and in only a few moments, the entire town had emptied itself out. It was a cruel, strange set of affairs to fall upon the town, but something else bothered Thistle as he mulled over all that he knew.

It didn't actually make sense. Not from the priest's point of view, anyway. If he wanted the skull, then presumably he'd either stolen it or found who had. If he wanted to sow death, the plague had already done that for him. Changing the form of the sickness had no redeeming value, save that it made for a temporarily bustling town. Kalzidar was indeed wicked; however, nothing in the myths made him seem like one to dole out pointless commands. The priest's actions seemed to have added no deaths, gained nothing not already easy to take, and provided no new opportunities. Thistle knew this couldn't be the case, which meant there were simply pieces of the puzzle that he'd yet to see. He'd have to catch a glimpse if he hoped to understand just what was going on, and unfortunately, there was only one place that came to mind for where he might get that chance.

"Copper for your thoughts." Eric walked over, wiping small beads of sweat from his brow. Loading the horses had been a simple but cumbersome task, at least for someone with his lithe frame.

"You're better off keeping your money," Thistle advised. "There's nothing pleasant in what's swirling about in my head."

"Then I'll share mine with you," Eric replied. "As I see it, we have at least three days, potentially six or more, to kill before Grumph and Gabrielle will return with help. The first of those should be spent rounding up food and other supplies that will spoil, and fortifying one of these places so that we can safely spend our nights there. I noticed a few with potential during the search last night, so we've got a nice head start there. Altogether, that will take us one, perhaps two days to complete, which means we should begin to consider what to do with the rest of our time in Briarwillow."

The sound of clacking armor filled the air as Timuscor began traipsing across the road. Unlike Eric, he wore no sheen of sweat from the recent labor. Beneath the heavy plates were thick, powerful muscles that nearly rivaled Grumph in terms of pure strength. Timuscor was physically built for knighthood, almost as if he'd been designed by the gods specifically to fulfill that role. It was a happy coincidence that Thistle and Eric had both noticed, but made no remarks on. The implications were more than either wanted to thoroughly discuss.

"You want to go look for the rest of the townsfolk," Thistle said, determined to get the matter resolved before Timuscor was in earshot. Strong and bold though their new friend was, he tended to prefer action over discussion, and there was no sense putting any ideas in his head.

"I think we need to, honestly. It wouldn't do much good for Grumph and Gabby to come back and find us with no clue as to where they need to direct those mages."

"They're mages," Thistle countered. "I suspect they can find that information on their own."

"But not what they're going up against, if the people of Briarwillow are even still alive, if the plague is still contagious, or any number of things. Look, if the mages do show up, we need them to succeed, for the good of everyone. I know you're trying to keep us safe, but we all knew that once we became adventurers, safety was not a luxury afforded to us anymore." Eric turned to the gnome and stared hard into his eyes. "You know better than the others how valuable information is. Let's collect a bounty of it for when our friends return."

There was little time left to talk, as Timuscor was nearly upon them. Thistle marveled at Eric, who was showing cunning and strategy far beyond what he'd displayed in his time as a simple town guard. Constant danger had sharpened the young man, carving out the instincts he'd never had the chance to utilize in his mundane years. It was impressive, and also just a touch frightening. Thistle couldn't help but wonder: if this was Eric after less than three months since leaving Maplebark, what he would he be like in a year's time? It was a thing to consider; however, it paled in comparison to the threats at hand. Much as he disliked admitting it, Eric was right. With time to kill and no way to leave, the best way they could possibly spend their time was gathering information.

"Aye, perhaps that might be for the best," Thistle agreed. "After we've fortified a base and gotten provisions, of course. I've got no desire to be out in the open when darkness falls. Just in case."

Chapter 8

The sun was past its halfway point when Gabrielle and Grumph rode past the last of the farms. Much as she wanted to push her horse, given its age and constitution, doing so might end up forcing her to walk the rest of the way. Despite their thorough search of the town, no one had come upon a single other steed—or pet of any kind, for that matter. The animals, it seemed, had not held out against the plague as long as the humans had.

She slowed her horse as the farmlands faded from sight. Getting clear of Briarwillow had been their most important task; with that accomplished, she could let the horse rest, even if only for a short while. Grumph's pace fell to match hers, and soon they were riding alongside the increasingly dense trees at a moderate pace.

No words passed between them as the sound of hoofbeats filled the air. Grumph was quiet by nature, obscured and deep like a pool of dark water tucked away in some ancient forest. As for Gabrielle, she tended to converse reactively, which gave her little grounds to begin a discussion. Sarcasm was wasted when one's companion stayed silent, after all. Besides, the truth of the matter was that Gabrielle didn't particularly mind the quiet. It reminded her of her days in the woods, when the goblins would "kidnap" her. She could spend whole days nearly undisturbed, practicing her tracking, hunting a quarry, or working on some mindless task to help the camp. Gabrielle had long ago found peace in silence, and she saw no benefit in shattering it pointlessly.

Of course, silence also came with the added benefit of helping one's ears stay sharp. Sometime after they'd put Briarwillow behind them, Gabrielle became aware of the slightest sounds of riders coming in their direction. She turned to Grumph, whose creased forehead told her quite clearly that he'd noticed the sound as well. From the sounds, the riders were pushing their horses far harder than she and Grumph were. If the gods were on their side, it might mean the strangers hadn't heard the comparatively quiet steps of their horses. But even if that were the case, it wouldn't be for long.

With no time to think, Gabrielle did what she specialized in: she took immediate action. Wordlessly directing Grumph with hand gestures, Gabrielle took them off the road and into the forest. She chose a section nearly devoid of brush for entry, then immediately steered them to the densest foliage she could find. Given how little time they had, the coverage they could find was sparse at best, and if any member of the coming riders knew how to track, they'd be found out instantly. Even if these were kingdom soldiers, patrolling the roads to keep them safe, Gabrielle preferred not to be seen. One kingdom's wanted adventurers were another's political bargaining chips.

She held her breath as the hoofbeats drew closer. Her hands gently stroked the mane of her horse, who, for once, she was glad was an older steed. If it had been young and excitable, the sight of the other horses might have spurred it into making noise. As things stood, her mount seemed completely content at being given the chance to rest for a few seconds. Grumph's might still prove to be a problem, but Gabrielle couldn't worry about that. All she could do was focus on the elements within her control.

At last, the riders came into view, pounding past the point where she and Grumph had left the woods. That was cause for relief, yet Gabrielle felt none as she observed the riders heading down the road. They weren't soldiers—that much was certain—and they didn't seem like any adventurers Gabrielle had ever encountered before. In her brief glimpse, she saw that they were road-worn, with mismatched clothing on their backs and too many sacks burdening their horses. They rode with weapons at the ready, scanning the road as they went, searching for . . . she knew not what. Not soldiers or adventurers, then, but they did resemble something Gabrielle had seen on a few unfortunate occasions.

They looked like a group of bandits, riding the kingdom's roads.

Once they were well past, Gabrielle began to move her horse back toward the road. A heavy, green-skinned hand fell across the blood-red armor on her shoulder, holding her in place.

"Wait." Grumph nodded down the road in the direction the bandits had gone, his eyes locked on the horizon.

"Why are we waiting? We should either hurry out of here now or go try to help Thistle and the others. You know they're heading toward Briarwillow, right?"

"Yet no one has visited in weeks," Grumph reminded her.

Gabrielle eased herself back into her saddle as his point hit home. Briarwillow was a town cursed by a magical plague, so far as anyone else knew. According to the citizens, no one had been there since the infection became common knowledge. What were the odds that this group of would-be thieves would choose the day it became deserted to pay the plague-town a visit? Much more likely they were taking advantage of the deserted roads and absent soldiers, waylaying anyone who attempted to escape imminent death in the disease-ridden town. Her blood grew hot at that idea, picturing the poor few that managed to get free, only to have their belongings, and perhaps their lives, taken by these opportunistic thugs.

"Not now." Grumph tightened his grip on her shoulder, bringing Gabrielle back to the moment at hand. She nodded her thanks; controlling the anger that dwelled inside her was a constant battle. Ever since it had broken free, she'd learned to be constantly aware of herself, not letting the rage take control unless she willed it to. Some days were more successful than others.

A familiar sound hit her ears, and she turned in the direction Grumph was still staring. Sure enough, the bandits were coming back, no doubt having hit the edge of the farm lands and deciding that they were close enough to death for their tastes. That meant they were running in a loop, from some point up the road to the edge of Briarwillow and back again. Gabrielle didn't know how long that journey took, or the number of times per day the bandits were making it.

What she did know, what she couldn't deny no matter how much she wished to, was that this made their already problematic plans all the more troublesome.

*   *   *

Timuscor laid a salvaged door on top of the wooden planks, which tripled the density of the basement's outer exit. Thistle stood nearby, holding up hammers and tools to assist with the fortification process as Timuscor worked to secure their second, weaker entrance. Thistle had many talents—wit, words, and wiles, to name only a few—but there was no denying that his stature was an impediment when it came to handling hard labor. Especially when paired with his warped limbs and hunched frame.

"Not quite in the center," Thistle advised him as Timuscor pulled back his hammer. "We want it to be difficult to break through, yet easy to slip out of. Should things go poorly for us, it always pays to have a few escape routes in place."

With a slight nod, Timuscor adjusted his one-handed grip on the door, sliding it to the right until Thistle made a sharp click on the back of his teeth. A few hearty blows got the first nail, already driven into the door itself, through to the planks on the other side. From there, it was a simple matter of slamming the rest in one after the other.

Timuscor enjoyed work like this. It was simple and straightforward, much like the clarity that came over him during a battle. No one was asking him to understand concepts that sounded like the ravings of a madman, or counter opponents that wielded mystical forces as easily as he wielded his blade. This, he understood. What's more, he excelled at it. Being in this strange group often left Timuscor feeling as though he were lacking, even if he couldn't particularly say how. They all seemed so good at so much: Grumph with quiet wisdom, Eric with his nimble stealth, Gabrielle with her fearsome axe, and then, of course, there was Thistle.

The gnome had hopped away from the stool he'd been perched on to hand off the tools, his small, armored footsteps clanging off the walls of the blacksmith's basement. It had been Thistle who suggested they hide out in the subterranean stone dwelling once night came. With a small furnace that fed to the outside for warmth, heavy walls and ceiling for protection, and ample spare weapons to set traps with, this simple hole had all the makings of a serviceable base. Timuscor and Eric had agreed, with the latter heading off to forage for supplies and the former staying to follow Thistle's directions.

When he had first met the party, Timuscor had been more impressed by Eric and the strange object he'd wielded to uncloud Timuscor's mind. Then, he'd grown an appreciation for Gabrielle, as they sparred and he saw the depths of her strength. Once Grumph began to speak—on the few occasions he did—Timuscor saw there was more to the half-orc than mere muscles, and that determination proved right the first time he witnessed his new friend cast a spell. Only Thistle had seemed odd amidst this group of gifted warriors. Small, weak, and with only a pair of throwing daggers to defend himself, Timuscor had assumed Thistle was nothing more than a tagalong the party didn't have the heart to cast aside.

That misimpression lasted only until the second night they were all together, when the wolves attacked. Massive beasts fashioned from claws, teeth, and murder leapt out of the brush at them, catching everyone off guard. Of them all, it was Thistle who was first to react, moving with a determined speed that Timuscor wouldn't have imagined his small body capable of. His first dagger caught a wolf in its flank, while the second managed to clip one beast across its furry throat. As he threw, Thistle let out a primal scream that drew the wolves' attention. Between the yelling and the blades, he succeeded in temporarily turning their wrath onto his too-small form. As those monstrous teeth clanged against his armor and claws stained with long-dried blood scratched for his throat, the others finally snapped into action, assaulting the wolves with such ferocity that, for a moment, Timuscor forgot that the beasts were the attackers.

When the battle was done, Thistle merely hauled himself up, checked to see if the others were hurt, and then healed his wounds with a single prayer and a brief glow of light. The others continued about as if little had happened, but for Timuscor, his world had been fundamentally altered. Thistle, the physically frail gnome he'd taken as a burden, had thrown himself into the fray without a moment's hesitation to protect his friends. What's more, he, that weak little man, had done so wielding the divine gifts provided only by the gods.

There was little that Timuscor could clearly recall from his life before meeting this group: a brief, rushed childhood, time training in the Solium army, that short stint with the awful people he'd been forced to call a party. But one element did shine through with curious clarity: Timuscor had always wanted to be a paladin. It was why he'd trained himself so hard, worked with all his might to master the art of battle. All in the hopes that one day, a god would find him worthy and call Timuscor to his service. Yet here he was, a pinnacle of power and battle acumen, unclaimed by any of the gods. Meanwhile, the weakest person he'd ever encountered wore the paladin's mantle without any pomp or grandeur. Timuscor was not envious of Thistle's achievement, but he did admire it. Clearly, there was something more a paladin needed, something he was lacking. Timuscor stayed close to Thistle, always watching, in the hopes that one day he would grasp what that strange element was.

That had been the plan, anyway. After several weeks, Timuscor had grown to understand that there were many things Thistle had that he didn't, the great majority of them mental. He knew there were strong paladins, though. Timuscor has seen them from a distance while training in the Solium courtyard. He could reach that goal; he knew it was possible. But not if he kept that aspiration to himself, it seemed.

"Thistle, may I ask you something?" With the others riding toward Cadence Hollow and Eric looting all he could, this was the first time Thistle and Timuscor had been alone for any true length of time. Timuscor was determined not to waste the opportunity.

"Certainly, and I'll do my best to provide an answer. I daresay that might be the only thing I can actually contribute in this current endeavor." Thistle pushed aside a set of rusty shields and pulled out a small short sword. He turned it over in his hands several times, then threw it in the middle of the basement floor and went back to searching for more useful items.

"Can you tell me, how does one . . . how did you become a paladin?"

"Found myself between a dragon's maw and claw, so when Grumble dangled me a lifeline, I grabbed onto it. Probably similar tales for many of the others out there, as well." Thistle glanced up from his digging and noticed the solemn, almost reverent expression on Timuscor's face. He quickly spoke again, this time with less frivolity. "I was called by my god to serve him, that's how I became a paladin. To my knowledge, it's the only way we can be made. They look amongst their devoted and find those who have traits they feel will make them worthwhile champions. In my case, Grumble didn't have a great amount of choice warriors to select from, hence why he was willing to settle on someone like me."

"The gods choose from their followers . . ." Timuscor looked as though he'd swallowed some bad berries and was beginning to understand the implications of what such a mistake entailed.

"Paladins serve the just gods, other kinds of servants belong to the wicked ones, but all of us are of their followers," Thistle confirmed. "If I may be so bold, Timuscor, which of the gods in the pantheon do you follow?"

"I don't . . . I've never really prayed to one in particular." Timuscor had tossed a prayer to Cecily, goddess of roads and travel, before going off on any journey, and he'd certainly dropped a few coins at the temple of Grithgow, god of battle, before dangerous missions, but he'd never taken a single god to call his own. It hadn't seemed necessary; paladins were warriors of goodness who made the world better. So long as one was on the side of the just gods, what did it matter who amongst them they bowed to?

"There's certainly nothing wrong with that," Thistle assured him. "As the many gods serve their functions, so can the prayers of a mortal be split to suit their needs. But, as far as paladins go, we hold within us a slim bit of our god's divine favor. From what legends say, to create a paladin is for the god to loan out a tiny fraction of their power. It's why they are so selective in making them, and why they tend to only choose from those they believe will serve them and them alone."

"I see." Timuscor leaned down and plucked another piece of lumber from the pile they'd gathered. "I always thought the gods merely made paladins of those who were strong and tried to do what was right."

"Sadly, the gods are more self-serving than you give them credit for." Thistle could see the disappointment in his companion's eyes, but there was nothing he could do to change the truth of the situation. Gods chose from their favorites; that was all there had ever been to it. "I think our world would be a better one if they did pick your way, though. There are certainly many out there who could do a great deal of good, if only given the means."

"Perhaps it would be," Timuscor agreed. "But it seems it's not our place to question the will of the gods."

"Nonsense. If anything, our entire role as mortals is to do exactly that. If we went along with everything they wanted, what would make us different from mindless pieces on a game board? The gods have their wills, and we have ours. Certainly they win more often than not, but we still have to struggle. Because sometimes, with enough determination and luck, ours are the wills that win out."

"Says the gnome who spent half the morning stuck to the road for trying to ignore his god's orders."

"I did say they won most of the time," Thistle reminded him. "But my point is simply this: we live in a wild world where anything is possible. Grumble himself was once nothing more than the abused servant of a mad wizard. If a simple kobold can ascend to divinity, then perhaps one day you can find a god willing to make you paladin without quite as much devotion as they usually require."

"How did you know I wanted to be a paladin?"

"Because, when most people find out how rare it is to be made one, they're relieved," Thistle explained. "As you've seen, it is a job that comes with many obligations which can shorten one's lifespan. You weren't relieved at all, though. You were disappointed."

Timuscor nodded as he hefted the next board into place. "It's been my dream for as far back as I can remember."

"Then keep pursuing it with all you have. Just because I only know of one path to paladinhood, doesn't mean it's the only one that exists. And, speaking on a personal note, I think it would do our ranks well to have one like you among us. You've got the spirit of a paladin, if not the actual abilities."

"Thank you." Timuscor couldn't bear to look at Thistle dead on after receiving such high praise; so instead, he focused on hammering in the board he was holding. The nails went right in after each powerful blow he delivered. Timuscor dearly wished it were so easy to grasp hold of his goal, a single, swift bout of effort followed by success.

He wasn't quite ready to give up, though. Timuscor would keep hammering at the door that barred him from his dream, banging against it ceaselessly until either the door shattered or he did.

Chapter 9

Gabrielle nudged her horse forward, weaving between the trees as best she could manage. There was no telling how much time they were losing traveling off the road, but it was certainly a faster alternative than meeting a full group of bandits with only herself and Grumph to fight them off. His spells were quick and her axe was strong, but neither of them was so confident of victory that they proposed the idea of taking on a needless battle. Despite Gabrielle's certainty that she could take down at least a few of the bandits in any skirmish, it wouldn't be enough to keep them alive. Dying on the road was bad for the citizens of Briarwillow, their friends stuck back in that town, and, most of all, Gabrielle herself. She'd made some peace with the fact that choosing the life of a barbarian warrior meant her death would ultimately come in battle; Gabrielle just didn't want it to be a pointless death.

Shadows of the trees stretched out before them like grasping fingers. Night was falling, and Gabrielle's mind was split with worry for her and Grumph, as well as for those they'd left behind. At least the others had shelter to work with; she and Grumph would just have to hope their luck at not seeing monsters held. Traveling through the woods made the prospect all the more risky; however, they'd still yet to encounter so much as a stray boar. Once, the goblins had told Gabrielle that the beasts of the wild were more connected with the magic that flowed through their realm than the sentient races would ever be. They believed animals could sense great power, and either gathered near it or ran away, depending on whether it was of light or dark. If her tribe was right, then it certainly didn't bode well for Briarwillow. Everything that flew, slithered, or crawled seemed to be keeping a wide distance.

Still, foreboding as it made the forest seem, Gabrielle was grateful for the unexpected solitude. If the forests had been swollen with monsters and the roads sieged by bandits, there was a very good chance they would have had to turn back. At least this way they were making progress, incremental though it was.

She was about to guide her horse through a moderate gap between a pair of thick-trunked trees when an unexpected scent wafted through the air. Gabrielle jerked her horse to a stop and held up a hand, indicating for Grumph to hold his position as well. The half-orc complied immediately, resting a heavy hand on the hilt of his demon-bone blade.

"I smell smoke." Her eyes scanned the forest, searching for the telltale flicker of a fire. They found nothing, nor did her ears pick out the sounds of men settling in for the night. If they were near the bandits' camp, then every one of them was displaying a mastery of stealth that had been unseen when watching them barrel noisily down the roads. It was possible—as were all things—but unlikely.

Moving as quietly as she could with an animal that weighed hundreds of pounds beneath her, Gabrielle started forward once more. The scent of smoke still lingered, yet no amount of searching would reveal its source. No flames, nor smoke, nor crackling of wood burning. It was as though she merely smelled the ghost of a fire. She noticed a thick grove to her right—trees lined densely enough that it might have hidden a few people taking rest, but not so close that they would have concealed the flickering light of flames.

Gabrielle halted again, this time lowering herself down from the horse as she did. A grove like that made too easy a place to lay an ambush, especially with the unexplained scent dancing in her nose. If it was filled with bandits, best to try and take them by surprise; if it was actually empty, then all the better. They'd need to make camp soon; the grove could just as easily be their hiding place as an enemy's.

She skulked through the forest, moving as softly as the wind's whisper. Eric might be quicker and quieter than she in the caverns and castles of the world, but she knew how to walk with silent steps in a forest. Behind her, Grumph stood, still mounted on his horse, hand off his blade and resting readily at his side. His movements would surely give them away, if indeed they did have any advantage of surprise, and they both knew it. Instead of stomping about, Grumph was readying himself to act if it was needed. While his spells weren't the most potent, a well-placed fire blast amidst the trees would provide ample distraction for escape.

As she drew closer to the grove, Gabrielle's straining ears finally caught something other than rustling leaves or the breathing of horses. It was a voice, muffled and light, yet with a whimsical tone. There were no words being spoken—at least none she could make out—only a slight, rhythmic cadence being mumbled. Gabrielle slowed her already tentative movements. The voice . . . was it humming? She couldn't be certain, but she did know the smell of smoke was growing stronger the closer she walked to the grove. Hesitating for only a moment, Gabrielle decided to see her plan through. If it was a bandit, there seemed to be only one, which meant she and Grumph could hopefully handle them without trouble. Perhaps they could even convince this mystery bandit to talk, gaining enough information to use the road safely.

Gabrielle quickly reached the distance where careful movements would work against her; skill could only compensate for so much of the noise her armor made. Better to charge in at once, taking her quarry by surprise while she still had the chance. With a single glance over her shoulder to Grumph, Gabrielle pointed to the trees and bolted forward.

She burst into the clearing, axe raised high overhead and a look of barely constrained fury on her face. Waiting for her inside was not a bandit, as she'd expected, nor was it some simple beast that had been making strange sounds. Instead, there was an elven woman with short, cropped brown hair and an expression of sheer panic at the mad, axe-wielding woman that had suddenly torn forth from the trees.

"Graaaa!" Gabrielle let out a yell before she'd even realized it was at her lips, the familiar fog of battle overtaking her mind.

"Gaaaaaaaah!" The elven woman shrieked, fumbling through a small pouch at her side and producing a silver rod. She pointed it toward Gabrielle, her hands shaking as she stared down the wild, blonde woman in the blood-red armor. "S-S-Stay back! I know how to use this!"

The unmasked terror in her voice cut through to Gabrielle's reasonable side, and it began to occur to her that perhaps this woman was not a holed up bandit after all. Pushing back against the waves of anger that were trying to fuel her, demanding she slam her axe into something's skull, Gabrielle began to assert her rational mind, and as she did so, the situation made much more sense.

Next to the elven woman's feet was a sleeping bag under a backpack. To the left of those things were a waterskin, a large satchel, and what appeared to be pieces of dead rabbit sitting atop a strange box boasting strange runes. As Gabrielle watched, she realized the rabbit was sizzling, as if being cooked over a fire, yet still none was in sight.

Slowly, she lowered her blade until it rested in front of her defensively. "Are you a bandit?"

"Am *I* a bandit? You're the one who just came tearing in swinging that axe all about." The woman's hand steadied slightly, but the silver rod was still wobbling through the air as she spoke. "Seems to me you're the one looking to rob and kill."

"Sorry about that. We've been hiding from thieves riding the roads all day, and when I saw you hiding here, I . . . well, I jumped to some wrong conclusions. I'm not here to rob or hurt you, though. My name is Gabrielle."

"I appreciate the words, Gabrielle, but I can't help noticing you're still holding that big axe at the ready."

"You've still got your silver stick pointed at me."

"You're the one who came bursting into my campsite."

"I suppose that's fair." Gabrielle leaned down and carefully set her axe on the lush grass of the forest's floor. She then rose back up, hands in front of her chest to show there were no other concealed weapons on her person. "See, no more axe."

"It's a start." Slowly, the woman lowered her rod, though she pointedly did not release it from her hand. "So, Gabrielle, was it? What brings you to these woods, invading people's resting spots?"

"On my way to Cadence Hollow. Had to stick to the woods in order to avoid the bandits," Gabrielle replied honestly.

"Same here. Are you cutting around Briarwillow as well?"

Gabrielle shook her head. "No, we're coming from Briarwillow. Things are . . . strange there. We need to get word to the mages at Cadence Hollow so that they'll help."

The woman snorted, an oddly melodic yet disgusting sound. "Good luck with that. Mages aren't exactly known for their altruism."

"Our friends are back there. We have to try."

"That a fact?" Looking Gabrielle up and down, the woman seemed to relax slightly, for the first time allowing herself to look away from her invader, even if only for the briefest of seconds. "Well, Gabrielle, you seem to be telling the truth, or at least, if you were a robber, I'd hope you would have come up with a better lie. Why don't we sit and talk for a few moments? Perhaps we might be able to help one another. This journey can be perilous, you know."

Gabrielle slowly lowered her arms. "That sounds like a good idea. May I ask what to call you?"

"Me?" The woman did a deep, wobbly bow that almost sent her tipping over. "I am Fritz. Traveling purveyor of potent potions, expert in enchanted items, and conjuror of the cheapest tricks you'll find anywhere between Baltmur and the Dragon Sea. I deal in anything with stoppers, runes, or switches, and all at very reasonable prices."

"Pleasure to meet you, Fritz." A sudden thought occurred to Gabrielle at the mention of magic, and she decided it was best to get it out of the way as soon as possible. "Before it comes as another surprise, I should probably tell you that I've got a friend traveling with me, and he's waiting outside the grove in case I need help. He's a peaceful fellow, but he's also a half-orc."

Fritz raised one of her barely visible eyebrows and looked Gabrielle over once more. "Are you sure you aren't secretly bandits?"

*   *   *

"More roasted turkey?" Eric held the platter up, only to have both Thistle and Timuscor wave him off. To be fair, they had managed to put a sizable dent in the massive bird. It was so large, in fact, that Eric deeply suspected the plucked foul was one of the rare dire animals that occasionally popped up. They were stronger, bigger, and all-around more dangerous than their more mundane counterparts. Also, as Eric had learned after they cooked it using the inn's oven, more delicious.

The three of them were huddled together in the blacksmith's basement, which they'd begun to think of as their temporary home while they were stuck in Briarwillow. They'd watched the last rays of the sun fade from the sky before barricading themselves inside. Thistle had built a very small hole into their back door, barely big enough to stick four nails through, which would serve as their way to see when the sun rose once more. Eric was keenly aware of the fact that they might be going overboard, especially since they had no reason to believe the people of Briarwillow would return, and he didn't give one steaming pile of bugbear shit about that fact. He much preferred being overcautious and alive to flippant and dead.

"Who's taking first shift?" Timuscor asked. He planned to take the middle shift, worst of the three as it broke up one's sleep schedule, himself.

"No one, as I can't say I see much need for holding watch tonight." Thistle picked at the remains of turkey on his plate, occasionally sticking one of the smaller pieces into his mouth despite the protests of his full stomach. "Anything trying to break in will make more than enough noise to wake us, and if it's powerful enough to tear through our fortifications before we can get ready, then I doubt we'd stand any real chance against it even if we were prepared. Better to get a good rest, especially since last night's was interrupted."

"It won't hurt us to hold watch anyway, just in case," Eric said.

"I greatly disagree," Thistle replied. "Weeks on the road have worn us down, and last night's lack of sleep is only compounding the issue. For what lies ahead of us, we need to be at our best. That means allowing ourselves the luxury of a restful evening or two, as well as properly prepared meals. I've agreed to your plans about looking for the missing townsfolk, but we are going to do it in a way that offers the best chance of returning alive. The first part of which is allowing our bodies and minds a chance to repair themselves."

"You can both rest; I don't mind keeping a long watch," Timuscor offered.

"Kind though that is, you need the rest as much as either of us," Thistle said. "Perhaps even more. With Gabrielle and Grumph gone, Eric and I will be trusting in your strength should things go awry. It serves all of us if you're in tip-top shape."

Eric considered trying to argue the point with Thistle, but as he did, an unwanted yawn wormed its way free from his mouth, essentially proving the gnome's point for him. Thistle was right; now that they'd finally stopped moving, they were all feeling the weeks of travel piled on top of them. For Eric, the idea of a whole night without having to feel constantly alert, even when he was dreaming, seemed so luxurious a commodity that he felt like he should make sure his coin purse hadn't suddenly grown lighter. Thistle seemed more hunched than usual, and Timuscor had dark, visible bags beneath his eyes. If they were going to try and refresh themselves, there wasn't likely to be a better opportunity than this one.

"Thistle has the right idea. We owe it to the people of Briarwillow to be in top form when we try to save them. It gives us the best chance of discovering something useful, not to mention staying alive long enough to relay the information when Grumph and Gabby bring back mages. Let's take tonight off, for everyone's sake."

Timuscor nodded, then took a bite of bread and chewed it slowly. A niggling suspicion in Eric's brain told him that the knight would still be sleeping with one eye open, no matter what they said. That was Timuscor's choice, though; Eric neither had the power nor the desire to force his will on another's mind. All they could do was make the case and provide the opportunity. What Timuscor did with it was in his hands.

"Thank you, Eric," Thistle said. "It's especially important, because tomorrow, we're going to be doing some traveling."

"We are?" Timuscor asked.

"Aye. As we were working today, I realized that the strange feeling Grumble placed in my stomach is doing more than weakening my appetite: it also seems to be slightly tugging me in a constant direction. Near as I can guess, that's the spot where the source of the evil is, and where we've got the best chance of finding Briarwillow's citizens."

"The gods have strange ways of passing information," Eric remarked. "Can you tell us where your gut is pointing you?"

"I fully intend to, but not until the morning." Thistle set his plate down in a box they'd brought with them to hold debris. "No need to set your minds alight with ideas just before it's time to shut them down. Once dawn breaks and we are ready to go, I promise to share all that I can with you two. The paladin senses are far from exact, but I have a few solid hunches of where we should start, if nothing else."

With the matter settled, Thistle laid down on his bedroll, gazing up at the thick ceiling separating them from the world above. Timuscor followed suit a few moments later, and Eric, the last of them to be awake, blew out their salvaged lantern before settling down on the floor as well.

The three of them lay there until sleep finally claimed them, their last moments of consciousness spent straining with all of their might to hear the first warning signs of footsteps traipsing through the town. Those sounds never came, and soon all three were completely dead to the world.

Chapter 10

"They're made by this group of wizards out in Thatchshire's capital. Cooks everything just like a fire would, but without the smoke or light. Perfect for the merchant or adventurer-on-the-go who wants to keep a low profile." Fritz sat beside her strange rune-covered box, reaching down periodically to rotate the roasting strips of meat Grumph had pulled from his pack. Darkness wrapped around them like a protective curtain, the only illumination coming from the nearly full moon that hung fat and white over their heads. Ordinarily, a fire would have been lit even with the risk of attracting bandits, but with seemingly no animals to keep at bay, it seemed more prudent to simply let the stars provide lighting.

"They started out as bigger models made for royalty and those with lots of wealth, but over the past year, the wizards focused on creating small ones like this that could be sold across kingdoms more easily. Since I was already going to hit the road to make my fortune anyway, I've been traveling across the lands, showing it off and taking orders for the wizards."

"Forgive me, I don't quite understand. You just travel around, hoping to come across people who are in need of a potion or enchanted item and willing to pay top gold for it?" Gabrielle was impressed by the way the box was cooking meat, but she didn't quite see how one could make a living off odd sales of circumstance.

Fritz shook her head. "Those sales do happen, especially when I go through towns with lots of adventurers, but I make a lot of my gold acting as a facilitator. Let's say a town in Alcatham has a really talented blacksmith-and-wizard duo cranking out quality enchanted weapons. Meanwhile, another town in Solium is seeing an uprising of gnolls, but their entire industry is based on farming. As someone who roams about and knows all the towns, I can connect the Solium town with the crafters in Alcatham. They buy a bunch of those quality weapons, sell them to the adventurers who come pouring through to kill gnolls at a substantial mark-up, and I take a reasonable chunk as my finder's fee. There are dozens of situations like that popping up every year. A little ingenuity and a lot of travel can make one a fair bit of gold."

"Industrious." Grumph sat further away from Fritz than Gabrielle did, and made a point not to make any motions that might come off as aggressive. Elves and orcs, even half-orcs, had a rather storied and bloody history where their interactions overlapped. While the sins of their ancestors certainly weren't theirs to bear, the fact remained that each race tended to be a bit wary around the other. Since they were the ones invading her camp, it only seemed fitting that he make the show of peaceful intentions.

"Thank you. It took a lot of time to work out the business model to a point of efficiency, but that's the one resource I've got plenty of." Fritz chuckled at her own joke and checked the cooking meat. Elves were not technically immortal—at least, not so far as anyone knew—but they did tend to measure their life spans in millennia rather than simple years. Only frequent wars and fertility issues kept them from overrunning the world. Delicately, Fritz pulled the slices of elk from her magic cooking-box, laid them on a small metal plate, and handed it across to Grumph and Gabrielle.

Each took a piece and bit into it, unsure of exactly what to expect. It turned out to be exactly what Fritz had promised: hot, cooked meat just like it came from a fire. Gabrielle was barely through her first piece when she reached for a second.

"That's good. I mean, *really* good. How much does one of those cook-boxes go for, anyway? It might come in handy with as much traveling as we do."

"Standard rate is two thousand gold pieces," Fritz told her. "Though there's currently a list of people waiting to get theirs that's about six months long. For an extra five hundred, the wizards will move your order to the front of the line."

Gabrielle was trying not to choke on her second bite of meat after hearing the words "two thousand gold pieces." Between the four of them, they had perhaps three hundred left from their winnings at the Appleram tournament. Aside from royalty, who had that much gold? And that much to spend on a useful, but ultimately unnecessary, magical item?

Fritz noticed the look on Gabrielle's face and smiled knowingly. "Magic items aren't cheap, you know. Besides, adventurers are always looking for ways to spend their treasure. You don't drag it all around in coin form, do you?"

"No . . . we don't." Sometimes, it still caught Gabrielle off guard to be taken for an adventurer. Even after all the effort to appear as one, and the actual progress in learning the skills needed to survive such a lifestyle, there was a part of her that continued to feel as though she were doing nothing more than playing a game of pretend, that someone would come along and call her out as the mayor's daughter dressed up like a warrior. "But we haven't come across that kind of gold in the first place."

"Ah, just starting out then." Fritz nodded as she pressed her finger to a spot on the side of the magic box. An instant later, the runes flickered out and the elven woman slipped the device into her satchel, where it seemed to vanish without so much as making a bump. "I've seen plenty in that position on my travels as well. Nothing to worry about; once you slay your first evil dragon or mad wizard, there's bound to be a bounty of gold for you to scoop up. Not quite sure why they always have huge stacks of uninvested income lying about, but they do."

Gabrielle and Grumph both had a pretty good theory about why the piles of gold would be lying about, but neither said a word as Fritz finished putting away her cooking tools. Savvy as the elven trader seemed, explaining what they'd learned about their world and how it was impacted by beings from another one would make them seem crazy at best. Even seeing what happened to Timuscor and experiencing some of the effects from The Bridge firsthand, Gabrielle still wasn't entirely convinced she believed that story. One could only imagine what Fritz would think, being shown no proof at all.

"Thank you for cooking our dinner," Gabrielle said. It seemed the safest place to steer the conversation, and it would lead to the point she actually needed to address. "Your help saved us a lot of trouble."

"Well, we are all stuck hiding in this forest together. Seemed only nice to help one another out."

"Perhaps we could continue to do so, at least until we reach Cadence Hollow. A third person to share night-watches with will let us get more rest, and help you as well. Plus, it would be better to have a third around, just in case we fail at avoiding the bandits in our next day's travels."

"The keeping watch part I can certainly help with, but I wouldn't count on me to do much in a fight," Fritz warned. "My specialty is wheeling and dealing, not bashing in heads. That's why I keep gear that lets me travel unobserved; I win the fight by not engaging in it at all."

"The best strategy," Grumph said. Fritz looked at him with a touch of surprise, evidently not expecting a half-orc to enjoy tactics that focused on avoiding violence rather than starting it.

"No question there," Gabrielle agreed. "Though, you obviously have a few backup tricks up your sleeves, judging by that silver stick you pointed at me earlier."

"Ah yes, my pre-charged wand, made to let even the most mundane of folks call forth the power of a magical spell." Fritz dipped her hand into the satchel and pulled out the silver object in question as though it had been resting directly in reach. "This one will do quite a number on whoever I shoot it at, but its magical core is depleted thanks to a pack of rock lions that attacked me. There's probably only enough left for one or two more uses before I have to overpay some mage to give it a recharge."

"All the more reason for us to travel together then," Gabrielle pointed out. "Grumph and I may not be the strongest warriors in all the kingdom, but we're a far sight better than nothing in a pinch. And we could really use someone who's as familiar with the area as you are."

"No argument here; I think working together benefits us all," Fritz said. "Even if I'm not sure that going to Cadence Hollow is in your best interests. Honestly, you're probably better off going back to help your friends. Mages are a notoriously self-serving group, and no one knows that better than someone who does business with them. Unless you're one of them, or there's some gain to be had, you've got a better chance of convincing a dragon to lend you aid than a mages' guild."

"But they do help out other spellcasters?" Gabrielle leaned forward, unintentionally signaling her interest so keenly she may as well have lit a signal fire.

"They help out others in their guild, but that only allows in conjurors of a certain level, not just random adventurers. Unless one of you is secretly a sorcerer, I'm afraid you're probably out of luck."

Grumph coughed discreetly in his hand, a sound that made a more primal part of Gabrielle's brain put itself on alert for danger. He looked at Fritz sheepishly—or at least as sheepishly as a half-orc is capable of, which is really more like a wolf swaddled in sheepskin—and pulled out the precious tome from his backpack.

"What about a wizard?"

* * *

It started, as all things ultimately did, in darkness. No light, no sound, not even a sense of self as he hovered there. Then came the noises: shambling, tepid footsteps and the shaking of the earth beneath countless bodies. A moon appeared, casting its weak light through the world, shining down on the battlefield below. The beams reflected off the shining armor of soldiers, marching beneath banners Thistle didn't recognize. They flowed across the land like a river of steel and determination, all converging on a single point on the plateau. Standing there, waiting for them at the center, stood a single man. His features were impossible to see, but the way the light dimmed as it drew near him told all that was worth knowing.

As the armies reached him, they let out cheers and yells before surging forward, weapons drawn and at the ready. Darkness dripped from his hands as he met their advance. The lucky soldiers were turned into little more than piles of pulped flesh in a single blow. Other poor souls fell into patches of shadow that slipped and whispered between their feet, tumbling into a void that wouldn't be so merciful as to offer a quick death.

Powerful though he was, the armies continued their attack, being replaced as quickly as they were churned through. With sheer, vast, sacrificial numbers, they began to turn the tide, landing strikes and drawing blood with increasing frequency. For every drop of blood they spilled, he took hundreds of their lives, yet they paid that toll without hesitation. At last, a soldier with a blade that shone bright in the moonlight slipped forward in the lake of pooling blood, missing an attack by chance more than skill, and pressed his sword through the lone man's heart.

A wave of silence burst forth, and every warrior around him fell to the ground, expressions as still as the graves they'd been sent to. The only one who survived was the soldier still shakily gripping the blade sticking out of the man's back. Slowly, they both sank to their knees, staring into each other's eyes as the life drained from one of them.

When the deed was fully done, the soldier pulled his sword from the man's chest, dark blood oozing down its blade. Cheering soldiers gathered around him, quickly dismembering the corpse lest it find new life through some unknown dark magic. As for he who had done the deed, the killer merely stared at the dark stain on his sword. It was impossible to know what was going through his mind, even as the others lifted him high in celebration.

But, for just a moment, there seemed to be slightest flash of grief flickering in his half-covered eyes.

*   *   *

When Thistle first woke, he thought for a moment he was still on that battlefield, bearing witness to terrible carnage. All he could see was darkness. No moon, no stars, not even the light of a dying fire to guide his eyes. Then, as Timuscor let out a soft snore, reality came rushing back to the gnome, just as the armies had overrun their foe.

A dream, then, that's what it had been. Unlike any Thistle had ever experienced before, save only for the time he'd come face-to-face with his own god in the land of slumber. It seemed like a fair bet that the two were similar, because they came from the same source: Grumble. That paladins were sometimes given visions from their gods was no great secret, though Thistle had always assumed they were more akin to directions than what he'd received. Go slay this monster, come save this village, that sort of thing.

The dream was still in his mind, clear as a true memory, not disappearing like morning fog as did most nocturnal visions. He could picture the banners of those armies in perfect detail, yet they still remained foreign to him. None of the kingdoms he was aware of used such symbols, save for one sigil he'd seen flying over a smaller unit. That one had looked, at least cursorily, similar to the crest of Solium with which Thistle was all too familiar. As for the others, they were utterly alien.

Either this meant his visions took place in the ancient past, before the current kingdoms had come into being, or it was somewhere Thistle had never so much as heard of. There was also the possibility that he had seen events that were yet to come, but if it was so far off that all the kingdoms would change, then Thistle highly doubted there would be any point in giving him such a dream. The other two were far more likely, not that this fact helped give him any idea of what he was supposed to actually take away from the vision.

A powerful, nearly unstoppable man being killed only under the combined might of several armies and the sacrifice of thousands of lives. Thistle wasn't certain how the vision impacted what had happened to the people of Briarwillow or why Grumble was keeping him in the town. All he had was a sole hunch, and he didn't at all care for the implications that came with it. Whoever this mystery man had been, whatever powers he'd been gifted with or tyranny he'd wrought, there was one fact that seemed uncomfortably clear from Thistle's vision.

That man's body had certainly had a skull.

Chapter 11

"You're sure this is the right way?" Eric scanned the landscape around them, searching for even the slightest signs of life. Nothing met his eye besides the worn dirt their horses were clomping across, the thin patch of trees to their left, and the mountain stretching upward in the distance, nearly hiding the morning sun as they rode toward it.

"As a matter of fact, no, I'm not sure at all," Thistle said, turning his head so he wasn't speaking directly into Timuscor's back. With Grumph gone, he'd had to burden himself on the second strongest of their remaining horses, which belonged to Timuscor. Had they been moving at a brisk speed, the extra weight might have been a serious issue, but by keeping to a careful pace, the steed was holding up well, even with a human and a gnome on top. "This whole enterprise is experimental by its very nature. I'm trying to guide us with a strange feeling in my stomach, which I'm only presuming to be a divinely inspired sense that tells me where evil lurks. You should probably prepare yourself for more misses than hits today."

"Someone's a little testy this morning," Eric muttered. He'd meant to do it quietly, but with nothing around to absorb sound, the words easily carried across to Thistle's ears.

"My apologies. I had . . . trouble sleeping." It had taken at least an hour for Thistle to finally grow tired again after waking from his vision, and the rest he did find was fitful and disturbed. Every time he closed his eyes, memories of the dream danced through his mind. Blood-soaked ground strewn with bodies, pits of darkness that seemed to stretch on infinitely, and the fierce eyes of the one man taking on thousands of others. Strangest of all was the moment he was finally felled, that last exchange playing itself out more times than Thistle could count before the sun finally rose.

"If you're feeling bad, we don't have to do this," Eric said.

"I'm afraid that's where you're wrong. I have to follow this instinct I've been given, no matter the cost that comes with it. That was the bargain I made when I accepted Grumble's power, and I'll not go back on my word. Especially not to a god."

"No doubt such a sturdy moral center is precisely why Grumble chose you in the first place." Timuscor spoke without turning back, keeping his eyes always on the path ahead. Thistle thought the young man's attitude had shifted, just a touch, since their discussion on the prior day. Whether Timuscor had given up on the idea of becoming a paladin or was committed to it all the harder, he'd clearly made a choice. Thistle didn't think it actually mattered which one he'd picked; so long as he was set in some direction, Timuscor would be better off than before.

"That, and I actually ran toward a demon instead of away. We worshippers of Grumble are not known for our bravery, so even such a small act stuck out to him."

"You know, I keep meaning to ask you about that, but then more important things come up." Eric steered his horse closer to Timuscor and Thistle, straightening out when he was only a few feet away. "I've heard you say that Grumble was just a lowly minion himself, and that when he attained godhood that's who he decided to look over. How exactly did a kobold minion become a god in the first place?"

"How does anyone become a god at all?" Timuscor added. "I'd thought they were all formed from the start, like the stars in the sky."

"Some were," Thistle said. "Mostly the gods of the races, like Mithingow, god of the gnomes. Or Adamus, god of humans. Legends say that they were born with the world, and they made their people of the land in their own image. From them sprang the sentient creatures that we collectively think of as 'people.' There were also primal, powerful gods who ruled over the elements themselves, though most of their names have been lost to history. They neither cared for nor about our kind, working only to ensure their element was in balance with the others. Those were the original gods, as the legend goes, but throughout the years since creation, a precious few mortals have found their way into the ranks of the divine."

"I know a few of those myths; my mother told them to me as bedtime stories," Eric added. "Longinus was a great hero who found godhood when he slew a demon that had eaten up half of the hells to increase its power. So much magic poured from its neck that when it rained upon Longinus, he was imbued with the power of the divine."

"If the demon had enough power to turn a human into a god, wouldn't the demon have been a god itself?" Timuscor pointed out.

"These are myths, mere stories spread about how the gods became what they are," Thistle told him. "I wouldn't expect too much accuracy from them. They're meant to capture a spirit more than details. None of the gods actually want to share how one climbs the steps toward divinity, for fear that others would follow in their footsteps."

"Which brings us back to my original question: what's the legend for how Grumble became a god?" Eric asked.

"Grumble's tale, like Grumble himself, is a simple one." Thistle leaned back slightly in the saddle, allowing him to speak without having to keep his head constantly turned. "He was the minion of a great, if overly ambitious, wizard. In the mage's plundering and research, it is said he came across a ceremony of tremendous power, one so ancient he could not discern its source. Wanting to see what it did, but not willing to put himself at risk, the wizard performed the ritual and threw Grumble in as the target at the last moment. No doubt he believed it was some sort of terrible curse or means to wreak horrible damage, thinking it would be of use against his enemies. We can only imagine his shock when his servant emerged, not only unharmed, but also blessed with divine power. He certainly would have used the power on himself, but Grumble never gave him the chance. Thus, the god of the minions was born."

"Do you believe that's actually how it happened?" Timuscor asked.

"I believe it's close enough that whatever details might be wrong are inconsequential. And, in truth, I've never cared much for how Grumble became a god in the first place. What matters to me is how he uses that status, and Grumble chose to watch over those who previously had none that cared for them. His actions and people tell far more about who he is than a legend of his origins ever could."

"He did seem pretty down to earth," Eric agreed. "I mean, for a god."

Timuscor turned his head so quickly it nearly sent Thistle tumbling off the side of the horse. "You too have met this god?"

"Sort of. We met in a dream. Or when I was dying; I've never been completely sure on exactly where I stood at that moment. Point is, yeah, we had a quick chat and he agreed to help Thistle heal me. All I had to do was promise never to set foot in my homeland again." Eric allowed his horse to drift slightly away from Timuscor's, a brief flicker of pain dancing in his eyes.

When he spoke next, it was not of gods or the sacrifices they demanded. "Thistle, I hope your gut is telling you to turn soon. At this rate, we'll be trying to ride horses up a mountain in the next hour, and even if Grumph were here, I don't think he has a spell for that."

"As far as I can tell, we are meant to keep heading directly forward," Thistle replied. "Though our proximity to the mountain does raise an interesting point: were we not told this was the place where the skull was first uncovered?"

"You think the people of the town came all the way out here, in the dead of night, searching for clues in the place where the skull popped up?" Eric didn't bother trying to sound skeptical; his words did the job well enough on their own.

"I have no idea if this is where the people of the town are or not; even assuming I am being guided toward a spot of powerful evil, there's

91

no guarantee Briarwillow's citizens will be at the same place. I do have one thought, however, about what it might be that's pulling me in."

"Do we want to know this?" Eric asked.

"Probably not, but I'm going to tell you anyway." Thistle's mind flashed back to the dream once more, and he shook his head until the visions sank back to the less accessible parts of his mind.

"My theory is this: skulls do not usually exist in isolation, at least not when fulfilling their intended function. More often than not, where there's a skull, there's a skeleton."

*　　　*　　　*

The last of the trees were only spots of green in the distance as they drew close to the mountain. In place of the lush foliage were small, determined plants that stayed close to the ground, not daring to reach up into the sky. From what Thistle could recall, this mountain marked the division between Alcatham's more bountiful pieces of kingdom and the Hooran desert, a vast swath of uninhabitable land separating Alcatham and Baltmur. Technically, both nations would claim it if pressed on the issue, but neither could find a way to actually make use of the desert's desolate miles. That relegated it to a matter reserved for royalty to bicker about, not for soldiers to fight for.

The mountain did make an excellent boundary, though. It loomed before them, nearly as wide as it was tall. Going around it would take no less than two days, and that was assuming one had good horses and no delays. It was a sprawling expanse of elevated rock that could make the world seem like it was closing in if stared at for too long.

Just as with the other lands around Briarwillow, there seemed to be no signs of life remaining. Aside from the occasional bug or a lone bird circling high overhead, the world around them was lonely and quiet, factors which made the trail of footsteps lingering in a section of loose gravel all the more puzzling of a discovery.

"There were a lot of them," Eric said. He'd dismounted from his horse, which was currently trying to choke down one of the tough shrubs as it hung around nearby. "I can't tell how many, though, or when these tracks were made. This whole area seems so undisturbed that it could have been two weeks ago, or it might have been just before we arrived. We really need Gabby for any sort of decent tracking estimate."

Thistle surveyed the area around them, finding nothing new that could have been missed in the dozen other scans he'd made. He and Timuscor had also dismounted from their horse, though theirs was a bit better trained and stayed close to the knight who'd been riding it. They were close, he knew that at least. His odd stomach feeling was practically growing stronger by the step. Something was around here, and it wasn't on the side of good. It was plain to see where logic dictated the source must be located; Thistle just didn't enjoy what those implications were. He'd always known it was a possibility, but he'd still held out hope that he'd be wrong. Not for the first, nor last time in Thistle's life, he detested discovering that his suspicions had been correct.

"It seems the people of Briarwillow have gone the way of the dwarf," Thistle sighed. He nodded his head slightly; there was no need to make a show of it. There was little chance the others could mistake his gesture to be indicating anything aside from the towering hunk of land that blotted out the eastern sky.

"Tunneling through mountains is a lot of work, even for an entire town working together," Eric pointed out.

"Aye, but discovering abandoned tunnels, now, that's a far easier task." Thistle ran his eyes along the mountain's slopes as carefully as fingers across a lover's face. "The skull was found here, we know that much already. It was discovered by people who were looking to mine for precious ore. Now, while it's certainly possible that someone chucked a powerful, cursed skull in a hole by a mountain, doesn't it seem far more likely that it was stored away in some sort of crypt or hidden dungeon, accidently uncovered by a pair of bumbling prospectors that carved through the wrong piece of rock?"

"It doesn't make more sense," Eric said. "But given what we know about the world, it does seem more likely. You think there are tunnels and caverns under the mountain, then?"

"Under or through, it makes no difference. Either one would provide an excellent place to store a cursed artifact that could wipe out entire towns. No one comes here in the first place; its proximity to the desert makes it a pointless path, and the mountain itself is a sheer annoyance. There's no challenge in scaling it or beauty to gaze at from its peak. It's the sort of place that lends itself to going undisturbed, which I suspect was exactly what someone was looking for."

"If you're right, that's still a lot of mountain to search," Timuscor said.

"Thankfully, we aren't searching as much as we are following a path. A wobbly, inconvenient one I'll admit, but a path nonetheless." Thistle found his eyes resting on a particular spot on the mountain's surface, dull and lifeless as every other inch he'd scanned. Yet, when his gaze fell upon this spot, the twisting in his gut doubled in intensity, nearly causing Thistle to gasp in surprise. He looked away and felt the sensation lessen, then turned his eyes back. Sure enough, the twisting grew stronger once more. It was at best a pointed sign, at worst a clue. Unfortunately, it also meant they'd have to leave the relative safety of daylight and descend into the uncharted darkness of the mountain.

"I want you both to know, going beyond this point is likely to be very dangerous," Thistle announced. "While I might not know precisely what's waiting for us inside there, I can say with certainty that it will be powerful. I realize that trying to discourage you both from coming along is a fool's errand and wastes precious time I don't have, so at least let me caution you. Be on your guard, be wary of your surroundings, and be ready to retreat at my signal."

"Paladins can't retreat," Eric reminded him. "That's what got us into this position in the first place."

"Perhaps, perhaps not. My god is one who rules over the minions, and we are not a stalwart bunch by our nature. Since I am working in preparation for attack, rather than committing to a charge, he may be willing to cut me a little slack. Even paladins should have the option of using strategy. Either way, it makes no difference. I said that you were to be ready to run at my signal, not that I was certain I'd be behind you."

Eric stared at the gnome with a look like he'd taken a sip of ale before it was done fermenting. "Thistle, you don't really expect us to abandon you in there, do you?"

"I dearly wish you would, if the need arises. Remember, I have the protection of a god with me. It's possible for me to survive things that you two might not. And, should that fail to prove true, I at least have the assurances of being escorted into the afterlife with a warm welcome and open arms. A paladin's career might be short-lived, but the retirement is top-notch. You two have no such assurances. You need to prioritize living above all else, if for no other reason than to warn the others."

"Let's see if the situation actually arises before we spend an hour arguing about it," Eric suggested.

"Good plan," Timuscor agreed. "Words are malleable and easy to forget, anyway. No one knows what they will do in a moment of crisis until they live through it. We will only see what actions we take when we are put to the fire."

"Well then," Thistle said, starting off toward the mountain. "Let's all try very hard to not end up running for our lives in the first place."

Eric chuckled. "It would make for a nice change of pace."

Chapter 12

It was hard to say what was more impressive: Fritz's strange, horseless miniature cart or the way the device pivoted and bucked through the trees without ever crashing. Neither Gabrielle nor Grumph had known quite what to make of the strange device when it was pulled, in miniature form, out of Fritz's seemingly bottomless satchel, and after hours of riding through the woods, they were still quite confounded by it. The one thing they both knew was that Fritz seemed to be having more fun driving her cart than they were riding their horses. Gabrielle almost opened her mouth to ask how much the wizards charged for a device like that, but then she remembered the price of a simple cooking box and thought better of it.

Gabrielle had never been poor, and she still didn't consider herself to fall into that category. Growing up in the mayoral mansions of Maplebark had shown her luxury, and the amount of gold they'd won since leaving town would have required years to work up to honestly. Still, seeing the fancy trinkets that Fritz made a living selling drove home for the first time just how much money was out there. If they stayed on this path of theirs, continuing to work as adventurers, there might one day come a point where she could buy one of Fritz's carts or cooking boxes without so much as a second thought. It was mind-boggling to try and picture, though still not quite as strange as the self-moving device tumbling across the uneven ground.

The forest had, thankfully, not grown any denser as they made their way parallel to the kingdom's road. Occasionally, they would veer closer to it than intended, alerted to the mistake only by catching a glimpse of the road through the trees or hearing the sound of other riders in the distance. Fortune was favoring them, but as with all things, it was bound to run dry sooner or later.

Shadows splayed over the ground like lazy fingers as the afternoon sun fell further from the apex of its rise. After nearly a full day of solid progress, the trees were finally becoming too thick to navigate

Fritz's cart through, and the horses were struggling as well. Foliage had become a true forest, which meant their only way through was to risk riding the road until the trees thinned once more.

"There's no way they won't have a camp around here," Gabrielle declared, trying for the fifth time to guide her horse out of the oaks it was stuck between. "With as much as they're riding the roads, this is the perfect pinch point to catch anyone who has been staying out of sight."

"The thick patch might run for miles," Fritz pointed out. She'd stepped out of her cart and was watching it shrink slowly back to a form no larger than her hand. "They can't be watching all of it."

"How long doesn't matter. Only where it starts." Grumph was still sitting atop his horse, as he'd seen where things were going and stopped trying to press forward unnecessarily.

"He's right. If they know this is the spot where forest travel becomes impossible, then they only need to be ready around here . . . probably a little ways up the road, some of them lying in ambush. If too big of a group goes through, they just stay hidden. Otherwise, they pop out and do some plundering."

Fritz frowned as she scooped up her cart and popped it into her satchel. "I find that unacceptable; most of what I have are loaned prototypes. Having to pay for them would seriously cut into my profit margin."

"We could try to sneak by," Gabrielle suggested.

"On an open road? How are we going to manage that? Do you two have some invisibility magic you've been keeping up your sleeves?" Fritz asked.

"No, not unless Grumph found any new spells in that book of his."

"Still five," Grumph assured them.

"Right, so we can't go invisible, but we can wait until nightfall and try to ride past," Gabrielle said.

"Pretty sure they'll hear us coming, which actually would have been a problem with the invisibility plan too," Fritz realized. "We could try racing by, running past whatever they have set up before they can get ready for our arrival."

"Horses are too slow." Grumph patted his mount affectionately, but it didn't change the truth in his words. His steed might be able to make it for a few hours more than Gabrielle's, but that was only a maybe. Both were older and had been on the road for weeks, with little chance to rest. If it were a sprint to town, there was a chance, but with at least another full day's ride ahead of them, there was no hope of outrunning prepared bandits.

"It's true; we wouldn't make it more than an hour or so going at full speed." Gabrielle tugged forward, finally freeing her horse. It snorted in either annoyance or gratitude—Gabrielle couldn't be sure. "Your cart might be able to, though."

"Sadly, they only run for around ten hours every day before they have to recharge themselves. As it is, I'll have to hitch a ride with you if we travel past nightfall," Fritz explained.

"We can't sneak past, we can't run past, and if we try to fight our way past, we'll probably get slaughtered." With a careful hand, Gabrielle guided her horse back to the leaner part of the forest, hoping it would manage to stay unstuck for at least a little while. "Any other options on the table that I missed?"

"Camouflage," Grumph suggested.

"It's an open road, and even if there were something to blend in with, I doubt I'd be able to whip up convincing outfits in a reasonable amount of time," Gabrielle replied.

Grumph shook his head and lowered himself down slowly from his horse. Reaching into his backpack, he produced a length of rope, followed by a small dagger.

"Wrong kind of camouflage. If we must walk through a trap, we go as predators. Not prey."

*　　　*　　　*

Finding the tunnel's entrance hadn't actually been difficult once they knew where they were looking. Had they been forced to comb the seemingly endless mountainscape, it could have taken weeks, perhaps even months, to locate what they were looking for. But with Thistle's strange stomach pointing the way, it was a relatively simple matter to locate the small opening concealed in a hanging rock's shadow.

Getting to the entrance had proved more problematic and required some moderate climbing from all parties involved. The horses were left at the base of the mountain—normally an equine death sentence as they'd be food for monsters, but with the area barren of other life, it seemed like only a moderate risk. Two humans and a gnome began making their way up the steep, rocky surface as carefully as they could, prioritizing sure-footedness over speed.

Eric, the only one of the three with human-sized limbs and not burdened by bulky armor, was able to scramble up well ahead of the others. Timuscor followed after him with Thistle bringing up the rear. The climb wasn't especially steep or high, merely burdensome, like everything else about the mountain. By his reckoning, Eric figured they'd be able to race down the mountain's face if they had to hurry out of there, though Thistle might need to do some healing after it was all said and done.

"Do we have a plan for how we're going to find our way around in there?"

Timuscor was staring into the narrow opening, straining to see more than a few inches beyond where the daylight ended. It was a futile effort; the mountain devoured what little light made its way into the waiting maw without so much as a hiccup.

"I think I may have a leftover torch from the dungeon." Eric began to remove his small backpack, only to have Thistle put a steadying hand on his shoulder.

"Hold on a moment, there's something I'd like to try." Thistle walked over to Timuscor and gently rested his hands on the shining shield strapped to Timuscor's back. "Grumble, god of the minions, you are sending us into darkness. To better serve your will and accomplish our mission, I beseech thee to light our path."

At first, it seemed like nothing happened; then a soft white light began to cloud the mirror-like surface of Timuscor's shield. It spread across the gleaming surface until every inch of the shield was glowing brightly. Unstrapping it from his back, Timuscor pointed it toward the mountain's opening, revealing a sloped tunnel moving downward.

"Handy trick," Eric said.

"More ostentatious than a torch, but it allows the wielder to keep their weaponry at the ready. To be honest, I wasn't sure it would work. Just something I've heard paladins were capable of."

"You really should talk to Grumble about getting a detailed breakdown of what powers come with paladinhood." Eric pulled his own short sword from its sheath and took one last glance at the daylight. He hoped he'd make it back to see the outer world again, but in his brief time as an adventurer, he'd already learned to take nothing for granted.

"I rather suspect that the discovery is meant to be part of the journey, though, if I ever get the chance, I will do my best to wring out as many details from him as possible." Thistle pulled the daggers from his belt and held them both tightly. Within seconds, the same light that had spread across Timuscor's shield was glowing from the blades in Thistle's hands.

"No prayer this time?"

100

Thistle shook his head. "Prayers do not always need to be said out loud, or even contain words, for the gods to hear them. They only need to be sincere." He reached forward, motioning for Eric's sword. "Would you like me to illuminate your blade as well?"

"Thanks, but no thanks." Eric pulled his sword back a few inches, keeping it from Thistle's grasp. "You two are already throwing off plenty of light, and I'd prefer not to have my only weapon turned into a giant glowing beacon. Just in case I need to move around unseen, you understand."

"A fine point." Thistle pulled back his hand and turned to Timuscor, who waited patiently at the tunnel's mouth. "As you have the biggest light and a shield, are you all right taking the front position? I'll use my daggers to light up anything that might be out of your range, or attack if some unexpected beast makes an attempt on your life."

"I was going to ask for the front, anyway." Timuscor drew his sword, longer and heavier than anything Eric could successfully wield, and headed into the tunnel without another word.

"Go after him," Eric urged the gnome, who seemed to be hesitating. "Don't try and keep me safe by putting me in the middle. You're the only one of us with any ranged attacks, so we need you able to throw in either direction."

"One of us really does need to learn how to properly wield a bow," Thistle muttered, hurrying to stay on Timuscor's heels. Eric followed, leaving the world of light behind as they plunged headlong into the empty darkness.

The path was narrow: too close for more than one moderately sized person to move through at a time, but not so close that they had to turn to their sides to make it past. Even Timuscor, the widest of the three of them, was able to make it through easily, so long as he paid attention to where he stuck his sword and shield. Whoever had made these tunnels had done so with humans, or human-shaped beings, in mind. As they walked, Eric kept his eyes peeled, scanning for any signs that the villagers had come through the same passageway. Sadly, with the light source ahead and only rock on all sides, there was precious little to work with in terms of clues.

It was hard to say how long they walked. With no sun overhead and only occasional dips and turns to measure their progress, time quickly became a slippery thing that slithered out of any firm grip Eric tried to lay on it. His best guess was that they'd been walking for under half an hour when they came to the cavern.

The expanse of open rock came from nowhere; Timuscor simply turned a sharp corner and suddenly there they were. A carved ceiling rose above them, barely reinforced by stone pillars that were half crumbled into dust. Four more tunnel entrances greeted the travelers, dark and foreboding, like hungry mouths ready to swallow their souls.

To Eric's surprise, there were also supplies resting in a corner: pickaxes, shovels, and a sack of stale bread all clumped up against each other. He picked up one of the shovels and brought it over to Timuscor's shield, where he could see it in detail. The tool was well-crafted, but otherwise unexceptional: wooden handle, metal spade, and a bit of wear along the edges. Definitely not from the same era as the pillars, else it would have rotted into rust and dust.

"I think we found the miners' base camp."

"Well, at least we know my hunch was on the right track." Thistle was standing by the tunnel they'd emerged from, carefully carving a series of notches just to the left of its opening. When that was done, he bent down and scratched a small arrow in the sediment that lingered throughout the cave, pointing down the tunnel. "Just so we don't get lost on the way back."

"Didn't the notches take care of that?" Timuscor asked.

"Aye, but the arrow is in case we don't have time to look for notches. It never hurts to have a clear path during an escape."

102

Eric agreed but said nothing, not wanting to restart their argument about whether running would be viable. Instead, he focused on trying to see if he could hear anything from the mouths of the new tunnels. Occasional sounds met him at first—water dripping or some creature scuttling through the walls—but nothing that provided useful information. As he reached the fourth tunnel, however, Eric noticed a distinct, rhythmic thumping coming faintly from its dark depths. There was no way to tell exactly what it was, but it was different. And different was what they'd come here looking for.

"I might have found something," Eric said, waving the others over. "It's faint, but there's definitely a noise coming from this one."

"Well then, I suppose it's our duty to go ask our neighbors to keep down the ruckus," Thistle said.

Timuscor led the way once more, with Thistle following and Eric a few steps behind. Unlike before, his attention was split, constantly turning back to make sure some unwanted guest hadn't joined them in skulking down the tunnel. No interloping figure appeared, even as they walked further and the sound grew progressively stronger. It was a tireless thudding, keeping in perfect rhythm no matter how long Eric listened. If it hadn't been so perfect, he'd have likened it to the beating of a heart, but no heart stayed that constant. Fear, joy, love, even boredom, all them could change a heart's tempo. This had no change, no variation. It was an empty, endless, perfect thudding, as dead as it was constant.

It did help Eric count the time, and as they came to where the tunnel opened up, he guessed they'd been going for only a quarter of an hour this time. They moved cautiously, knowing full well that the glowing metal in their hands would make them unmissable targets. This far in, there was no other way for them to see, though. It was a risk they'd have to take if they wanted to actually learn anything from the trip.

The tunnel opened up into a large, sprawling cavern. It seemed to run down for miles, far deeper than where the mountain met the ground. The three of them stood on top of a sloping path that ran from

103

their location to another section of cave far below. The distance was impossible to judge, but it was not so far that they were unable to make out the activity taking place. Hundreds of bodies were lined up together, a massive piece of what appeared to be another stone pillar held above their heads. The people were slamming the pillar into a white, ornately carved door over and over. Each blow seemed to have almost no effect, but the slight crack in the spot they were striking told a different story.

What was most disturbing was not the act itself, nor the pillar, nor even the mysterious door. It was the people who were hitting it. They didn't turn toward the light that Timuscor was shining down on them, didn't even seem aware that their cavern had been invaded. All they did was hit the door, over and over, their pale skin stretched across nearly visible bones, milky dead eyes set firmly on the target before them.

Dead, the lot of them. Or, rather, undead. Eric had heard stories, but he'd never actually witnessed such monsters in person. Beside him, he felt Thistle stiffen. That was when he knew, even before the gnome's softly whispered words filled the air, the grief in them nearly palpable.

"Though it pains me to say so, I believe we've found the citizens of Briarwillow."

Chapter 13

Grumph moved carefully between the horses, daring only to peek up from the ground in brief intervals. The ropes binding his arms, or at least appearing to do so, ran from their wrappings around his back and up to Gabrielle and Fritz, each tightly holding an end. Occasionally, a drop of blood from the wound he'd opened near his eye would drip against his pupil, stinging and blinding him for a few horrid seconds. Gabrielle had tried to talk him out of adding the wounds with his dagger; however, Grumph remained steadfast in his dedication. They all looked far worse than they actually were, but no one would believe these two women had captured a half-orc without beating him into submission first.

Unfortunately, Grumph was all too familiar with exactly what being a captive looked like. He pushed those memories away as he trudged along the road, though. It was imperative that he appear beaten and defeated. If their charade was to sell, he couldn't show the fire that would be brimming in his eyes were he to allow himself to dwell.

For their parts, Gabrielle and Fritz were both filling the roles excellently. They would glance at him occasionally, only to make sure he wasn't up to no good, and otherwise treat him like one of the saddle bags. It showed concern for him as property but none for him as a person, just as he'd instructed. Gabrielle rode with axe out, dangerous though it was, and appeared constantly at the ready for a fight. This part was the easiest to sell, as Gabrielle truly was a hair's breadth from spilling blood if she were attacked.

Their goal was not to make the bandits believe the fight was unwinnable; that was impossible to accomplish with only three travelers. Rather, their goal was to make the bandits see a target where the risk outweighed the reward. Bounty hunters might be flush with gold, but not when they were out working. Dragging in a quarry meant that they were on their way to a payday, not carrying ample sacks of coins. It also painted the picture of two women who were capable at what they did, at least enough to bring down a fearsome foe like Grumph. Certainly, the bandits could overwhelm them; however, in doing so, they would lose at least some of their men. For a hefty amount of treasure, that might be worthwhile, but with targets that seemed both tough and broke, it might be a gamble not worth taking. At least, that was what Grumph was hoping for.

Dusk had fallen upon them and nearly given its seat to night when the bandits finally appeared. With as much noise as Fritz and Gabrielle were making, there had been plenty of time for them to get ready. That, too, had been intentional; prey snuck about, predators announced themselves.

"Evening, fellow travelers." He appeared to step out of nowhere, though in truth, he'd merely been carefully tucked behind a tree. The man wore simple vestments, made for utility over pomp. A short sword hung strapped to his hip, next to a crossbow and a set of daggers. A white-toothed smile that could not have been friendlier rested on his handsome face, assuring them that all would be well.

Gabrielle tightened the grip on her axe.

"Evening." They didn't slow their horses, nor give any signs of fear at this stranger's appearance. Gabrielle appeared more annoyed than anything, and Fritz somehow managed to seem bored with it all.

"Tell me, dear travelers, do you come from Briarwillow? I'm on my way there now to check on the citizens, and would dearly love to know if there is news."

"Urthos." Gabrielle jerked the rope, and Grumph took the cue to stumble, nearly letting his knee smash into the road's rough surface. "This one thought it could hide out in the wildlands."

Even knowing that Gabrielle was playing a part—an act that all their lives might very well depend on—Grumph felt a familiar fire of hatred stoked as she called him "it." With all the mental fortitude he'd acquired over the last dozen years, Grumph smothered the flames as best he could, keeping his eyes to the ground. He could easily bear this much.

Grumph had endured far, *far* worse. Still, if things did go awry and the fight turned to blows, he at least knew there was ample fuel in him to cause pain.

"And a fierce-looking brute he is. Must have been a lot of trouble for you two to bring down by yourselves."

"Hardest part is tracking these things," Gabrielle snapped. "You with the kingdom or something? We got the bounty papers, if you need 'em." She motioned to Fritz, who began rifling through the satchel she always kept close at hand. It wouldn't have surprised Grumph if Fritz really did have forged bounty papers somewhere deep down in that thing, but luckily, their bluff wasn't called.

"No, no, as I said before, just a simple traveler. Though one that has run into some problems with his horses and equipment. If you were feeling so generous as to offer a bit of gold, I might be able to get back on the road." Nothing in his face was pleading, nor did his smile seem humbled in the slightest. This wasn't so much a ruse as it was a cheap coating of words, one meant to be seen through.

Gabrielle barked a harsh laugh, lifting her axe slightly so that it was in a more defensive position. "Gold? You think we'd be hunting these damn things into Urthos if we had gold? No, traveler, if you were to try cutting us down, and somehow the gods allowed you to succeed, all you'd discover is a few bits of copper, some half-molded trail rations, and a few of your own limbs clutched in our hands. You'll find that we're not inclined to part with what little we have."

"That is unfortunate, for you see, I have many hungry mouths depending on me." From the trees stepped more of the bandits, roughly a dozen walking freely into the road. There were certainly more hiding that they couldn't see; the man seemed too experienced to make a mistake like playing all his cards at once.

"So it seems. Well, gents, I'm happy to give the first one of you who comes close something to put in your belly." Gabrielle spun the axe in her hand once, lest there was any doubt about exactly what she was offering. A smile danced on her lips, though it was unlike the wide grin of the bandit standing in front of them. Hers was angrier, hungrier than he could have ever managed. Already, the blood was burning in her veins. She didn't have to pretend that she wanted a fight in the slightest; it was all Gabrielle could do to hold herself back.

"I've got seconds, if the first doesn't fill you up." From a sheath at her side, Fritz drew Grumph's demon-bone sword. Even in the faltering light of day, the bandits could see its sickly-pale color and the few dark stains running along the edge as she held it at the ready. This was not the weapon of someone who'd made a purchase; it belonged to one who had killed.

"Gracious as that is, I fear it won't be enough for so many of us," the bandit leader told them.

"Perhaps not, though I'm sure we can serve at least a few of you. The rest will be welcome to our meager copper and dirty rations. Surely those will be of great comfort to you while you dig the fresh graves." Gabrielle turned down to look at Grumph, her grin deepening. "Oh, and I suppose you'll also get to play with this thing. He'd wild as a boar, won't care if you're friend or foe. Perhaps we'll let these ropes go, if you decide you'd like to dine with us this evening."

Gabrielle allowed a little slack in her rope, and Grumph seized the moment, jerking on the bindings he was actually holding in place and surging forward, nearly pulling the horses with him. His eyes flew up from the round and he snapped his jaws so loudly that his teeth ached. It had the desired effect, though, as all of the nearby bandits took at least a half step away from him. Were he riding with the girls, composed and normal as usual, they'd have never shown him such instinctual terror. There was something about dealing with the wild things of the world, some part of them that remembered a time before lighted cities and sturdy homes. That piece knew that, in the face of animalistic ferocity, all ideas of battle and civilization burn away. All they could do would be to try and kill the monster before it killed them, and that was far more terrifying than committing a simple robbery.

The tug on his arms gave Grumph the signal to let himself be pulled back as Gabrielle re-asserted her authority. He made a show of struggling against it until the butt of her axe slammed into his shoulder. It looked worse than it felt, but it still felt pretty painful. Seemingly broken by his captor, Grumph plodded back into his starting position, head once again hanging in shame.

"So, will your men trade their lives, or that of their friends, for a handful of copper? Or should we keep riding? In truth, I'm fine with either option, as I'd imagine your head will likely catch a fair price as well." Gabrielle leaned forward slightly on her horse, meeting the bandit leader's eyes as she spoke. Her axe was angled just right for a charge, letting him know that if they attacked, she would see to it he was one of those amongst the corpses.

The moment seemed to stretch on interminably, until at last the bandit leader lowered his head into a slight, but definite bow. "My apologies if we seemed too aggressive. All we requested was charity, and if you have nothing to give, then we can hardly ask it from you. Please, ride ahead, and may the goddess Cecily bless you on your travels." He took a step to the side, moving out of Gabrielle's path, and nodded at his men to do the same.

Neither woman waited for any more signal than that, starting the horses forward and making Grumph jog to keep up. Their weapons never left their hands, nor their eyes the bandits, yet none of the men made so much as a single motion to attack. All they did was stand at the side of the road and watch as two women and one half-orc moved slowly out of sight.

Only when they'd been going for ten minutes past spotting any of the bandits did Fritz finally speak, and when she did, her voice was heavy with relief. "I cannot believe they actually let us go."

"You shouldn't," Gabrielle replied, her eyes still locked on the woods. "Because they didn't. They're following us now, still planning on attacking."

"Wait, why? If they were going to kill and rob us, wouldn't they do it when they had us surrounded?"

"We were ready." Grumph spoke softly as he jogged, wary of being overheard. "We were dangerous."

"These aren't adventurers willing to risk their lives for some small score or thrill," Gabrielle explained. "Time and terrain are on their side, so instead of trying to fight us when we might take them down, they'll be patient and wait until we make camp. Even with one on watch, we'll be far easier targets than we were back there."

Fritz let out a long, annoyed sigh. "Forgive me, but I fail to see the point in all of this then."

"It's simple: they had an ambush for us waiting on the road, which we wanted to get past. Now, it's our turn to be ahead. And if there is one thing that my tribe taught me well, it's how to fight superior foes when they're coming for you."

"I'm sorry, your 'tribe,' you said?" Fritz asked.

Gabrielle blushed for a brief moment, then covered it with a heavy shrug. "It's a . . . long story."

"Yet one I think would be fascinating to hear," Fritz replied. "You know, assuming we live through the night."

"Consider it a deal. In the meantime, can you pull out your cart and switch horses with Grumph?" Gabrielle asked. "If we want to pull this off, we need to cover a lot of ground before they catch up."

*　　　*　　　*

Timuscor pulled the door shut, barring them safely inside the blacksmith's basement. Their ride back had brought them into town after sundown, but none had really been afraid of something overtaking them in the darkness. They'd watched the undead townsfolk slam the door for countless minutes, and nothing was distracting them. Whoever had bound them to their task had made certain to keep them working hard.

Of course, knowing that also made their fortified base seem like something of overkill, but as Thistle pointed out on the ride back, knowing one threat was gone wasn't the same as knowing all of them were gone. Given that a horde of undead was only a short ride away from where they were staying, prudence and safety were by far the smarter bets to make.

"Does anyone have any idea of what we're supposed to do?" Eric was pulling out leftover turkey from the prior day's meal, all inclination to cook worn out of him by the day's sights and travels. "Thistle, didn't you have some experience with undead?"

"I did, and they were awful," Thistle admitted. Given that it was the tale of how he'd met his wife, hiding that expertise from his companions had ultimately proved impossible. "Horrid, mindless beasts, and that's if you're lucky. The most powerful of the undead actually retain their minds, or at least a dark reflection of them. They are by far the most dangerous enemy one can end up facing, and if you're lucky, you only end up being killed by them."

"Wow, that is really depressing," Eric said. "I was actually asking if you knew any ways to turn them back or drive them away. Glad to know we're in a 'hoping for death' situation, though."

"Oh." Thistle took a seat next to Eric while Timuscor began stripping out of his armor. "My apologies. Seeing them down there and being around such concentrated, evil energy . . . I fear I might be a touch off my game tonight."

"I forgot to ask you about that; did you get any more directions while we were inside the mountain?" They had explored one of the tunnels briefly, only to find it led to a dead-end. By that point, it was decided they had best come back the next day, as none of them wanted to be in that mountain full of undead once the sun had set. It might not have any effect on the monsters, but no one was particularly eager to find out for certain, not even Timuscor.

"Sadly, no. Once we were inside, there was no sense of a place I should be going, only an increased intensity, like my sense was letting me know I'd arrived." Thistle paused, thinking back to the show they'd sat quietly watching for part of the afternoon. "Were I to make a guess, however, I would think that whatever is drawing us to the mountain might lie beyond those massive doors."

"The ones the undead were trying to bust down?" Timuscor asked, slowly freeing himself from the silver container that kept him safe in battle. Nearby, his shield still cast the barest of glows. The enchantment Thistle had cast was apparently temporary, which was actually a relief as they moved closer toward trying to sleep.

"Those indeed," Thistle confirmed.

"Great, so all we have is an army of undead and apparently impenetrable doors standing between us and whatever you have to do to get out of this town." Eric took a bite of cold turkey and chewed slowly. "I think I'm starting to miss the demons."

"It's not quite as bad as all that," Thistle said. "The undead are trying to force their way through something that was clearly meant to be opened either by magic or mechanism. If we can figure out what actually grants entry, then we'll be halfway to getting through."

"Sure, we'll just have the hundreds of undead down there, who you described as 'horrid, mindless beasts.' And that's assuming none are the more dangerous, intelligent kind," Eric pointed out.

"Fine, so we'll be a quarter of the way there once we crack the doors."

"That's all I'm saying." Reaching around his back, Eric pulled his pack forward to serve as a makeshift pillow. "How do you plan on popping open those doors, anyway?"

"Someone built that place, and given its proximity to the mountain, I'd guess that the person lived in Briarwillow," Thistle said. "In fact, Briarwillow may have first sprung into existence as a place to shelter those constructing the caverns. Tomorrow, we raid every house for books, diaries, scrolls, the lot of it. If there are any records to be found about what's down there, this is the town they would be in. With a little help from the gods, and a lot of reading, perhaps we can uncover some clues as to how those doors work, or even what dwells beyond them."

"You ever wonder how many other paladins out there prefer research to fighting?" Eric asked.

Thistle shook his head and tore off a hunk of cold turkey. "Can't say it's ever crossed my mind. All I can do is be the best paladin I'm capable of, and I'll take knowledge over a sharp dagger any day of the year."

Chapter 14

The bandits were stealthy, by most definitions of the word. They moved carefully, with lanterns covered and feet sure. No telltale snaps of twigs gave them away. Any rustling they made could have easily been little more than the wind or some stray beast. Words were locked away in their mouths; only simple hand gestures were used to convey directions, and even those were infrequent. They had a plan, and these were woods they knew. Little correction was required as they skulked toward the smoldering fire that marked the campsite.

What struck Gabrielle as she stood, hunched over, her axe gripped firmly in hand, was that even now, they still moved like predators. No fear clouded their movements, at least not the kind of terror that came from knowing dangerous things might be lurking just out of sight. Grumph had been right to walk them through the ambush point as predators, but now was the time to remember what it meant to be prey: to be quiet, and meek, and fearful. People often thought of prey as helpless creatures, merely walking meals for the beasts that hunted them. Too often they forgot that a herd of deer could kill a wolf. Being prey didn't make them helpless, it just meant they had to fight smarter.

Worried as she was for her friends—as well as herself— Gabrielle couldn't help but feel a thrill of nostalgia as she watched the figures creeping through the woods. It reminded her of hunting with her tribe, when nearly every animal in the woods was more dangerous than the goblins that fed upon them. She'd always admired their coordination, how boldly each member of the tribe undertook their roles. They had understood what it was to be weak and knew that only by working together could they hope to triumph. Her tribe had taught her much, and as the bandits came within striking distance of the camp and Gabrielle eased up from her perch, she was thankful for every bit of their education.

Her first blow took one of the stragglers in the back of his neck, cleaving through his vocal cords before he could cry out. Gabrielle caught his body before it made any ruckus, laying it gently down onto the forest floor. Soon, the true melee would begin, but every bandit she could turn into a corpse before then would give them a better chance of success. Fritz was ordered to stay silent and still for as long as possible, and Grumph was waiting to start things off properly. Only Gabrielle could take a few of their enemies before things got going. It was her gift, and her burden.

Another fell beneath her axe, though this time, she had to wiggle it out after putting the bandit on the ground. The damn thing needed sharpening—needed a complete repair job, if she were being honest with herself. As fine a weapon as it once might have been, her stolen axe hadn't been made to deal with the caliber of foe she'd been up against. The demon scales alone had left several chips in the blade.

Once she pulled her weapon free, Gabrielle realized the others were too close together for her to risk taking any more. It was all up to Grumph now; only he would know the perfect time to get things rolling. Angling herself carefully, with the fake campsite just at the edge of her peripheral vision, Gabrielle reached into her mind for the bubbling well of anger she'd inadvertently dug.

All those years spent—nay, wasted—splitting herself between duty and desire had formed a central core of frustrated rage in her heart. It had simmered in there for years, building pressure against the bonds of self-control she'd placed against it. When her tribe was attacked, being shredded by demons before her eyes, the pressure had finally been too much. Her anger had burst forth, and ever since, there had been no putting it back in its cage. All she'd managed was to delay it, deter it, and direct it. Tonight, there was no need for holding back. Her world would turn into blood and battle the moment Grumph started things off. As much as Gabrielle hated to admit it, these were the sort of situations where she was most useful.

Even worse, she was beginning to develop a taste for them.

The blinding flash of light from her left was the final lock left to fall away, and Gabrielle let the rage pour out of her as she turned toward

115

the site of the fire. Bandits were stumbling about, their night-adjusted eyes temporarily blinded by the massive blast of fiery light Grumph had conjured. They groped about, searching for each other or something solid to grip on to.

Where they met Gabrielle, they found only death. Blood splashed against her armor as hard, blunt blows rained down on the bodies. Nearby, she could see Grumph crashing through those on his side, the pale blade of his demon sword flashing in the moonlight as he plunged it into bandit flesh.

Part of Gabrielle had wondered if she'd be able to fight these people like she had the demons. After all, those were mere monsters, but these were fellow humans. As she turned her axe and slammed it into a bandit's stomach, pulling wide to send his innards spilling out, she realized there was no hesitation in her strikes. Bandit or demon, human or beast, none of it made any difference. The bandits had made this a situation of predators and prey. Only living mattered. Everything else was nothing more than an afterthought.

A sword turned her blade away, and Gabrielle felt a half-aimed thrust bounce off her armor. Twisting to strike back, she cleaved into a bandit's arm, but failed to separate his head from his torso as he scurried backward. The effect of Grumph's flare was fading, and their vision was returning. With a quick sweep of her area, Gabrielle could see there were four surrounding her and three cornering Grumph. It would be a hard, bloody fight, but ultimately, the bandits would likely come out victorious.

Gabrielle smiled, joy and rage melding inside her as she looked at the sneering, confident faces surrounding her. All the corpses at their feet, and yet still they only thought like predators. She knew better, had been taught better.

One of her favorite lessons, in fact, was how the best traps always sprang more than once.

"Now!"

* * *

Gabrielle's voice echoed through the trees, reaching the ears of Fritz, who stood waiting for the signal. There had been precious little time to work with when they finally veered back into the woods, and Fritz had been doubtful that they could make anything that would really turn the tide of battle. She'd been a bit more convinced when Gabrielle suggested Grumph use his fire spell to blind them, but it had been the second part of the plan that drew Fritz the rest of the way in. Besides, it wasn't like she had any other choices for making it out of this alive; at least, none that wouldn't be prohibitively inconvenient or expensive. Though this one wouldn't exactly be cheap, either, if things went awry.

Bursting forth from under the brush they'd used to conceal her cart, Fritz and the device barreled forward on a direct course for the cluster of bandits that had formed up around Gabrielle. She sped forth, unhalted by trees, for they'd chosen this clearing well. It limited places the bandits could hide, while allowing her to run over them with minimal obstacles to steer around. Of course, the cart wouldn't actually do much damage to anyone it hit; the devices were made lightweight to minimize the magic needed for powering them, and Fritz herself was a slender elf that only added a few pounds. What it did manage to do was scatter them, breaking their formation as they leapt out of the way to avoid being smashed.

That, in truth, was the core of the plan. Together, there was no question the bandits would overwhelm Grumph and Gabrielle, but fighting them one on one at least offered the adventurers a chance. Death was still a firm possibility; however, this method at least reduced it from being a certainty. Given their situation, that was an important step in the right direction.

Fritz jerked her wheel to the side, lifting the cart up on two wheels for a moment as she reoriented and came speeding toward the bandits by Grumph. This time, they weren't quite as taken by surprise, and one was clearly lining up his crossbow to take a shot at her. Grumph's sword burst out of his chest as the bandit's arms fell limply to his sides. Dangerous as a trader in an enchanted cart might seem, it was utter folly to turn one's back on a half-orc brandishing a blade.

Another hairpin turn put her on track for Gabrielle's group once more, but just as she drew close, Fritz yanked the cart off-track, veering toward Grumph's group and clipping a bandit's hip. He went spinning off to the side as Fritz reoriented herself. If she wanted to stay alive and effective, she had to be unpredictable. Simply circling in a pattern would get her killed. If they never knew when she was coming, they had to split their attention between her and whichever member of the group they were fighting. Against Grumph and Gabrielle, that was showing itself to be a death sentence.

This was proven by the pair of fresh corpses lying at Gabrielle's feet. Her victory hadn't come without a cost, though, a sight visible as she raised her axe at a new foe. That strange red armor was stopping the blades from cutting her, but the force of the blows was still taking its toll. By Fritz's count, Grumph should be down to his last opponent, which meant Gabrielle needed help the most. One of the bandits, a man who she thought looked like the person they'd spoken to on the road, was too close to Gabrielle for her to try and ram. The other, thankfully, was shifting his position in the dark, trying to flank the axe-wielding woman. Fritz was having none of that, and set herself on a crash course with her fresh target.

His reflexes were impressive as he threw himself clear of the charging carriage. Sadly, his legs weren't quite as powerful as his reactions, and a sickening crunch filled the air as Fritz sped over what she suspected to be his arm. He let out a howl of pain and scrambled up from the ground, all thoughts of Gabrielle forgotten.

Fritz glanced about, quickly realizing that both Grumph and Gabrielle were already fighting what seemed to be tough opponents. As the bandit advanced on her, blade gleaming at the end of his working arm, Fritz knew what she had to do. This too had been discussed and strategically accounted for, with everyone agreeing on a best course of action should the situation arise.

118

With a quick twist of the wheel, Fritz barreled out of the clearing, trying desperately to get somewhere safe. The bandit snarled in rage, and then raced after her. Her cart was faster, but outside the clearing, she had to deal with veering around trees and every detour cost her valuable seconds. A peek over her shoulder showed the bandit keeping up, racing through the brush like a man possessed. Fritz swallowed hard and turned her attention back to driving.

This was going to be a close one.

*   *   *

Unlike the others, the bandit leader fought with a shield—at least, Gabrielle assumed he was their leader, given that he'd been the one to speak to them on the road and was proving to be the toughest opponent she'd faced. The man was nimble, dancing around like Eric, yet his blows were almost as heavy as Timuscor's. Had she not spent so much of her time training with the both of them, there was a good chance this fight would have already ended, and it would not have been in her favor.

"You're better than I expected." He twirled his sword effortlessly, moving it as naturally as he shuffled his feet. From what Gabrielle had seen sparring against Timuscor, she'd guess they had similar training. Probably a soldier once, one who had discovered that being a robber paid better than stipends from the kingdom.

"You, too. Can't say the same for your men," Gabrielle sneered at him, trying to hold on to the anger that was beginning to ebb under the onslaught of pain and weariness. Having anger might be constant, but using it as fuel was taxing. She could only keep it up for so long, and they were drawing near the end of what she could manage. Her axe, handle half-slick with blood, was beginning to feel heavier with each passing moment. Gabrielle tried to force those thoughts out of her head. This was what she did; this was the role she served in their party. She had to be strong enough. There was no other choice.

119

The bandit leader's eyes darkened at the mention of his downed friends. "They were pups, nothing more than trainees I'd taken here to show the ropes. Hard to find a better training ground than a deserted road, after all. Pups though they were, they were still members of our outfit, and you're going to suffer for cutting them down."

"Bring it o—"

Gabrielle's taunt was cut short as the bandit leader charged, blade gleaming in the moonlight. He was fast and strong, but Gabrielle had fought faster and stronger—although not the two rolled together. The axe seemed to move almost automatically, deflecting the more dangerous blows and letting her armor absorb the weaker ones. As they fought, she kept her mind on the task at hand, always waiting for the right opportunity. Weary as she was getting, her next true attack would be the one that decided the match. If she couldn't finish things, he would eventually overwhelm her.

It was when the bandit leader was shifting backward, angling for a new wave of assault, that Gabrielle saw what she was looking for. His shield had dipped—just for a moment—as exhaustion finally began to extract its payment from him. Fast as he was, she knew she could get the axe through his guard. There was no time for contemplation or thought. All she could do was act.

Gabrielle swung her axe, and as she did, she poured every remaining drop of rage she could into the blow. Her muscles, filled with weary fire only moments before, roared with life as they sent the blade of her weapon on a direct course with his neck. She could feel it, even before contact was made. This was a mighty blow. This would cleave that grinning face from that nimble body in a single motion. Victory was hers.

That thought was shattered, along with the head of her axe, as the bandit leader slammed his shield into her weapon. Even with him pushing back, the force of the blow still sent him reeling, and he had to scurry backward lest he fall completely prone in front of his enemy. He

120

looked at her with newfound respect, even as Gabrielle gazed at the shattered remains of what had once been her trusty weapon.

"A good strike," he said, marveling at the dent his shield now boasted. "But an amateur mistake. Pretending to be tired, drawing your opponent out: it's one of the first things any real warrior learns. You've clearly seen some fighting, but I'd wager none of it was against other humans."

Gabrielle lifted the broken axe, now little more than a staff with a hunk of metal on the end, and stared at him angrily. Without her weapons, she would surely die. That much was obvious. Still, she refused to die groveling or in mid-retreat. Gabrielle would die fighting, even if it was futile. That too was the goblin way.

"You've got potential," the bandit leader said, circling her slowly. "And I've got a few openings in my crew. If you're willing to swear allegiance, and prove it, then I might be willing to spare your life."

"How sweet. Too bad there's no way I'm sparing yours." Words, nothing but empty words, and they both knew it. Yet Gabrielle still felt better as they left her mouth. She hadn't been strong enough, but she could still die an honorable death. And perhaps, if she was very lucky, she could spill a little of his blood on her way into the next life.

"Foolish girl, don't you even know to take an offer of kindness when it's offered to you?"

"Don't you know not to lose track of how many people you're fighting?" The words came from behind the bandit leader, but before he could twist around to see who had spoken, a green, flickering light engulfed his whole body. He screamed in pain, throwing himself to the ground and trying to quell the magical fire that was already charring his flesh. His flailing neither spread the flames nor extinguished them. The screams of the bandit leader drew the attention of his last remaining cohort, giving Grumph the chance he needed to slip the blade between his enemy's ribs.

The horrible yelling grew louder and louder, and then fell silent. Moments later, even the crackle of flames died away. Only then did Gabrielle turn to face her savior, the silhouette that stood several feet away, shadowed by the trees.

Fritz stepped into view, a sizable bruise on her cheek, a cut on her arm, and the silver rod she'd pointed at Gabrielle clutched firmly in her hand. Before their eyes, the silver began to darken, losing its luster until the rod was pitch black. Fritz let out an annoyed sigh, and then tossed it unceremoniously into her satchel.

"Well, I'm out of shots, so I really hope everyone is dead."

Chapter 15

"That was brutal." Tim set down the damage dice he'd had ready in his hand. The first of his attacks had killed the final wyvern, and finally ended their protracted battle at the cliff's base.

"Seriously. Chalara is down to three points of mana." Cheri eyed her little brother suspiciously from across the table. "Russell, you wouldn't have tacked on some extra monsters in that battle just because we've been doing so well, would you?"

Russell raised his right hand into the sky. "It's all exactly as the module outlined, GM's honor. You all just happened to choose a path that took you down one of the tougher encounters."

"Well, let's try and avoid another one of those. Chalara is looking beat to hell right now. How's Wimberly? That fall off the cliff did a lot of damage."

"She's alive," Bert assured his fellow players. "But it was touch and go for a while there. Definitely going to need to drink some healing potions."

"Save them, if you can," Tim warned. "We've got a long way to go before we get to this wizard's castle. I can heal you up at least part of the way."

"Gelthorn would also appreciate divine mending, as she currently has two arrows stuck in her shoulder," Alexis mumbled, just as she did every time she left the safety of speaking as Gelthorn.

"Heal Gelthorn first. Wimberly sees less action in combat; this one was just bad luck." Bert flipped to his inventory page, making sure he had enough items of healing to get the gnome gadgeteer back to a functioning state. "I've been meaning to ask this, but having Wimberly get so beat up reminded me. What happens when your character dies? Is there an item we bust out to fix it, like super-healing?"

Russell shook his head, but it was Cheri who answered the question. "Dead is just that: dead. Sometimes, in really high-level games, there might be ways to bring them back, but even in the *Spells, Swords, & Stealth* world, death is a lasting consequence. It's what adds a bit of real danger to our games. No one wants to lose a character they're attached to."

"Wait, so if Wimberly dies, I can't play anymore?" Bert looked torn between shock and tears, with no one sure which side he'd fall on.

"You could still play," Russell assured him. "Just not as Wimberly. We'd have you roll up a new character and the party would meet you somewhere down the line. Truthfully, I'm amazed this hasn't come up already. The four of you have been playing very well to avoid losing any party members so far."

"But it looks like things are getting tougher," Tim pointed out. The number of dead wyvern tokens scattered across the dry-erase map was proof of how dangerous their evening's game had been. If a few rolls had gone slightly askew, they might very well be burying at least one of their party's members.

"That is the nature of a campaign. You go up levels, get better gear, and generally become stronger. Meanwhile, the monsters become more dangerous, and the treasure more worth claiming. I've looked through the module's campaign, and while it's not impossible for everyone to live to the end, it's going to take a fair bit of luck on your parts," Russell admitted.

"Damn, one bad fight and your character is gone." Bert shook his head in amazement. "This game has some high-ass stakes."

"Just like life," Cheri said. "Except we can't just roll up new characters."

"True," Tim agreed. "But we also don't have to fight monsters all the time."

Cheri snorted and took a sip of her drink—this time, one made sans booze. "Can you imagine if we did? No rerolling lives *and* dealing with monsters on the daily? That shit would be the worst of both worlds."

*　　*　　*

This time, he was not overlooking an ancient battle filled with kingdoms and people he'd never seen before. Nor was he in the church where Grumble had first appeared, a dream corollary to the place Thistle had spent so many wasted years as little more than a floor polisher. Instead, dry leaves crunched beneath his feet and cold wind slithered across the stone markers around him. He'd never been to this place before, or, if he had, he couldn't remember it, but Thistle knew where he was the moment he looked around.

This was a graveyard, a sprawling one that lay beneath the glowing light of a full moon. Nothing stirred around him, nor did creeping shadows appear at the edges of his vision. The place was still, quiet.

Dead.

"If you're trying to tell me I'm going to die, you can just say it," Thistle called, his voice bouncing off the gravestones as it went tumbling down the rows. "Though I do respect the theatrics, they are unnecessary. I knew what I was signing up for. If that time has come, so be it."

At first, only silence and his own echo greeted him. Then, the sound of more crunching leaves came, and Thistle turned to find a familiar kobold stepping from behind one of the more massive tombstones.

"Other gods send paladins coded messages all the time."

"And that's lovely for them, but I am a minion at heart. The best orders are clear ones, because there is less chance of erring in their execution and earning a pointless death."

"I'm also pretty sure other paladins show their gods more respect, when they deign to speak with them."

Thistle sighed, but bowed his head anyway. "Oh mighty Grumble, god of the minions and the lowly, would you please be so merciful as to tell me what in the name of the high heavens is going on?"

"See, that wasn't so hard." Grumble stepped forward and hooked a scaly claw under Thistle's chin, lifting it up from its bowed position. "Sadly, I can't give a direct answer on this one. You've stepped into something that other gods have stakes in, which means the divine protocol is in effect."

"Dragonshit. You're talking about politics, aren't you?"

"Unfortunately, yes," Grumble admitted. He released Thistle's face and began walking down the aisles of tombstones, motioning for his paladin to follow. "How much we can intervene with our followers usually depends on how much other gods want us to succeed or fail. In a case like this, where gods are working toward conflicting goals, we use what's known as 'divine protocol' to keep things fair. No one is allowed to just tell things directly to their followers, but we can send visions that you try to interpret. Crappy as they might be, they're still better than nothing."

"Interesting. Certainly explains why Mithingow was often so cryptic, even with her high priests." Thistle paused for a moment, turning the information over in his head. "How is it you can tell me about this, then?"

"Strangely enough, no one ever actually bothered putting conversations about divine protocol under the restrictions of divine protocol," Grumble said. "The other gods keep it secret because they think it makes them seem more mysterious to talk to their followers only through coded visions."

"And you?"

"I think it makes us seem like asses. But even gods have rules they have to follow." Grumble ran a hand over the spines that covered the top of his head. "The most I can pull off is this, showing up to at least explain why I can't explain."

"The effort is appreciated. I was beginning to wonder if I'd done something to incur your wrath," Thistle admitted.

"Well, you're a little too free with the 'strategic repositioning' at times, but when things get serious, you've shown yourself to be a surprisingly heroic follower. So: now you know that I'm not angry with you; I just can't do more than show you seemingly random visions. What's say you try and make the most of this one?"

Thistle looked around, expecting to see the landscape shift or a new set of events burst forth from the stars. Instead, he was greeted with the same graveyard and one divine kobold staring at him with a toothy grin.

"Is . . . is this the vision?"

"No, I brought us here because the chilly air and creepy tombstones really gives the place a homey feel. *Of course* this is the vision."

"Forgive me, I don't think I'm seeing whatever the message is meant to be here," Thistle said.

"That's all right. This one might take a while. Let's stroll around a bit. I can't offer you any help, but I can listen while you try to puzzle through things." Grumble turned down a new row of tombstones, and Thistle followed.

The gnome's mind whirred as he struggled to understand what Grumble was trying to tell him. No, that was wrong. Thistle shook the notion loose before it had time to take root in his mind. Understanding would come later; at the moment, he just needed to grasp what he was seeing. First actually get the message, then try to translate it. Details were what mattered at the moment. The graveyard itself was unfamiliar

127

and bore no distinct features, so it couldn't be the place that was important. That left the tombstones themselves, or rather, what was written on them.

Each stone was bone-white, jutting up from the ground and bearing inscriptions in elegant handwriting. As Thistle began perusing them, he quickly noticed that nearly all of them listed the dead as goblin, ogre, or kobold. These three species may as well have been called the minion races, so far as Thistle was concerned. While every creature could be tempted, cajoled, or outfight forced into the work of servitude, those three races were by far the ones used most frequently. Given that this was a vision sent to him by the god of the minions, though, it made a fair amount of sense to see so many in the graveyard.

Thistle continued reading the inscriptions, looking for a pattern in the names or dates. Nothing leapt out at him, until he came across an inscription that stopped him suddenly in his tracks. He leaned closer, feeling a tickle in his mind as the word called forth memories long forgotten.

"I knew this one. Crasku, a kobold I worked with under a half-mad sorcerer."

"Did you now?" Grumble's voice betrayed nothing; he merely listened with a curious gleam in his wide, reptilian eyes.

"Crasku had ideas for fixing up some of the traps that had been set in the lair. He spent weeks going over his design updates, drawing up proposals, and even making a few small-scale models."

"That's quite industrious. How did that go over?"

Thistle remembered too well the way things had played out; it had been early in his minion career and taught him a lesson that he never let himself forget. "The sorcerer listened for less than five minutes, then threw Crasku into one of the flaming spear pits and said, 'Looks like the current ones are working fine to me.' After that, he laughed, pointed at a random kobold, and told them to fish the corpse out before the scent of charred kobold stunk up the lair." He didn't know when, but Thistle realized he'd clenched his hands so tightly that his nails were on the verge of cutting into his palms.

"My, what a bastard." Grumble stepped over and looked at the headstone, wiping away a small smudge with his hand. "Crasku was a good minion, but he broke one of the cardinal rules we live by."

"Be unseen," Thistle muttered. "Those who stick out are cut down."

"You have no idea how far back that expression goes." For the barest of moments, Grumble's good humor slipped away and Thistle could see the pain and anger still lingering inside him. Then it was gone, the cheerful kobold with the power of a god back in his rightful place. Strangely, Thistle was more comforted by the momentary slip than he was bothered by it. Being a minion was pain, fear, and danger all wrapped up into one cowering existence. It felt good to know his god still remembered that. He shared in the pain of his people, and it made him a better god for it.

"Well, lovely as it's been to catch up with you, I think we've had enough of this place." Grumble straightened up, still a few inches shorter than Thistle, and nodded toward the horizon. "Sun will be up soon, and you've got a lot of reading to do, from what I hear."

"Wait, did I get what I needed to from the vision?"

"You got what you got," Grumble replied. "Now it's up to you what you make of it. I'm sure you'll figure something out, though. I've got high hopes for you, my paladin." Grumble reached up and touched Thistle's head with a single scaly finger.

The graveyard fell away, swallowed by an empty void, and suddenly Thistle realized he was sitting straight up on the basement floor, staring into the darkness of their sealed off base. With a groan, he lay back down, but something in him told him morning would come too soon.

He needed to solve this puzzle and get free of Briarwillow; otherwise, he was never going to have a peaceful night's sleep.

Chapter 16

Unlike Briarwillow, Appleram, or any of the other smaller towns they'd traveled through since leaving Maplebark, Cadence Hollow was not a city built on farming. Certainly, they'd ridden past one or two fields of crops once they finally broke free from the forest, but it was nowhere near the sprawling lands that most villages boasted. Cadence Hollow had begun its life as a hub of commerce, a place where people gathered between their respective towns to sell goods and buy items not available at home. From there, it had grown slowly but steadily into a city built not on corn or labor, but on money.

Gabrielle marveled at the well-cared-for streets as they trotted into town, noting all the shops and booths lining the sides were already opening their doors. Not since the capital of Solium had she seen such opulence or grandeur. This was a city of means, where she imagined almost anything was available to those with the right amount of gold. It was no wonder the robbers had been attacking people on their way here. People coming to Cadence Hollow would certainly have coin to spend, or worthwhile wares to peddle.

She spared a look at Fritz, who was back to being cheerful in spite of the bandages adorning her body. The elf had somehow managed to best her bandit in the confusion of their chase, a fact which Gabrielle found curious, if not outright suspicious. No words were spoken of it, however, as Fritz had returned and proceeded to save Gabrielle's life. If that didn't earn their traveling companion the benefit of the doubt, nothing would.

"Ahh, it feels good to be back in Cadence," Fritz said, wheeling her cart around a pair of dapper men standing in the street. They gave it a look of interest, but seemed otherwise unsurprised by her magical moving device. "Up the street is the temple; there are plenty of priests there who are willing to call down divine healing—in exchange for proper donations, of course. We're coming up on a turn that will take you up to the local Alcatham guard outpost. I'll handle explaining things about the bandits; they know me around here. Ooooh, five streets up is a bakery that sells buns that will knock your shoes off. I'm being literal here; they use enchanted dough to pull it off. Then there's the bar—"

"We need the mages' guild," Grumph interrupted. "Please."

"Fun as a lot of that sounds, I'm with Grumph. It's been three days since we left our friends; the sooner we can get the mages' guild to help us, the better off I'll feel," Gabrielle added.

Fritz furrowed her brow, but seemed to be resigned to the fact that they were set on sticking to business. "All right, we can go to the guild. Let's stable your horses and pop by the temple first, though. You don't want to deal with those people at half-strength. Trust me."

"Fritz, you've been a good friend to us and a great help in getting here," Gabrielle said. "I can't ask any more of you. If you just tell us where the mages' guild is, that will be plenty. We'll go handle our problems, and you can get back to work."

"Sadly, that's not going to work for me," Fritz replied, steering her cart to the side and narrowly missing a stationary wagon filled with apples. "The mages' guild isn't a place I can just give directions to. It's hidden in ways that require you to know what you're doing if you want to find it, which means I have to walk you there personally. Don't feel too bad, though, I would have had to stop by anyway. Those fogies are both my source and best customers for a lot of this merchandise." Fritz patted her satchel tellingly. "Besides, I didn't just help you out of the goodness of my heart. Seeing the show is half of why I came all this way with you two."

"There's a show?" Gabrielle asked.

"Are you kidding me? When a half-orc that looks like he can lift a horse walks in petitioning for membership, those old dicks are going to shit goblins, and that won't even be half as fun to watch as when Grumph shows them he can actually cast. Mages might have a lot of power, but a lot of them also have their heads crammed up their asses. This is going to be something worth witnessing."

Gabrielle turned to Grumph, who seemed impassive to the idea. He was, no doubt, already accustomed to such treatment. She could still remember when he'd first come to Maplebark and begun building his bar, when Gabrielle was just a child. Half the citizens lobbied her father to throw Grumph out, believing he was a spy for a clan of hunters or would draw villainous types to their town. It had been years of patient, constant work in Maplebark before he was accepted as one of the community, and even then there had been a few holdouts. Grumph was used to walking into places where he wasn't wanted or trusted; Gabrielle had no doubt of that. She wished they had a better method to petition for help, but Fritz seemed to think this was their best way in the door. Strange as the elven peddler was, she clearly knew more about mages and their guild than either Gabrielle or Grumph.

"Well, we thank you for taking the time to help us," Gabrielle said at last. "Let us cover the cost of your healing at the temple. It's the least we can do after you saved my life."

"I'd say we saved each other's lives, if you look at the big picture," Fritz replied. "And you should keep your gold. If the mages say no, your next best bet is hiring mercenaries, and those do not come cheap. Besides, someone needs to buy a new axe."

Gabrielle's hand moved on its own, resting against the wooden shaft strapped to her back. It was all that remained of her axe, the tool she'd had since the day they left a goblin camp with new roles. She knew that without its blade, the staff was broken and largely useless, but she couldn't bring herself to simply toss it aside amidst the corpses of bandits. Her blade had died in battle, and noble as that was, she intended to at least dispose of it properly. That would come when time allowed, however. At the moment, their sole objective was getting to the mages' guild and doing whatever was necessary to secure their assistance.

"Later," Gabrielle said, letting go of the broken weapon. "First horses, then healing, and after that, we find the mages' guild. I'll have a shopping spree if there's time."

"Time is the one thing I don't think you'll have to worry about," Fritz warned. "Mages aren't exactly known for doing things quickly."

"They'll make an exception." Grumph didn't sound as though he were being hopeful as much as he was making a threat. Truthfully, Gabrielle wasn't sure which category the words actually fell into, but she was glad to hear them nonetheless.

With their friends in gods-only-knew what kind of danger, every minute was precious.

*　　　*　　　*

"Look out!"

Thistle leapt to the side at the sound of Eric's voice and narrowly missed being crushed under the collapsing tower of books stacked up beside him. He cursed as he saw them fall, not due to the danger or near-miss of being assaulted by literature. No, Thistle was angry because he'd just finished organizing that stack, and the toppling undid at least half an hour of his work.

"I keep you telling you we should take out the ones you've gotten through," Eric said. He was standing in the doorway, a fresh stack of books tucked under his arm. Sunlight streamed through the expansive window behind Thistle, lighting the young rogue like the love of the gods was shining down upon him. It had taken nearly half a day for Thistle to find the best reading nook in Briarwillow, and the cobbler shop's bedroom had won out due to the massive windows that brought in sunlight from all angles.

"And I keep telling you that it's imperative we keep all the books around," Thistle countered. "There are parallels in the diaries, similar notes in the stories. I can't see how it connects yet, but I refuse to lose the chance at following a bit of intuition because the book I need isn't at hand."

Eric stared at Thistle for a long moment, and then set his newly found books in the pile that Thistle had designated as "incoming." The gnome had been reading for nearly a day straight, even bringing a lantern and a stack of books into their basement when night fell. He was beginning to seem a bit frayed at the edges, more nervous and edgy than Eric had ever seen his friend before. Both he and Timuscor knew Thistle hadn't been sleeping well—they'd heard him tossing in the night and jerking awake—but Eric suspected that their ordeal in Briarwillow might be taking more of a toll than he'd expected.

"You know, if everything is going to plan, Gabby and Grumph should be arriving in Cadence Hollow today," Eric reminded him.

"Has it been three days already? My my, that means we only have three left, at most, to figure this all out." Thistle wandered over to a small desk and picked up a book that had been left lying face down. "I'd best get back to reading."

"Or you could take a nap." Eric watched as his words bounced right off Thistle, who was already absorbed in the book he'd picked up. "You know, catch a little shut-eye. Relax. Get some sleep."

"I'm familiar with the concept of sleeping," Thistle said dryly. After a moment, he sighed and lowered the book, pinching the bridge of his nose. "Forgive me, Eric. My dreams have become anything but restful, and I fear I've begun taking out the resulting crankiness on those I hold closest."

"It's okay," Eric assured him. "These dreams, though, are they . . . I mean, is it paladin stuff?"

"Unquestionably." Thistle set the book down and allowed himself to fall back onto the comfortable chair where he'd spent hours already, reading until his eyes grew blurry. "Grumble has been sending me visions, ones which I have yet to understand. There is one thing that's become abundantly clear to me over the last three days, though, and it's why I'm driving myself so hard to unravel the mystery of that cavern."

"If you can share, I'm willing to listen."

"Based on what I've seen so far, and a dream conversation with Grumble, I don't think he's held me here simply because paladins are not allowed to run." Thistle leaned forward, looking out the eastern window to the mountain that loomed nearby. "Whatever this is, whatever we're supposed to be uncovering, I think it has to do with minions. I'm not being held here as just *a* paladin, I'm being held here as *Grumble's* paladin."

"What do magic disease, a cursed skull, and undead villagers have to do with minions?" Eric asked.

"That, I have yet to figure out," Thistle admitted. "And, as it stands, it doesn't seem like I'll be getting any clear answers from above. Hence why I have committed myself so heartily to these books. I will devour every scrap of information in Briarwillow to uncover what might lie beyond those doors. Perhaps it's madness, but I feel that's the piece of this puzzle that will allow me to lay the others in their place."

"It might very well be madness," Eric agreed. "But it's not like Timuscor or I have any better ideas. Try to sleep when you can, at least. We need everyone for when the others get back, but we especially need you."

"I promise I will do my best." Thistle lay back in the chair, but also scooped up his book and opened it once more.

With a last glance at his frayed friend, Eric slipped out of the room and back into the town. All he could do was continue to hunt for the books of Briarwillow and pray he found the one Thistle needed before the poor gnome exhausted himself into insanity.

*   *   *

Gabrielle was both impressed and disgusted after they left the temple. It was true that the priests had done an impressive job of healing the wounds they'd sustained in their fight with the bandits, but the cost was so exorbitant that she nearly choked when they asked for the donation. The gold coins they demanded by no means bankrupted her and Grumph, but when weighed against what the gold could have purchased if they were living in Maplebark, her hands shook at the decadence. It was no wonder those who could magically heal never made trips to the smaller villages: only the truly wealthy could afford such services, and they would send for priests when needed. The whole thing left her with a dirty taste in her mouth and a new appreciation for Thistle's generosity with his gifts.

So lost was she in thought over what they'd done that it wasn't until Fritz was leading them past a fountain featuring warring mermaids for the third time that Gabrielle realized they seemed to be just ambling about, rather than on course for the mages' guild. She held her tongue as they walked up and down the streets, passing many vendors who waved at Fritz while ignoring Gabrielle and Grumph. Only when they rounded the fountain for a fourth time did Gabrielle's curiosity finally overtake her.

"Are we lost?"

"In Cadence Hollow? You'd have an easier time finding gold on the ground than getting lost. The whole place is a giant series of circles with interconnecting roads," Fritz told her.

"So why are we walking past this fountain again?"

"Remember when I said you couldn't just go to the mages' guild? Well, this is how we get there. While they have incantations or some such that let them just appear outside the door, we mundane folk have to follow the proper route. I know it's a little long, but rest assured that we're almost there."

Gabrielle trusted Fritz, both out of earned respect and simple necessity, so she continued to trudge along behind the elf as they turned down a small alleyway, took a corner that led them onto a street filled with merchants selling jewelry, then down a road that she was reasonably certain would take them back to the fountain. That turned out to be wrong, though Gabrielle felt certain that it shouldn't have been, as the road split off into three different paths. Fritz took the left one, which led to an identical split where she took the right one, bringing them again to a split, at which Fritz took the left path one last time. This path was long and winding, impossibly so given the intersecting nature of Cadence Hollow's streets, and ultimately ended abruptly in a small alcove.

Around them seemed to be nothing but a featureless wall, jutting up far too high to match the rest of Cadence Hollow's buildings, with a single unmarked door set opposite the point of the street's end. No one needed to be told what lay beyond that door. Even if she hadn't been aware of their destination, Gabrielle could practically feel the magical energy in the air. The hairs on her arms were standing on end, and her skin felt like it was almost crawling beneath her armor.

"Here we are, the mages' guild," Fritz announced.

"You mean an outpost," Grumph corrected.

"Well, yes and no. You're better off thinking of the guild as one place with a whole lot of doors in and out. From what I've heard, you can't access every part from every entrance, but they'll all get you in the basic areas. For what you're trying to do, this should be plenty."

"So, what do we do?" Gabrielle asked. Given all the twists and turns it had taken to even reach this point, she imagined the tasks for opening the door would be even more complex. Grumph, it seemed, didn't share her opinion, as he immediately started forward.

"We knock. It's polite." The half-orc raised one of his meaty fists and gave a firm, but gentle slam on the rough wooden door. A thud echoed through the alcove and bounded down the alley they'd taken, where Gabrielle had no doubt it would magically die out. It was an impressive sound, made somewhat less so when nothing happened in the moments after the thud faded.

"Good instincts," Fritz said, walking up and joining Grumph at the door. Gabrielle followed suit, lest she get accidently left behind. "But you also have to state your purpose. For example, if I were to knock, I would say I was here with a delivery of magical goods. There are lots of wards in place, so if you lie about why you're here, or say something that doesn't deserve entry, it won't open."

"Can't we just walk in after you?" Gabrielle asked.

Fritz shook her head. "The doors open to where you'd go for your business. My place is very different than where they welcome new mages. It's a lot higher up the chain, and they might kill you just for stepping in without proper permission."

"Guess Grumph will have to ask his own way in." Gabrielle turned to the half-orc, who seemed to be stricken with a sudden case of hesitation. He raised his hand, preparing to knock once more, then lowered it several inches and turned to Fritz.

"Giving help isn't a reason, is it?"

"No, not inherently," Fritz admitted. "Maybe if you were coming offering lots of gold, or trading something the mages cared about, that would be a different story. Requests for charity do not open the door, though. You can draw your own conclusions as to why."

Grumph nodded, turning back to the door. "And no lying?"

"No lying. Whatever you tell the door, it must both be a valid reason to open as well as be true in your heart. If either part is lacking, that door won't budge."

A long moment of silence passed through the alcove as Grumph stared at the door. Despite his seemingly impassive features, Gabrielle had known her friend long enough to sense when he was giving an issue exceptional thought. His brow furrowed slightly, and his bottom lip pulled back less than an inch, revealing a slight glimpse at his wide, sharp teeth. Though she didn't know exactly what he was thinking, she had a hunch that he was trying to find a piece of truth in himself. Saying they wanted Grumph to join the guild to get in the door had been one thing, but now it wasn't something they'd be able to fake. He had to decide for himself if that was something he could truly find reason to want.

Finally, Grumph reared back his arm and slammed it into the door, this time far harder than the first. As he struck, his stony, half-orc voice roared out, stating his business with such ferocity that anyone nearby might have mistaken it for a declaration of war.

"My name is Grumph, and I am a wizard! I have come to become more powerful, in hopes that I will never again be helpless while a friend dies. I will study under the mages' guild and learn all that you can teach. Open this door, for I have come to join!"

His words hung heavy in the air, lingering like lost dreams moments after waking. For an instant, it seemed nothing would happen, that all their work had been for nothing. Then, torturously slow, the door's knob began to twist to the right.

"Good job, Grumph. I think you pulled it off," Fritz said. "Welcome to the Guild of Illustrious Mages."

Chapter 17

Grumph was not an easy half-orc to surprise or impress. His travels and life, even before meeting Thistle, had taken him to strange, unexpected places on more than one occasion. Deep down, he considered himself to be worldly; at least, worldly compared to the companions he'd made throughout his life—ones who'd never so much as crossed an ocean, let alone the entirety of their landmass. So he was neither shocked nor taken aback by the vast, cavernous hall they found themselves walking through. Nor was he stricken with amazement when the floating lanterns before them began to light themselves, or when the runes in the floor started glowing, guiding them along their path. None of it surprised Grumph, but he was still able to gaze upon the magic in pure wonder as it occurred. To be ready for the curiosities of the world and yet still be able to marvel at them was something Grumph prided himself on, and there was so very much worthy of being marveled at as their footsteps echoed through the impossibly vast hall.

"If I'm being honest, this sort of makes your spells look pretty crappy by comparison," Gabrielle said, turning briefly to Grumph as her head spun around, constantly taking in the new sights of their surroundings. Vast, intricate tapestries were hung along the walls, showing massive battles as well as simple men sitting around work stations.

"Time and resources can turn any talent into spectacle," Fritz replied. "Just as every warrior could once only lift a single stone, even the greatest of mages once started with the simplest of spells. Besides, this place has existed for thousands of years, with each new generation of mages inheriting and adding to it. I'm pretty sure there are enchantments woven in here that none of the modern mages would be able to replicate."

"Your confidence overwhelms me with esteem." This voice belonged to neither Grumph, nor Gabrielle, nor Fritz. Instead, a new figure shimmered into view before them. He looked to be neither fully elf nor human, with slightly long ears that stuck out well below his short blue-blond hair. Robes adorned his body just as a slightly annoyed sneer decorated his face. He looked the three of them up and down slowly, the dissatisfaction all but sparkling in his eyes. At last, he spoke again, this time with a touch of confusion in his voice.

"Is this some sort of a joke, trader? I received summons that a new mage had come to apply for guild membership, yet all I find is you and a pair of warriors. Useful business tool or not, I do not take lightly to having my time wasted."

"Chill out, Ferdy," Fritz replied, unbothered by the man's condescending tone. "I'm not the one who opened the door. That would be my friend here, the wizard Grumph." Fritz's arm fell across Grumph shoulders, lest there be any confusion about which of the two she was referring to.

"My name is Ferdinand De Corslo, and I will be speaking to the council of High Mages about this stunt of yours." The mage's fists were curled up into balls, and Grumph could see a flush already creeping up his pale neck. "Just because you make us a bit of money, you think you can come around here, acting as an equal, undermining our sacred rites and laws, making a mockery of us to suit your whimsy. Well, this time—"

Ferdy was cut off as Grumph finished the spell he'd been casting under his breath, which caused a bucket of water to appear and fall to the ground only a few feet in front of the ranting mage. His next words died on his tongue as he stared at the conjured item, going back and forth from Grumph to Fritz to the bucket, and then repeating the cycle over and over again. When at last he spoke, the red was fading from his neck and his hands had become only half-fists.

"Fritz, did you use one of your trinkets to do that?"

"She didn't. I cast the spell." Grumph stepped forward, not that he doubted Ferdy would mistake his voice for either of the women's. It was simply time to set himself apart and push the issue. If they were going to be turned away, then he'd rather see it happen sooner than later. At least that would give them some chance to regroup and, perhaps, think of a new plan. They didn't have time to piss away on pointless chatter that would yield no results. Or, to be more precise, their friends didn't have that time.

"Did you now? Then, would you be so kind as to cast another?" Ferdy's tone was somewhere between sarcasm and genuine interest, his head cocked to the side like a dog being shown a bone he is uncertain he'll be allowed to chew on.

Grumph went more slowly this time, being deliberate with his motions and the muttering of words across his tongue. Even now, they still sounded like gibberish to his ears, but after countless hours of study, they had become familiar gibberish. He drew the magic through himself, weaving it with thought, word, and motion until at last the desired effect manifested into being. A golden spear seemingly made of light appeared in his right hand. With a thought, Grumph reshaped it into a hammer, then a short sword, before finally settling on a falchion.

"You can cast," Ferdy said, his tone somehow still neutral. "My apologies, Fritz. It seems you did nothing to befuddle our wards after all. One who can wield magic is indeed fit to request membership. Whether he will be granted it or not depends on just how powerful he is. You may dismiss your spell, Grumph the wizard. I accept you as a caster, and, as such, you may follow me to the chambers of the Apprentice Committee. They will determine your worthiness from there."

"I look forward to it." Grumph began walking forward, noting that Fritz and Gabrielle were doing the same. Unfortunately, he was not the only one to recognize three sets of footsteps where there should have been one.

"Unless you two would like to show me some spells as well, you have no business following me any further," Ferdy snapped, turning to the warriors and the trader. "Fritz has permission to be here in her capacity as a vendor for our wares, but you, red-armored thug, have no such rights. This is a place of magic, not a bar room for you to trash. Go back out through the door you came in."

"What the hell did you call me?"

Grumph found himself slightly thankful that Gabrielle's axe had been shattered, as her hand reached back and gripped the handle of the broken weapon. If she'd had anything worth swinging, he had little doubt she'd have tried to make the mage eat his words, along with her blade.

"Ferdy, my rights as a trusted vendor also afford me the privilege of lodging for myself and any servants that may be in my employ." Fritz had moved swiftly, placing herself between the fuming barbarian and the smug mage. "Gabrielle here is working as my bodyguard; she and Grumph helped me escape a mess of bandits on the way to Cadence Hollow. Under guild law, she has every right to stay so long as she is with me or in my quarters."

Grumph half-expected Ferdy to start a fight himself with the way he was glaring at Fritz, but instead, the half-elf merely nodded, albeit with aching slowness. "So she is. Be sure she doesn't stray from your side, though. We have no need for wild dogs wandering in these sacred halls, and they shall not be tolerated." He turned to Grumph, barely-contained rage still seething in his eyes. "If you wish to be a mage here, then you must start with two things: follow me right now, and rethink the sort of people you ally yourself with."

With a twirl of his robe, Ferdy was off, nearly stomping down the cavernous hallway at a brisk pace. Grumph spared a single look back to his friends, and then hurried to keep up. A few verbal slights were nothing compared to the need of their friends back in that cursed town. By now, they might have taken sick or been overrun with possessed citizens or who knew what manner of calamity. Grumph was the only one who might be able to bring back help, and he would be damned if he let some insipid spell-slinger stop him from accomplishing his goals.

Grumph had seen too many gravestones bearing names he knew. He would give all he had to keep another from being made.

$$* \qquad * \qquad *$$

Fritz clapped her hands together, startling Gabrielle, who was still watching the mage and Grumph walk down the hall.

"Well, that went about as well as it was ever going to. You want to get some food? After weeks on the road, I could go for a nice meal."

"What the hell was that guy's problem?" Gabrielle almost felt actual pain in her head as she went from dealing with that asshole to Fritz's cheerful voice.

"Don't mind Ferdy, he just doesn't like me because the higher ups in the guild tend to trust me more than him." Fritz patted her satchel tenderly. "First rule of the world: nothing out there—not rank, nor skill, nor prestige—nothing matters more to those in charge than who's making them the most money. Ferdy hangs around and does work for the council, trying to move his way up the ladder legitimately. Meanwhile, I show up, the barest of magical talents to my name, and I'm rubbing elbows with the archmages because my sales are financing new wings on half their towers. Sort of pisses him off."

Gabrielle thought the prospect over for a moment, and then a rogue question slipped into her head that she couldn't help asking. "When you say new wings, are you talking about sections of the buildings or literal wings that would make the towers fly?"

"Depends on the mage in question," Fritz replied. "Anyway, food? Grumph is probably going to be a while, but there's no reason for us to starve. Besides, with Ferdy shutting us out, we'll have to depend on the gossip mill to know how your friend is doing. No better place to constantly run into mages than a cafeteria."

"I . . . I guess that makes sense. But how do we get there?" Gabrielle pointed off toward where Grumph was fading into the distance, and then back toward the door through which they'd entered. "This place is just one long hallway, and your buddy was pretty clear about us not following."

"Oh, this? This is just for the rookies and tourists. Big, grand impressions designed to keep up the image of the all-powerful guild of mages." After a few seconds of digging through her satchel, Fritz produced a small golden key that seemed to almost glow in the lantern light. "I've got the portable shortcut system right here."

Fritz walked over to a section of wall—smooth stone just like the rest of the hall—and held up the key. In seconds, a wooden door much like the one they'd entered through had bloomed into view. With a simple twist, Fritz spun open the knob. Before Gabrielle could register so much as a single sight, a wall of scent hit her like a charging ogre: roasting meats, cooked vegetables, countless sauces she could only briefly recognize from the fanciest of galas her parents had drug her to, plus an array of tantalizing odors she'd never so much as caught whiffs of before. The rumble from her stomach echoed through the vast hall, so loud that the tips of Gabrielle's ears turned red in embarrassment.

"No need to feel bad; if yours hadn't drowned mine out, you'd have heard quite the symphony from my gut as well," Fritz said. "But let's go actually enjoy the food, rather than torturing ourselves by merely lapping up the scent."

Gabrielle needed no more convincing than what had already been delivered. She followed Fritz through the door, stepping into a vast room that was bigger than the entire estate where she'd grown up. Ornately decorated tables were set up in all directions, with only a few people—nearly all them in robes—sitting about. Gorgeous sunlight streamed through sculpted windows, pouring across the tables and perfectly lighting the food. A vast circle stood at the back of the room, filled with pots and dishes that were nearly overflowing with all manner of morsels. Periodically, a few mages would make their way around the circle, piling plates high with as much of the assortment as they could manage, though inevitably, it was only a fraction of what was present.

"Can you explain this to me?" Gabrielle could feel her jaw hanging open just as she could sense the curious stares locked on her, but she paid neither any mind. There was too much here to be amazed by for her to allow such trivial concerns to cloud the experience.

"Everyone likes good food," Fritz said. "And, like I said, one building with many doors. This place feeds pretty much all of the mage outposts in the world, which is also why it's such a great place to gather information."

She pointed over to the circle of food, which Gabrielle noticed was not being depleted no matter how much the others took for their plates. "As for the technical side of things, spells that summon food are pretty common, but what they conjure is often very basic. Some mages like to tinker about, though, and a few of them managed to create spells for delicious, savory meals. Pair that with a good enchanter and you have a self-filling pot of stew. Rinse and repeat for everything up there. As for the tables and chairs, a few replication and self-cleaning spells took care of seating. That's pretty much all we needed. Oh, except for the sunlight. That's imported."

"Imported?" Gabrielle took a deep breath, nearly setting off her stomach as she did, and tried to focus. "If I ask you to tell me how that's possible, will I even understand the explanation?"

"Maybe, but I don't really get it myself, so the odds aren't great," Fritz admitted.

"Then let's not bother. Right now, it's taking all I have not to dash over there and eat straight out of the cookware."

"I won't say you'd be the first, but it generally never goes over well. Let's stick to plates and silverware for now." Fritz led the way to the circle of food, where she immediately began piling things on her plate with reckless abandon.

Gabrielle tried to show a bit more restraint at first; her years as the mayor's daughter had left her mother's voice constantly in her head, reminding her how a proper lady should act. Eventually, pragmatism overtook habit, as the dishes she wanted to try were more than would fit neatly on a plate. Even caving as she did, Gabrielle was forced to finally walk away with no fewer than a dozen items she still wanted to sample but simply could not fit on her dish.

She and Fritz sat down at one of the tables that were unoccupied, which were by far the majority. Despite the trader's promise of people to talk to, the cafeteria seemed largely deserted to Gabrielle, though that might have been a matter of perspective. In a place so huge, even several hundred people might seem paltry.

"How does sitting alone help us find out what's happening with Grumph?" Gabrielle asked. It was a testament to her friendship that her plate was yet untouched, concern for the half-orc outweighing even the temptation of culinary decadence.

"Obviously, it doesn't," Fritz replied. "But we actually have to wait for something to happen first. Remember what I said: mages do things slowly. Until his first meeting is over, there's no news to get. I hate to break it to you, but this is largely what it's going to be like while you're here. Whether he makes it or not, Grumph is going to have to fight this battle on his own. The most we can do is cheer him on and pray to the gods he finds a way to pull things off."

"I'm not a fan of sitting idle," Gabrielle said.

"There are other things to do in Cadence Hollow," Fritz said. "In fact, after lunch and my meeting, I'll even help you with the most pressing one. Literally, it's pressing against your back."

Gabrielle didn't need to reach up and touch the remains of her axe; she knew too well the weight to which Fritz referred. Much as the idea of simply buying a new one saddened her, deep down she knew it was inevitable. Without a weapon, she had no place alongside the others. Her strength had already come up lacking in the last fight, and that was when she had her axe. Now, without it, she felt almost powerless, closer to the Gabrielle who had sat in the sitting room with her family than the one who had prowled the forest with goblins.

"Thank you for the offer." Gabrielle picked up her fork and began to eat at last. "I'd like that very much, actually. After we hear about Grumph, of course."

"Of course."

Chapter 18

The fire was beginning to die out on its own when a purple cloud appeared over it, raining fat droplets that extinguished the remaining cinders with a sizzling hiss. A woman, waving a wand with a glowing purple tip, looked on carefully until the fire was completely out, and then flicked her wand upward and caused the cloud to vanish.

"If you let it burn itself out, the chamber will stink for days," she explained to the other two people in robes, tucking the wand back up her sleeve.

"Let the record show that Grumph, wizard and mage guild applicant, has now cast two spells in front of the admissions committee, and two in front of his escort, Ferdinand De Corslo." It was Ferdy who said this, speaking to a small man, nearly gnome-sized, who was rapidly scribbling things down on a scroll. "Though they require little mana, they were executed within the realms of acceptability. Grumph, you may continue when ready."

"I have one more." Grumph's voice was a harsh contrast to the almost-but-not-quite lyrical sounds of Ferdy's half-elven tones. "But people need to be hurt for it to work."

Around Grumph were Ferdy and two others, all three observers resting on a curved stone that rose from the floor and wrapped around half the room. They were sitting no less than eight feet in the air, staring down at Grumph as he conjured his spells in the designated area across from them. Thus far, neither the elven male nor the human woman with the wand had said much, preferring to let Ferdy handle the talking, most of which was simply giving Grumph instructions to cast his next spell. They were judging him; that much had been made abundantly clear by the room's setup. Grumph had come in expecting to be evaluated, though he'd hoped they might be a touch less overt about it all.

"Also, casting it drains me. A lot." There was nothing to be gained by hiding his limitations. This was not a point he was going to be able to bluff his way past, not with people who knew so much more about magic than he. If Grumph wanted to have a shot, all he could do was his best and pray it was enough.

"Can you elaborate on why you need people who are injured?" The elf spoke for the first time, face resting on the elegant, long fingers that were crossed beneath his chin.

"It helps them up. Gives them strength, for a time." Grumph had only managed to cast this spell once before, yet the memory of it was seared in his mind more clearly than all the others. Clutching the strange, unnatural artifact had torn open his mind, showing him the world in ways he didn't yet understand. In that moment, the spell he'd been struggling with became so clear, so simple, that Grumph would never be able to forget it.

"Interesting. One moment." The elf's eyes closed as he muttered a few words under his breath. When next his lids parted, his irises had gone from the golden color of honey to a glowing green like fresh summer grass. "You may now cast, Grumph. I'll be able to see the magic, even if there are no targets to use it on."

Grumph nodded; it wasn't as though he had much choice aside from trusting these people. With a moment of calm to focus, he pulled up the memory of that spell, weaving it into the world even as he felt the strength begin to leave his body. Part of him feared that he'd taxed himself too much by casting his other spells first. That worry gave no aid, though, so Grumph pushed it aside. He had to believe he could cast the spell, because he *had* to cast the spell. Too much rode on it. Failure was not tolerable.

"*Rouse.*" The final word left Grumph's lips as a whisper, the only piece of the spell that actually made sense to him. He felt the spell form, then burst through the air as it found no target for its energizing gifts. All three of the mages staring at him seemed to perk up and stiffen, no doubt taking in a bit of the spell's effects, but it was only the elf who rose to his feet, staring at Grumph in disbelief and wonder.

"*That* was not a beginner's spell. We have mages far above your skill level who would struggle to cast it, yet your form was flawless. How have you managed to master a spell clearly so far above your experience?"

"My friends were being attacked. They needed help. We were going to die, so I made it work." Grumph agreed with Thistle's philosophy on lying: it was far better to merely tell selective truths. Not only did it allow one to keep a story straight, but it was a way around any spells or wards that watched for those who crossed the threshold into falsehood.

"Forced growth through immediate peril." The human woman seemed interested for the first time since Grumph had walked in the door. "Not unheard of, but pretty damn far from common. Let's step back a moment, though. You said you were a wizard?"

Grumph nodded, wary of what question might come next.

"So that means you had to have someone show you the spell first, written out in a scroll or book. Where did you get that spell in the first place?"

"In a book from another wizard."

"Was this other wizard your teacher, the one who showed you how to work magic in the first place?" Ferdy asked.

"No. He was dead, though not by my hand. I took the book and read."

If Grumph's spell had shocked them, this announcement nearly knocked the committee over dead. Ferdy's eyes bulged like Grumph had socked him in the gut, and the elf's features grew tightly pinched. Even the woman seemed stunned, and Grumph suspected she'd only been paying half attention throughout his interview.

"Grumph, I didn't feel this needed spelling out, but it is a serious offense to lie to the committee during your request for membership into

152

the mages' guild," said the elf, at last. "Knowing that, would you like to . . . rephrase . . . your claims?"

"I do not." Grumph met the man's skeptical eyes with no fear. Every word he'd uttered so far had been honest, if perhaps not as in-depth as they could have been. He had no backpedaling to do, and even if that weren't the case, he'd still have held firm. Retreating here would lose him all chance at victory, of that he had no doubt.

"So, you are claiming to have found a spell book, and with no instruction or tutelage from any other wizard, taught yourself to cast the spells you've shown us merely through study?"

"Yes, I did."

The elf looked at Ferdy, who was still wearing a face of shock even as he shook his head. This raised one of the elf's eyebrows as he looked back to Grumph. No longer was his face merely pinched, though; it had begun to relax, and curiosity was twinkling in the still-glowing irises of his eyes.

"Either you are telling the truth, or you've found a way to compromise our wards. Whichever is correct, they would both provide reason enough for you to find a place at the mages' guild. You probably don't realize this, but self-taught wizards are extremely rare. Most need to be shown, physically instructed, to master the art of even the most basic of spells. As overseer of the Apprentice Committee, I, Talcia the sorcerer, hereby approve your petition for trial membership."

"What is a 'trial' membership?" Grumph had an uneasy feeling as Fritz's words echoed in his mind, cautioning him that mages were not prone to doing things quickly.

"We allow you access to the guild, to the teachers and books that all full members get, and you use those to improve your skills," Ferdy explained. "When you feel you're ready, you can undergo the trials to gain full membership, which grants you all the rights and privileges of the mage's council."

153

"I see." Grumph turned the situation over in his head, carefully considering the options laid out before him. "Privileges . . . like the right to ask for help?"

"It would depend on the circumstance, but we do look out for our own," Talcia assured him.

"Briarwillow has a magic plague caused by an artifact. Whole town has vanished in the night. Friends are trapped there, and the paladin sensed great evil. That kind of help?"

Talcia tapped his hands against the stone before him, clearly weighing Grumph's words. Nearly a full minute passed before he responded, and when he did, his words were measured and careful.

"In that situation, with a great mystery to solve and the chance at scooping up a powerful artifact, I would likely authorize the use of two to four fellow mages for one of our full members. This is, of course, all dealing in hypotheticals, since it will be months—"

"I'm ready," Grumph interrupted. "Let me take the trials."

By this point, he'd so worn the three out in terms of surprises that they were scarcely able to manage more than a slight stirring at his declaration. Talcia seemed more cross than bothered; he'd obviously anticipated something like this when he gave his answer.

"You can't just jump from apprenticeship into the trials," Ferdy protested.

"Is there a time limit?" Grumph asked.

"Well . . . yes, but it just says you have three years from your apprenticeship to undergo the trials. And that's because most mages spend as long as possible preparing for them. No one ever wants to do them early," Ferdy admitted.

"I do. Please." Grumph met the eyes of each of his judges one by one, hoping they could see, and would care about, the sincerity in his request. "Unless you will lend aid to a trial member."

"We would not," Talcia replied immediately. "What you've described is a dangerous situation. Either the expedition would be led by a member of the guild or paid for properly, which I doubt you can afford. However, I will not allow you to step right into the trials. That would be a waste of potential, especially since your last spell channeled out all of your mana. Tell me, Grumph the wizard, did you know that's why it drains you? You're literally turning the mana you've gathered into physical energy for those you aid. Were you aware of that?"

"No." Grumph refused to look away; he and Talcia stared at one another like punches were about to be thrown.

"I thought not. Such are the limitations of self-education. That said, I do not have it in my power to stop a trial member from undergoing the trials, so let me make you a deal. Your friends are in Briarwillow, which is three days' ride from here, yes?"

Grumph nodded, he was too familiar with the journey for his tastes by this point.

"Then I want you to spend two of those days preparing for the trials. Let yourself learn and be taught by what we can offer. On the third day, you may attempt the ordeal itself. Should you prevail, I will personally see to it that you are sent back there by magic, saving you the trip."

"How much do you think he's going to learn in a couple of days?" Ferdy asked.

"I have no idea," Talcia admitted. "But I also do not know how he taught himself to cast, and to manage such a difficult spell at that. With a few days, he might just surprise us. And, if nothing else, it will prove to be entertaining. You know how the mages love a good show. What do you say, trial guild-member Grumph?"

155

"If I make it, I get help." The offer of transport was nice, but useless if he wasn't bringing mages back with him. Talcia seemed smart, which made him dangerous until Grumph had a better sense of the heart that lived below the cunning brain.

"Agreed. Your expedition is authorized on the condition you pass the trials," Talcia replied.

There it was. Everything they'd hoped for. Everything they needed. Everything his friends were counting on him to provide. And all that stood between Grumph and his goal was a single ordeal. Granted, an ordeal that real spell casters spent years studying and preparing for, but it was still a lone obstacle. One last problem to solve and they could get back to the others. Even if Grumph died undergoing the trials, he would do so without regret. After all his years alone, he again had people he loved enough to risk his life for. This was what it meant to have a party.

This was what it meant to have a family.

"It's a deal."

*   *   *

Fritz looked up from her fourth slice of pie, not noticing Gabrielle gaping in wonderment over where this slender woman could possibly be stuffing all the food, and nodded to a cluster of robed people who were coming through one of the many doors in the cafeteria.

"That might be something. They're chittering like mice over there."

"Do mages requesting membership make that much of a stir?"

Fritz grabbed a napkin and wiped away a trace of cinnamon-coated apple from her mouth. "Normally? No; we get them fairly regularly. Half-orcs, on the other hands, are quite the rarity. To my knowledge, there have only been a handful of them in the guild's history."

156

"You seem to know an awful lot about this place for not being a mage yourself." Gabrielle's tone wasn't accusatory, not exactly, but there was certainly a barb buried in her seemingly innocent words.

"Actually, I am a mage—a sorceress, to be specific—just not a very good one. And of course I know all about it: information is just another form of currency to the right folks. Now, do you want to sit around here asking me obvious questions, or shall we go cozy up to that group and see what they know about Grumph?"

"Doesn't seem like that will be necessary," Gabrielle replied, pointing to another one of the doors that had just opened. If she had drawn stares with her red armor and fierce expression, Grumph had the entire room's rapt attention strictly on him. He seemed to pay them no heed, however, merely walking briskly through the tables, Ferdy at his side, on a direct path for Gabrielle and Fritz.

"How'd it go?" Fritz asked, leaning back in her chair.

"Your traveling companion made quite the impression," Ferdy informed her. "Not only was he accepted as a trial member, but he's requested to undergo the trials to become a full member in a mere two days' time."

A long whistle escaped Fritz's lips as she stared at Grumph, while Gabrielle felt a rush of panic and energy not unlike what she experienced pre-battle. "That sounds dangerous. Why do you want to take some test?"

"If I win, we get what we need." Grumph saw no point in adding more to it than that. The facts were laid out quite simply: this was the best path forward, so it was the one he would take. Danger was irrelevant, so long as it only applied to him.

"The longer I hang around you two, the more fun you turn out to be," Fritz chuckled. "Taking on the trials with only a couple of days to study, that's a gutsy move. Especially since there's no complete win for you in it."

"Wait, he can't beat whatever these trials are?" Gabrielle asked.

"Oh, he can pass them, theoretically," Fritz explained. "But I mean there's no real win for him here. If he fails the trials, he'll end up seriously hurt, possibly dead. On the other hand, if he passes the trials with only a couple of days to train under his belt, every mage in here with any sort of ego is going to hate him for showing them up, and mages collect ego like dragons collect gold."

"We worry later," Grumph said, angling toward the food. "First we eat. Then I train."

"Like I said, more and more fun with each passing day."

Chapter 19

Timuscor flipped over the rotted out barrels, revealing a small chest. Once upon a time, he'd have hoped to find gold, or gems, or even a magical trinket when he discovered such prizes. Now, he gritted his teeth and said a silent prayer to no god in particular that he would find only a single type of treasure contained within: books.

In the basement of yet another home, digging about through a family's collection of memories and antiques, books were all that Timuscor searched for. As tiring as it was to scour the town for something that seemed so meaningless, every trip back to Thistle made Timuscor feel shamed at even considering a complaint. All he had to do was find the things. Thistle was devouring them, reading each at least once, but likely far more times than that. Timuscor had always imagined that a paladin's duties were simple, straightforward tasks: fight the monsters, protect the innocents, save the villages. Watching Thistle, Timuscor had begun to realize that what it meant to be a paladin, more than anything else, was devotion.

Not just to a god, though that certainly seemed a necessary trait, but also to the jobs they were given, the problems they were expected to solve. Paladins couldn't walk away if a task was too big. They were stalwart, committed. Even if the job was beyond their strength. Even if it wore them down and began to tear them apart. Thistle wasn't sleeping well, if at all. Neither Timuscor nor Eric knew how much longer he could keep up this pace of study. If all went well, which seemed unlikely by this point, the others would be back in a few days. Perhaps they would bring some news or information that would let Thistle put his mind to rest. As for Timuscor and Eric, all they could do was keep the search going, hoping to find whatever book Thistle was searching for.

Using the butt of his hilt, Timuscor smashed open the paltry lock and popped the chest open. A few gold coins, two rings, a locket, and a diary. Timuscor took only the coins and the book, as the owners likely wouldn't be making any purchases from beyond the grave; touching the jewelry, clearly stored here with love and intent, felt too much like grave-robbing. He shut the chest closed once more, stuffing the goods in his bag.

Maybe this would be the book that set Thistle free. It wasn't likely, but hope was important, especially in times like these. Timuscor didn't know if he could do it, were he in Thistle's shoes. His was a mind built for battle and combat; poring over countless words would have been a living hell for him. Deep down, Timuscor suspected that were he to become a paladin—as he'd always dreamed—he would have found his own way to come at the problem. Not necessarily better or worse than Thistle's, just one that played to his individual strengths. The longer he observed the gnome and his toiling, the more certain Timuscor became that each paladin had to find their own way to serve. It was all meaningless conjecture, though, at the end of the day.

Much as he might dream of holding the same mantle as Thistle, it seemed none of the gods were offering.

*   *   *

"Given how little time you have to work with, we're going to have to get you a tutor." Fritz yanked the key out of her satchel and held it to one of the many doors leading out of the cafeteria. She twisted the knob to reveal what looked like the entrance to a stately manor. Ushering Grumph and Gabrielle through, Fritz immediately shut the door behind them. "And not just one of the mages everyone uses. You can't get a half-assed education. Not if you want to have a shot at making it through the trials."

"Can you tell us what those 'trials' actually entail, please?" Gabrielle noted the size of the room Fritz had taken them to, as well as the corridors and large staircase, and then pushed such observations out of her mind. Grumph's well-being was far more important than the strange workings of the guild's doors. "Maybe if we have an idea of what he's in store for, it will help Grumph better prepare."

"The trials are actually very straightforward," Fritz replied. She headed for a sizable chair and nearly fell into it, sending a small could of dust into the air as she landed. Her hands spread as she motioned for them to take seats as well.

"Grumph will have to prove he has skill, power, and determination: what the guild considers the three greatest traits for any mage to possess. How they test that tends to vary, as using the same trial for everyone would let applicants tailor their studying to passing that ordeal, rather than preparing for whatever might come at them. I've seen them set up elaborate dungeons, create magical puzzles, even summon dangerous beasts. They've got at least a hundred different trials that I've seen used, and people are constantly coming up with new ones."

"Guess that means knowing what we're facing is out," Gabrielle muttered as she sank into one of the chairs.

"Well, yes, but in a way, Grumph might have utilized one of the better strategies I've seen a wizard take," Fritz added. "One of the biggest problems with the trials is the fear. As you spend your years studying, you see others go through their ordeals, and each time, you find something that you're underprepared for. Mages end up spreading themselves too thin, trying to have the perfect spell for every situation instead of getting a few flexible ones down pat and learning to adapt their thinking. Grumph doesn't have the option of overthinking or getting in his head. In a way, that makes jumping right in sort of brilliant."

"Thanks," Grumph rumbled.

"Of course, most mages *also* use that time to build up their spell catalog and mana reserves, which means you're going into this thing with a severe handicap," Fritz tacked on. "That part is significantly less brilliant."

"Let's get back to how he might stand a chance," Gabrielle suggested. "You mentioned something about getting him a tutor?"

"Right, that. While I might be useless with a spell book, I do have a few folks around here that owe me some favors. If I can get one of the more experienced wizards to teach Grumph, he might just be able to master a few new tricks before the trials."

"How many tricks?" Grumph remained standing, forcing down the urge to pace. Now that the immediacy of the moment had passed, he was stuck in the looming shadow of the task before him. If he let the fear, or even the reality, of what he was facing into his mind, there would be no driving it out. His only hope was to focus on strategy, thinking about what he could do rather than what he might be facing.

"That depends on you," Fritz said. "Given that you puzzled through your book without any help at all, it's obvious you've got a pretty keen mind. Still, spells get harder the more powerful they are, and the first casting is always the toughest. If you were to work constantly, with minimal sleep or distractions, and we got you a hell of a tutor, you *might* be able to learn two new spells. Maybe three, if they weren't too difficult."

"Two or three new spells. Doesn't seem like a lot," Gabrielle noted.

"It's not. Most mages know around thirty or so when they undertake the trials," Fritz agreed. "But let's not get too far ahead of ourselves. Before anything else, I need to see if I can find someone willing to train you." She hefted herself out of the chair and headed for the door, golden key already in hand.

"Gabrielle, you're going to stay here per guild regulations. Grumph, as a trial member, you can go to the cafeteria or the library; just say where you're heading when you hold the doorknob. Feel free to explore around; I rarely spend any time in my quarters, anyway."

"Wait, this is where you live?" Gabrielle turned about, admiring with new appreciation the sprawling area they were sitting in. She'd assumed Fritz's quarters would be a room with a cot, and perhaps a window. They were in the front room of what was clearly a large estate.

162

"Nah, this is where I stay when I have to visit the guild." Fritz smirked, clearly enjoying Gabrielle's shock, and gave the barbarian an exaggerated wink. "Remember what I said earlier: all people really care about is who's making them their money."

With that, she swung open the door—briefly revealing a stone room with a torch burning off to the side—and vanished as it swung shut behind her. Just like that, Gabrielle and Grumph were alone for the first time since they'd run into the strange peddler and stuck in a mansion-sized room somewhere in the magical halls of the mages' guild.

"When this is all over," Gabrielle said, still eyeing the surroundings with awe, "I might seriously have to consider a career change. Think Fritz needs an apprentice trader?"

*   *   *

When Dejy took a seat at the Table of Mages, he'd expected many things. Respect, certainly, along with a fair bump in access to the treasury, plus the duty of using his tremendous power to handle the more problematic situations that vexed the guild. After all, the Table was as close to a ruling body as mages could handle, and those on it were expected to be equal parts powerful and devoted to their fellow spell casters. Dejy had expected a great many of the things he dealt with frequently, but one had taken him completely by surprise:

Dejy hadn't counted on the amount of paperwork members of the Table had to endure.

Expedition forms, demands for financing, incident reports, and a seemingly endless string of mages requesting judgment from the Table on who was at fault in some petty feud. As an archmage, Dejy knew no fewer than a dozen potent spells to summon fire, and staring at the stack of parchment on his desk, it took every bit of self-restraint not to call upon them.

He ran his fingers through the thick, dark hair that adorned his head. Most members of the Table were either elven, and therefore looked ageless, or human, and wrinkled as forgotten grapes. Dejy was considered a prodigy, having made it to his station within the guild by the age of thirty—no small feat for a human. Of course, there were also whispers of backroom deals and secret alliances that accounted for his seat, but he paid no mind to those. Dejy, as well as those who had attempted to test their strength against him, knew he had more than enough power to back up his status. Some days, he wished one of the upstarts would actually give it a try. Anything to get a break from the monotony of paperwork.

Across his massive office, which was nearly choked with all manner of knick-knacks and decorations, his door slowly opened without as much as a knock. Dejy made sure an annoyed, sour expression rested on his face as the figure stepped through the now open door, though inside, he was actually delighted by the visit. Few people had the gall to walk in on him without proper formality, and the one he knew would be coming was a pleasant distraction. Still, appearances mattered, so he scowled at the elven woman as she shut the door behind her.

"Fritz." It was a greeting, accusation, and statement all rolled into one. His elven guest gave a polite nod that in no way took away from her mischievous smirk and crossed the room until she was nearly at his desk. The trip was a quick one, though, in the process, she nearly took a tumble over a half-rusted set of armor and a stuffed, formerly possessed dragon toy.

"Dejy, you really need to clean this place up once in a while."

"They're all subjects of study." There was no thought or fumbling for his excuse as Dejy defended his lifestyle; the words came automatically. Given that he had this fight at least once a week with some member of the guild, it was more habit than discussion for him. "At least, they would be, if I ever had any time to myself."

"Poor Dejy, so talented and powerful that he got his wish of taking a seat at the Table, only to learn it came with actual responsibilities." Fritz giggled, a demure sound she'd never have allowed

164

most of the other mages to hear, and pressed a hand to one of the many stacks of paper on Dejy's desk.

"Did you think it would be nothing but uncovering great ruins, studying ancient magic, and getting decadently drunk on the private reserve wine?"

"Maybe not *all* that stuff, but a little more would be nice," Dejy grumbled. "You know, running that errand for you was the first time I'd left my quarters in nearly a week? I have assistants bringing me food, and they never seem to remember what my favorites are."

Fritz smiled, all too aware that purposely bungling menial tasks was a tried and true way to avoid having to do more of them. Rather than point that out, however, she turned the topic toward more productive means. "If you ran the errand, I take it you got my message? I had to send it in a bit of a hurry."

Dejy rolled his eyes, a motion that was almost sublime in its practiced perfection, honed from years of dealing with bureaucratic nonsense. "No, it didn't make it through, that's why there just happened to be an admission committee assembled when you brought some stray wizard to our door. You're welcome, by the way."

"Oh Dejy, you know I couldn't get a thing done without you . . . which is actually part of why I'm here. Tell me, did you bother to keep tabs on how the admission went?"

With an audible thump, Dejy slapped his hand on the hefty stack of papers resting in the bin marked "Completed." Big as it was, it was dwarfed by the other, presumably uncompleted heaps of documents still scattered about the desk. "Does it look like I had time to watch some rookie mage petition for membership?"

"I thought you might have heard something. After all, it's not every day we get a half-orc inside these halls." Fritz's smile didn't deepen as she watched surprise ripple across Dejy's face, though she failed to keep the humor from dancing in her eyes.

"A half-orc?" Dejy leaned forward, inadvertently smudging the document he'd been working on when Fritz walked in. "Where in the kingdoms did you find a half-orc that thought he could be a mage?"

"Thought nothing," Fritz corrected. "Grumph was granted trial membership by the committee, and he's ready to start training for the trials. Though, to be honest, he could use a tutor."

Dejy sat back in his chair, studying his elven intruder carefully. What she was asking would no doubt cause a great drain on the little free time he had. Tutoring a wizard, especially a new one, was a time-consuming task, one he would have ordinarily refused outright. But training a half-orc . . . that was something different. Only a handful of the guild's mages weren't gnomes, human, elf, or half-elf, and the majority of those were dwarves. Half-orcs were in the guild's history books, but with incredible rarity. Magic often tended to be a defense for those who are physically weak, and as such, the powerful half-orcs rarely had the need to develop skills for it. The chance to teach one, to see what they were capable of, would appeal to any mage. Curiosity, as much as power, defined what led one down the path of magic.

"I might be able to fit something in. Perhaps sessions once a month . . . no, every two weeks. They won't be tremendously long, but I feel confident I can help shape his training even with so little time."

"That would be great and all, but there's one problem: Grumph is only training for two days, and then he's taking the trials. So we'd pretty much need you around to teach him as much as you can before then."

A soft choking sound escaped the back of Dejy's throat as he reeled at that revelation, eyes bulging like Fritz had socked him in his stomach. "Two days? You found a half-orc wizard that managed to qualify for the trials, and he wasn't willing to wait more than two days?"

"There are some external time constraints. Friends in need, that sort of thing," Fritz replied, unfazed by his reaction. "I'll explain it all once you decide you're on board, but I need to know if you're willing to help. With only two days to train in, he needs an archmage, a wizard of incredible knowledge and power. Naturally, you were the first one who came to mind."

"My ego is a mighty beast, but not even I am foolish enough to believe I can teach someone all they need to know in a mere pair of days," Dejy protested.

"Then don't teach him everything, just enough to get by." Fritz lifted a stack of documents from the desk, fanning them out before her and letting them scatter like leaves in the wind. "He and his companion are interesting and might surprise you. Besides, won't it be more fun than sitting in here, scribbling on these pages?"

"Even if I wanted to neglect my duties, we both know it's impossible. There's work to be done here, and it doesn't halt just because you need a favor."

"Fair enough. Let's not call it a favor; let's call it a trade." Fritz slapped her hand on the desk and scooped up one of Dejy's spare quills. "You go train the half-orc, and I'll cover for you on the paperwork. All you'll need to do is scratch out a few signatures so they're official; I can handle everything else."

Dejy rubbed his thumb against his cheek, considering the proposition. "You have to do all of it: enough to buy me a solid week off. And that's a week on top of the days I spend training your friend. Think you can manage that?"

"Please, some of us have enough practice to plow through this stuff faster than an attack from a gelatinous blob. You worry about helping Grumph pass; I'll tend to your precious paperwork."

"If you can pull that off, then we've got a deal," Dejy agreed. "Give me an hour to get things in order and to pop by the cafeteria for a proper meal, and I'll be at your quarters to pick up the apprentice."

Fritz nodded, turning back toward the door. Before she had her key fully raised, Dejy called to her, and for the first time, his voice was absent of the purposefully affected authoritative tone.

"Do you really think he'll be able to pull it off? I mean . . . two days."

"Honestly, I have no idea," Fritz admitted. "He's self-taught, which means there are many basics for him to learn, and the spells he knows already are fairly limited in use. Grumph is determined, though, and that counts for a lot, especially in the trials. At the end of the day, I'd say he has a shot. The guy's got talent, if nothing else. And you know that when I see talent in someone, I expect great things from them."

Fritz scanned Dejy's office—his vast, impressive office that he had been given as part of his promotion to the Table—and smiled. For a moment, time seemed to slip, and Dejy no longer felt like he was the prodigy mage talking to a simple trader. Instead, he was just a stupid farm boy standing in the middle of a dusty road, catching his first sight of the elven woman walking through their town. Her robes were splendid white with golden trim. Even if he hadn't known what that signified at the time, Dejy could tell, even as a child, that it meant she was important. From atop her steed, the woman scanned the crowd, a look of polite boredom on her face . . . until she saw Dejy. Then, and only then, did the elven woman grace them with a smile, one that was meant just for him.

"Tell Grumph to be ready. If I'm going to train him, I'm going to see to it that he passes those trials."

Chapter 20

"Knock knock."

Russell looked up from the books spread across his bed to see Cheri standing in the doorway of his room, a glass of what he could only hope was iced tea in hand.

"You're supposed to actually knock, not just use the words."

"Pretty sure that only applies if the door is closed," Cheri countered. "Anyway, I wanted to let you know that Tim texted you; he's stuck in traffic, so he'll be late for the game tonight."

"You're definitely not supposed to be snooping around on my phone."

"Well then, don't leave it in the living room where you know your nosy big sis can notice it." Cheri took a long sip from her glass, clearly scanning the array of documents and hand-scribbled pages on Russell's desk. "Soooo . . . whacha doing?"

"Preparing."

"Yeah, you're running a module, which means most of the stuff you need is already done. Plus, we both know you don't wait until the last minute to prep for game. Come on, you're not me. Thus, I am forced to ask once more: whacha doooooooooing?"

Russell gritted his teeth as she stretched the last word, moving it in the sing-songy harmony she knew annoyed him. Tempted as he was to kick her out of the room or threaten to kill Chalara out of spite, part of him was also grateful she'd broached the topic. There was something he'd wanted to talk with her about, share with her, ever since she came back from college; he'd just never found a way to work it gracefully into a conversation. Plus, he worried she might think he was crazy, which would only match the suspicions he was beginning to carry about himself.

169

"Cheri, you've played *Spells, Swords, & Stealth* for longer than anyone else I know. Has anything . . . weird . . . ever happened during one of your games?"

"Are you kidding? Only all the fucking time. I remember one time, we were in the middle of slaying a nest of elder worms when one of those little shits grabs my barbarian in its mouth and swallows me whole. Now I've got her hacking through a giant, acid-filled stomach, when what should I come across but—"

"No, not . . ." Russell sighed, putting his hand on the module book. Next to it were handwritten copies of each section, scrawled out over and over again in several notebooks worth of paper. "Not *in* the game. During it. Like, things started happening here, in the real world, that were hard to explain."

"We once got a free pizza delivered by mistake, but something tells me that's not what you mean." Cheri stepped fully into the room, setting her tea down on Russell's dresser. "Why? Did something happen to you?"

"Yes. I mean, maybe. One thing, definitely, but there might be more to it. Look, do you remember Tim telling us about the time his die broke during our last session?"

"Given how freely he busts that story out, yeah, it's familiar."

"Well, weird as that was, there are probably a lot of explanations for it," Russell admitted. "Tricks of the light, some unstable gunk getting accidently put in the die when it was made, a prank by one of the others that no one has owned up to yet . . . there are lots of rational ways to explain it away. But there was more to it that just the die. During that game, when we were playing the module—and this is where I'm going to lose you, but—I swear to God it seemed like the book was changing."

"Changing how, exactly?" Cheri was looking at him not with worry, or terror, or concern as he'd been so afraid she would. Instead, it was curiosity that filled her eyes, and Russell suddenly remembered why there had been a time when he looked up to his older sister like she walked on water.

"I, um, I thought you'd be a bit harder to convince," Russell said.

"Don't get me wrong, I'm not saying I'm wholly buying what you're selling, but you're not really the type to go this far for a silly joke." Cheri gestured to the piles of handwritten pages, turning a few over to prove her point. "Plus, you're a terrible liar, just overall. And, come on. If I wasn't at least a little open to, if not hopeful for, the idea of the magical and unexpected, why would I keep playing these games?"

Russell nodded and picked up his older book, the first module they'd run that took place in the kingdom of Solium. In it were maps, encounters, quests, and magic all spread across a powerful, if perhaps not completely good, kingdom. And near the end, at the spot where several quest lines converged, lay a dungeon holding a mysterious artifact that several teams fought to reach first.

Eight teams, to be exact, which Russell *knew* was one more than there had been the first time he read it. This time would be different, though. This time, he was keeping records.

This time, there would be proof.

*   *   *

"Magic is everywhere." Dejy stood in front of Grumph, who had only his spell book, a quill, and a stack of parchment to write on. Dejy, on the other hand, was surrounded by stacks of books, dozens of scrolls, and a glowing rectangle pinned up on the stone wall behind him. No one else was in the room, or allowed in for that matter; Dejy had personally requisitioned a solitary space in the library for the next two days. On the far wall of their room was a pair of small doors, one leading to a room for handling the necessaries, and another with a pair of beds to catch brief sleep in. Aside from Fritz bringing them food, the two were on complete lockdown. There were to be no distractions: only training.

171

"Now, that's all well and good in a philosophical way, a nice view to have on the world, but when I say magic is everywhere, I'm not talking about it in an abstract sense. Magic literally flows through everything in our world. You, me, the books, the table, even something as ineffable as the sunshine. All of it is connected to the stream of magic circulating about, pumping through our world like blood through a heart."

Grumph nodded, but said nothing. This concept was far from unheard of; the basics of everyone being connected by magic were essentially common knowledge. Of course, that was like saying the fact that sunlight made one warm was also common knowledge: being aware of it and understanding how it worked are two very different levels of awareness.

"Sometimes, we can create pools in the stream, if we stick with the analogy." Dejy reached back to the glowing rectangle and began to draw with his finger, creating bright blue shapes seemingly out of nowhere. He made a stick-figure person, then a sloppily drawn sword. Around them, he drew little arrows that went into and out of his creations, easily discernible as the stream he was talking about.

"Everyone has a little magic built up inside them. However, mages—be they wizards, sorcerers, warlocks, shamans, or any other obscure classification of spell caster—have the ability to create pools of this energy—called mana when it's out of the stream—in themselves. As magic flows through us, we skim a little off the top and keep it for ourselves, not unlike an unscrupulous tax collector. However, we are merely borrowing the mana, as we give it back in the casting of spells. The more training you have, the more mana you can hold in your pool and the more magic you can wield before waiting for the stream to refill you. With me so far?"

Though writing furiously on one of his pieces of parchment, Grumph managed a quick bob of the head so that Dejy knew he was keeping up. Nothing was terribly hard to grasp in Dejy's analogy, yet still Grumph took careful notes. He'd done enough work at building and brewing to know that the fundamentals of every craft were the things that came up again and again.

"Good. Now, enchanted items are ones where a mage has constructed an artificial way to restrain or direct the magic as it flows through a tool, not unlike a dam. A simple enchantment might be the ability to have a sword be sharper when swung. In that case, the mage merely creates a spell that is being fueled by the magic already weaving through the sword. If one were to make something more powerful, they could create a pool in the sword, filling it with their own magic, so that the sword could be lit on fire. Anyone could use the blade, though a mage would be needed to refill it after the power was used. The most powerful kind of enchantment would be not only to give the sword a pool of its own and the ability to light on fire, but also to connect it to the stream in a way that allowed for it to refill automatically, just as a mage would. It takes a very gifted mage to create those sorts of items."

"Am I to enchant something?" Grumph was enjoying the lesson, though he'd slowed his writing as he began to wonder how learning to make magical items was relevant to a wizard of his level.

"Not for a long while," Dejy assured him. "But I wanted you to have a firm understanding of how magic and your own ability to store mana work. As it stands, your two biggest weaknesses are the limited number of spells you can cast and how little mana you're able to store. While I plan to train you on the former in classes and practice, deepening one's mana pool is more difficult. It's akin to trying to build up strength: a matter done best with time and effort."

"So I work around it," Grumph said. He'd expected this much; despite all the effort he'd put in on their weeks of travel, his spell-casting power was growing slowly. Dejy's analogy was spot on. It was like gaining muscle; slow, deliberate work was the only way to succeed.

"Well, I guess you could do that," Dejy agreed. "Or we could try and forcefully deepen your pool, which was what I had in mind."

Grumph said nothing. He merely waited patiently for the man in dark robes to explain. Dejy dug about in his pockets until he produced a white stone with runes etched across it. Power seemed to radiate off the object, and Grumph had to fight to keep from staring into its alabaster depths.

"This little beauty is called a Mana Stone. Rare as all get-out, but being a big-wig in the guild has its perks. They're fashioned for use in war time, meant as a tool to consolidate power. Mages can funnel mana into the stone, like they're refilling an enchanted item. Then, any mage who knows the command can draw the power into themselves. A dozen weak spell casters can trade their power to an archmage, who will wield its combined might to tremendous effect. Luckily, as no one has made war with the guild in a few centuries, we now mostly use them for big enchanting projects. Or, in today's case, training."

"You want to drain my magic." Grumph eyed the stone suspiciously, beginning to notice slight curves and imperfections on its surface. The longer he looked, the more it appeared less like a rock and more like something far more insidious. Bone was white too, after all.

"Quite the opposite," Dejy replied. "The best way to deepen a mana pool is by draining and refilling it over and over. You're going to burn through your mana learning the spells, and I'm going to fill you up using the stone. In that way, we tackle both of your biggest weaknesses in the same go."

"Seems . . . too easy," Grumph admitted.

"Trust me, it isn't." Dejy slipped the stone back into his pocket, and, as he did, a weight seemed to rise off his shoulders. "The reason we don't use Mana Stones more frequently is because employing them hurts. A lot. Some to the one who gives the mana, but more by far to the one who receives it. They're made that way. Power should never be freely taken from others. If mana is being forcibly moved around, then a toll has to be paid."

174

"Good." Grumph felt his esteem for the guild, or at least whoever crafted the stones, rise. The ability to take and wield another's power, magical or otherwise, was not thing that should be done lightly. It was reassuring to know he was joining with people who understood that. "I can handle pain."

"I rather thought you might be able to," Dejy said. "But that comes later. First, we've got to get you emptied, and to do that, we're going to start working on spells. Keep your quill at the ready, there won't be time for going backward."

Grumph did just that, a flower of excitement blooming in his chest. For the first time since he'd picked up that dead wizard's book, he was moving past the mere guise of being a mage. He was learning, growing, and surpassing the wizards he'd been pretending to be. While he was still worried for Thistle and the others, there was a simple truth in him that could neither be contained nor denied.

Grumph couldn't wait to see where this new path took him.

*   *   *

Eric and Timuscor watched the sunset as they tore into a plate of vegetables and leftover dire turkey. The meat was finally beginning to run out, and come tomorrow, Eric would have to dedicate at least a bit of his time to searching out new foodstuffs. That didn't particularly bother him, as he was running out of places to search for books, anyway. What did nag at the back of his mind was that Thistle still refused to leave that office of his, even for meals. The plates Eric would bring up were occasionally picked at, sometimes even half-eaten, but there was no way Thistle was putting enough down to sustain himself. Not even gnomes ate that little.

Plucking a piece of breast from the nearly picked-clean carcass on the plate before them, Eric took a moment to enjoy the sight of dusk glowing across Briarwillow's empty streets. Amidst the worry and uncertainty and fear, he'd managed not to notice how hauntingly beautiful a place it was, now that all of its citizens had been removed.

175

Sitting in the street, mouth full of turkey and back to the hall, it finally hit Eric that there was a silent majesty to Briarwillow in its abandoned state. He wished Thistle were with them to share in the sight. Actually, he just wished Thistle were with them at all. Without the gnome's guidance, Eric was realizing for the first time how much they depended on their paladin, and he was feeling more lost with each passing hour.

"If everything went well, they should be heading back around now," Timuscor said, breaking the spell of silence cast under the waning sun's light.

"I'd hope they wait until morning," Eric replied. "Though, I suppose, if they've got a squad of mages, perhaps night travel isn't as difficult."

"Part of me was hoping to see them popping out of some magic portal today, assuring us they'd gotten help."

"Nice as it would have been, if they just make it back safely, that will be enough for me." Eric spat out a small piece of bone, which bounced off the stones in the road before coming to rest several feet away. "They'll get us help. Maybe not what we were hoping for, but they'll find some—"

A thunderous slam, followed immediately by crashing steps, halted the words on Eric's tongue and dried up his thoughts. It was coming from the building behind him, the one where Thistle had been holed up for two days straight. There was no mistaking the noise for anything but what it was: quick, furious steps by gnomish legs navigating a human-sized house.

Moments later, the front door burst open and Thistle came all but exploding out of it. He looked around, eyes wild and a small book clutched tightly in his hands, before he finally noticed his friends resting their backs against the house's front wall.

"Timuscor!" Thistle waved the book he was holding, thumb firmly gripping his spot in the pages, and rushed over to the knight who still had an apple halfway to his mouth. "Timuscor, where did you find this book?"

"In . . . in a basement. Of a house. Near the edge of town." Timuscor, a man whom Eric had seen put himself in the most dangerous positions of every expedition without a second thought, was clearly rattled by this small bundle of half-mad energy.

Thistle took in the information like it was a blow to the head, then scurried into the street, gesturing down the twists and turns.

"Which way? North? East? We need to go back there!"

"Thistle." Eric stood from his restful position, dusting off his pants as he rose, and stared his friend in the eye. "Enough. We've held our tongues while you twisted yourself into madness upstairs, but the sun is already setting. There's no time for an expedition out to the edge of town, not if we want to make it back safely."

"But I need to see what else is in there," Thistle protested.

"Why? What makes that place so much more special than any of the others? You need to tell us what you found in that book if you expect us to keep helping you with this. Was it a way to open the doors?"

"The doors? Ah, right . . . the doors." Thistle shook his head, clearing away some of the cobwebs and calming himself down. When he looked at Eric again, there was still a lunatic sheen in his eyes, but some semblance of awareness had also returned. After the past pair of days watching Thistle grow worse, Eric took it as a marked improvement.

"No, I've found nothing about the doors, or the caverns, or the mountain's purpose," Thistle admitted. "But I may have gotten a lead on something, at long last."

"If it's not one of those three, what's there left to learn about?" Timuscor asked.

"The starting point for all of this madness, the first piece of the puzzle we ever encountered." Thistle raised the book until it was level with his head, and then tapped its corner to his face, just above the ear.

"I may have found a lead on the skull. Or, to be more precise, the skull's original owner."

Chapter 21

Gabrielle was grappling with something she hadn't had to face for a very long time. Not since Maplebark had she faced this adversary, before the adventurers died in Grumph's tavern and thrust her into a perilous new world. This was not an enemy she could easily battle; it would not be merely beaten into submission, not even if she still had her axe.

For the first time in months, Gabrielle was fighting boredom. With Grumph in training, Fritz handling business, and her status as a non-mage confining her to Fritz's quarters, there was little for her to do. Worse, there was almost nothing for her to be afraid of. Fear and caution had defined her life since they left Maplebark: watching the roads for signs of monsters, sleeping uneasily lest they be ambushed before they could wake, living in constant readiness for action. It all took a toll on her, consuming a vast amount of mental energy. Now that she was safe, that energy came bounding back, and the only place she had to direct it toward was, unfortunately, aimless worry.

She worried about Grumph passing his trials. She worried about Thistle, Eric, and Timuscor stuck in the strange, cursed town of Briarwillow. She worried about her family, her mother and father in Maplebark as much as her tribe in the forest. They'd worked so hard to be sure the king of Solium had no reason to raze their precious town, but with no way to check in, her imagination filled Gabrielle's mind with images of slaughter. Yet, it wasn't even for the family she couldn't see that Gabrielle worried the most. That honor was reserved for herself.

Gabrielle worried—feared really—that she was nearing the edge of how well she could continue to fulfill her role. The others were getting stronger: Eric more confident in his stealth, Thistle gaining new paladin powers, Grumph getting an education under proper mages, and Timuscor was already a handy fighter. All it felt like she had were anger issues and a broken axe. She hadn't even been able to best a lowly bandit in matched battle. Since the day Grumph took the spell book and she the axe, Gabrielle had feared that she wasn't strong enough to fill the role of barbarian. At the rate her party was growing, it seemed that fear would be realized sooner rather than later.

These were the sorts of thoughts muddling around in her head when the door opened and Fritz came bustling through, arms piled high with scrolls and parchment.

"Afternoon!" Fritz said, dumping the lot of her load unceremoniously on the floor.

"Afternoon," Gabrielle replied, staring uncertainly at the clutter of paper now littering the floor. "Do you need a hand with that?"

"This? Gods no; if I never see another order slip or receipt it will be too soon. There are a lot of things I love about being a kingdom-trotting trader, but the paperwork is far from one of them. I pay a few of the lower-ranked mages to swing through here and keep things organized." Fritz walked over the papers, stepping on more than a few, and sank into one of her many living-room chairs. "So, how was your first day by your lonesome?"

"To be honest? Strange. I really didn't know what to do with myself, having no one to fight and no danger to watch for. I mostly explored your estate," Gabrielle admitted. She hadn't even taken the time to don her armor that morning, instead wearing simple traveling clothes built for comfort. It was nice to move so freely again, but at the same time, she felt . . . wrong. Too light, too vulnerable. She missed the weight of her armor and the power it carried.

"You mean my quarters," Fritz corrected.

"Ten bedrooms, two kitchens, three living rooms like this, and a massive outdoor garden. I may not know magic or trading, but I know an estate when I see one. Makes me wonder how one trader could possibly be worth this much to a guild of magic users."

"I always say it's the three Cs: Consistency, Customer Service, and Cunning. That last bit comes in handy for making people see the

180

need for enchanted items, even if they have more mundane solutions. Speaking of, didn't you and I have a shopping trip on the books?"

Gabrielle could see it was a deflection—she'd spent enough time around Thistle to know conversational misdirection when she saw it— but she decided not to push the issue. After all, Fritz had helped them every step of the way; without the elf, they likely never would have made it to Cadence Hollow, let alone gotten into the guild to ask for aid. If Fritz wanted to have some harmless secrets, it was no place of Gabrielle's to try and pull them out of her. So long as they remained harmless, of course.

"That we did. Do you know of any good smiths in town? I'd like to get an axe that's a bit sturdier this time around."

"Good smiths? Gabrielle, this is Cadence Hollow, a town built on merchants and money. Short of a kingdom capital, here is where you can find the most amazing, well-crafted weaponry in the land, coupled with whatever enchantment you might happen to desire."

"Well, that sounds wonderful," Gabrielle said.

"It is. Unfortunately, given how you reacted when I told you the price of some of my wares, I doubt you'll be able to pick up those sorts of items," Fritz clarified. "But we can still find you something nice. Plus, if I do say so myself, I am one demon of a haggler when the occasion demands. Mark my words, you shall have an axe by this day's end."

"If that's the plan, then we should probably get going." Gabrielle rose from her own chair, mildly surprised at the ease of the action until she remembered her demon-scale garb was tucked away in one of Fritz's bedrooms. "Let me go put on my armor."

"Heavens no, that's the last thing I want you to do." Fritz hopped up out of the chair and grabbed Gabrielle lightly by the shoulder. "Once they know you can actually *use* the weapon, they've got the power in a sale. We're shopping for this like it's nothing more than a trinket, a bauble to set over the fireplace. First rule of negotiation: never give away any more information than you have to."

"I'm fairly certain that's also one of the main rules in battle," Gabrielle said.

"That's only fitting. After all, negotiation is a battle of its own. Only we fight with money instead of weapons. Come, my little barbarian; come and see my battlefield."

*   *   *

Thistle laid the map out across the desk, sending the sides spilling over the edge until they hung down like flat, wagging tongues. He paid these no mind, as his eyes were on the center continent—one with which everyone in the room was intimately familiar. His small hand traced a line across it, beginning at the Endless Ocean and going north until a finger rested directly on the kingdom's name, surrounded by hand-drawn etchings of mountains.

"Baltmur," Thistle said, tapping it gently. "A small kingdom surrounded by mountains and cliffs, built into rock. Between it and the nearest kingdom, Alcatham, is the massive Hooran desert. And the city on the edge of that border is us, right here in Briarwillow."

"Everyone knows about the Hooran desert," Eric said. "It's said to be one of the deadliest places in all the seven kingdoms."

"Aye, so it is, but have you ever stopped to think about why it's there?"

"Do deserts need a reason to exist?" Timuscor asked.

"A few days ago, I'd have said no. But after my literary binge, I'm afraid I find myself less certain on the subject." Thistle reached over and tapped the book that lay just in front of Eric and Timuscor, which he'd read through at least four times. "In this diary, one of the citizens details a story passed down through their family from generation to generation. The story goes that countless years ago, long before the seven kingdoms as we know them were formed, a man with dark, terrible powers arose, intent on conquering all the other lands. He was met by the combined might of the existing kings and their armies in the stretch of land between what we now know as Alcatham and Baltmur. Through the will of the gods and the righteousness of the men, they triumphed over this man at the cost of many lives. The land they fought on, however, was so stained with blood and dark magic that the very grass wilted. Death took root there, and was the only thing that would ever grow again."

"And you . . . what? Think the man in the story is the skull they found?" Eric asked. "Thistle, I know we're at the point of grasping for straws, but that's still a long leap to take."

"It would be, except that I saw the battle this story describes." Thistle stared down at the Hooran desert, wondering for the first time what secrets might be buried beneath its dark, shifting depths. "One of the dreams Grumble sent me was of the final encounter. The man I saw was beyond powerful; he laid waste to many of the soldiers that tried to bring him down. It was only through numbers that they succeeded in stopping him." Even as he said it, Thistle felt a pang of doubt. Had it been sheer numbers? They hadn't just overwhelmed him; it had been the lone soldier with a lucky blow who ultimately brought him down. The lone, remorseful-looking soldier.

"Okay, so they kill this powerful guy, one so strong that they needed whole armies to take him down," Eric said, "then, fearing someone will try to bring him back or use his remains for magic, they create a tomb inside a mountain and hide all evidence of it. I think I see where you're going now."

"You're on the right track, but there is a critical piece of the story you've overlooked," Thistle told him. "For one, it seems highly unlikely that the skull was found behind those doors; otherwise, we'd have seen more bones and relics in the miners' belongings. But beyond that, there's a greater issue at hand, one that raises far more questions than it answers."

"The skull had runes carved into it." Timuscor's voice was soft yet heavy as he struck upon the realization Thistle had been leading them up to. "That's what the townsfolk said when they described it. And no matter how powerful he was, he couldn't have mutilated his own bones while they were inside him."

"Precisely," Thistle agreed. "I do not believe his remains were sealed for fear of someone turning them into magical components. I think that work was already done, likely on the day he fell. I'd wager that inside that tomb is an array of cursed, magical items, all made from this mystery man's bones."

"A treasure-trove of death," Eric muttered, "that the god of darkness sent a priest to retrieve."

"So it seems," Thistle confirmed. "Which means, I'm afraid, that we must go back to the mountain and check on the status of the doors. If they are near to breaking, then we may not have the luxury of waiting for the others to arrive."

*   *   *

A softly whispered chant fell from his lips, and the pain that was stabbing at his skull like a dagger between the eyes faded. There was no mystical or mysterious cause for this annoyance; he knew all too well what was giving him the massive headaches. It was the banging. The endless, tireless, ceaseless banging as those undead husks of humans slapped at the doors with their giant pillar. Five days they'd been at it, and the priest who wore no name was beginning to wonder if this wasn't secretly a test from Kalzidar to judge just how dedicated he was to the cause.

True, they were making progress. What had once been a sturdy, impassible set of doors had chipped and cracked, their bulk slowly wearing away beneath the relentless assault. The things were enchanted halfway to the heavens, but at the end of the day, everything would break if given enough time. Especially when a priest of Kalzidar was on hand, weakening the enchantments that protected those damned doors.

He leaned against the cool, dark rocks as he watched the undead work, a piece of parchment in his hands that he began to fold. Folding was his art, his hobby, his way to pass the intolerable hours of boredom that came from sitting in the darkness watching the undead work. Sometimes, he would sleep or reach into his bag and gobble down some simple trail rations or wander down to a deeper portion of the cave to use the necessary (though this practice had caused him to miss some quite interesting visitors when they stumbled across the site), but at no time did he ever leave the skull sitting in his lap. It still ebbed with darkness, even after all these days, exerting its power on the toiling corpses that were cursed to obey its whispered commands. That skull was their unmaking in every sense of the word; it had taken away their lives, dragged their remains from the peace of slumber, and commanded their movements completely. The villagers of Briarwillow had no more will left in them. So long as he held the skull, only the priest's will existed, and his was the will of Kalzidar.

Two more creases and his paper creation began to take on a shape, that of a long-legged spider. Idly, he wondered what sorts of treasures would lie beyond the barrier. A skull that could weave blankets of disease only to raise and control its victims as undead was already quite powerful. But the human body held many more bones than just a skull. With such power distributed to the followers of Kalzidar, the god of darkness would no longer be worshipped only in the shadows. His brothers and sisters in faith could sweep the land, driving the followers of the supposed "just" gods from the light. And as one who heralded the beginning of this new age, no doubt the priest himself would receive his choice pick of the magical tools, along with a prestigious position of power in the new hierarchy.

All in good time, of course. First came the actual acquiring of the bones—those lovely bones Kalzidar showed him in his dreams—and for that to pass, he would have to endure the constant banging for some while to come. Though, perhaps not too much longer. As he watched, another piece of the door's ornate white stone fell away. Soon, the crack would reach the other side, and then it would only be a matter of making it wide enough for him to pass through.

185

The nameless priest watched the work and grinned. He finished his paper spider, tossed it into the bag next to him where hundreds of other folded animals already lay, and took out a fresh sheet of parchment. He wouldn't have to make many more of these. The time was almost at hand.

Only a day or so more, at most, and Kalzidar would have his prize.

Chapter 22

"This time, we'll get lucky. I can feel it."

Gabrielle did not share Fritz's optimism or energy as they pushed open the door to yet another weapons shop. Had she been in possession of an axe, she might have used it to intimidate the elven trader into giving up their search and returning to her quarters for relaxation and a nice meal. But sadly, Gabrielle did not have an axe with which to make threatening gestures, which was why she only stifled a sigh and scanned the room, working to find a few remaining shreds of hope still in her.

After half a day of shopping, the issue was not that they hadn't found an axe. They'd seen dozens, if not hundreds, of axes already. No, the problem was that this was Cadence Hollow, which was where the best goods and wares were bandied about. Gabrielle had seen axes that could summon beasts under her command, blades sharp enough to cut solid stone, weapons that might control the very elements if needed. What she hadn't seen was one even remotely in her price range. Asking the owners for regular, non-magical weaponry had elucidated blank stares, followed by scrutinizing glances asking just how much she was looking to spend. Once that number came out, they quickly lost interest in her, turning their attention to other customers or ledgers of bookkeeping that had suddenly become very important.

To Gabrielle's thinking, she was ready to part with quite a substantial amount of gold, more than several years' wages for the people back in Maplebark. But this was not Maplebark, and the concept of money in Cadence Hollow drove home just how different the scales with which they measured wealth were in this world.

The shop they'd wandered into this time was a bit smaller than many of the others, with fewer weapons strewn about and tacked on the walls for display. Gabrielle had been a bit taken aback with how willing everyone seemed to display—and let her handle—items of such immense value, until Fritz explained that the mages' guild set up and maintained powerful anti-theft enchantments in return for a cut of the profits. That familiarity had given them a bit of an in with the owners so far, but it was nowhere near enough to get the prices down to where Gabrielle needed them. Still, she felt a faint flicker of hope in her heart as they scanned this new shop. It seemed poorer, not as well maintained as the others. Perhaps this owner would find her gold worth taking.

"Gustav! How's my favorite weapons dealer?" Fritz called. A squat, muscular man standing at the counter glanced up from the short sword he was polishing and suddenly went pale. His eyes darted about, clearly searching for an exit, only to realize that Fritz was between him and the door. Carefully, he turned toward the back door, which no doubt would lead to a storage room in the rear. It didn't seem likely that he'd have an exit there, but from the way he was nervously clutching the blade, Gabrielle suspected he might just try and hack a way out through the walls.

"F-F-Fritz," Gustav stammered, a thick accent that Gabrielle didn't recognize coating his words. "No one t-told me you were back in town."

"That's because I pay better than you, so when someone tells them to give a heads up when I return, they come to me to see if I can make a better offer. And I did." Fritz smiled, her grin like that of a cat watching a mouse with its tail pinned beneath a barrel. "But today, I'm not here to talk about those 'magic' arrows you sold me. I'm here helping my friend Gabrielle shop for a new axe. So why don't you be a good little shopkeep and show us what you've got? Heaven knows you need the business; there are some debts you'll need to repay very, *very* soon."

Gustav swallowed, then looked down at the sword in his hands as if he were considering jamming it into his own belly to save someone else the trouble. Either he had too much hope or lacked the courage, because he laid the sword down carefully on the counter and turned to Gabrielle.

"R-right, an axe. Gal your size, something light that you can swing with one hand, no doubt."

"Wrong." Gabrielle was tempted to put some fire in her voice as she corrected him, but in truth, she was afraid that the already sweating man might keel over if she added to the pressure Fritz was exerting. "I need a two-handed one. A battle axe. And I'd like if this one could be sturdy."

"Are you su . . ." Gustav's voice trailed off as he caught sight of the look in Gabrielle's eyes. Evidently, that was enough to prove her certainty, as he quickly pulled a book from below the counter and flipped through its pages.

"Battle axe, two-handed," he repeated, pages fanning the sweat on his forehead as he searched for the right entry. "Here we are." A stubby finger ran down the length of the page, stopping as he read the section slowly, visibly mouthing the words. "Right now, I only have three axes that fit your needs. One is heavily enchanted for sharpness and durability. Another can pass through solid objects like armor, but still cut flesh. And the last . . ." Gustav leaned down, reading his entry more carefully. "Oh no, that one's no good."

"What's wrong with it?" Gabrielle asked.

"Um, nothing, per se," Gustav said slowly. "It was sold to me by a trader who found it deep in an ancient temple. Definitely magical, and strong at that, but it seems to have . . . compatibility issues."

"For the love of the gods." Fritz shook her head, and Gustav seemed to shrink back into himself, cowering slightly. "'Compatibility issues' means cursed in trader-speak. And cursed items are *supposed* to be turned over to the guild so they can either destroy or de-curse them."

"But they don't pay for them!" Gustav protested. "And I can't just get rid of it without recouping some investment."

"Which is why you spend the money on keeping curse-detecting tools on hand," Fritz snapped, sending Gustav shrinking away. "Be glad

189

you came in with me, Gabrielle. Otherwise, he'd have tried to unload that thing on you."

Gabrielle contemplated the curious exchange of the man who looked like he could singlehandedly lift a cart being verbally tossed about by the slender elven woman and decided it was probably time to intervene. "How cursed is it?"

"W-w-what?" Gustav's stammer had returned with Fritz's newest tirade, but a slight glimmer of hope seemed to spark in his eyes at the question.

"The axe. How cursed is it? Like, will it turn me into a bugbear or just give me sore feet?"

"Gabrielle, I see where you're going, and this is a bad idea," Fritz cautioned.

"Really? Because I still need a weapon, and aside from the cursed one, both of those other weapons sound really expensive." She turned to Gustav. "Were either of them less than ten thousand gold?"

"My goodness no." Gustav shook his head, looking downright incredulous at the suggestion. "Far more than that paltry sum."

"There you go; another shop where I can barely afford to walk in the door. So, let me ask for the third time: just how cursed is this axe you've got? The one you now have great reason to sell for a deep, deep discount."

Gustav swallowed, glanced at Fritz, and then spoke. "The few people I've talked to who used it report that it's sometimes painful to hold, like it's slowly burning their hands, and that when they wield it, the pain grows worse. Gloves don't seem to help, either. Worse than all that, though, they say it feels like it clouds their judgment. Riles them up, tries to whip them into a frenzy of bloodlust."

Gabrielle weighed those words carefully, imagining what it would be like to have even more fury in her head. It could be an asset to

190

her as a barbarian, there was no question about that, but it might make her lose the delicate control she was able to maintain. It was a risk, certainly, though one that was perhaps worth taking.

"I'd like to see it for myself."

This time, Gustav didn't budge, he merely stared at Fritz, who was in turn looking hard at Gabrielle. At last, the elven woman gave Gustav a small nod, and he nearly disappeared as he hurried into the back room.

"You don't have to do this, you know. There are other shops, and at least one of them will have a mundane axe."

"Maybe I don't want a mundane axe anymore," Gabrielle replied. "You heard what he said: the axe is cursed, *and* it's strong. If the second part outweighs the first, then it might be worth it."

"Magic, especially curse magic, is very dangerous," Fritz cautioned.

"Good." Gabrielle allowed a slight smirk to tug at the edges of her mouth. "I like things that are dangerous. Especially when I'm not supposed to."

Before another word could be said, Gustav lumbered back in. In his hands was a long wooden box, one that would have been quite unwieldy in a weaker man's grip. Gingerly, almost reverently, he set it down on top of the table and pulled off the lid. Fritz and Gabrielle both stepped forward without intending to, peering into the box's depths and getting their first look at the cursed weapon.

It was large, slightly bigger than Gabrielle's first axe, yet the crafting was impeccable. Even with only a glance, Gabrielle could tell it was perfectly balanced. The head was pitch black and double-sided, each blade somehow seeming sharper than its twin. Runes were etched into the head and haft, seeming to glow a touch red when the light hit them just so. Gustav might be, and certainly seemed to be, a liar about many things, but it was clear he hadn't embellished about this weapon. It was powerful. Gabrielle could practically feel its magic humming across her skin as she drew nearer to it.

Reaching out slowly, half-expecting Fritz to try and stop her, Gabrielle wrapped her hand around the dark wooden center. The instant her fingers made contact, she could feel the pain Gustav had warned her about. It was constant, but not overwhelming. She'd gotten worse aches after hard sparring sessions with Eric and Timuscor. Then again, he'd also said it got much worse when used in actual battle. Pushing the pain aside, she tightened her grip and pulled the axe free from the box, holding it carefully and giving a few gentle swings.

Despite the curse, it felt *good*: strong, light, as if it had been crafted especially for her. The longer it was in her hands, the more certain she was that this was a weapon she could wield. It would help make her stronger, hopefully strong enough to close the gap between herself and the others. If she could aid them, keep them safe, be of value to them, then it was worth the risk.

A shadow seemed to dash across her mind, like a strange sound in a field at midnight. She'd nearly let herself forget about the mental component of the curse. Now that she was searching, Gabrielle could feel the foreign presence dancing about at the edge of her consciousness. Its full heft, it seemed, would have to be fully discovered on a battlefield, as she had no intention of slicing up Fritz or Gustav just to test it. Though perhaps Fritz might not mind if Gabrielle took a few chunks out of the nervous man's flesh.

Gabrielle blinked in surprise. Where had *that* come from? It was a short-lived question, as the obvious answer was still clutched firmly in her hands. More dangerous than she'd expected, it seemed. Only a thought, though. Gabrielle could handle errant thoughts. It was actions that truly mattered. She spun the axe one more time, and then turned to face Gustav.

"I'll take it. But throw in a good sheath. I don't want to hold this more than I have to."

"Really?" Gustav seemed taken aback, but he quickly recovered. "I mean, of course; how could you resist such a fine, rare treasure? Now, let us simply arrive at a fair price for such a magical, one-of-a-kind item as what you are holding there."

"No, Gustav, let *us* arrive at a fair price for the item you'd rightfully have to turn over to the guild free of charge," Fritz interjected. She looked at Gabrielle and gave a wry grin. "I'll handle things from here. You might want to wait outside, though. It's going to be bloody."

*   *   *

As soon as Gabrielle was out the door, axe resting once more on the counter, all the tension drained from Gustav's face. He calmly took out a pair of dark leather gloves and lifted the weapon from his display, dropping it back into the box.

"The stammering was a bit much," Fritz said, watching her friend work.

"Do not make demands of an actor and then critique his performance. Besides, she seemed to buy it just fine."

"Only because she's gotten used to seeing people afraid of her, so it didn't faze her to see it in others. You happened to hit her blind spot, that's all." Fritz reached into the bag at her side and produced a swollen pouch, the tip of a gold coin poking slightly out the top. "You did your job, though, and I appreciate that."

"Seems like a lot of work to unload an axe on some adventurer," Gustav noted, though he accepted the coins without protest. "Bribing all the other traders to hide the cheap stuff, getting her desperate enough to accept a cursed axe, why not just hand it to her straight out?"

"Would you use a cursed weapon if you knew there were other options out there?" Fritz countered. "It needed to be her only real option if she was going to accept it, and that axe can only be taken willingly."

Gustav carefully placed the lid back over the box, and then pulled off his gloves. "What's the deal with this girl, anyway? You got a grudge against her?"

"Quite the opposite. I'm growing more fond of Gabrielle by the day," Fritz said. "That's why I don't want to see her meet an early end at the tip of some bandit's blade or beast's jaws."

"Rather see some cursed weapon do her in?"

Fritz chuckled, resting her hand lightly on the box that contained Gabrielle's new killing tool. "Not at all. This axe might bear a cost for wielding it, but it will also do far more to keep her safe than some silly enchantment of sharpness. If she can master this weapon, that woman will truly become a force to be reckoned with."

"And if she doesn't?"

"Well, then I suppose she wasn't as interesting as I thought," Fritz replied. "Now, go get her sheath. This transaction is officially complete."

Chapter 23

The morning sun was just beginning to approach the middle of the sky (marking the sixth day since their friends had ridden out of Briarwillow and into a danger they could only imagine), when Eric, Timuscor, and Thistle reached the opening in the mountain. They'd left after breakfast, making their way straight toward their destination without stopping, save for only a brief respite so that Thistle could make their tools glow once more before crossing into the darkness. It was a tense, worried ride, as each of them wrestled with the fear that they would come across an opened door and an army of undead wielding incredible dark magic. Few words were said as they took the plunge into the lightless void of the tunnel, and silence became their only tongue as the last vestiges of daylight slipped from their view.

Even moving slowly, making as little noise as possible given that two members of the party were covered in clanging metal armor, they still reached the junction point in only a few minutes. Once they knew where they were going, it was easy to navigate the general area. Though primed to be attacked once they drew closer to the actual site, they were struck with shock when Timuscor entered the cavern and cast the light from his shield on a pale, clearly undead figure who let out yelp of surprise and then put its own hands over its mouth.

"They've spread." Timuscor drew his sword without another word, stepping aside so that Thistle could have a clear shot at the monster before them. The small paladin had a dagger pulled back, ready to let fly at the thing's chest, when he realized something was wrong. Their undead foe wasn't attacking them, or screeching at the others for help, or even trying to run. It was just standing there, looking as scared as they felt, unsure of what to do. And the longer Thistle watched it, the more he began to think it looked a touch familiar.

"Kendal?" At Thistle's words, the undead man's eyebrows rose in surprise, and he slowly lowered the hands that were in front of his mouth.

"You're that gnome who came around bothering us with all the questions." His voice was roughly, almost gravelly, but the surly tone was exactly how Thistle remembered it from nearly a week prior, when he'd chatted with Kendal and Gurt to learn what was happening in town.

"Aye, that I am. And you were the only one in the village not ready to dance a jig about suddenly seeming to be cured," Thistle replied. He reached over and carefully tugged on Timuscor's arm, lowering the sword so it wasn't quite as threatening. "Suppose you were right in that regard."

"Never been much for doing things just 'cause they seemed like what I ought to," Kendal admitted. "Guess that's why I'm the only one of them trying to fight this."

"Only one to fight . . . ? Wait, Kendal, are you saying the others still have their minds?" Thistle's heart hammered in his chest as he absorbed the information. Dispatching mindless undead was one thing—it was more mercy than murder—but to kill those who were under another's control was a dark act, even if it was in self-defense.

"Some of them, I think," Kendal replied. "Hard to tell. Hard to think with this voice whispering in my head all the time, telling me to go work with them, telling me to pound on that damned door." He pressed his fingers against the side of his head, accidently scraping away a fat piece of skin and exposing his skull. "Obeyed it for a long while, but finally got strong enough to duck out when that ass went to the bathroom."

"That ass?" Eric asked. "The voice in your head?"

"Don't be stupid, boy," Kendal snapped. "The voice is from the skull. I can never get away from it. I was talking about the man who's been watching us, using the skull to control us all. Same lyin' bastard that claimed he was curing us."

"The false priest," Thistle whispered. His mind whirled, adding this new information to what they knew. If a servant of Kalzidar,

196

especially a nameless one, was down there, then he was dangerous. With enough power to control an entire platoon of undead minions, that danger increased exponentially. If those undead still had minds and were innocent victims . . . well, that was a situation that might truly be unwinnable.

"Kendal, we've come to try and help," Thistle said, speaking slowly, as if he were just realizing this himself. "But if we're going to set you all free, I have to know as much as possible about the priest: what he does, and what he's after."

"What are you going to do?" Kendal didn't bother masking the doubt on his face, just as he wouldn't have if he'd still been alive.

"I don't know yet," Thistle admitted. "But we're edging closer to a solution, and we've got friends who should be rejoining us soon with help."

Kendal sneered. "If you haven't noticed, we're sort of beyond helping at this point."

"Maybe so," Thistle agreed. "I won't promise that there's even a way for us to aid you, given the situation. But we can at least try to make sure it doesn't happen to anyone else and take some vengeance for you on the man who did this. Vengeance is a paltry substitute for salvation, but at least that much we can accomplish."

"Vengeance, huh? Should have said so first. Spite's one thing I've never had trouble getting behind." Kendal took a few steps closer and began to tell them everything he'd seen since they first left Briarwillow.

*   *   *

Many of the people in robes stared at the red-armored woman as she made her way through the coliseum, too awestruck by her surroundings to take note of their curious gazes. She only moved forward when the elven woman behind her jabbed her lightly in the back to get her plodding along once more. At least a few hundred of the guild's mages were in attendance, though, by Gabrielle's estimates, the massive stadium they were in could easily seat thousands. Yet coming had required nothing more than Fritz waving that key of hers at another door. The longer she spent around the mages and their guild, the more disconnect Gabrielle felt from the harsh reality of life on the road. She was glad it was ending soon; already, she sensed her body trying to grow soft and complacent from the constant comfort.

Though the coliseum itself seemed mundane—if a touch ornate with all the decorative gold and velvet cushions—what lay in its center was another story. Where ordinarily Gabrielle would see horses and knights preparing for jousts, or perhaps a few warriors readying to spar, she instead could perceive only fog. It was like a massive cloud had descended from the sky, formed a perfect orb, and settled itself into the coliseum's ground like an opaque marble in a socket. Of course, the four mages standing equidistant from one another along the fog's edge, visibly muttering and making frequent hand motions, explained away the curiosity while also doing little to help Gabrielle understand it.

"It's to keep the test a mystery," Fritz said, nudging Gabrielle forward yet again while nodding to the fog. "Otherwise, some of the older mages might see the setup and instantly know which of the trials the applicant was going to face."

"Why do they need to keep it a mystery from us? Only Grumph should worry about being surprised. The other apprentices will get different trials, and all the full mages have already passed theirs. Do they think you'll try to help him somehow?"

Fritz snickered under her breath. "Oh, it's not about integrity on our part. At least, not that kind of integrity. It's just that we *love* betting on these things, and knowing what the test will be ahead of time tends to swing odds in the old-timers' favor. This way, people can only bet on what they know about the mage. Keeps things a bit more even."

"I should have expected that." Gabrielle finally began moving again, heading toward a section in the middle that Fritz seemed hell-bent on reaching. "Any word on how the bets are going today?"

"It's an interesting split," Fritz replied. "Most of the gold is going down that Grumph will fail, which is hardly something he should take personally since he is trying to undertake this after only a few days of training. But of those that are betting on him to succeed, a lot of them are the older, wiser mages in our guild. Sort of makes you wonder what the smartest bet really is."

"Wish I'd known; I still have a few gold left. I'd have put them on Grumph to succeed." Fritz had gotten Gabrielle a better deal than she'd ever expected, allowing her to leave the shop with her new axe strapped to her back and a healthy amount of gold still in her purse. Fritz certainly lived up to her bragging, though Gabrielle was beginning to grow uncomfortable with how much she and Grumph owed the elven trader.

"Much as he'd have appreciated it, I think you've already got enough riding on this," Fritz told her. "Besides, I dropped a thousand gold on him to pull it off."

"A *thousand*?" Gabrielle nearly leapt out of her armor and whirled to meet Fritz's surprisingly calm, placid face staring back at her.

"Didn't I tell you? The smartest mages are betting on Grumph to win. Why wouldn't that include me?"

"But . . . a thousand gold."

"Is mine to do with as I see fit," Fritz assured her. "I like a good gamble, and after seeing you two fight those bandits, I know better than most how capable our half-orc friend is. Now, hurry up and quit gawking, otherwise we're going to miss the start of this thing."

Gabrielle complied, finally hustling at a pace to Fritz's liking. They eventually reached a section of seating in the middle, filled with gold cushions rather than crimson ones. This was the most sparsely populated area in a coliseum that was already woefully under-filled, with only a few other robed men and women scattered about. Some of them started to rise when they saw Gabrielle entering the area, but a single glance at Fritz and they lowered themselves back into their seats.

There was, however, one man who did not slump back down. Instead, he hurried down the steps, taking them two at a time to arrive quickly at Fritz's side. Rather than chastising her as Gabrielle feared he might, the man leaned down and spoke to Fritz in an almost conspiratorial whisper.

"It's about time. I thought you would be late."

"I always arrive at exactly the right moment, you know that." Fritz didn't bother whispering back; instead, she took the man's arm and turned him so he was facing Gabrielle. "Now, Dejy, don't be so excited you forget your manners. Be a dear and introduce yourself to my friend, Gabrielle."

"Ah, so you're the fearsome barbarian with the heart of a dragon," Dejy said, a surprisingly handsome smile lighting up his face. He bowed slightly, then rose and met Gabrielle's uncertain gaze with a cheerful wink. "I'm the one who has been training Grumph for the past few days. He's told me all about you and your friends back in Briarwillow."

"How many days did it take to get all that out of him?" Gabrielle found it hard to imagine Grumph having long, in-depth discussions with anyone. His stoic tongue was one of the most constant and endearing features about her friend.

"You'd be surprised how much comes out when people are sleep-deprived and suffering from mana drain," Dejy replied. "Ours was not an easy training program, and we were both pushed to the very edges of our limits in undertaking it."

"Is he going to be okay for the trials?" Fritz asked.

"Nothing to worry about; I saved our last few hours for potions and rest," Dejy assured her. "Though I can't guarantee how he'll do, of course, he's at least going in with a clear head and full pool of mana."

"A what of what?" Gabrielle looked at Dejy like he'd begun speaking another language halfway through his sentence.

"If you think of food as energy to use with your muscles, mana is energy to use with your magic," Fritz explained. "Dejy just means he has the magic equivalent of a well-fed stomach."

"Oh. He should just say that, then."

"He should, shouldn't he?" Fritz turned slightly to face the fog, staring at it for a long moment before resuming the conversation. "Anyway, can you tell us how things went? Were you able to teach him any more spells?"

"Grumph gained a good handle on two and has come close to figuring out a third," Dejy told them, a bit of pride at his teaching skills creeping into his voice. "Whether or not he can pull those out in the heat of battle instead of a classroom is something we can only see in the doing."

"Going to tell us what those spells he learned are?" Gabrielle asked.

"Not planning on it." Dejy smirked, a mischievous glint dancing in his eye. "Far be it from me to steal my student's thunder. He should be the one to show you what he's learned."

Gabrielle began to protest, but before she could, a voice bounded through the coliseum, reaching every ear without overpowering a single one. Though the voice was utterly foreign to her, Fritz and Dejy both perked up as though they recognized it—and had in fact been waiting—for it to appear.

"My fellow mages, today we have gathered to bear witness to the testing of one who wishes to join our prestigious ranks. He casts spells through the style of a wizard, and his skill was great enough that he was judged to be capable of undertaking the trials. After only a few days of study, he has exercised this right, and before you all, today he will attempt to prove his worth."

"Talcia sure does love to hear himself talk," Fritz muttered. Gabrielle nodded, despite not having the slightest idea who Talcia was. Assuming it was the man speaking to them currently, she was inclined to agree. She wanted to see Grumph, to know what he was facing, far more than she felt like tolerating this pretentious preamble.

"Should our ambitious wizard be successful, he will become a member of the Guild of Illustrious Mages, with all the rights and privileges pertaining thereto. Should he fail . . . well, wielding magic is a dangerous endeavor, as we all know too well. Without further ado, I present to you Grumph the wizard, undertaking today's trial: Shattering the Tempest Crystal."

Fritz sucked in a breath through her teeth, and Dejy spat out a word that Gabrielle didn't understand but could infer was some sort of swear simply by his tone. The fog began to clear, revealing what looked like a set of half-crumbled runes, a dark stone tower, and shapes slipping about in the shadows. She couldn't yet see Grumph, though that didn't worry Gabrielle half as much as her fellow spectators' reactions.

"This is bad," Fritz said. She and Dejy shared a look that needed no translation. A glance meant to convey "We're in deep shit" pretty much looks the same no matter one's language, gender, or race.

"Tell me what this means," Gabrielle demanded. She almost reached for the axe that Fritz had made her leave behind in their quarters, now knowing why the elf had been so adamant about not bringing a weapon.

"Shattering the Tempest Crystal is regarded as one of the most difficult trials a mage can be given," Dejy explained. "Grumph will have to try and make his way past magical traps and barriers, climb the tower in the center of the field, and destroy the tempest crystal before it can create a magical storm that will destroy everything else. Oh, and there are also worshippers of the crystal trying to stop him at every turn."

Gabrielle stared at both of them for a few brief seconds, and then did something neither expected. She visibly relaxed, turning back toward the field, where the last traces of fog were dying away. There, she could finally make out her friend, standing stalwart in the mid-afternoon sun's blazing light.

"Is that all?" Gabrielle asked, leaning forward in her seat as she realized the show was about to begin. "For a minute, I thought Grumph was actually in trouble."

"I know you have faith in your friend, but he only knows a few spells, and not nearly enough to circumvent all those dangers," Fritz reminded her.

Gabrielle shook her head, refusing to take her eyes off the field. "No, Fritz, you don't get it. I was scared this whole time that he'd be given a test demanding lots of magical knowledge or power, because then, he might have come up lacking. This trial doesn't outright require any of that, though. All it asks is that Grumph survive and complete his goal."

"How do you think he'll do that with such limited magic?" Fritz asked.

"I don't know," Gabrielle admitted. "But don't make the mistake of thinking Grumph is the contents of his spell book. My friend was dangerous long before he ever learned to cast."

Chapter 24

Unlike nearly every other mage in the coliseum, Grumph wasn't wearing robes. Instead, he wore a simple shirt, sturdy pants, and comfortable boots. Dejy had offered to have some proper mage attire crafted for him while they studied, but Grumph had politely declined. Robes were well and good for creating an impression of power and mystery; however, they came up severely lacking in terms of practicality. He might have looked more impressive in robes, but Grumph knew he could actually *be* more impressive with his usual attire. As he'd walked into the fog-covered field, his instructions hurriedly whispered to him by Talcia before the announcements, Grumph was thankful for this decision. Rough as the task before him already seemed, he could hardly imagine having to do it while tripping over a bunch of flowing fabric.

It was obvious they were going hard on him with this trial, not that he'd expected any less. When one declared that they would do in mere days what others spent years preparing for, there was a lot of room for egos to get bruised. Someone, somewhere higher up the echelon, wanted to make an example out of him for daring to insinuate that it would be so easy to join the ranks of the other mages. All he could do was hope that they hadn't gone so far as to rig the whole test to be impossible to pass. As long as Grumph had a legitimate chance, he felt there was hope. A single arrow could slay a dragon, if shot straight through its eye and into the brain. No matter how slim the chances, it could still happen. Grumph clung to that thought as the last vestiges of fog faded and Talcia's voice filled the air once more.

"Wizard Grumph, are you ready to begin?"

With a single motion, Grumph yanked free his demon-bone sword from its sheath, holding it before him with both hands, ready to attack the first thing that came within striking distance.

"My spells are prepared."

Despite this being the proper reply, he could still hear the ripple of uncertainty amidst the mages watching from above. Weapons were allowed in the trials, but most expected them to be the last resort of mages whose mana had run dry. Drawing a blade from the start was unusual, even insulting, to those looking on. Grumph paid them no mind, however. If this caused a ripple, he imagined some would suffer from full-on cases of fainting by the time his trial was done. Talcia, at least, seemed unfazed as he spoke for what would be the last time until a result was rendered.

"Then I hereby officially commence this wizard's trial."

The words had barely faded before Grumph was off, dashing headlong into the ruined buildings without so much as a single spell of caution or protection cast. It wasn't as though he'd learned either of those to begin with, and Grumph had decided from the start that he had exactly one strategy available to him that hadn't existed for the previous test-takers: he was not accustomed to thinking of himself as a mage. Therefore, he reasoned that if he could do things as unwizardly as possible, acting in ways they'd never have anticipated, he might just take the creators of the trial by surprise. It was, obviously, sheer madness and the longest of shots, but it was also the best he had, so Grumph followed through on the plan, barreling past half-eroded buildings as fast as his mighty legs would carry him.

A real wizard would still be back near the start, casting spells that would shield him from damage or help him avoid danger entirely. The enemies—artificially created magical constructs, as Talcia had explained—would no doubt be trying to move into position, expecting such a late start. Grumph hoped he was sprinting past a great many of them, catching them too off guard to react to a half-orc dashing straight up the middle. It was a strategy that would buy him very little gain, if it even worked, but Grumph had built an entire tavern from the ground up. A little here, a little there, and soon the impossible could be made to take shape.

His luck held for almost a full minute as he darted through the ruins, cursorily appreciating the amount of effort his fellow mages had put into creating the scenery. Unfortunately, just as he got clear of a small cluster of burned out homes, he hit a massive blast of wind that caught his foot and nearly sent him hurtling into the air. Only Grumph's weight saved him, as the heft of his body allowed him enough time to fling himself backward, out of the upward tornado's range. He quickly righted himself and paused for a moment to contemplate the obstacle before him.

Wrapping around the next section of the runes, for as far as Grumph could see, was a tremendous upward billowing of air. It was ceaseless now that it had begun, shooting up from the ground with such force that even standing too near it made Grumph feel uneasy. He'd barely put more than a toe into the skyward stream and it had taken all he had to yank himself free. Charging through was impossible: he'd be hurtled out of the coliseum entirely, and when he finally came down, even if he survived, he'd have failed the test. Fire and ice spells were of no use, nor was his bucket of water. With no allies to invigorate, the rejuvenating spell was off the table too. He had his new ones, but those took a lot of mana to execute. Grumph knew there would be more obstacles than just a wall of wind before the day was done. An idea tickled the back of his brain. It was risky, and would burn precious mana if it failed, but if he pulled it off, he could get past here with only a single spell.

The sound of stirring from behind—regrouping enemies, no doubt—made Grumph's decision for him. Hesitation was not a luxury available to him; only action would see him to victory. With a single wave of his free hand and a few whispered words, Grumph summoned the golden weapon of energy he'd called forth several times before. It appeared as a sword, but Grumph immediately willed it to turn into a spear. The light shimmered and then obeyed, stretching out and taking its new shape. Holding his breath and dropping a prayer to the gods for luck, Grumph stabbed the energy weapon into the fiercely blasting wind, waiting to see if it would be ripped from his hands.

Instead, there was nothing—not so much as a tug on the massless weapon. The breath inside Grumph came whooshing out in an explosion of relief. He'd noted long ago that this weapon had no weight despite its power to injure when wielded, but he hadn't known if that would be enough to spare it from the wind-wall's thunderous blasts. More scuffling from the rear reminded Grumph that while his gambit had worked so far, there was still work to be done. Focusing on the shape of his magical weapon, Grumph pulled it back and changed it to something he'd never had cause to call up before. As the new shape formed in his hand, he heard the first tittering of excitement from the crowd as they realized what he was creating. Grumph ignored them, as well as the sound of approach from behind, instead sheathing his demon sword and swinging his new weapon high overhead. He would likely only get a single shot at this.

He had to make it count.

*   *   *

"An anchor on a rope," Fritz muttered under her breath, watching in wonder as the display before her eyes unfolded. "Dejy, has anyone ever gotten past the wind wall using an anchor on a rope?"

"Can't say they have," Dejy replied. "Though I should also add that I can't recall a time when anyone tried. Most attempt to cast a flying spell and navigate through, or else try a weak teleport spell, if they've got the chops for it."

"Do those work?" Gabrielle asked.

"Depends on the mage. Flying through one of those is pretty hard: takes a lot of control. And the whole field of the coliseum is warded to interfere with teleportation, otherwise these would be too easy. You can break through a ward, but it takes a lot of skill and drains loads of mana," Fritz explained. Her eyes weren't on Grumph, but rather on the humanoid figures clattering through the ruins in pursuit of their prey. The things were always bunched up near the start, so Grumph's sprint had caught them by surprise. His lead was dwindling, though; they'd be on him in moments. Fritz was so caught up in watching Grumph's pursuers that she actually missed the throw that would be spoken of for weeks afterward amid the mages who were—and those who would falsely claim they had been—at the trial.

"He hooked it!" Dejy leapt up, completely forgetting his station and raising his arms high in the air. "Fritz, did you see that? He got the anchor around the corner of a building on the other side!"

"Of course I saw it," Fritz quickly lied, turning her attention back to the half-orc. It was clear from the glance over his shoulder that Grumph knew time was almost up. With a firm grip on the glowing golden rope in his hands, he gave it a test tug, pulled tight the slack, wrapped it around his forearms, and stepped boldly into the wall of wind.

He was immediately hurled upward, but stopped after only a few feet, his rope and anchor holding even as the building they were attached to seemed to wobble. A cheer went up from around them, even the mages who were betting on Grumph's failure forgetting themselves at the impressive display. None of the three who were friends of the half-orc joined them, however. They knew he was far from safe. Grumph still had to pull himself to the other side of the wind.

And the longer they watched, the more the building he'd hooked seemed to be shaking.

*   *   *

Wind screamed in Grumph's ears, pulling on them so hard he feared they'd tear away. Never had he been more grateful to be born a half-orc, whose ears were small and close to their skulls. Had he been an elf, he'd likely either be bleeding from the sides of his head or pulled free from his tenuous tether to the ground. Focusing through the pain and sound and terror took nearly every bit of self-control Grumph had.

He moved his hands slowly, steadily, one at a time over each other as they pulled more of the rope to his body. Tempting as it was to try and hurry down the line to safety, he didn't have that much faith in the stability of the ruins he'd hooked the anchor to. One good jerk might be enough to yank him free. As it stood, he was already hoping against hope that it would last until he'd finished crossing over. Also that his arms wouldn't get torn free from his body under the wind's relentless assault.

It was impossible to say how long he was stuck in the center of the howling barrier; there was no time in that world, only sound and pain. He might have been in it for only seconds or for several minutes. All he knew was that when his right hand reached out to grab a new section of rope and found itself suddenly beyond the wind, Grumph nearly dropped his lifeline in sheer shock. Recovering quickly, he continued his effort, slowly but surely extricating himself. Now that he was almost out, he could see how close the building was to giving way. He fought against the panic swelling in his brain, screaming at him to hurry things along. He was so close now. This wasn't the time to lose it all through primal emotions like fear.

At long last, Grumph fell a short way to the ground on the other side of the wind wall. He lay there for a brief moment, panting as sweat glistened across his dark green skin. The effort had been exhausting, far worse than he'd realized when he was midway through doing it. What he wanted was a good ten minutes to rest comfortably before continuing on his journey. What he got instead was the sound of something moving in the ruins ahead of him, the noise jolting him up from the ground.

More enemies. Of course there were more—he hadn't imagined they would only be in the first section—but this time, there was little hope of outrunning them. Even if Grumph had had enough energy on hand to pull it off, he'd taken too long resting once he breached the wall. They'd no doubt gotten into position, blocking off any of the exit routes he might have taken.

With his right hand, he redrew his demon-bone sword, while with the left, he shifted the form of his golden weapon, turning it into a compact hammer with a sizable head. Weapons in both hands meant casting would be impossible, but Grumph preferred to get a sense of his enemies before resorting to spells anyway. Swinging a blade took no mana, after all.

The first of the creatures finally burst forth from behind a half-shattered building. It scurried forward on a set of six legs, a long set of curved blades mounted on the front like pincers. Grumph momentarily mistook the thing for a beetle with its wide, flat back and rapid leg movements. Beetles didn't tend to be a metallic gray in color with glowing magical runes on their backs, though. Nor were their legs and pincers fastened with bolts, and they certainly weren't the size of well-bred guard dogs.

More followed the first, at least half a dozen appearing in the span of seconds. Grumph wasted no time, refusing to let them surround him; he charged forward and met the first head-on. Lifting his golden hammer high overhead, he brought it down like he was trying to split the very earth, aiming for the rune that he imagined was the thing's power source. The blow struck true, slamming into the false-beetle's back with tremendous force. Instead of sending it to the ground or cracking the rune or even shattering the creature outright, something utterly unexpected happened.

The golden hammer in Grumph's hand shimmered once, then fractured into pieces, and finally vanished entirely. Grumph quickly backpedaled, but the creature took the opportunity to advance, slashing at his legs and leaving Grumph with a few shallow cuts for his trouble.

Grumph turned the situation over in his head several times, trying to understand what had happened while also bringing his blade around to a defensive position. The spell-weapon lacked any kind of physical mass, which was why it had been able to cross the wind wall; that meant the odds of the not-beetle being so tough it shattered the hammer on its own were negligible. The thing had been composed almost entirely of magical energy.

Grumph nearly stepped back into the wind wall as the truth struck him. This was a test for mages, one meant to show more than their skill with attack spells. What better way to do so than giving them an enemy they couldn't simply blast into oblivion? As soon as the idea hit him, Grumph knew it had to be right.

These bladed, deadly creatures he'd been set against were more than mere crafted obstacles. The damned things were also resistant to magic.

Chapter 25

"I really hate those little bastards," Dejy said, watching as Grumph's weapon was destroyed in a single swing. "Had to fight a few for my own trial. What do they call them? Constroids?"

"That's the name for all magically powered creations. This type has a specific term, but damned if I remember what it is," Fritz corrected.

"You both seem to be taking the fact that Grumph just lost one of his weapons, along with some flesh from his legs, with a very carefree attitude." Gabrielle was trying not to get worked up, but as she watched her friend backpedal, trapped between a wall of endless upward wind and seven large machines that were slowly surrounding him, it was hard to keep the worry out of her voice.

"Constroids are a big pain for most mages because they're heavily warded to resist magic," Fritz explained. "Nothing is magic-proof, of course, so some mages beat them by using enough power to blast through the wards. For most, this is a challenge that requires strategic thinking like they've never encountered. When magic is one of your tools, you rarely need to reach for anything else. Lots of mages can't adapt to a situation where their default tactics are useless and fall to these things."

"Are you trying to make me feel better? Because you are doing a shit job if so," Gabrielle snapped.

"What she's saying is that these are a big hurdle for most mages. But Grumph isn't like most mages, now is he?" Dejy pointed out. "He's more accustomed to handling problems without his magic. And I'm extra calm because I happen to know which spells he has tucked up his—well, never mind, looks like he's about to show us himself."

Gabrielle and Fritz looked down at the field, where Grumph was completely surrounded by the constroids. Despite what had happened with his hammer, he was clearly casting a spell with his free hand.

Several of the other mages nearby chuckled, muttering something about rookies, but Dejy was grinning from ear to ear.

"I had a feeling that would come in handy."

*   *   *

"One of the fundamental keys of magic is to learn what you do best. Some wizards are naturally adept at fire spells. Others excel at summoning. Play to your strengths, in other words. But since we don't have time to test you in every discipline, we'll have to use that strategy slightly differently."

Dejy's words echoed in Grumph's head as he wove the spell. It had been the first one his teacher had decided he should learn, and therefore the one he'd gotten the most experience in casting. True, that was very little compared to the time he'd spent with the ones from his book, but Grumph had thrown his first spell without instruction in the midst of a demon attack. Some oversized metal bugs weren't nearly enough to rattle his concentration as he finished the last of the gestures and let the final word of command fall from his lips.

He could see the crowd lean forward, their faces expectant as they waited to witness his spell fizzle out against the well-defended opponents closing in on him. They were quickly disappointed, as no massive fireball or blast of force appeared from his hand. In fact, to the untrained eye, it looked like Grumph hadn't managed to actually call forth any magic at all. Only those who recognized the spell, or had the keen eyes to watch his body, understood what Grumph had done.

His muscles were already beginning to swell as the first creature leapt for him, pincers at the ready, aiming for his chest. Grumph met the metal monster with his blade in midair, cleaving through the creature as though it were formed from rotted wood. Powerful as he was, this was a feat far beyond his usual limits. Dejy's first spell had been one that played to Grumph's most obvious strength: his actual physical strength. For a short while, he had surpassed his natural limits, and the power surging through his muscles made him feel almost invincible.

The "almost" was important, as three of the creatures came forward at once. One managed to reach up and leave a gash on Grumph's arm. He quickly retreated, only to find two more were moving around to flank him. With the wind wall at his back, the room for maneuvering was quickly shrinking. Strong or not, he'd be cut to ribbons if they all managed to flank him at once. Grumph cursed the wind behind him for cutting off his escape, then immediately tossed out a prayer of thanks as a new idea formed.

Leaping for the two that had circled behind him, Grumph whipped his blade around in an exaggerated motion. As he'd expected, the nearest one raised a pincer to block. This didn't bother Grumph in the slightest as he slammed his sword into the appendage, hitting with such force that he knocked the monster off its legs and into its adjacent partner. Grumph didn't let it end there, however; he kept right on pushing those two metal monsters directly into the wall of wind.

As soon as they hit, they were gone, flung up toward the gods, to do with as they saw fit. Grumph spun around, facing the other three. They spread out, joining with a fourth that had been hidden amidst the ruins, but it was no use. Without the advantage from flanking him, and now that Grumph had a quick way to dispose of his enemies, he made short work of the remaining opponents.

Two more were sent into the sky, while the remaining pair was chopped into pieces by his magically augmented strength and his sword forged from the tail of a demon. In truth, Grumph hadn't known if demon-bone was strong enough to cut through metal, but he was grateful to find such to be the case. Not only did it make his job easier, but it meant he didn't accidently break his blade as he hacked them to pieces.

When large hunks of the defeated creatures littered the ground at his feet, Grumph turned to the next section of ruins. There would be more of them, no question, but so long as he stayed fleet of foot and aware of his surrounding, he felt confident he could handle them.

What worried him more were the dark, swirling clouds beginning to form around the tower in the center of the field. He knew

214

there was a built-in time limit to this trial, and hoped he hadn't lost too many minutes to battle. On sheer impulse, Grumph reached out his with free hand and picked up one of the least damaged segments of metal beetle. The vast majority of its back still held together, making it just about the right size for a shield.

Grumph's legs pumped, the magic of his spell still filling him with power and energy as he sprinted across the fabricated remains of what had once been a small town. Part of him wondered if this trial was based on something, perhaps a legend or an ordeal one of the older mages had actually endured. It all seemed a little too real, felt a touch too specific for it to be something they'd cooked up merely to test the spell-slinging skills of applicants. He heard more rustling from amidst the tattered remains of the city, but not a single metallic enemy popped out. Perhaps they would have, had he been moving more slowly or weakly. Grumph was in no mood to find out; he merely plowed ahead as fast as the swollen muscles in his body would permit.

The spell, while potent, had the drawback of consuming a fair chunk of mana and only lasting a short while. By the time he cleared the last of the buildings and found his next obstacle, his muscles were already shrinking back to their normal size and the fatigue borne from constant exertion was beginning to take its toll. Grumph was sweating again already, an issue that increased exponentially as he stepped out of the ruins and was nearly bowled over by the wave of heat coming off the ground.

Unlike the wall of wind, there was no chance of being caught unawares by this trap. Before him stretched a wide expanse of rock so hot it almost seemed to be boiling in a few places. Even from at least thirty feet away, he could feel the heat. Up close, he imagined it would be like standing in an oven. Reaching back to one of the buildings, Grumph snapped off a piece of dilapidated wood and tossed it out into the burning expanse. No sooner had the wood touched the ground than it burst into flames, turning into cinder and vanishing from sight within seconds.

He stared at the spot where the wood had been, and then raised his hand and cast the first spell he'd ever learned—one that summoned a blast of ice magic to strike his target. The ice hit and, unlike the wood, managed to hold its shape for almost a quarter of a minute before dissolving into first water, and then steam. So, magic could resist the effect, but only for a time. The cold spell didn't take much out of Grumph's mana, but he in no way thought he'd be able to cast it quickly enough to hop from frozen spot to frozen spot. He went to scratch his head with his left hand and nearly banged his cheek with the makeshift shield still clutched in his grip. Grumph looked at the remains of the metal beetle, remembering how easily his magic hammer had been dissolved when it touched the creature. Yes, the wind wall had lifted them easily, but they were likely being hit by the effects of the magic there, not the magic itself.

Carefully, trying not to breathe the hot air, Grumph came as close to the edge of the burning land as he dared and rested part of the metal body on the near-boiling ground. Pops and sizzles greeted his ear, like he was throwing cold water on a stove, but the remains of the almost-beetle seemed to hold their shape. After as long as Grumph could bear to stand so close, he pulled his shield away. It was unscarred, not so much as a singe on the dull gray exterior. The ground, however, looked as though it had been forcefully cooled and was now almost normal in color. That effect quickly faded as it began to burn once more.

Grumph retreated from the heat, head spinning as he contemplated his options. He had a means to move across the ground, sort of, but there was still the issue of the overwhelming temperature to deal with. Adding to his troubles, the clouds near the tower were growing larger, the sound of distant thunder rumbling on occasion. One idea, one admittedly terrible idea, came to Grumph and he seized it. With time running short, he'd have to take some chances.

Setting down the creature remains on the ground, Grumph lifted his blade overhead and went to work.

*   *   *

216

"Not a new idea, but always a classic," Fritz noted.

"He's trying to make the constroid into shoes, isn't he?" Gabrielle asked.

"That he is," Dejy confirmed. "Looks like he's using the innards as straps to secure the bottoms to his feet. Smart; you'd be amazed how many were wily enough to use the materials to cross this challenge but didn't bother making good fastenings. Of course, he's only solved one of the problems so far; that heat will knock out anyone who spends too long in it, even if they can walk safely."

"Oh, you haven't figured that part out?" Gabrielle grinned, savoring the feeling of being the one to have insight for a change. "Grumph solved that issue before the foot one."

"'Solved' is a rather strong word," Fritz countered. "I don't think anyone has ever gone that route for coping with heat before."

"Then Grumph will get to have some fun bragging rights," Gabrielle said.

Dejy stared at the both of them, utterly perplexed. "What in the nine hells are you talking about? How is he going to deal with the heat?"

Fritz held a finger up to her mouth, which was twisted into a spiteful grin, and nodded to the field. "Shhh. Let Grumph show you himself."

Dejy crossed his arms and mumbled something about disliking sarcasm, but watched as his student finished crafting the makeshift metal shoes and turned toward the burning landscape once more.

*   *   *

This was going to hurt. No matter how Grumph came at it, no matter what tricks he employed, there was no getting around the fact that this would be a painful experience. Grumph readied himself for that as he moved carefully, halves of the not-beetle's back bound to his feet with the bits of flexible metal that had been inside. He had experienced pain before, more than he cared to think about or would ever admit to. This wouldn't be so bad. At least it was finite; there was a clear end in sight. Compared to languishing in an ink-dark cell, knowing only pain and fear, it was nothing. Grumph could handle far worse than this.

He stepped to the edge of the fiery ground, sheathed his blade, and began to cast. It was his ice spell, the one he'd thrown at a demon to steal its attention away from Thistle. That night seemed like a lifetime ago, despite it being only months. Then again, perhaps it was a lifetime, for the Grumph that had been lying on the ground, desperately trying to form some half-hearted spell, was a far cry from the one who wove magic from the air, calling forth elemental forces to serve his command.

Grumph finished casting and turned his hand so the blast would hit his target. It was not the ground he tried to freeze, however, nor was it the metal covering his feet. Instead, Grumph blasted himself directly in the chest. The sensation of cold that overtook him was so powerful he began to shiver; his skin felt like it was burning and numb all at once. Without wasting a moment, Grumph stepped forward into the inferno.

The heat was oppressive, powerful, and smothering, but it served only to ameliorate the cold that was clinging to him. Opposing forces went to work on his body, and the result was a middle ground that, while nowhere near comfortable, was at least tolerable. Grumph hurt in every direction—cold in his chest and fire licking at his appendages—but he could continue. That was all he'd wanted, all he'd dared hope for. After a few steps, he began to cast again before the magic of the first ice spell had fully worn off, once more hitting himself center mass with the attack.

It was slow, tortuous going, but Grumph persisted step by step. As he neared the end, his head was swimming from the heat and his chest felt like chunks of his skin were going to come off. Still, he cast one last ice spell, forced himself to keep walking forward, and finally burst through to the other end of the fiery lands.

Grumph collapsed onto the ground, unable to move as the ice spell finally dissipated. Had more of the creatures come for him in that moment, he would surely have been torn to pieces. Thankfully, it seemed whoever designed the trial had some compassion in them, as Grumph was let be for the few minutes he allowed himself to recover. At last he pulled himself to a sitting position, yanked off the remains of the metal creature, and took in his surroundings.

Only a few ragged buildings were in this new section of the field, likely tossed in purely for atmosphere. They were dwarfed by the stone tower that jutted up from the ground like the scolding finger of a buried giant. Its great height was surrounded by a swirling mass of pitch black clouds, its face constantly illuminated by crackles of lightning.

He'd made it to the final section of the trial. Now, he just had to hope there was still time. Grumph rose to his feet, took out his sword, and lumbered forward with all the strength he could still muster.

Chapter 26

Gabrielle had begun to notice a slight, subtle shift in the mood of the crowd watching Grumph. At first, they'd been a bit set against him, which had come as no surprise given what he was trying to do and how many almost certainly had gold riding on his failure. But with each successive encounter and ultimate triumph, more and more of the other mages seemed to be cheering when Grumph managed to survive. By the time he all but fell out of the fire pit and collapsed, several of the robed individuals leapt up and cheered as he lay on the ground recovering.

"I thought it would be harder for him to win people over," Gabrielle said. "I mean, considering . . ."

"The half-orc thing?" Dejy cocked his head to the side, as though the idea genuinely hadn't crossed his mind. "I suppose there is the enmity between their kind and elves to consider, but the only ones who make an issue out of it are those that choose to. We have no issue with half-orcs joining the mages' guild; it's just that very few ever try. For whatever reason, their culture doesn't put as much importance on learning to weave magic as others."

"Well, now I feel like I come from a town full of assholes. When Grumph first showed up, lots of people in the village acted like he was going to start gobbling up children and burning crops," Gabrielle admitted.

"That is . . . a little behind the times," Dejy agreed. "But a half-orc moving to town, and one joining our guild are different things. A town is merely a collection of people who live in proximity to one another. A guild is something far more interconnected. No matter who we are, what race or region we hail from, or what gods we pray to, we are all magic users. We all seek to grow stronger, and swear to protect others of our kind and the guild that houses them. Your town saw a powerful, dangerous being move close and assumed it meant danger."

Dejy pointed down to the field, where Grumph was rising to his feet amidst the scattered applause coming from his fellow mages. "What we see is a powerful, dangerous being who is striving to become our guildmate. Our friend. Our brother. We can cheer for Grumph because his success is our gain."

"And what a gain it will be, if he can make it in time," Fritz added. "The storm is going to begin soon."

"Hope you taught him a few more tricks that he's hiding up his sleeve," Gabrielle said.

Dejy didn't reply; his eyes were fixed on the half-orc, on his student, as Grumph barreled past the few tattered buildings and reached the base of the tower. The last leg of the trial had begun, and he'd be damned if he glanced away for even a moment of it.

*   *   *

Gauging one's remaining mana was a lot like trying to figure out how many more times a barrel could be lifted overhead before one's muscles would give out and they'd take a nasty bruise on the skull. It was doable, but only with countless hours of practice and a complete knowledge of personal limitations. Grumph had a firm grasp on the latter, though he was severely lacking on the former. Thus, as he reached the base of the tall stone tower, he was uncertain how many spells were still left in him. Amplifying his strength had taken a large toll, and while the ice spells weren't especially draining, he'd been forced to cast a half-dozen of them. He estimated two or three weaker spells were still available, and perhaps one more use of the new, more potent ones.

Thankfully, the door wasn't warded and opened with a single shove. For a moment, Grumph allowed himself a heartbeat of relief. Once indoors, he should at least have some cover in case the storm started. Then he felt the blast of wind and cold water splash across his chest. Stepping in, Grumph understood the error in his logic immediately. He'd assumed that the tempest crystal was conjuring the storm outside the building, allowing it to reach full power before bursting.

What was actually happening was that the storm had been forming in the building all along; the bits in the sky that Grumph could see were merely the parts that had started to leak out. A barrage of raindrops pelted his skin and harsh winds tore at his clothes. It was like stepping into a burgeoning tornado, one not quite yet at deadly strength. Thunder roared in his ears from overhead; brilliant blasts of lightning half-blinded him and made it impossible to see where they struck. He blinked through the rain, trying to find a path forward. What his eyes missed, his feet discovered—chiefly by smashing his toes directly against a hard stone step.

Muttering curses, Grumph raised his leg and felt around. Definitely a raised stone, with another higher above it. Stairs. Stairs that were leading up higher into the flashes of sharp white, deadly lightning, but also leading up toward his goal. After coming this far, there was no way Grumph would allow himself to be halted by mere drizzle and a chance of painful death. It took far greater dangers than that to dissuade a half-orc with his mind made up.

Climbing as fast as he dared—which was not terribly fast at all, since he was half-blind and moving across slick wet rock—Grumph began ascending the stairs. With nearly every step, he could feel the storm intensify, rain pelting him like it was trying to get down to his bones. Idly, he wondered what sorts of spells the other, more experienced mages had cast as they endured this part of the trial. He had one that would make the climb easier, but it would do nothing to protect him from the elements. Besides, without knowing what lay ahead, Grumph was hesitant to use up the last of his mana. Great as the strides he'd made with Dejy were, he was still, at best, a novice wizard, and his pool for holding mana reflected that.

Grumph took another step upward and was nearly hurled back by a fresh gust of wind. Only a frantic scramble and his powerful grip allowed him to hang on to the spiraling staircase. Once he'd gotten hold of himself, Grumph tried to ascend once more, only to be pushed back yet again. Not coincidence then. The storm was designed to blow him away after reaching a certain point. Much as he loathed parting with the last mana he could draw, there was no point in saving it for some unknown obstacle ahead if he couldn't make it past this one. Retreating a few steps back down, Grumph raised his hands and began to cast.

"Most mages think of casting only in terms of the spell's school. Summoning, conjuring, illusion, you get the idea. Personally, I like to split them into offense, defense, and non-combat. As I see it, you've got plenty of offense in your arsenal already. Normally, I'd teach you a non-combat or two to make life easier, but since your trials are around the corner, a defense spell is probably a better use of our time. I'll let you decide what you'd like to learn, though. A spell that will increase your toughness, giving you some magical armor against enemies, or one that will help your movement, allowing you to take positions in a battlefield that were impossible before."

Grumph hadn't even hesitated when Dejy made him the offer. Armor could be purchased, wounds healed, and blood would dry eventually. Magic, to him, was not simply a tool to make him a better warrior; Grumph already had confidence in that department. Magic was a means to do the impossible, and as Grumph finished his casting, feeling so much mana whisper out of him that he nearly got light-headed, he was grateful for his choice. Armor was well and good, but what he needed here was the power to climb.

Pressing his hand against the tower's wall, Grumph felt the newly familiar sensation of bonding. He lifted himself up, adding his feet and other hand to the tower's smooth stone surface. Just like that, Grumph was no longer standing on the stairs; instead, he held himself on the wall like a cockroach searching for abandoned bits of food. Tentatively, he reached out, willing one hand free and affixing it to a new point on the wall. Then he moved his legs, then an arm again, and so on, until he was weaving his way around the tower at a pace perhaps a touch quicker than he'd managed on the stairs.

The testing point came when the wind's force suddenly doubled once more, driving raindrops into his face as if he'd dunked his head in a bucket. It was as powerful as before, but this time, Grumph wasn't pushed back. His magic, binding him to the wall at his desire, was stronger than the storm, and he continued climbing, following the route of the stairs.

Grumph considered trying to bypass the spiral of the staircase entirely and begin climbing straight up, but when he stretched a hand out toward the center of the tower, he felt the unmistakable tingle of electricity. Jerking his hand back quickly, Grumph continued on the longer path. There was no way to be sure without testing it, but he felt reasonably certain that there was lightning waiting in the tower's center, waiting to strike all who left the stairs, be it by choice or accident. He might be wrong, of course; however, Grumph saw no reason to chance it when his current strategy was holding up. He was brave, not pointlessly death-seeking.

The first time lightning struck the staircase, Grumph was so shocked he nearly went toppling from his perch on the wall. Only the fact that he was too surprised to mentally release his bond saved him, leading to him flopping about before realizing that he was magically connected to stone. After that, the strikes became more frequent, fat bolts of electricity slamming into the stone stairs, blinding Grumph even more than the rain and wind already had. At first, he was terrified, cautious of every movement, afraid the next bolt would be the one that finally hit the wall. However, after ten strikes, Grumph realized that none of them had deviated from the staircase. It was another layer of obstacles, just like the torrential wind that tried to blow him away. Most mages had likely found a different solution to the wind problem and were then in a position to cast a shield or ward against the lightning. By sheer chance, and perhaps the grace of the gods, Grumph's remaining spells had felled two wolves with a single strike.

Grumph's last surprise in the tower was a bump to the head. Since he was climbing up parallel to the stairs, but not actually treading on them, he had no idea that they'd finally come to an end and thus, smacked himself headlong into a wall. Groping about carefully, he inched his hands down from his horizontal perch until he finally felt a surface other than rock. Wood, weathered and beaten and who knew how old, but wood nonetheless. He ran tired fingers across its surface until they seized what he'd been so desperately searching for: the knob. Twisting it without delay—for if this too was a trap, then Grumph had no more spells to counter it—he barreled through into the new room.

For an instant, Grumph thought he'd died. The sudden silence and peace after having all his senses being assaulted made it feel like his body must have ceased functioning. Then reality set in, and he understood that he was finally, however briefly, out of the storm. Before him was another set of stairs, though these were made of simple wood and rose thirty feet up to another door. He was in the last chamber before the top of the tower, where the crystal rested. Much as he wanted to feel relieved, there was only anxiety burning in his chest.

He'd come so far, managed to do so much, but the cost to make it had been great. His mana was completely tapped out, his body was beaten and exhausted, and his mind was growing fuzzy with fatigue. There would almost certainly be one last obstacle to overcome, and Grumph wasn't sure how he would do it. Stepping forward, he tested the wooden beams to make sure they would hold his weight. Though creaks and groans met his ears, the foothold seemed stable enough.

With nowhere else to go but up, Grumph began to climb once more.

*　　*　　*

When the door opened and Grumph stepped into view at the top of the tower, there was nothing subdued about the cheer that rose from the crowd. Many, including Gabrielle herself, leapt to their feet, screaming support as best they could. The half-orc looked like he'd been through hell, albeit a wet one. Soaked to the bone, clothing half-shredded by wind and rain, and visibly limping, Grumph was hardly the picture of health as he tottered through the door and looked at the glowing crystal.

225

"Think he has anything left?" Fritz asked.

Dejy shook his head. "If he made it past the tower's insides, he had to use the Wall Climbing spell I taught him. After all the others he cast to get there, I'm honestly amazed he's still on his feet. There's no way he was any mana left to draw on."

"It's not like he needs it though, right?" Gabrielle pointed to the center of the field, where Grumph was slowly approaching the crystal. "It's over. He made it. Now he just has to smash the thing."

"Not quite that simple, I'm afraid," Dejy replied. "The crystal defends itself with lightning that surges into anything that touches it. One hand on the surface and most men will be dead. Ram it with a sword or spear, and it'll race back to the wielder, likely killing them. I'd hoped he would hang on to the constroid remains all the way to this point, as those might have been used to bash the thing to pieces."

Gabrielle tapped her leg as she stared at her friend. "Did any of you ever actually ask Grumph about that weapon he carries? I mean, was it inspected or vetted or even drawn in front of you?"

"Not that I know of," Dejy said. "I didn't feel much magic from it, and mages are allowed to bring weapons and tools into their trials. But unless it's enchanted to be lightning-proof, I doubt it will change anything. All metal conducts those bolts."

"Maybe so," Gabrielle agreed. "But what about the bones of a demon?"

*   *   *

No one had to tell Grumph that the crystal was trapped; the singe marks and occasional small crackle of lightning emanating from it conveyed that story perfectly well. Just to be sure he understood how the trap worked, however, he decided to do a test. Ripping off a button from the tattered remains of his shirt, Grumph gently tossed the scrap of metal at the shining white crystal hovering five feet off the tower's floor.

The blast of electricity was blinding as the button hit, and only a small scrap of melted metal fell to the floor. Pretty good trap, by Grumph's reckoning. It would blast anything that touched it, which meant magic was the only way to shatter the thing unharmed. He drew his sword, testing the heft of it in his hand. Grumph had never tried to attack the demons with lightning during their battle, though he was certain some of the other adventurers at the tournament had. He dearly wished he could look back in time and see how that had worked out. Everyone knew demons were immune to fire, and lightning was just very concentrated fire from the sky, when one thought about it, so it seemed like there was a decent chance demons might be resistant to getting shocked.

Grumph realized he was merely trying to find enough justification for the theory to get up the courage and swing. Maybe demons were resistant to electricity, maybe they weren't. Either way, he was about to find out. Grumph had pushed himself harder in the last few days than he'd needed to for years, and he'd done it all because his friends were counting on him. One crystal—and potential death—were all that remained between him and helping the others. He'd already made it through three or four potential deaths just in the last hour. What was one more on the pile?

Raising the blade high overheard, wishing he still had the magically enhanced strength, Grumph took precise aim. He would likely only get a single shot at this; it wouldn't do to crack the thing without breaking it. Grumph took a deep breath, gathered every ounce of strength still remaining in his body, and swung like he was trying to chop through a giant's leg.

In the brief moment before his blade made contact, Grumph wondered if Talcia would still honor their bargain to send aid if he died making it into the guild.

*   *   *

The brilliant white explosion blinded all who'd been watching Grumph's swing, which was to say damn near everyone in the coliseum.

Eyes were rubbed and stars blinked out of sight as they tried to make out what had become of the intrepid apprentice wizard working so hard for membership. By the time their vision returned, the tower was obscured by the funneling clouds that were drifting out of it, dissipating into the sky. Hushed whispers overtook cheers as they waited for any sort of movement or sign. As seconds stretched into minutes, the whispering became less hushed and more frantic.

"Come on, Grumph." Gabrielle had her hands clenched so tightly that her armor rattled. She stared, unyielding, at the cloud-obfuscated tower, waiting for any sign of her friend. Fritz laid a hand on Gabrielle's forearm, but said nothing. There were no words for moments like these.

Only prayers.

"My fellow mages." Talcia's voice filled the air, stoic and inscrutable from the first word. "I must inform you that today's applicant, Grumph the wizard, succeeded in destroying the Tempest Crystal and passing his trial for entry into the Guild of Illustrious Mages. However, he was not able to escape the resulting blast unscathed. Thus, it is my duty to deliver some unfortunate news."

Gabrielle felt her heart shatter in her chest, but before she could even feel the impact of Grumph's loss, Fritz slapped her gently on the back and put her elven face directly in Gabrielle's.

"Talcia's a dick," she whispered excitedly. "A dick, and a showman."

Before their eyes, the clouds burst apart, revealing the announcing mage in question supporting a singed half-orc who was clearly unable to stand on his own. Grumph was swaying from side to side, one good thump from passing out, but unmistakably alive.

"The bad news is that we're going to have to call some priests in to patch this guy up before we can throw his guild acceptance party!"

Everyone in the audience leapt to their feet and cheered, even Gabrielle, despite the fact that she was mentally calculating how to jump and mercilessly pummel an announcer mage.

Chapter 27

"Absolutely not." Talcia crossed his arms and glared, an expression he'd perfected over decades on the admissions committee.

"I don't think you get to just turn me down. I outrank you by quite a bit," Dejy pointed out. "And I say I'm going to be in the group you send to help Grumph."

"Dejy, you're an archmage and have a seat at the Table. This guild depends on you; it needs you. We can't let you go gallivanting off on some wild adventure for who knows how long. Think of all the responsibilities you have to attend to here," Talcia reminded him.

"You mean paperwork," Dejy muttered darkly.

The pair sat in Fritz's quarters, along with the elven trader herself and Ferdy, who'd tagged along with Talcia despite having no invitation of his own. With Grumph being healed by priests, and Gabrielle refusing to leave his side, it fell upon the older mages to fulfill their end of the bargain made several days prior. Grumph was owed magical transport back to Briarwillow and a team of two to three mages to lend aid with their situation there. Mages, by and large, were not always the most trustworthy of sorts, but they prided themselves on keeping deals with fellow guildmates. It was the only way to trust and live in peace with each other.

"Dejy can push the issue if he really wants—he does outrank us all—but I think the Table will ultimately agree with Talcia on this one," Fritz said. "You went and got too important in the guild; now, they can't survive without you."

"Come on; he's my student, doesn't that get me something?" Dejy asked.

"A student of two days," Talcia reminded him. "Not exactly a long-lasting bond. Why do you even want to go on this trip, anyway? From the sounds of things, it's either a simple fix or nothing at all."

"I think he just got accustomed to the excitement and is dreading going back to his normal work." Fritz anticipated Dejy's glare and met it with a playful wink. "There's nothing to worry about, though. After the spectacle Grumph put on, I imagine we've got plenty of mages who would jump at the chance to go into the field with the guild's newest member."

"That's a little too true," Talcia agreed. "I'm having trouble deciding who to actually assign. Haven't seen this many volunteers since that nymph island asked us to come help with their locust problem."

"Why not keep it simple?" Fritz asked. "You and Ferdy are both accomplished mages, and clearly interested in keeping tabs on Grumph for a bit, so go ahead and put yourselves on the team. Since you're both part of the admissions committee, it's well within your rights to watch over a newly joined guild member. Plus, I'll be coming along as well."

Ferdy snorted from his seat near the door. "You think Talcia will really waste a spot on someone like you?"

"Talcia can do what he pleases. I never proposed I'd go in as a member of the team," Fritz countered. "You seem to forget; I'm an associate of this guild, not a member, which means I can go where I want whenever it suits me. Those two are my friends, and quite fun, so I'm tagging along."

"Don't bother arguing. Gods have lost their wills trying to make Fritz change her mind," Dejy cautioned. "I'd like to second her on you going, Talcia. If I can't keep an eye on my student personally, I'd like someone skilled, who I trust, to be there with him."

Talcia was quiet, mulling over the requests set before him. "Perhaps that would be for the best. And Ferdy, if you can hold a pleasant tongue to Fritz, you can come along as well, but I won't have you annoying us all with pitiful barbs."

"Personally, I find them quite charming," Fritz said.

"And no instigating him," Talcia added, pointing at his fellow elf.

"What makes you think I want to go on such a pointless assignment?" Ferdy asked.

"Please, kid, you forcefully tagged along to this meeting, and your eyes practically popped out of your head when Fritz suggested you go. If you want people not to know your desires, work on your poker face," Dejy said. "So, Talcia and Ferdy as the mages, Fritz because she wants to. Anyone else?"

"I think keeping it to the two of us is best." Talcia pulled a piece of parchment from his robe and scanned it carefully. "Everyone else who has come forth has their own desires or agenda, wanting to glom on to the momentary acclaim Grumph has after his success. I'd rather work with people who can put the job first. And Fritz, I suppose."

"Thank goodness, I was worried you were going to drag some dullards into our party," Fritz replied. "Guess all that's left to do now is arrange some transportation. We've got people who're familiar enough with Briarwillow to cast a Teleportation Tunnel, don't we?"

"The town is only three days' ride from here and has some of the best pumpkins in Alcatham; we've got gobs of mages who are familiar enough with it to open up a way," Dejy told her. "I want status reports every few days while you're there, though. Keep me in the loop about how my student is doing."

"If you continue tossing around the word 'student' like that, people are going to think you've actually taken Grumph as your apprentice," Talcia warned. "And we all know how the great and powerful Dejy feels about having an apprentice."

"Maybe I've just been waiting for one worth teaching." Dejy snapped the words on reflex, his contrarian impulse refusing to allow someone to pin him down, though once the words left his mouth, he wondered if there wasn't a bit of truth to them. Not that it mattered; he was an archmage with duties to the guild, and Grumph was set on adventure. There was no way to train him as a proper apprentice, even if Dejy wanted to.

He spared a glance at Fritz, who'd moved on to determining where they should open the tunnel on their side, and allowed himself a moment of honest envy. She could go where she pleased without a second thought, owing her time to no man or guild. Just like that, she'd decided to go along with the adventurers, while he'd been completely shut down. Dejy loved his position and power; he'd worked hard to claim them. But there were days he wished for the freedom he'd had as a simple traveling wizard.

On those days, he understood Fritz and what she'd done just a touch better.

*　　　*　　　*

"The wizard's tower lies ahead, visible even over the massive trees that reach into the sky." Russell read from the module's book while also checking his notes. The party was getting close at long last; they'd nearly made it to the tower, which would serve as a massive final dungeon. This was the point when things had started to slip off the rails last time. And he refused to be caught unaware again. "From the size, Gelthorn gauges it to be roughly another day's travel until you can reach the entrance."

"Thank Longinus," Tim said. Timanuel's refusal to retreat had nearly gotten him killed several times already; he was anxious to be out of the forest and into a closed off area where running wasn't meant to be an option. Plus, after all the effort of getting past the monsters and traps, he was pretty darn curious about what was inside this tower.

"Hold off on the thanks, we're not there yet," Bert cautioned. He peered down at the map, analyzing the trees and paths Russell had drawn. After getting a feel for his GM's battle style, Bert was beginning to notice when the board was set for an ambush. Nothing jumped out at him so far, but he checked how many alchemical bombs Wimberly had on hand, just to be safe.

"We'd have been there six games ago if *someone* would have let me cast the teleport spell," Cheri groaned.

"You're trying to break into a wizard's stronghold; doesn't it seem like warding against people popping in uninvited is the first thing he would do?" Having access to the module, Russell actually knew that teleportation blocking was in fact the first spell the wizard had laid on the castle, making it the oldest and strongest amongst his many precautions.

"It wasn't so bad. We got to travel through lots of forest." Alexis still spoke at the same, barely audible volume when out of character, but the others had learned to fall silent when they saw her lips move, making it far easier to pick up her words.

Russell half listened as they recounted their adventures, his mind occupied as he flipped ahead in the module to the adventure that lay before them. On top of scanning for changes, he was also doing his best to memorize each bit of information, in order to host an enjoyable gaming session for his players. After all, the hook for the adventure was a pretty cool one. Once they actually made it into the tower, they'd have to deal with all manner of distorted realties and strange chambers before they reached the final floor. And in there, things would go really off the walls.

Russell was so focused on tracking his party's adventure that he'd failed to look at any other portion of the module. It was a shame, really. If he'd thought to examine the entire book instead of just the part he was playing, he would have gotten some scrap of proof that he wasn't crazy.

But he also would have learned that the situation in Briarwillow had turned out to be far more complex than a simple plague.

*   *   *

All healing magic was not created equal. After the bandit fight, Grumph and Gabrielle's exposure to the priest's divine mending had been minimal, since all they'd had were a few scrapes and bruises. Grumph's session following his trial was far more in depth, giving him his first chance to really get a sense of the energy flowing through him. It was much different than Thistle's—that became clear immediately. When the gnome healed them, they were filled with a sense of comfort and familiarity, like receiving a hug from a long distant friend. The priest's magic was colder, more detached, akin to an emotionally closed off parent offering some small word of praise. It was possible the difference came from their roles, priest versus paladin, or because they worshipped different gods, but Grumph highly doubted it. Lying on the table as the priest removed his hands from the half-orc's chest and motioned for his sack of gold, Grumph realized that just because someone could call upon the power of the kind gods did not mean they themselves weren't something of an asshole.

That said, there was no dispute to be had with the quality of the work. Grumph slowly lifted himself into a sitting position, surprised at the lack of pain in his body, only to be nearly knocked back down as Gabrielle wrapped him in a massive hug. She squeezed for all she was worth, which was quite a bit after the constant training she'd been undergoing, and Grumph had to gently slap her arm repeatedly before she finally let him go.

"You are out of your gods-damned half-orc mind, you know that, right?" She released him, stepping back to look him over and make sure the priest hadn't missed anything. "I mean . . . the fire part alone . . ."

Grumph winced at the memory, then checked himself for burns or frostbite, but found none. It truly was as though he'd never undergone the trial at all, save for the fact that half his clothes were torn, burned, or shredded by wind. As he looked around, he realized something else was different: neither his blade nor its scabbard was hitched to his belt.

As he began to search the sheets, Gabrielle reached around her back and presented the missing weapon, tucked neatly into its sheath. "It survived, but I think barely. Obviously, that wasn't a real tempest crystal, but Dejy told me they still had to layer a lot of magic onto it to create the effects. Just smacking the hell out of it—no one does that, especially with demon . . . you know what, see for yourself." She held out the blade and Grumph accepted, drawing his trusty tool slowly from its scabbard.

The shape was much the same, but the pale-white of the bone was stained dark across the front, like it had been dipped in soot. Across the once razor-like edge were dozens upon dozens of small nicks and fractures. As he peered closely at the almost-shattered edge, Grumph thought he saw a small spark zip between two of the raised portions.

"No idea if it will still cut anymore," Gabrielle told him. "We could probably get you a new one, but things in this town are crazy expensive."

"It's fine." Grumph tucked the blade back into its sheath and went to strap it on his belt, only to realize said belt had been fried in the explosions. Some shopping, it seemed, would still be in order. Grumph bit back a curse at the thought. He'd worked so hard in order to return to the others as soon as possible. Any delay, no matter how small, twisted in his gut like an angry dagger.

The door to the small room—and its lonely bed and dresser—opened for the first time since the priest and guild attendant had left. Funneling through the small opening was Fritz, Talcia, Ferdy, and Dejy. Talcia and Ferdy had changed out of their ever-present robes, and were now wearing clothing closer to what Grumph had been when starting his trial. Packs and bags weighed them down, and Talcia walked with a large, ornate wooden staff covered up and down with runes. Fritz was dressed much as always, although she was carrying her satchel once again. Dejy was largely unchanged, save for the sizable, sheathed axe that hovered several feet in front of him and the pack gripped loosely in his hand.

"And there's the talk of the guild!" Fritz called, walking over and giving Grumph a healthy smack on the shoulder. "Not too shabby of a show you put on. I daresay the next applicants we get are in for a rough time, now that you've set a two-day bar in front of them."

"Let's please not try and make this an expectation," Talcia said. "I do not want to see our best and brightest next generation killed off by trying to recreate this feat."

"Technically, if they're the best and brightest, shouldn't they be able to pull it off?" Dejy turned to Gabrielle and made a motion with his hand, causing the axe to sail toward her. "I believe this is yours. Fritz said you'd need it for the journey, but that I shouldn't touch it. Care to explain?"

Gabrielle accepted the weapon, noting the slight pain in her palms at its touch, and slipped it onto her back. "I got a bargain."

"Interesting." Dejy walked over to his student, who was still sitting in bed and beginning to feel a bit embarrassed about it. "Grumph, I brought you your personal effects. The rest of your belongings are being loaded onto your horses, which we'll be meeting outside in a few minutes."

"Already?" Grumph was happy with the news, but it did take him off guard.

"Talcia made it clear how important time was to you, and given what you did today, I'd say you earned having your wishes honored." Dejy set the backpack carefully down on Grumph's lap, as though the modest bundle of leather was going to inflict a wound that wind, fire, and lightning hadn't. "There's a fresh change of clothes in there, as well as a formal set of guild robes. I know they aren't your usual attire, but you should still have some, and, as your teacher, it's my privilege to provide them."

"I'm amazed they stock robes in Grumph's size," Gabrielle said.

"They don't, actually," Dejy admitted. "I had these specially commissioned after my first day working with Grumph. Something told me he'd be needing them."

"Thank you." Grumph accepted the backpack, and then looked up at the man he'd spent the last several days cooped up with. It would have been easy for Dejy to half-ass the training, to brush Grumph off as unimportant due to his race or station. Even as a favor to Fritz, he could have taken it easy; after all, no one expected the half-orc to succeed. But he hadn't. Dejy had worked as hard, if not more so, than Grumph. "For everything."

"It's not often a man, mage or not, gets to be part of something as incredible as what happened today," Dejy replied. "Thank *you* for livening things up around here. I wish I could be there for more of your journey, but I'm thankful to have been witness to at least this much. And anytime you're in a town with a guild outpost, stop by and see me. I'm sure I'll be here."

Everyone pretended not to notice how depressed Dejy got on his last sentence, and Fritz plowed past the moment by beginning to hustle everyone out the door. "Come on, come on, we're off to the courtyard. Give the man some privacy to change. Grumph, when you're ready, just open the door. It's already set to bring you where you need to be."

Fritz grabbed and shoved everyone through the door before shutting it behind her, leaving Grumph alone for the first time since he'd stood on the floor of the coliseum. He opened the bag and pulled out the fresh clothes on top. There, just below them, was his all-too-familiar spell book, but next to it was another tome, one he'd never laid eyes on before. Lifting it from the pack, he pulled back the cover and read the first page, a toothy, half-orc smile growing with each passing word.

Since I can't be around to train you like a proper teacher, I thought I'd send along a study-aid. This should help you keep learning, even without me around to help.

Grumph flipped through a few of the pages, then closed the book and set it back in his pack. Much as he wanted to study and learn, there would be time for that later. Assuming they survived, of course. Climbing out of bed, he began to dress, wondering what the others would say when he, Gabrielle, and several mages stepped out of thin air.

*   *   *

"You owe me two gold," Thistle said, nudging Eric in the ribs. The glowing green circle that had appeared in the center of town was the first sign that Grumph and Gabrielle had succeeded, and the party members in Briarwillow had quickly hurried out of the smoked meat shop where they were having dinner to greet their returning friends. It was also theoretically possible that some enemies were teleporting in to try and kill them all, but after what Kendal had told them in caverns, Thistle found it unlikely. Whatever else could be said about the threat they were facing, he seemed the type to work alone.

First to step into view was an elven man none of them recognized, riding a large steed; he seemed unsurprised to find them waiting. Next came a familiar blonde in blood-red armor atop a tired horse, though the dark axe jutting up from her back was a new addition. After Gabrielle came a female elf with no horse, carrying a large satchel, eyes twirling about as though she were trying to take in every detail. Following her was a half-elf with a sour expression on his pale face, and, lastly, looking as though he'd had to duck in order to make it through whatever passage he was using, rode the unmistakable bulk of their half-orc companion.

"Good to see you made it, old friend," Thistle called, watching with curious fascination as the green glow flickered before fading completely.

"Glad you survived," Grumph rumbled in his deep, half-orc tones.

To those watching from the outside, it seemed a subdued reunion, but both Grumph and Thistle had no need for a grand show of affection. Their bond was forged over years of friendship and tested by constant danger. Each knew the joy they felt at seeing the other's safe presence, just as they knew the loss they would feel were that friend ever to be struck down. Words were useless in the face of such sentiment, so there was no need to try and involve them.

"Looks like you had quite an interesting trip," Thistle said.

"There were moments."

"And I shall hear all about them, but I'm afraid I must request that we relay our tale to you first. Time, it seems, has sided with the enemy."

Chapter 28

After introductions were made all around, relaying the tale of what had happened in Briarwillow since Grumph and Gabrielle left was a relatively short task, especially since much of the time had been spent doing tedious research that could be skimmed over. The telling of the discovery of the hidden mountain catacombs slowed the story greatly, as Talcia had an abundance of questions about this hidden piece of history. Likewise, Gabrielle and Grumph both perked with curiosity when Thistle began describing his visions, and Ferdy nearly fell out of his chair when Thistle detailed his discussion with an actual god.

It was once they got to the return visit that questions fell away, however. All attention became rapt as Thistle detailed their discussion with Kendal and the chance that the citizens of Briarwillow might still have sentience within the prisons their corpses had become. Thistle ended by sharing what little information Kendal had been able to impart about the priest of Kalzidar and his habits, actions which were so infrequent as to barely be considered as such.

"A whole town's worth of undead, completely under his control," Gabrielle muttered.

"Correction: a whole town's worth of undead, completely under his control, who might be innocent in this whole affair," Eric added. "Meaning that if we butcher them, we're the bad guys."

"Better the bad guys than the dead guys," Gabrielle countered.

"Perhaps neither is needed," Thistle interrupted. "Now that you've brought people with more specialized skills than we have, I feel as though we should ask the mages' opinions on how to handle this situation."

Talcia and Ferdy exchanged a long glance before the elder mage looked back at the table. "There are spells that allow us to bind the undead, ones both Ferdy and I are familiar with, but you've described at least a hundred down there, perhaps more. If their will is being suppressed, then it would be difficult for them to break free of any binding spells, but it is possible. However, it would still take constant casting and a tremendous amount of mana to hold that many for any measureable length of time."

"Could you teleport them away, like how you brought us here?" Gabrielle suggested.

"I'd have to look to be sure, but if this room is as well-protected as you say, there are almost certainly wards and enchantments meant to stop the use of teleportation within its walls." Talcia reached out and grabbed a hunk of smoked meat, turning it over in his hands rather than biting into it. "Still, binding his army, taxing as it may be, would allow one of us the time to study the door and perhaps perceive a way to open it."

"But there would still be the priest to deal with," Eric reminded him.

"That, I assume, you five would be capable of handling," Talcia said.

"Aye, he's our problem, no question about it," Thistle agreed. "Though the door may not be much of an issue for long. Kendal felt like they were about to crack the thing within the day, and that was hours ago."

"So maybe we let them." Eric had a glassy, far-off look in his eye as the beginnings of a plan started to take shape. "If we can't pick the lock, let's have someone else open the door for us. We sneak back into the caverns, keeping watch from up high. As soon as they manage to break open the door, one of the mages handles the undead, and we attack the priest. Door is open, and we're all set to go recover the bones."

"It's pitch black in there," Timuscor reminded him. "And if we use light, we won't be hidden for long. It was only luck that allowed us to pass through the first time."

Fritz yanked open her satchel and began to rummage about. "I might have something for that. Salve of the Owl; real useful stuff. Smear it on under your eyes, and you can see in the dark for hours. Ladies in some of the northern kingdoms have taken to using it as a fashion accessory, so I always keep a few bottles on hand."

"How much?" Gabrielle and Grumph both asked in unison. Thistle, Eric, and Timuscor looked aghast, while Ferdy and Talcia merely chuckled. Anyone who knew Fritz for more than a few hours knew to check the price before mentally making a purchase.

"Just this once . . . on the house," Fritz said, pulling free a large bottle filled with dark yellow liquid. "Grumph made me quite a few coins with his little show today. Think of this as his cut."

"That is very generous of you." Thistle's eyes lingered on the elven woman for a half-second longer than necessary, and he quickly pulled his gaze back to the table. There was something familiar about her, yet he was certain they'd never met. A mystery, no doubt, but one reserved for a time when they had less pressing concerns to deal with. "That still leaves us a slight logistical hurdle, however. The entry point where the tunnel lets up is quite high over the alcove where the door rests. Once they break it open, we'll have to make a charge that takes several minutes, during which we'll be completely exposed. This means we can be attacked, or the priest can slip through the doors and gain a vast head start. While we may not know exactly what lies behind the door, we can be certain that he will be easier to defeat before he finds it."

"Talcia and I can cast from a distance," Ferdy said, speaking for the first time since introductions. "One of us can start handling the undead as soon as you give the order. That takes them out of the equation even during the long run."

"As for slowing the priest, well, you're pretty good with those daggers," Gabrielle pointed out to Thistle.

"Good, but not nearly good enough to trust our entire plan to it." Thistle mentally conjured the interior of the caverns once again. Making those throws, even in the best of circumstances, would take the blessings of the gods. Under the conditions of battle, with everything hinging on him, even the gods might not have the necessary power. "We need to find a way to delay him. Otherwise, he'll vanish before we can reach the door."

"I have an idea." Grumph looked to Ferdy and Talcia, who both wore expressions of polite curiosity. "Already got a great delay," —he patted Gabrielle on her armored shoulder, causing a soft rustle of leather to echo through the smoked meat shop— "she just needs . . . traction."

*   *   *

In comparison to the multitude of plans that had been hatched throughout the history of their world, it was not a great one. In comparison to the ones created just in that year, it still fell pretty far short. In comparison to the drunken ravings of men soaked through with mead about how they would slay a dragon and become the new king, however, it was downright coherent.

As they crept into the caverns once more, Salve of the Owl smeared beneath each of their eyes, every member of the party knew their roles. Talcia and Ferdy were waiting for the signal that would come from Eric, who had the keenest eyes of the group, at which point they would both begin binding the undead until all were stopped. Then, Ferdy would keep the spells going while Talcia joined the others. Grumph and Thistle had the simple job of rushing forward when Eric gave the signal, sprinting downward headlong into danger, trusting the mages to contain the army of undead that would surely rip them apart if not subdued. Eric, of course, was to watch for an opening in the wall so he could give the all-important signal, and then join Grumph and Thistle in their near-suicidal charge. Timuscor would make the descent alongside Eric, ensuring that, if anything slipped past their first wave, the rogue still had some protection. Fritz planned to hang back, watch the show, and perhaps pick up a trinket or two from the bound corpses, though she didn't share this last part with the others.

Only Gabrielle had a unique role to play, and though she'd be waiting on the signal too, when she heard it, there would be no time to think. She would be leaping directly into the fray, which, truth be told, was exactly what she'd have requested if she were the one coming up with the plan.

All of that action would come at once, but until then, they were stuck waiting around for the wall to actually break. Once they reached the cavern where the tunnels connected, Eric went on ahead by himself to scout the situation. If things had changed or the priest was on watch, he had the best chance of making it in and out without tipping their hand. They had very little working in their favor so far; losing the element of surprise might cripple them completely.

Grumph settled into as soft a place as he could hope to find in a cavern and tried to rest. Between the time in bed, the healing, and the meal, he'd managed to regain a fair bit of his mana after the day's trials, though he was far from full capacity. Every minute he managed to relax and recharge meant another step closer to more spells, so despite the tense situation, he forced himself to stay calm and gain genuine rest.

Ferdy and Talcia seemed intent as they reviewed their spells, both closing their eyes and muttering under their breath as they mentally prepared for the coming battle. As sorcerers, they called forth magic in a different manner than the book-bound wizards, and while they lacked the expanded spell arsenal of said wizards, they more than made up for it with larger mana pools and versatility in combat.

Gabrielle sat at the far end of the cavern, gently pressing her hand to, and then pulling it away from her new axe. Each time, the pain greeted her, and with every gripping of the weapon, she grew more accustomed to it. When the battle started, she couldn't afford to be caught off guard by the magical burning across her fingers and palms. Even a second of hesitation could be the difference between life and death. With so much riding on her, the least she could do was wield her weapon well. Hopefully that would prove to be enough.

245

Thistle prepared in silence, as he usually did before they headed into a dangerous situation. He checked his daggers, tried to think through parts of the plan that might go awry, and braced himself for the very real possibility that this might be the adventure that killed him. Death was not a thing Thistle feared anymore, at least not on an intellectual level. After all, his service to Grumble essentially assured him the world after this one would be pleasant, and besides that, he dearly missed his wife. No, what scared Thistle was losing the others, or leaving them on their own. Without his healing, and perhaps a touch of guidance on needed occasions, they would be facing a far more difficult road ahead. So Thistle plotted, planned, and prayed that when the sun next rose, it would be on all of them, alive and well.

Timuscor watched the others going through their pre-battle rituals and considered tending to his—mostly just stretching and warming up a little so he didn't jump into a fight cold—but then changed his mind. Slipping off down one of the dead-end tunnels, Timuscor made his way carefully through the carved out sections of rock until he was far enough away that he hoped the others wouldn't be able to hear him. Digging his sword into the ground, he used it as leverage to slowly lower himself to his knees. It was the first time he could remember ever taking such a position, the slurry of his half-formed memories providing no prior occasions that he could recall. Releasing the sword and lowering his head, Timuscor began to whisper into the darkness.

"There is no god in particular that I dedicate this prayer to, though I have no interest in serving those of wicked or evil intentions. I am Timuscor, a knight of no small experience, a dedicated warrior, and a man who wishes to join the ranks of paladins. I am not a devout man, and I do not anticipate that changing any time soon. Even so, it has always been my dream to be a champion of virtue and decency. Thus, I offer my services to any of the righteous gods that will have me. I will not dedicate my life to you or your teachings. I will not put on false airs and act as though I have always been a devout man who has not made mistakes. I will not be a pawn in whatever godly games you might be playing. But I will do my part to make this world a better place. I will wield my sword against those who are cruel and dark, while protecting the innocent with my shield. I will fight, to my last breath, against those that would see evil done upon this world. If that is enough for you, any of you, then I will join your service. If you cannot welcome me as a paladin on those terms . . . well, then perhaps it is not the calling I thought it was."

Gripping his sword and pushing himself back up, Timuscor looked around the pitch-black tunnel he could still magically make out, waiting to see if any sign was coming from a particularly enterprising divine presence. Nothing happened, which lined up well with Timuscor's expectations, and he moved quickly back down the tunnel and into the cavern. There was no way to know if the gods had been listening, or even if they cared; yet Timuscor still felt better for having said the prayer. He'd laid his terms out in the open for any who were interested. He'd taken a genuine step toward his dream, and it felt unexpectedly freeing.

Timuscor entered the cavern only a few minutes before Eric emerged from his tunnel, eyes wide and breath just the slightest bit labored. He quickly motioned for everyone to gather around him, and the party wordlessly did as they were told. Within seconds, Eric was encircled by the motley arrangement of races and classes that comprised his group of friends. At last he began to speak, his words whispered and hurried.

"It's close. I mean, really close. I'm honestly not sure if we're going to have time to get everyone in position, but it's worth it to try. We need to move, though, starting right now." He paused, glancing around to make sure all were in attendance. "Anyone need to do anything or cast any spells? Once we step into that tunnel, it's all stealth and silence until they crack open the door."

Ferdy and Talcia both nodded, stepping over to Gabrielle and beginning to mutter different spells under their breath. They laid their hands upon her while the others started following Eric down the tunnel. There was no more time to rest or prepare. Soon, the bloodshed would begin, and each party member had no doubt that a fair share of the crimson liquid ultimately staining the ground would belong to them.

Chapter 29

Eric had not exaggerated the door's severely deteriorated condition. The constant, ceaseless pounding from a town's worth of undead villagers had taken a slow but steady toll. Looking on from their respective positions, even those with the weakest eyes could make out the large crack that had formed directly in the door's center, just underneath where the pillar was being driven into its alabaster face. Only Eric and Talcia could tell that it didn't go all the way through, however, meaning they still had a precious little amount of time to work with.

From the corners of his eyes, Eric kept track of the others' movements, hoping that they would be ready when the undead broke through to the other side. He dared not look away, even for an instant, for once the door was breached, every second they had would be crucial. Still, using peripheral vision and some mental mapping, he felt confident that nearly everyone was in position. Gabrielle was the only unknown, as, by virtue of her role, she was impossible to track. Despite the fact that she was the most important piece of their plan, she was also the only bit that no one could be sure was ready. All they could do was have faith that she'd manage.

A loud crash filled the air as a hunk of white rock broke off from the door and tumbled to the ground. The others tensed, ready for action, but Eric held up a hand to steady them. It was close, but they hadn't quite broken through yet. All they'd really managed to do was widen the crack to where a human-sized adult could pass through, whereas before, only Thistle would have been able to make it without contorting. Grumph was still going to have to duck and turn sideways unless they broke off more from the side, but the rest would be able to pass through easily. Eric considered that to be good and bad news, as it meant the evil priest tucked away somewhere in the shadows would have an easier time slipping in as well.

The undead went back to their work. The constant racket had started to cause a headache behind Eric's almost-unblinking eyes. He ignored the pain and focused on watching for a particular piece of movement. It was a skill he'd learned and perfected during his guarding days: a telltale rustling in the bushes, shadows scampering across a courtyard, all were signs of an impending goblin raid. Often, catching those small motions was the only way to gain any warning whatsoever, and Eric had worked tirelessly to learn to watch for them. Now, he pushed the rest of the world away and let the eroding door fill up the entirety of his mind, every chip, nick, and scratch carefully documented in his brain as they were being formed. Nothing went unnoticed. Then, after several more minutes of pounding, he finally saw what he'd been waiting for. The deepest section of wall within the crack splintered and began tumbling backward. Eric couldn't make out exactly what was on the other side, aside from a stone wall, but it was enough. He was seeing what lay beyond the door. The time for watching had come to an end.

Eric let out the loud, piercing whistle once used to alert the other guards of impending goblins. This evening, under the mountain adjacent to a deserted town, it signaled his friends that the way ahead was clear and the battle had begun.

*　　*　　*

It was not dignified, fun, or enjoyable for either adventurer, but necessity had demanded a compromise of dignity when the plan was being formed. Thus, as Grumph barreled forward, charred sword gripped firmly in his right hand, his left was clutched around the belt of Thistle, who swung to and fro in the half-orc's powerful grip. To his credit, Thistle didn't let the embarrassment of being handled like a child show on his face, focusing instead on the enemies' reactions and trying to figure out if the plan had gone awry yet.

All plans eventually fell apart; it was in their nature. Reality never complied with expectations, and one who expected plans to be pulled off perfectly was often left unprepared when chaos overtook the calculated order. By Thistle's estimates, the greatest strategists he'd ever met or seen could make a plan that lasted five steps. His own works, on the best of days, usually made it to three. Step One had been sneaking in and watching for the break in the door. Step Two was the mages binding the undead so they didn't swarm and murder everyone. Step Three was stopping the priest, ideally through non-lethal means, but given that he'd slain an entire village, no one would feel too bad about putting him down for good. Step Four was, of course, recovering whatever artifacts lay beyond the door, and Step Five was really hoping that Grumble gave them some direction, or the others came up with something. Thistle didn't imagine wandering between kingdoms as wanted fugitives holding a cache of cursed artifacts was a solid long-term strategy. He'd neglected to share Step Five with the others, for obvious reasons.

From what Thistle could see as Grumph hurtled across the rocky terrain, hurriedly driving them closer to the door and the hundred or so undead guarding it, Step Two seemed to be going well. Bright green light was wrapping around the townsfolk of Briarwillow en masse, pinning down whole groups of them, one after the other. Talcia and Ferdy were living up to their claims so far. Thistle made a mental note to write them a proper thank you letter if they, and he, managed to survive this insane errand.

As Grumph rounded another bend, putting him on the direct slope toward the door, a fresh figure finally came into view. He had simple gray clothing, a bag slung over his shoulder, and a wand gripped tightly in his right hand. In the left hand, so dark that Thistle almost didn't see it against the backdrop of shadow, was the skull. Even without having previously glimpsed it for himself, Thistle knew this had to be the item that had started Briarwillow's misfortunes: it seemed to pulse with dark energy, power rippling through the arcane runes etched across the black bone.

The priest looked at them and smiled. Despite seeing him head-on, the smile was the only thing Thistle could manage to make out on his face. He could see the other features, but in his mind, they instantly became muddled and unremarkable. Blade to his throat, Thistle couldn't have picked this man out of a crowd. It was all he could do to keep focusing on him as Grumph barreled closer. As they drew near, the priest lifted his wand and began to mutter under his breath. Thistle didn't know

250

what sort of divine power this servant of a wicked god was calling upon, but he had a feeling it wasn't going to be an enjoyable to experience. Step Three should have kicked in by now. If the plan had gone awry already, then this would be as far as they got. Thistle refused to look away from the man who was likely trying to conjure a hex of death as they sprinted toward him. He would be ready for when Step Three began.

Thistle would have faith in their barbarian.

*   *   *

Eric's whistle had come so suddenly that Gabrielle nearly went tumbling from the wall she was slowly climbing across. Only the magic of the spell and her reflexive grip kept her from going bouncing down the sheer edge of the vertical rock surface. Much as she wanted to swear under her breath at the signal coming before she was ready, Gabrielle instead focused on scrambling down as quickly and quietly as she could.

Having the mages use spells to make her invisible and able to climb rocks had seemed, in the moment . . . well, actually, the idea had struck Gabrielle as at least half-mad. For their group, though, half-mad wasn't so bad, which was why she'd agreed to her role in the plan. What she hadn't counted on, what certainly no one had anticipated, was that climbing down a wall was tough, spell or no. Doing the same task while invisible, unable to see where her hands and feet were going, compounded the effort tremendously. Ferdy's magic was certainly all that allowed her to climb into position unattacked, but it was also slowing her down. By the time Eric's signal finally came, she was close to being in position. Just not close enough.

Hustling across the slick surface, sticking to it only by the grace of Ferdy's wall-climbing spell, she began to prioritize speed over silence, especially since Grumph and Thistle were making a commotion as they began charging down the long, sloping path. She watched as the priest slowly rose to his feet from his seat on the ground, seeming more amused than bothered by the interruption. He plucked a wand from somewhere within his robes, but never once allowed the skull to leave his possession. A half-folded piece of parchment fluttered from his lap, knocked into the air as he stood. She had no idea what it was; she just hoped that it didn't dispel invisibility or climbing magic. Not that it would matter if she didn't hurry. Soon, Thistle and Grumph would be directly in his sights, at which point they'd be sitting ducks for whatever foul spells he called down from Kalzidar.

Angling herself diagonally so she drew nearer to his position while still getting closer to the ground, Gabrielle moved hand over hand as quickly as she could. All thoughts of stealth were gone from her mind as she scrambled to get to her target, the sounds of her movements easily covered by the wailing of the undead as they were blasted by binding magic. For a man losing his army, the priest seemed oddly unbothered. Indeed, as he raised his wand and began to mutter, aiming at Grumph and Thistle, who were now in plain view, he almost looked cheerful for the distraction.

There was no time left, and she wasn't nearly close enough to scurry down and mount any sort of attack, not before he'd be able to get off a shot or two at her friends. Gabrielle let the image of her friends being burned by some imaginary magic fill her mind, kindling the ever-ready anger that dwelled inside her. Even the mere idea of her friends being hurt made her angry, and she embraced that rage like a long-lost lover. Fury began to pump through her veins. She was going to need every scrap of it to get through the next few seconds. Her anger had proven a potent weapon many times before, and the way it helped her fight through pain and injury could not be overlooked.

Gabrielle just hoped she was angry enough to block out what was coming, because it was going to hurt like hell.

*   *   *

Nimble as he was, Eric couldn't match the head start or raw leg power of Grumph as the half-orc tore across the steep terrain. It was all the lithe rogue could do to catch up with Timuscor, whose heavy armor stole speed from his well-trained feet. The two men rounded the bend of the final slope well behind Thistle and Grumph, unintentionally giving themselves a spectacular view of what would be a very confusing few seconds for a cocky priest on the verge of finishing a spell.

On the wall directly above the priest, Gabrielle suddenly blinked into view as she drew her axe and kicked off from the rock she'd been magically bound to only seconds before. Even from as far away as he was, Eric could tell she was too high. Something had gone wrong; she hadn't had enough time or had gotten into the wrong position. Either way, this wasn't a fall she could roll through on landing and come out unscathed—all the more so because it was clear that she had no intention of trying to avoid injury. Gabrielle was coming down with all her weight on the blade of her axe, a dark-bladed weapon that was quite different from the one Eric had last seen her fight with. If it found its mark, the priest was going to be in for a very unpleasant surprise, but no matter how things went, Gabrielle was likely to crack a few bones on landing. Not the biggest issue, since Thistle could patch those up, except for the fact that she'd then be injured, possibly defenseless, and next to the priest of a wicked god whom she'd just hurt and pissed off.

Eric pushed his legs for all they were worth, sailing past Timuscor and closing the gap between himself and Grumph. They wouldn't arrive in time—that was impossible—but they might be able to make a difference.

If they hurried.

*   *   *

The pain in Gabrielle's hand seemed almost nonexistent as she leaned down on the axe, hair whipping past her face as she built up speed. Whether she hit or she didn't, it almost didn't matter at this point. Whatever the outcome, she was guaranteed to break this asshole's concentration, and that was all that really mattered. Of course, given that he'd killed an entire town and was likely trying to do the same to her friends, Gabrielle very much still wanted to hit him, so she shifted her angle slightly as she drew near. In a moment, she'd be on him; how true her strike would be was in the hands of fate.

Gabrielle expected the next thing she hit to be either the priest's flesh or the hard rocky ground, so she was taken by surprise when, only a few feet above his head, Gabrielle's axe was suddenly stopped by an opaque black shield that flickered into view. It sparked as the blade pressed against it, slowing her down without pushing her back. The priest started visibly, looking up at her in shock even as his lips continued mouthing the important words of the spell. She'd taken him by surprise, but the wily little fuck had been protected from the start. For an instant, their eyes locked, and his arrogant smile turned into a disdainful sneer.

The edges of Gabrielle's vision began to blur, and she became dimly aware of the taste of blood in her mouth. He was mocking her, laughing at her for not being strong enough. The kindled rage inside of her roared, building upon itself until it was a burning inferno. Gabrielle could barely think straight with how angry she was. Her fury wasn't even at the priest—though, given the chance, she'd gladly make him a recipient of it. No, Gabrielle was angry at herself. Everyone was counting on her, and she was going to fail them. She needed to be stronger. She would do anything to be stronger.

A sound like a champagne bottle being uncorked popped in her ears, and suddenly she was falling again. Her axe had torn through the opaque shield as though it were a piece of silk; it was already unraveling around her as she passed through the hole. It was hard to say for certain who was more shocked, the priest or Gabrielle, as the blonde in blood-red armor came bursting through the shield, axe first. Both were certainly caught off guard, but one was more experienced in dealing with the unexpected. As the priest allowed his purely instinctual reactions to take over, lifting his arm to block the falling woman, Gabrielle acted with intent, swinging her blade down with all the force her muscles and falling momentum could impart.

Gabrielle slammed into the ground first, knocking the air out of her lungs and at least bruising several of her ribs. She was followed immediately by the priest's arm, the rune-covered black skull still clutched firmly in its grip. From nearby, she could hear the thunderous

254

stomps of a half-orc running, meaning that her friends were almost there. She smiled through the pain, of which there was a significant amount, and muttered softly to herself:

"Step Three: complete."

Chapter 30

There is nothing in the world quite like seeing a limb lopped off. In his years of traveling with adventurers and the time spent afterward working as a minion for various would-be evil masterminds, Thistle had been fortunate enough only to witness such an event a handful of times. As Gabrielle smashed into the ground with a worrying thud, followed by the priest's left arm, Thistle was struck with both the sadness of seeing it happen once more and at the poetic irony that their enemy now lacked the necessary fingers to tick off Thistle's dismemberment count.

The priest stared at Gabrielle and his arm for a moment, dumbstruck by what had just happened. Thistle was a bit curious about that as well, since, last he checked, Gabrielle didn't have any items that could cut through magical shields. Pain seemed to finally beat out shock, and the priest let out a furious howl that sent a chill down the gnome's short spine. Quickly touching his wand to the stump, the priest stopped the bleeding and turned to face the charging half-orc with a savage look in his eye. That savage look turned immediately frantic as he realized he was trying to stare down a gods-damned charging half-orc with a blade in one hand and an armored gnome in the other, all while the remains of his magical barrier crumbled around him.

Grumph released Thistle with little warning, sending the diminutive paladin tumbling across the ground. Thistle used the momentum to propel himself back to his feet, pulling both daggers free from their sheaths and quickly reorienting himself through the slight dizziness of being chucked about. He'd landed only a few feet from a cluster of undead villagers who were illuminated by a glowing green light that seemed to have pinned them to the ground. Spinning on his heel, Thistle quickly spotted the priest, just as the one-armed man ducked Grumph's blade, muttering a spell as fast as he could.

"I think we'll have none of that." Thistle let fly with a dagger, scoring a glancing blow across the priest's torso. It certainly wouldn't bring him down, but it was enough to make him lose focus. Against an opponent like Grumph, such mistakes were costly, as became clear when the half-orc managed to slice a chunk of flesh from the priest's hip.

Thistle heard the others coming before he saw them sprint past, Eric several paces ahead of Timuscor, short sword already drawn, the armored knight bringing up the rear and ready to deal damage. He chanced a look at Gabrielle, who was stirring but didn't seem to be in any hurry to rise from the ground. Eric and Timuscor rushed to Grumph's aid, and in seconds, they had the priest surrounded, his back pressed to the same sheer rock wall that Gabrielle had scaled and leapt from. Thistle started to move forward so he could join them, but thought better of it. Aside from Gabrielle's painful fall, things were going almost perfectly to plan. Tempting as it was to join the others for what seemed like an easy victory, Thistle had seen too much to grow arrogant. When a battle seemed won, that was often the point when things went completely to Hell.

Almost as if the priest had been reading Thistle's mind, he dropped the wand, which vanished as soon as it left his hand, reached into the bag at his side, and hurled out what appeared to be folded pieces of parchment, screaming some gibberish word as he did. The air around the pages contracted and grew dark, then burst outward with such force that it knocked Eric backward.

Standing there, blocking the priest from Eric, Grumph, and Timuscor, were a pair of ten-foot-tall paper wolves, whose folded teeth and claws still looked plenty sharp. While the others' stares were locked on the parchment guardians, Thistle looked back at the priest, who seemed to have regained his smile in spite of being one arm short. His hand was once again clutching a wand, though it still hovered close to the bag from which he'd plucked his helpers. Thistle couldn't help but notice that the bag seemed *exceptionally* full.

He muttered a command word to summon back the dagger he'd already thrown. It seemed a good wager that he was going to need every weapon he could get. Before Thistle could choose between his targets, the priest struck first. The spell that emanated from his wand wasn't one of destruction or shadow, nor was it a hex. Instead, he struck with the most potent weapon available in a cavern of complete darkness.

The priest's wand lit up like the sun, flooding the room in light and utterly blinding almost everyone.

*   *   *

By virtue of busted ribs and slowly refilling lungs, Gabrielle was one of the few people staring at the ground when the blast of white light tore through the cavern. All she saw was a slight flash in the side of her vision, enough to let her guess what had happened without filling her dark-adjusted eyes with spots and tears. The priest was going to make a run for it; otherwise, he'd have used the chance to cast an offensive spell. Gabrielle didn't know exactly what his plan was, whether he was going to break for the door or try for an all-out escape, but she was certain of one thing: he was damned sure going to do it without his arm.

Ignoring the protests of her aching body, Gabrielle reached forward and gripped the limp elbow of the priest's severed arm. She pulled it closer to her, noticing that the skull was still firmly clutched in his lifeless fingers. Evidently, he'd really been holding on to the thing; even being parted from its body hadn't been enough to halt the hand's efforts. She'd only managed to drag the arm a few inches closer when another hand wrapped around it, this one pulling upward. Gabrielle was jerked partway up, bringing her gaze directly into that of the priest's. He didn't seem quite so cheerful or cocky now, as he tugged at the bloody appendage, staring down at Gabrielle with utter contempt. For a moment, she feared he was going to cast a spell, but then she realized he couldn't. Everything he'd thrown thus far had required hand motions or the use of a wand. With one arm chopped off and the other holding on to it, he was temporarily helpless.

Gabrielle, however, was under no such limitation. Pained as she was, it took almost no effort to lift the axe still clutched in her right hand. The priest's eyes darted back and forth between his limb and the blade that had done the severing, quickly doing the math. A barbarian's grip was no small obstacle, and while he might have been able to tug the arm free with enough time, every second he spent trying to wrest it from her clutches increased the risk of being hacked by her axe, and left him vulnerable to the others regaining their sight. With one last yank on his arm, the priest sneered at Gabrielle and released his grip. The sudden loss of his force sent her tumbling back toward the ground, but not before she was able to make out where he was heading.

It seemed the priest wasn't quite ready to call it quits, even after losing an arm and a skull, albeit the latter far less painfully. Rather than casting some sort of spell to teleport away or break out through the mountain to the outside world, he was darting past the bound undead, even leaping over them in some cases.

The last Gabrielle saw of him, the priest slipped through the break in the door and vanished.

*   *   *

Paper wolves, as it turned out, weren't as strong as their real-world counterparts. Nor did they hold up to being sliced nearly as well. The claws and teeth, however, were for far more than mere show, as Timuscor learned when they sliced across a piece of his leg not guarded by armor. His flesh instantly parted, sending blood streaming down his silver leg-piece, but he paid it no mind. Instead, he stepped to the side, taking one of the wolf's strikes on his shield and blocking Gabrielle from an attack she wasn't even able to see coming. This was his role, what he could do that none of the others could.

Timuscor pushed back on the wolf's leg, swinging down with his sword in the moment it lost balance. A large scrap of paper fell to the ground, followed by a few splatters of ink, and suddenly his opponent was down to three legs. It loped away from Timuscor, allowing its twin to take up the fight. Before it had a chance, Eric appeared, seemingly stepping out of nowhere and taking out the lower halves of the second wolf's hind legs with a single sweep of his short sword. It teetered backward, desperately trying to regain balance, but Timuscor seized the opportunity, rushing forward and driving his sword through its paper throat. He and Eric hacked the rest of its body to pieces, just to be on the safe side, and then turned to dispatch the remaining three-legged enemy.

They found Grumph standing next to a wrinkled, soggy mass of wet paper, holding a bucket that both were certain he hadn't brought with him. He'd taken his boots to the congealed mass and there was little left of it but ink and water running away from the remains in diluted rivers. Timuscor quickly spun about, searching for the priest so that they could finish their work, but the slippery son of a bitch had vanished in the commotion. All Timuscor spotted was Talcia, making his way slowly down the slope, Fritz a few feet behind, and Thistle bent over Gabrielle, hands resting on her back. As the gnome muttered a prayer under his breath, a soft light, unlike the fierce blast the priest had unleashed, began to glow across her. Moments later it stopped, and Gabrielle rose to her feet, axe in one hand and severed arm in the other.

"He went through the door." Even after the healing, Gabrielle's words seemed half-choked as she struggled to get air moving in her lungs. "Fucker tried to take the skull back, too."

"The skull . . . you mean the one that makes everyone around it sick and flat-out kills anyone who touches it?" Eric asked.

Everyone but Thistle took an involuntary step back as they remembered just what the artifact only a few feet away from them was fabled to do. Gabrielle stared down at it, a fleeting look of panic dashing through her eyes, but then calmed down and gave a noncommittal shrug.

"Technically, the priest is still the one touching it. That's got to count for something."

"Perhaps, but the proximity effects aren't likely to be so easily skirted," Thistle reminded her. He turned slowly, taking stock of his party as they recovered. Spotting the wound on Timuscor's leg, Thistle quickly marched over and laid a hand on it.

Timuscor felt a surge of warmth, almost like a hug for his soul, and the pain was suddenly gone, like it had never been there at all. He'd seen the gnome heal others before, but this was the first time he'd ever experienced such power firsthand. It was nothing like he'd expected and only hardened his resolve to one day wield it for himself.

"We have a hard choice to make," Thistle said, turning back to the others. "Right now, there's a chance that if we ditch the skull and run, we might not have been around it long enough to fall sick. But if we do that, then the asshole that used it to kill a town is going to get his hands on whatever lays through that door, uncontested. We can chase him, but it means a higher chance of the skull's curse hitting us, to say nothing of what other horrible magic was walled off behind that door. I have to go—you all know that—but you each have a choice. Make it quick, though; every moment we spend out here gives him more time to find whatever he's looking for."

"I already got one arm; kind of feel like going for a matched set." Despite her words, Gabrielle lowered the appendage to the ground, clearly eager to put some distance between the skull and herself.

"We fight together." Grumph's voice echoed off the stone walls around them, making him seem all the more imposing.

"I'm with Grumph," Eric said. "Since the beginning, we've been in this together. May as well fight magical diseases with one another."

"I will always follow." Timuscor meant every letter of his few words, for he truly would walk with these crazy people to the ends of the earth if needed. There were no words for why; he couldn't put such a complex sentiment into something conveyable. All he knew was that ever since he had met them, it was the first time he'd truly felt alive. Everything before was murky and unreal, as though someone else had been guiding him around. Being with these four made him feel free, and that was something Timuscor would gladly die for if the need demanded it.

"Though I doubt you were really talking to me, there is no way I'm letting such a historical find pass by without exploring it," Talcia said.

"And I'm here to loot everything that's not nailed down," Fritz declared. "Looks like there's a lot of non-nailed stuff in there."

"Then we go now," Thistle told them. "Can Ferdy keep up the undead binding?"

"He had it well in hand when I left. Plus, it might not be bad to have him come down and stand guard over that." Talcia nodded to the skull, which somehow seemed to be smiling more than a fleshless face normally did.

"Call him down, then." With that, Thistle began walking briskly between the undead, making a beeline right for the entrance.

Timuscor was about to call out for him to stop, in case the priest was waiting inside to ambush them, but he realized Thistle already knew that was a possibility. The gnome was purposely putting himself in danger to make sure the others would have forewarning. Moving quickly, his once-cut leg now bearing weight effortlessly, Timuscor hurried to catch up. He couldn't very well stop a paladin from standing in harm's way, but he could stand beside him. Perhaps, if the gods were kind, Timuscor might be able to shield or help him, even a little bit.

Behind them, the others followed suit, plunging into the unknown as they carefully squeezed through the broken door.

*   *   *

Russell carefully laid out the figurines on the dry erase map, keeping to the diagram in his module perfectly. The fights so far had been wonderful ballets of constructed combat, and he'd found a healthy degree of respect for whatever author had planned them out so perfectly. In every encounter, there was a very real chance of death, yet a party with enough tactical sense, and perhaps a touch of luck, could emerge unscathed. Of course, things were getting tougher now that they'd reached the tower; the myriad of monsters defending the front door was a testament to that. Still, he'd skimmed the pages, and if his players kept

262

up the level of fighting they had so far, they stood a good chance of pulling off a victory.

"We're finally here," Tim muttered, watching from his seat as what lay before Timanuel and the others was placed into existence. "Just have to break in, and we'll be set."

"That's a lot to break through," Bert reminded him. "I'm just glad Wimberly took the time to build plenty of her mobile rolling-bombs." The large man glanced down at his character sheet and was clearly struck by a realization as he skimmed his inventory. "Hey, Russell, this Earhorn of Whispers I found a while back, am I allowed to use it to listen to what's going on inside the tower?"

"Technically, yes." Russell laid down the last metal figurine and sat back in his chair, quickly consulting the module book to make certain his answer was correct. Technically, as Game Master, he always had the right to overrule something he felt hindered play, but the items his players had picked up were well-balanced, and thus far had only served to keep things a bit more interesting. "As long as you point it at the tower and jam the other end in your ear, you get a check. It's going to be a high one, though, fair warning."

"May as well go for it." Bert tossed a die across the table, where it bounced several times before coming to a rest next to Cheri's glass of soda.

"Ten," Cheri informed them, before rolling the die back across to Bert.

"Which, with my bonuses, adds up to eighteen." Bert caught his D20 and set it back in the pile with the other matching dice in his set.

"Ouch, close, but no cigar," Russell said, skimming the book's page. "You'd have needed a twenty to make out even whispers, and that's the last shot you're getting. I mean, unless you want to burn a round of combat."

"Screw that, Wimberly has traps to set," Bert announced.

263

Russell flipped back through the module to where the battle was set up, moving away from the page detailing what was needed to hear inside the tower. Had Bert made the check, then Russell would have turned to the next page and perhaps gone a bit pale upon reading the description. The mages inside were, according to the module's current text, discussing what to do, if anything, with the strange artifact they'd gathered together to study. Though they had yet to touch or activate it, their studies indicated it had curious properties that might influence the world around them, though they weren't sure how.

One mage did have a working theory, however. He thought this artifact seemed to be linking to worlds other than theirs . . . almost as if it were some sort of bridge.

Chapter 31

Passing through the door, or rather the crack in its center, was like stepping into a new world. No longer was the party surrounded by crudely carved tunnels and haphazard caverns. The walls in this new place had been built with care, intricate designs woven into the white rock, not unlike those upon the door that had barred them from the catacombs. Along the tops of the walls stood chiseled torches that burned with blue flames and cast flickering light across the tiled stones in the floor.

Eric held his breath as he entered, waiting for a spell from the priest or some unseen trap to suddenly strike, killing or wounding them while they were all bunched together. Neither came, and for a moment, Eric allowed himself to feel relieved. Then his gaze traveled forward, noting that the short hallway came to an abrupt end branching into three tunnels, each with torches burning down as far as his eyes could see. There was nothing else to see, no other clue as to which way they should go—nor, as might have been more useful, which way the priest traveling ahead of them had already gone.

"Seems we're supposed to pick a direction," Talcia observed, he and Fritz being the last to make it through the crack.

"Ordinarily, that would have been the prudent move, but I'm afraid prudence is not a luxury the time-strapped can afford." Thistle looked the group over, his eyes darting back and forth so quickly that Eric could practically see the wheels in his small head turning. "Finding whatever is hidden here is goal number three, catching the priest goal number two, and, obviously, surviving is goal number one. Best chance at two of those is to split into three groups. We need a capable warrior in each, along with someone who has at least a passing familiarity with magic. So, Gabrielle, Eric, and Fritz will take the tunnel to the left. Timuscor and Talcia will go up the middle, leaving Grumph and me to take the tunnel to the right."

"Why are we in the group with three?" Gabrielle asked. Even as she spoke, Eric knew she already had to be aware of the answer. Thistle had done a quick patch job on her, but their barbarian was far from at full strength. It was amazing she was even able to walk around after the fall she'd taken; asking her to carry the full weight of combat was too much.

"Because we had uneven numbers, and you're the only one hurt so far." Thistle wasn't cruel about the answer, but he didn't bother pulling punches either. Gabrielle took the answer silently, though the scowl on her brow spoke scrolls' worth.

It was possible she might have fought him more, but with time working against them, there was no chance for discussion. Thistle had scarcely managed to get the orders out before Timuscor and Talcia were heading for the center tunnel. Grumph began to move too, and Thistle hurried to catch up. Eric was quickly left standing alone with a fuming barbarian and an elven trader who, he noticed, was trying to pry one of the stone torches off the wall.

"What are you doing?"

"Torch that never runs out of fire is pretty useful to a lot of folks. I can get at least a hundred gold or so for this." Fritz gave a firm tug—which failed to so much as rattle her prize—before giving up and letting go. "Unfortunately, it looks like whoever made this place knew that. The thing is really jammed in there."

"Let's go." Gabrielle, it seemed, was done taking slight and had decided the best way to show everyone up was to get the job done. She cut a brisk pace toward the left, moving so fast that Eric and Fritz had to break into light jogs to close the gap between themselves and her. The axe she'd come back with was tightly gripped in her hand, ready for use at the slightest provocation. A dozen questions rested on Eric's tongue, stopped only by the forceful closing of his lips. He wanted to know where she'd gotten it, how it had cut through that magical shield, and why he'd seen her wince when gripping it. All of that would have to wait, though. At the moment, the only things that mattered were finding what was inside this place and making sure the evil priest didn't get his scheming hands on it.

Well, scheming "hand," actually. Eric chuckled to himself at the piece of dark humor. Good-hearted as he was by nature, seeing the thralled corpses of over a hundred innocent people had removed any sense of empathy he might have felt for the villain in gray robes.

*   *   *

Kalzidar, in his divine wisdom, bestowed upon his devout followers the ability to block out large amounts of pain. This was done less as a kindness—after all, he wasn't really *that* kind of god—and more as a necessity. Those who worshipped evil gods tended to be self-serving, meaning they were prone to betraying others of their ilk if it would save them from pain and torture. Dulling their sensations of injury allowed them to withstand such circumstances, and thus helped evil flourish. Of course, there were limits to what a blanket blessing bestowed on his servants was able to do, a fact the priest was realizing as he skittered down the stone hallway, trying to ignore the throbbing pain in the stump where his arm was supposed to be.

He didn't know how that bitch with the axe had cut through his shield, and the charred, broken remains of the talisman that had conjured it weren't giving him many clues to work with. In the span of a few minutes, he'd gone from being the leader of an undead army, protected by a magical barrier he'd spent weeks crafting, to a one-armed fugitive desperately trying to fulfill his god's wishes before a group of do-gooder adventurers came to claim the rest of his limbs.

His hand hovered near the bag still stuffed with folded paper creations. Tempting as it was to unleash them on his pursuers, he might as well be leaving hand-painted signs that told them which way he was going. Better to save attacking for when the time demanded it. So long as he could stay hidden and ahead of them, he had a better chance at uncovering the treasures hidden in the tomb. Once those were in his grasp, he'd once again have the advantage.

And this time, he was going to tear them apart before they even had a chance to react.

*　　　*　　　*

Timuscor and Talcia said little as they hurried down the stone hallway. Torches were always burning, no matter the twists and turns their path took them on. Idly, Timuscor wondered if they'd been lit ever since this place was constructed, or if the act of entering these catacombs had somehow activated them. Magic made no more sense to him than the softly muttered ramblings of a drunkard, so he'd have taken either explanation at face value, had Talcia offered it. However, since Timuscor never bothered to ask such a question, Talcia naturally didn't provide an answer.

Instead, the elven mage held his staff out, mumbling words on occasion and sending a pulse of light racing ahead. It seemed to do nothing, as they could already see up to their next turn, but with each successful pulse of light, Talcia looked relieved . . . at least until he cast it again. After the fourth iteration of such an event, Timuscor could hold his tongue no longer.

"We can already see just fine."

"Of course we can." Talcia sounded like he was humoring a child, answering in agreement to an obvious statement that they both knew was true.

"Then why do you keep trying to light the way?"

"Light the . . . ohhhh, I see your confusion. No, my boy, this is not a spell to merely throw a bit of light. I'm casting a minor incantation to illuminate any sources of potential danger ahead. Hidden traps, magical runes, anything of that sort will glow if hit by my spell."

"That seems quite useful."

Talcia shot the armored man a wink before raising his staff once again. "Some of us in the guild got our experience the old-fashioned way: by doing stupid things like raiding ancient vaults for clearly cursed items. It paid to have a few utility spells under my belt." He began to cast once more, holding the end of the incantation until they turned the next corner before releasing his spell forward into the new area before them.

It flew forward as before, but this time, it quickly widened, as, after only a few feet, the tunnel opened up into a massive square room. It was filled with decorative tiles across the floor, walls, and ceiling, with nothing inside save for a single exit at the other end of its sizable expanse. Just as Talcia and Timuscor were registering how vast the space before them was, the spell hit, and everything lit up like a winter bonfire. Every single tile began to glow, flickering as Talcia's spell ran over them.

The two men stood there, dumbfounded by their predicament, as the spell came to an end and the final tiles joined their brethren in the illuminated display. No surface was unstained by the magical glow, leaving Talcia and Timuscor with quite the problem.

Going forward meant passing through an entire room full of traps, and going back meant possibly letting their quarry get away. Slowly, the sound of his heavy armor rattling with every movement, Timuscor turned from the room to face Talcia.

"I don't suppose you have a spell for this, too?"

*   *   *

"It strikes me that perhaps you left out some details when telling of the time you spent in Cadence Hollow." There was no accusation in Thistle's tone; such emphasis would have been pointless with Grumph. The two had known each other far too long to bother with petty sniping. Thistle was merely stating an observation; how Grumph responded was up to him.

"We were in a hurry."

"Aye, that we were, old friend. Tell me this, though; do you know where Gabrielle got her new weapon from?" Though Grumph was going at a moderate pace, Thistle jogged alongside his friend to keep up. The option of being carried was, of course, still viable, but outside of an emergency, the gnome couldn't bring himself to bear such indignity.

"No," Grumph admitted. "I was training."

"Perfectly understandable, given the task you had to accomplish, though I do wish we knew more. The way it cut through that shield was, well, fascinating, to put it mildly." Thistle kept his tone neutral, but in truth, he was bothered by far more than the blade merely breaking through a barrier. When it had done so, for just the briefest of instants, he'd felt a surge of nausea in his gut. Admittedly, his stomach was already churning from being so close to cursed artifacts and a priest of Kalzidar, yet he was certain the sensation had increased in that moment, if only for a heartbeat. That matter, unfortunately, would have to wait until they managed to finish the task at hand and, hopefully, escape the damned mountain.

A turn in the tunnel led them to an open room, occupied only by what seemed to be a makeshift altar. Thistle threw up his hand the moment it came into view, stopping Grumph from going forward before he had laid so much as a toe in the room. Thistle could just make out an exit on the other side, but he was under no illusions that reaching it would be quite that easy.

"Trap?" Grumph rumbled.

"Almost has to be, doesn't it?" Thistle stepped carefully forward, still holding up his hand to keep Grumph from moving, and laid a tentative foot on the room's floor. His breath held in his chest as his small heart hammered so hard he could feel it in his ears. Thistle thought he saw a flicker on the altar, but it was gone so fast he felt unsure. Walking carefully, one step at a time, he went further into the room, all the while expecting to activate a hidden trap or encounter some monstrous beast. Instead, he was greeted by a very sizable amount of nothing.

Thistle weighed his options as he slowly lowered his hand. It seemed as though they could pass through here unaffected, which should be a good thing. Perhaps the priest had come this way and already tripped whatever trap had lain in wait. But there were no scratches, scorch marks, blood, or corpses to attest to any sort of fight. It didn't add up, and a tickle in Thistle's brain demanded he try and make sense of this. Perhaps it was worth a few minutes to examine the one clue they had to work with: the altar.

Thistle approached it just as Grumph stepped past the threshold, and this time, he was certain he saw a flicker run across its white stone surface. Again, though, that was all that came. Thistle couldn't imagine someone had constructed this labyrinth sealed behind a door and hidden in a mountain all to make one of the traps be a very brief light show. It was possible that time had weakened whatever was set up, but given how well the rest of the area had been preserved, Thistle rated that as low in probability.

Stepping all the way up the altar, and only realizing as he got within touching distance that perhaps the flicker had been the lure to draw him in and he was about the spring the trap on himself, Thistle pushed ahead and leaned down, examining the markings carved expertly in the stone surface. Most of it appeared to be either runes or a language so long forgotten it might as well be gibberish to him, but one symbol stuck out. Carefully crafted at it was, the drawing held a cursory association with one he recognized. Given the age of the piece, though, that was unlikely to be a fault of the artist. After all, symbols, like language, changed and evolved over time—even a symbol of something as simple as a broom strapped to a dagger.

"Well, this explains a bit." Thistle leaned away from the altar and looked over at Grumph, who was staring at him, patiently waiting for something resembling an explanation. "I could be wrong, of course, but I feel fairly certain that this is an altar to Grumble."

"Here?" It was hard to discern the tone of doubt in the half-orc's rough voice, but Thistle picked it up easily as he noted the skeptical expression on Grumph's face.

"Yes, here. In fact, I think this room is very likely trapped or warded to the high heavens, but you and I didn't set it off because of what we are." Thistle moved away from the altar, brain buzzing as it incorporated this new information into what he already knew. Deep within the depths of his mind, a picture was beginning to take shape. He hadn't bothered noting it before, but this vault was incredibly well made, as if it had been done by those with ample experience building such places.

"A paladin and a wizard?"

"No: a gnome and a half-orc who have both spent their time under the boot heels of others. At one point or another in our lives, we have both served as minions." Thistle jerked a thumb back to the altar, which sat quietly, summoning no terrible guardians or calling down ancient curses. "This is only conjecture, but I think this room is meant to be a screen, not a wall. Only certain people are supposed to get through."

Grumph didn't bother asking out loud for an explanation. He simply raised a bushy eyebrow and waited for Thistle to get to the point.

"I am beginning to think that the people who turned our mystery man into a skull, and the people who sealed whatever lays inside here are not one and the same," Thistle said. "This place was never meant to be opened. It isn't a treasure chest waiting to be uncovered; it's a tomb."

"For whom?"

"That is the question, isn't it, old friend." With a quick step, he headed toward the exit door, Grumph quickly following pace. Thistle hadn't thought it possible to be more motivated to hurry than when chasing a priest of Kalzidar seeking unknown magical items, but it turned out there was one thing that could put more spring in his step than even that dire situation.

272

The one thing that could move Thistle like nothing else was answers.

*   *   *

"Fuck me." Gabrielle stared across the chasm—a hundred feet long if it was an inch—and the slender stone bridge that ran its length. Navigating such an obstacle would have been tough enough when considering the glinting spears at the bottom of the drop waiting to be soaked in blood. But the swinging blades suspended on chains slicing across the bridge at irregular heights and intervals made it functionally impossible.

"Now would be a really good time for more wall-climbing magic," Fritz said.

"Actually, not sure that would help." Eric pointed over to the walls separated by the yawning pit and dancing blades, drawing the elven trader's attention to the dozens of small, razor-like bits of metal jutting out from the stone surface.

"By the gods . . . someone really doesn't want people to get past this part, do they?"

"Unfortunately, I don't think it was enough." Gabrielle gestured forward, where, after a few seconds of searching, the others saw what she was staring at.

There, stuck on one of the swinging blades midway down the bridge, was an unmistakable piece of shorn gray cloth. The priest had come this way, and worse, he'd made it past the obstacle, which meant they were going to have to do the same.

Even if they didn't have the damnedest idea as to how.

Chapter 32

"Are you sure this will work?"

"'Sure'? Sure seems like an awfully certain word for what we're trying here. I'm hopeful, though. That good enough for you?"

It really wasn't, but Timuscor didn't bother telling Talcia that. After all, they had so few options. "Hopeful" would have to do. It was better than certain death, so there was that to be said for their plan, but Timuscor couldn't help thinking mages were supposed to be a bit more skillful than this. Talcia's idea had merit, certainly, but it came up completely lacking when checked for grace or subtlety.

"Okay, as soon as I summon the boars, you take off running," Talcia instructed. "I've enchanted your speed as high as I can, so if we're really lucky, you'll be moving too fast to be caught in any of the traps you inevitably spring. Meanwhile, I'm enchanted to weigh as much as a handful of feathers, so I'll just hang on for the ride."

"Explain to me again why we're murdering a bunch of pigs," Timuscor demanded.

"We're not . . . the pigs aren't real, okay? They're just magical shells in the shape of boars, same as with most summoning spells. As soon as they take too much damage, they'll vanish back into mana. And we're 'killing' them because they're the advance guard. They run ahead, hopefully setting off most of the traps before you get there, meaning we have a safer journey as tiles reload."

Timuscor shrugged his shoulders, a motion which sent Talcia, who was gripping onto them with both hands, tumbling about. "Still seems cruel, but if you insist."

"Seeing as neither of these spells last very long, I'm afraid I have to do just that," Talcia replied. He raised one hand, gesturing in the air as words fell furiously from his mouth. With a snap of his fingers and a hurried motion to grab back onto Timuscor's shoulders, the spell was done. Seconds later, a sounder of boars erupted from nowhere, appearing just past the line marking the end of the tunnel and the start of the room. They hit the ground running, and it was a good thing they did, as chaos immediately began to burst forth all around them.

"Go!" Talcia needn't have bothered with the command; Timuscor was already bolting forward, careful to stay behind the boars without getting too close to them. It was a smart strategy, as their stampede was triggering blasts of fire, flurries of arrows, whipping vines bursting forth from the ground, swords dropping from thin air, and more manners of potential death than Timuscor could even pay attention to. He quickly stopped trying to catalog them and focused on avoiding the multitude of obstacles instead.

The boars, in what was a shocking turn of events, so far as Timuscor was concerned, were actually proving to be quite helpful. Every trap they sprang stayed in place for at least a few seconds, giving Timuscor time to charge through or around it while the magic reloaded. Additionally, the creatures were cutting such a rapid pace for themselves that few of the deadly explosions or attacks were managing to hit them. By the time they, and soon after, Timuscor, made it halfway across the room, it seemed as though they were going to get to the other side easily.

That was right about when the boar in the lead on the far left stepped on a tile and was suddenly suspended in a giant glacier of ice which spanned several other tiles and nearly engulfed another boar's leg. The one who had suffered a near miss swerved to the side, dodging more traps like before, and then vanishing in a cloud of mana as a massive explosion burst forth from under it.

"What the hell!" Timuscor jumped to the side; he hadn't even been close to the boar, but the explosion was so large he could feel the heat on his face.

"I guess whoever made this accounted for the possibility that someone might try to just race through. Seems some of the tiles are meant to be undodgeable." Talcia sounded remarkably calm, though, if

275

Timuscor had been able to turn his head back and look, he'd have seen the elf was several shades paler than he had been only moments before.

Another boar suddenly found itself under a veritable waterfall of swords, letting out a single sharp squeal before mercifully dissolving into energy. There were only two left, and unless Timuscor was mistaken, the remaining duo seemed far less enthusiastic than they had when the charge began. On the upside, they were nearly three-quarters of the way through the room. On the downside, at the rate they'd been losing pigs, Timuscor would soon be racing along solo.

"Do you have a plan or something?" Timuscor yelled, striving to be heard over the swarm of arrows that had appeared in midair and turned another boar back to mana. The lone pig grunted harshly, and then lowered its head and hurtled forward, charging for all it was worth.

Talcia leaned over, putting his mouth only a few inches from Timuscor's ear, and screamed to be heard over the explosions roaring behind them. "FUCKING RUN!"

This plan, at least, Timuscor didn't need explained to him. Forgetting about staying behind the boar, he pumped his legs, putting every ounce of muscle he could into upping his already magically-augmented speed. There was no more strategy or observation. All that was left was to try and accomplish the impossible: to outrun every fiery, sharp incarnation of death this room could throw at him.

Timuscor was dimly aware of metal bounding off his armor, heat burning from the side, and something grabbing at his ankle, but he paid none of it any mind. Injuries could be healed, so long as they survived. A moment's hesitation, a stray thought aside from just running, and everything would be lost. His legs ached and his lungs burned, yet Timuscor dared not slow down. A few feet ahead of him, the final boar sank out of sight as a swamp of thick, dark goo suddenly appeared beneath its hooves. There was still time for Timuscor to dodge it, but doing so would mean sacrificing precious, precious speed that he didn't have the stamina to regain, not to mention sending him careening around to untested areas. If he'd focused very hard on footwork, he might have successfully redirected his momentum and made it around the swamp.

But Timuscor never even tried. In truth, it was only afterward, when he was in midair, that the thought would occur to him. For Timuscor, set as he was on going forward at any cost, never slowed down as he neared the swamp of the strange, thick goop. Instead, he ran faster, putting every last bit of strength he had in his legs. When at last he reached the final step before he'd go plunging into that dark liquid, Timuscor leapt for all he was worth.

It was a valiant effort—powerful strength combined with an earnest heart to propel him further and higher than he'd ever jumped before. That said, Timuscor was still just a man, and a man in heavy metal armor at that. As soon as his feet left the ground, it was apparent he'd fall short. Below him, the dark goop bubbled and shimmered, almost as though it was waiting for him.

With no time to think—an act that would only have been a hindrance to a man like Timuscor—the knight reached over his shoulder, grabbed Talcia by the wrist, and hurled the elf forward like he was tossing a sack of grain onto a pile. The sorcerer, already a slender man made exceptionally lightweight by his spell, whipped through the air, flying well over the remaining tiles and slamming onto the floor of the tunnel that marked the room's exit. Timuscor, satisfied that at least one of them had made it, closed his eyes as his descent began, waiting for the sickening splash as he fell into the goop.

In place of a splash, he was treated to an earsplitting clatter as his armor collided with hard stone. Slowly opening his eyes—first the right, followed by the left—Timuscor looked around to find that the swamp had vanished. He rose slowly to his feet, waiting for another trap to spring, but none did. Movement came from his left, and Timuscor spun around, hand on the hilt of his sword, only to find the final boar ambling about, hacking up wads of the black goop that vanished when they hit the ground.

"How in the nine hells did you know someone making it to the exit would deactivate the traps?" Talcia stared at him from the ground where he'd landed, not daring to move lest he accidently turn the room back on.

"I . . . um . . . lucky guess?" Timuscor finally pulled himself together enough to accept that he wasn't dead, and that, if he left the tiled floor quickly enough, he might be able to stay that way. On impulse, he whistled for the boar to follow him as he headed for the exit, which the wild pig did, albeit with a healthy amount of snorts and grunting.

"Damn good guess." Talcia pulled himself up from the ground as Timuscor and the boar stepped into the tunnel. He considered dismissing his sole remaining summons, but decided against it. Mana spent was mana spent, and they might find a use for it before the spell's time ran out.

Timuscor only nodded, then reached down and scratched the boar behind the ears. He was still in something of a shocked state, going from certain death to tentative safety in such a short span of time. Plus, unlike Talcia and his joy, Timuscor was haunted by a worry that was growing louder by the moment.

When it was time to leave, how on earth were they going to get back through that room?

*   *   *

"Both of you are completely insane, you know that, right? I mean, when we ambushed the bandits in the forest and Grumph volunteered to be the bait, I sort of suspected you might all be a touch off, but this . . . this is a whole new level of madness."

"How do you have the strength to talk?" Eric asked, working hard to make his jaw unclench. Every muscle in his body was aching, and they were only halfway through the trek.

"Fritz has a gift," Gabrielle grunted. Despite the added weight of her armor, she was actually holding up the best of the lot, having worked

278

so hard on arm and hand strength that her task was, while not easy, certainly within the realm of doable.

The two adventurers and lone trader hung upside down from the rail-thin stone walkway they'd been meant to pass over. Its leanness, no doubt intended to be an extra difficulty to overcome as one dodged around swinging blades, also made it possible for a determined, somewhat suicidal traveler to wrap their legs around it and pull themselves across from underneath, inching forward a bit at a time.

It had been Eric's idea, thrown out more as a joke than a real possibility, but Gabrielle had leapt upon it almost as quickly as she hurled herself onto the walkway and flipped down to its underside. With the priest so close by, there was no chance she was going to let him get away.

One plus of the method was that it took the swinging blades almost entirely out of the equation. Low as many of them went, none came so far down as to hit the gripping feet or hands, even if it didn't always feel that way while they shuffled underneath them. Of course, the trade-off was that crossing in such a manner was physically exhausting, even for those in relatively good shape. Before they'd even made it to the halfway point, all three were dripping in sweat from the constant physical exertion. This made keeping a grip tougher, which in turn made it all the harder to move with each passing inch, which tired them out even more in a circle of torture that, had it been the architect's intention, would have been sheer genius.

As Gabrielle reached forward, sliding herself along beneath the path of yet another swinging blade, she struggled against the dull ache in her left side. Thistle's healing had gotten her back on her feet, but it was either going to take several weeks or more magic before the effects of her fall were entirely removed. Pushing herself forward, she ignored the throbbing from her ribs. Blocking out pain was a talent she was quickly cultivating into a skill, one she had suspected would require mastery sooner or later.

The trio inched along, Fritz following Gabrielle, and Eric in the rear, boxing the elf in just in case she lost her grip. It had sounded noble when Eric suggested the lineup, but as they passed the halfway mark and drew closer to the three-quarter point, Eric was fairly certain all he'd be able to do if Fritz fell was perhaps tilt his head and watch her descent. All the reflexes in Solium couldn't make up for the fact that it was taking every ounce of his strength just to hang on. Thankfully, Fritz seemed to be having an easier time than he, her lithe body no doubt less burdensome to haul across the chasm. Eric simply focused on the motions he had to make, blocking out the constant noise of the blades swinging overhead and the twinkling of the spear tips in the darkness beneath him. All that existed were his hands and legs, tugging his body forward bit by bit. After a while, he fell into a rhythm, and the strain on his limbs began to grow more bearable.

In fact, Eric got so lost in his rhythmic movement that he failed to realize Fritz had stopped. It only entered his awareness when he reached forward to grab the beam and instead wrapped his hand around Fritz's slender leg. She yelped, kicking her leg slightly, and he quickly released the grip. For a moment, both of them hung there, panic trying to loosen their holds on the precious stone beam. Each was ultimately able to gain firm grips once again, and as soon as she had hers, Fritz whipped her head around to face Eric as best she was able.

"What the hell?"

"Sorry, I got lost in my thoughts," Eric admitted. Now that his focus was broken, the weariness in his arms and legs came shooting to the forefront of his mind. He could feel his fingers trying to shake and willed them to stay steady for just a bit longer.

"Well, cut it out. We can't afford for anyone's focus to stray. Not in this place." Gabrielle, unlike Fritz and Eric, spoke from an upright position, as she'd finished hauling herself onto the platform at the rail's end. This was why Fritz had stopped, and as Eric glanced at the beautiful, life-sustaining platform, he felt new strength flow to his hands. With salvation in sight, he wouldn't let his life come to an end here.

280

With Gabrielle standing, it only took moments for her to haul Fritz off the beam. Eric quickly followed, alternating between rubbing one hand with the other every few seconds as soon as his grip was allowed to be broken. There was little to see on the new platform; it looked essentially identical to the one they'd stood on across the chasm. All that mattered was the doorway leading into a new section of tunnel, one where they knew the priest had a significant head start on them.

Wordlessly, Gabrielle drew her axe and motioned for the others to follow. She took off at a jog, hurrying onward toward her quarry. Eric followed quickly, with Fritz bringing up the rear. After a few feet, they took a turn and the room of blades and death was out of sight, as if it had never been there at all.

The only reminders of their ordeal were their sore limbs and the swooshing sound of swinging blades that followed them down the tunnel's depths.

Chapter 33

After several minutes of walking, Thistle and Grumph once more emerged in a room. This time, however, there was no altar in the center, nor was it full of trapped tiles and swinging blades. Instead, the room was bare, save only for more torches and three other doors. Above each was a single symbol, and as Thistle turned around, he noticed the tunnel they'd emerged from bore a marker as well: a simple drawing of a sun.

"Ours leads to the surface." He turned, noting each of the other three symbols as he did. One was of a sword, the second of a shield, and the third of a book. "What do you think, old friend? Challenges, or rewards?"

"Maybe both." Grumph stared at the etchings carefully, trying to discern something from their design that might give away what lay at the end of each tunnel. No amount of squinting or head tilting revealed anything of note, however. The drawings were so crude that there was no detail to discern. They simply were what they were: a sword, a shield, and a book.

"Offense, defense, and magic. Or maybe it's strength, stamina, and intellect. Perhaps it's literal in that we'll simply find a sword, shield, or book at the end of each path." Thistle frowned; while this no doubt made a fine riddle to confuse those who were treasure-hunting, it didn't help him, since he had no idea what he was even looking for. The only clue already given was the altar they'd passed, hinting that perhaps this was more than merely a place to store magical weapons.

"Let's see here . . . any mage worth their salt would go after the book, wouldn't you say?"

Grumph nodded. Books and magic were practically synonymous; whatever lay down that route would certainly appeal more to a spell caster than blades or shields.

282

"And almost every warrior puts more stock in their blades than their shield," Thistle continued, looking at the other symbols etched into the wall. "Even if we expand the interpretation and assume some might look at it and expect to find armor, by and large I'd say the warriors of the world would go after the sword first. Especially if we assume it was adventurers expected to be stumbling upon this place."

"Probably was," Grumph agreed. He could already see where Thistle was going with this, but when the gnome got into a puzzle, it was best to let him work it all the way out.

"Meaning that the shield is by far the least likely of the three to be chosen by anyone. Or rather, the least likely to be chosen first. And, assuming there are more traps and dangers down each path, the odds of someone getting a second shot wouldn't be likely." Thistle turned to face his friend, only to find Grumph staring at him expectantly, clearly waiting for the big reveal. "Right then: so anything these builders might have *really* wanted to keep hidden would best be stored down the path with the shield on it, which means I think that's the one we ought to follow."

Grumph stared at the gnome, not moving so much as a massive foot in the direction Thistle was pointing. There was more to this—he could tell just from the expression on his friend's face—and given the stakes, he didn't plan on following until he was all the way up to speed. Thistle was getting a little too comfortable with keeping things close to the vest, and while that was fine around the others, he wouldn't tolerate it. They were partners, equals, and Grumph had no intention of letting Thistle forget that.

After a long moment—so lengthy that Thistle began to grow visibly uncomfortable under the fearsome, half-orc stare—Grumph finally rumbled out a couple of clipped words.

"What else?"

"Nothing else. That is to say, nothing else of substance," Thistle admitted. "Perhaps I might have the slightest of hunches, but even for a hunch, it is unsubstantiated and quite flimsy. More visual similarity than actual observation, if I'm being forthright."

"Tell me anyway." Grumph trusted Thistle with his very life and had for many years. But with that trust came the knowledge that Thistle, like most people too smart for their own good, could often twist logic to suit what he already thought. The rationale for going down the path with the shield seemed solid enough, but Grumph wanted to know all the factors that had gone into forming the decision. He would judge for himself just how sound they were.

"Very well; though, bear in mind that I warned you how insubstantial of a hunch this is." Thistle gestured up to the shield, pointing to the lower half of it. "Do you see how the shield is curved on its lower half, almost elliptical? Granted, this was drawn countless years ago, but to me, the shape seems a bit off. Added to that, if you mentally flip it over, the symbol looks far less like any sort of shield I've ever encountered and begins to look more like . . . well, like a gravestone."

Grumph could see the resemblance as soon as Thistle pointed it out—in fact, he couldn't unsee it no matter how he turned his head. It was strange, certainly, but far from inexplicable. It wasn't until Grumph thought back to Thistle telling him of his vision-meeting with Grumble that the pieces finally fell into place.

"He took you to a graveyard."

"Aye, that he did. Perhaps—no, probably—that fact and the symbol's appearance are nothing more than a coincidence. All the same, when coupled with our earlier analysis of what the most likely path to be chosen is, I can't shake the sense that this is the one we're meant to head down."

With the sound of heavy footsteps echoing off the stone walls, Grumph began moving toward the door with the shield over it, Thistle quickly falling into place at his side. It might be just a coincidence, Thistle hadn't been wrong about that, but it didn't feel like one. In fact, the more Grumph thought about it, the less like a coincidence any of this seemed. A hidden catacomb with an altar to Grumble, and when it finally opened, one of the few paladins of Grumble just happened to be outside the door?

"I think Grumble played us."

"Such was my suspicion when we laid eyes on the altar," Thistle agreed. "Though, when gods do it, it's called 'divine guidance' rather than hoodwinking, even if the latter is a far more accurate description."

"How long?"

"Hard to say; we are talking about a god, after all. Probably not before the goblin camp, since up 'til then I wasn't even a pawn. Almost certainly since we crossed into Alcatham, though. I've no doubt we were herded toward Briarwillow. Perhaps one of the roads we thought too risky wasn't actually so bad, or reports of trolls blocking a pass were exaggerated. Knowing Grumble, I'm sure he used a light touch, but we'd be fools to believe we came upon this place by ourselves."

"True." Grumph nodded. He tried to cast his mind back to their journey. As dangerous as things were on the open road, their path to Briarwillow had been almost boring. It should have struck him then that perhaps the only reason they were finding such an easy way was because it suited someone else's desires. "Lot of effort to get us here."

"Do you think so? I actually just had a far more disturbing thought, old friend. One that I will happily keep to myself, if you'd prefer not to lose any sleep should we survive this." Thistle looked up at Grumph and waited, not continuing until the half-orc chose to hear what came next.

After a few seconds of contemplation, Grumph nodded for Thistle to continue. No matter how bad things might be, there was no situation Grumph could conceive of where ignorance kept him safer than knowledge.

"It occurs to me that yes, Grumble might have gone to all this trouble to get us here, thus fulfilling some sort task for him, but there's also another option. Perhaps we are nowhere near what he ultimately wants us to do, and this is simply another step on the path he's herding us down."

Thistle had been right: that one was going to cost Grumph some sleep.

*　　　*　　　*

"Three doors," Gabrielle announced. "Sword, shield, and a book." She glanced back over her shoulder as Eric and Fritz entered the room, eyes catching the crudely etched drawing above their door. "And a sun above ours. So, quick thinking, people: which one did the evil priest take off down?"

"Seeing as he was wielding a wand and magic, I'm taking a wild guess that he's the book type," Eric said.

"Maybe, but after Gabrielle chopped his arm off, he might be looking to upgrade his defense," Fritz pointed out. "Shield seems like a solid bet to me."

"We don't know that these indicate what lies down the tunnels. It could be monsters, or magic that test the skills associated with the symbol. I doubt he wants anyone testing his defense right now." Eric paused, remembering that he was talking about a mage. "Or probably ever. The guy was only wearing robes."

"Robes, and a magic shield that I chopped through," Gabrielle reminded him. "But I'm with you; he seems like the type to grab a weapon before armor. Book is probably our best guess."

"Let's just hope that if there is some sort of magic down there, he hasn't found it yet," Fritz said. "He seemed awfully skilled with magic already."

"All the more reason to hurry." Gabrielle didn't wait for the others to bring up any more points of discussion. She started jogging for the doorway, quickening her step as she entered the tunnel.

Faced with the options of continued debate, thus leaving Gabrielle to charge through a labyrinth alone, or simply just following the barbarian, Eric and Fritz made the choice that, while not exceptionally rational, was as rational as they could manage under the circumstances. They broke into a light run, hurrying to catch up to Gabrielle before she found another split in the path and left them on their own.

*   *   *

Talcia, Timuscor, and the summoned boar all entered the new chamber with great hesitance, even after Talcia cast another of his danger flash-spells and found it completely safe. Bolting across an entire room of deadly traps left one's nerves a bit on edge. This was especially so for Timuscor and the boar, who hugged the sides of the room while Talcia tried to decide which path they should go down.

"The book seems the most personally interesting for me, but we're supposed to be looking for either artifacts or the priest, so I've got no idea which way either of those might be," Talcia admitted after several moments of contemplation. "Any thoughts?"

"It's all the same to me," Timuscor said. "I tend to let the others figure this sort of problem out. We could always let Mr. Peppers choose; he seems to have good instincts."

"Who in the nine hells . . . wait, did you name the pig?"

"Well, he *looks* like a Mr. Peppers, doesn't he?" Timuscor nodded to the snorting boar, which was currently sniffing the ground in front of the door with a sword over it.

"You do know that within the hour he'll dissolve back into the mana he was conjured from, right?" Talcia looked back and forth between the knight and the pig, wondering if he'd accidently let himself be paired with a madman. "I just don't want you to get attached."

"Who's getting attached? Things have names; now the boar does, too. Come on, I think he wants to go down the sword one."

"I don't recall ever agreeing that letting the pig choose was a good idea," Talcia pointed out.

"Mr. Peppers likes the sword tunnel, and I want to trust his instincts. He was the only one of the five to make it out of that room, you know. That makes it two to one, so we out-vote you." The matter evidently settled in his mind, Timuscor headed toward the tunnel under the sword symbol, pausing to scratch Mr. Peppers on the top of the head as he passed.

Talcia weighed his options carefully. He could argue the point, insisting that they not follow a summoned pig down a mysterious tunnel, but the truth of the matter was that he didn't have any idea which path would be a better alternative. Plus, strange as Timuscor might be, he'd tried to save Talcia's life when he thought they were both about to die. That certainly earned him a bit of leeway, at the very least.

All of those things aside, though, Talcia was not a rookie on his first adventure. He knew well that a mage's lifespan was often defined by how motivated those with physical prowess were to keep them alive. Given that Timuscor was the one with the armor, shield, and muscles, it seemed prudent to stay on his good side for as long as possible.

"Wait up, I need to check for danger," Talcia called as he followed the knight and the boar down the tunnel. He watched his steps carefully, for while he was reasonably sure summoned animals didn't go to the restroom, it wasn't an incorrect assumption he wanted to coat the bottom of his boot with.

*   *   *

Blood stained the priest's gray robes, testaments to injuries that had been incurred in crossing the bridge and later sealed away by magic. That power was running low; by his estimate, he might be able to mend one more small wound, but anything serious would have to be handled the old-fashioned way. In his current state, there was a good chance those damned adventurers could get the better of him if they caught up, especially if they were able to manage a half-competent strategy. Given how well their ambush had gone, he'd have been a fool to discount such a possibility, and the priest of Kalzidar was not a fool. A merciless, twisted, self-absorbed sociopath, certainly, but not a fool.

All that remained now was to try and fulfill his mission. If there were artifacts to be had in these trapped tunnels' depths, then perhaps one would allow him to turn the tables on his pursuers. If they were useless to him, he could only hope that Kalzidar would reward him with more magic for completing his task. Gods, wicked or just, had to reward those who did their duty, for no mortal served without proper compensation. How he would revel in using his master's power to turn the adventurers to ash. First would be the woman in the red armor, that bitch who'd taken his arm. She would be first and last, as he would make her spend decades cursing the day she had ever crossed him.

Another turn in the tunnel's winding depths and suddenly, he had arrived at his destination. The priest stepped carefully into the new room, wand at the ready, and examined his surroundings. As he gazed upon the splendor before him, a dark, curved smile sliced its way across his face.

He'd been hoping for power, and he was not disappointed.

Chapter 34

It became apparent that, though there were many paths through the tunnel they'd taken, Thistle and Grumph were slowly closing on one of the few possible destinations. This was demonstrated by the half-dozen tunnels that merged into their own as they continued downward, continuing on their trek to whatever awaited them at the path's end. Both were alert, lest they be mistaken for enemies by their friends or caught off guard by the priest, but with every tunnel that joined into theirs, it seemed more apparent that Thistle had been right about at least one thing: no one cared to go down the path of the shield.

At last, the ground beneath their feet leveled off, and stretched out before them was the largest room they'd seen since entering the catacombs. With high ceilings and broad walls, it felt almost like stepping back out into the world above, where one wasn't entirely surrounded by a mountain. Thick stone rectangles jutted up from the ground at regular intervals, wrapping their way around the entire length of the room. Each was slightly taller than Grumph, and nearly twice as wide. Resting in the center of the floor, surrounded on all sides by those rectangles, was a stone table. Though neither Thistle nor Grumph could make out the top of it from the end of the tunnel, they both immediately headed for it. Each was aware the room might be trapped, just as they understood that both of their skillsets were better suited to reacting to such threats rather than trying to discern them.

Nothing sprang at them as they walked noisily across the floor, only the echoes of their footsteps caring enough to greet them. In no time, they reached the table, and wordlessly, Grumph reached down, gently gripping Thistle by the back of his belt and lifting him onto the structure. It was a testament to how absorbed Thistle was by their surroundings that he didn't even bother to mumble complaints, but instead merely fixed his gaze on the table's surface as soon as it was in view.

Etched into the stone top were dozens of tiles, all with various runes and symbols carved into them. Lining the edge of the tiled surface were solid squares, each with their own unique marker. Additionally, there was one other solid square in the center, this one being the only blank piece present. At a glance, it was clear that this was a puzzle meant to resemble the very room they were standing in. Thistle reached out slowly, gripping one of the tiles with his small fingers. He found that he could slide the stone puzzle piece freely, but that it refused to lift even the slightest of inches away from the surface. Releasing it, he turned his attention back to the board as a whole, taking it in and trying to see the patterns that lurked within the chaos.

"I suspect," Thistle said at last, gesturing absentmindedly to the stone rectangles, "that these are all meant to be treasure chests. From what I can see, this puzzle can be solved in any number of ways, but each one only allows the center piece to be linked to a single other rectangle. Presumably, that opens our metaphorical chest, allowing its contents to be plundered, and likely triggers some sort of resetting mechanism that kicks us out, tries to kill us, or simply bars us from opening any others."

"So, we guess?"

"That was my first instinct, I'll admit, but as I studied, another thought occurred to me: this puzzle is exceedingly easy. Too easy, if we're being frank. It's like filling your house with silver so robbers will be too busy plundering to notice the gold under the floorboards." Thistle leaned forward, nearly toppling from his perch on the table's edge as he studied the pieces carefully. "I think that, just maybe, there is another puzzle hidden within this . . . that I might be able to loop the pieces in such a way that the center piece connects back to the center piece."

Grumph reached forward, ready to grab the gnome if his eagerness proved greater than his balance. "What will that do?"

"Possibly nothing. Perhaps kill us. But if the gods are on our side, then there is the slightest chance it might open up something the common grave-robbers and looters were never meant to uncover. The only way to find out is to give it a go."

They were already deep in a hidden catacomb that might or might not be housing countless relics of dangerous power, guarded by a horde of barely restrained undead outside, and trapped in the labyrinth with a powerful servant of a wicked god. Really, what was one more chance at death compared to what they were already facing?

"Do it," Grumph rumbled.

Thistle, needing no more encouragement than that, knit his eyebrows together as his forehead creased and his brain went to work. Seconds later, he moved the first tile and became utterly absorbed in his task.

*   *   *

Gabrielle was only saved by the glimmer of movement she caught out of the corner of her eye. Reacting without thinking, she jerked back around the corner and into the tunnel they'd been emerging from. The blast of what looked like black lightning struck where her foot had been only moments before, cracking and singeing the stone. Before the others could say a word, Gabrielle barreled forward, sprinting past the entrance and into this new room. If they stayed in the tunnel, whatever was attacking them could pin them there and have easy shots to pick them off. Better to keep the targets spread out and moving. Plus, if it went for her, then the others would have time to slip out as well.

The room around her was massive, filled with a half-dozen unnatural contraptions. Each was wide and complex, comprised of metal parts with arcane runes scrawled across them. The only element she recognized was drawn over the tops of holes in the contraptions' fronts: crude images of body parts.

"Elegant idea, isn't it? A very practical way to limit how much anyone can take from here."

The priest's voice drew Gabrielle's attention, and she jerked her head around to find his location. It was easily discovered, as the man in blood-stained gray robes was making no effort to hide. He stood proudly, slightly off-center in the middle of the room, cocky smile fixed firmly in place once more. For once, however, his arrogance was not his most striking feature.

No, that honor went to the skeletal black arm fixed in place where his left one had once been. It ran all the way from the shoulder to the fingertips and seemed to crackle with pulsing, dark energy that zipped between the symbols carved into the dark bone.

"How . . . ?" Gabrielle didn't know what words would finish that question, but she did understand, on an instinctual level, that this would change the fight she'd been expecting into something dangerous and different.

"The machines don't actually check to see that the whole limb is there. They just make the cut and give you your prize. As I said, ingenious and brutal, which is fitting. Magic like this always comes at a price." The priest nodded to a machine near him, one showing an image of an arm over a hole that was, unlike the others, completely sealed up. "You actually did me a favor, you know. If not for your crude attack, I might have hesitated in doing what was necessary."

Gabrielle took a step back, shifting her body weight and preparing to dodge whatever attack he threw next. The priest made a gesture with his right hand and that damned wand appeared in it once more. He raised his skeletal left arm, pointing the palm toward her, and tilted the wand slightly off to the side. The bastard was planning to box her in. Licking her lips, Gabrielle raised her axe, doing all she could to appear menacing. If his attention wavered off her, even for an instant, it could be disastrous.

"Truly, Kalzidar has rewarded me for my loyalty. I was hoping you'd be the one to find me. There is so very much I cannot wait to do to you." The priest took aim and prepared to strike, but just as energy gathered on his left palm, a noise came from behind him. He tried to spin around, which turned Eric's deadly strike at the heart into a stab through the priest's right shoulder. It was still enough to earn a scream of pain as the blessed short sword carved out a chunk of gray-garbed flesh.

"What is it with you people and arms?"

Even as Gabrielle tried to rush forward, hoping to capitalize on the window Eric had opened with his attack, she could already see that things wouldn't go that smoothly for them. Raising his left hand overhead, the priest made a fist and slammed it to the ground, sending a shockwave of dark magic blasting outward. Despite her charge, Gabrielle was still far enough from the center that it did little more than push her back.

Eric, being right next to the source, was not so lucky. He was sent sailing back in the air, a short-lived flight stopped suddenly when he slammed into the nearby wall. His short sword clattered to the ground as he slid down the stone and landed in a crumpled heap. Not so much as a stir of movement could be seen from his limp form.

"See what happens when you try to—" The priest's words cut off in mid-taunt when he managed to pull himself up and get a good view of Gabrielle; what he saw stilled his tongue and left him seriously questioning many of his life's choices leading him to that point.

Gabrielle's anger, the thing she'd been slowly trying to learn how to coax and control, tore through her at the sight of her oldest friend in the world lying motionless on the ground. Not since the night she saw her goblin tribe being slaughtered had her rage been so intense or so focused. Her body, moments ago singing with pain and soreness, felt as light as a dagger and ten times as deadly. The axe, still burning her palms, felt as if it were thrumming full of energy, begging her for the sweet taste of blood on its blade. All of this made for quite a terrifying sight, but it was not what had caused the priest to go silent. His quiet came from a fact of which even Gabrielle herself was unaware.

As fury took hold of her, coursing through every inch of her body, Gabrielle's golden locks had turned pitch black, and the axe in her hand had started to glow. Though the priest didn't know what these things meant, he'd been around magic enough to know they certainly weren't good signs. Given time, he might have been able to formulate a hypothesis on which magics were in effect, but time, like a normal left arm, were items not afforded to him that day.

With a scream that would make the very specter of death shrink back, Gabrielle raised her axe and charged.

* * *

"Last piece." Thistle stepped carefully around the table's edge, rechecking his work to make certain everything lined up. As dangerous as it was to try and complete a puzzle like this in an irregular fashion, trying and failing would likely have even worse consequences than success. "Be ready for anything, I suppose."

"Always am." Grumph smiled a toothy, half-orc grin as he carefully pulled his blade free of its sheath and brought a spell into his mind.

Thistle finished walking the length of the table, then, as carefully as he could manage from his bent over position, he slid a finger over the last tile out of position and pushed it into place. As soon as it went in, an audible *click* rang through the air, and the table began to shake beneath Thistle's feet. He leapt back and was snatched out of midair by Grumph, who immediately started walking backwards.

Before their eyes, the table Thistle had been standing on slid to the left, revealing a stairwell descending steeply into the unknown. After a few moments, the table stopped shaking and went silent, only its new position proof that a change had happened at all.

"Gold under the floorboards," Grumph said, recalling Thistle's earlier analogy.

"Seems someone else agreed with my way of thinking." Thistle started forward, and then paused to see if Grumph was following. The half-orc took a shortened step, not to overtake Thistle, but to show that he was committed to seeing things through to the end.

The two went down the stairs, more of the stone torches bursting into blue flame as they went. It was a short trip; unlike the tunnels above, this was not meant to be a winding excursion. They'd moved beyond the part of the dungeon meant for show and into the section only the designers were intended to see.

After just a few moments, the stairs came to an end, and the duo found themselves in a small room with a single altar in the center. Glowing runes encircled the stone, weaving around it before splitting off and going under the walls, presumably to other parts of the dungeon. Power hung heavy in the air, so tangible that Thistle almost felt as though he'd be bowled over by it. Instead, the gnome steeled his resolve and continued forward.

Resting on top of the altar, beating softly, was a dried-up heart. If one peered very closely, they would notice the slight tear in its center, like it had been pierced by a blade. As they watched, both noticed that, with every beat of the ancient organ, the runes around it pulsed slightly. Thistle tossed one of his daggers across the circle, half expecting to see it turn to dust or explode into pieces. Instead, it landed with a dull clatter on the floor. Thistle called it back, using the same high-pitched whistle as always, but found that the dagger stayed just where it was, resting on the ground.

"Interesting. Either things in the circle can't be taken out by magic, or once something is in there, it can't escape. Suppose we'd best see which it is."

Before Grumph could stop him, Thistle hurried forward, passing over the runes just as his dagger had and remaining wholly intact. He scooped up the weapon and returned it to its sheath. He readied himself to try and escape, but then realized how much louder the heart's beating was now that he was in the circle. It was entrancing. Without meaning to, the small paladin turned his head upward to where the heart lay. Every contraction and expansion seemed to pull him deeper, each motion of the magically animated organ drowning out the logic trying to tell him that this didn't seem exactly right.

Thistle hadn't even realized he was reaching for the heart until his hands entered his field of vision. Even as he understood what his arms were doing, there was no stopping it. Working without his approval, his hand wrapped around the heart and lifted it from the altar.

The room around him seemed to explode in light, and Thistle felt the entire world fall away from under his feet. He didn't know where he was anymore, but it damned sure wasn't the dungeon.

Chapter 35

Using magic was, in many ways, like riding a horse. Mastering it took skill, practice, and effort, all in the hopes of slowly getting better a bit at a time. That said, no one had ever become so good at directing a horse that they understood exactly what the animal beneath them was thinking; nor could they predict every technique being developed by other riders in the world. So it was with magic. Knowing what magic could do, and how one could use it when it submitted to their power, was not the same as understanding everything it was capable of. Magic was like a wild animal, able to be bent to the will of a firm hand, but truly a servant of no one.

The priest, as an experienced practitioner and student of the arcane arts, knew this fact well, which was why he tried to scramble out of the way of Gabrielle's axe as she came screeching at him, murder blazing in her eyes. Defensive spells sprang to mind, but he had no idea what the magic she was wielding might be capable of. Worse, he deeply suspected she didn't have the slightest idea herself, and that made what she was doing downright insanity.

Unfortunately, all the rational thought in the world didn't change the fact that Gabrielle had been training herself for—and had gained crucial experience in—melee battles, while the priest usually hid behind enchantments and lackeys. He backpedaled as quickly as he could, weaving between the machines as the furious barbarian swung that sizable axe like it weighed no more than a sentiment, tearing huge chunks out of the stone wherever she struck. Ducking under one of the limb-severing mechanisms, he took the brief respite to let his wand dissolve and grab some folded creations from the depths of his bag.

Rolling around the other side, he hurled the parchment in the air, spat a command, and watched as the creatures expanded into large forms directly between himself and Gabrielle, who'd rounded the machine and was prepared for another charge. Hopping up to his feet and assuming a carefree demeanor as best he was able, the priest turned to face Gabrielle, now that he had some defenses in place.

"It was a . . . cute effort, but now I think—"

For the second time in so many minutes, the priest was unable to finish his taunting. This time, however, it was not based on groundless uncertainty, but on a sudden need to focus on running away. Gabrielle, seeming to scarcely notice the giant paper spider and paper snake on their respective sides of her, had plowed forward, hacking away at the enchanted obstacles with no regard for her own safety. She cleaved the snake in two with a single blow, ripping its head from its body and sending both pieces fluttering to the ground. The spider managed to tear at her armor with a mandible before the axe sliced into its belly, rending it in half.

As his creations died, the priest re-summoned his wand and scampered to put some distance between himself and the crazed barbarian screaming for his blood. Clearly, the paper servants weren't going to be very effective unless he overwhelmed her with them, and even he could only animate so many at a time. Casting was his only shot, but after all the healing and getting past the blades, his mana was running low. With no other option left, the priest decided to take a gambit he'd have never tried under ordinary circumstances.

Gabrielle rounded the corner of a machine just as he flipped his wand into the air; this time, he did not let it dissolve, but caught it with the skeletal fingers on his left hand. Instantly, the wand began to glow and crackle, as it could barely contain all the magical energy pouring through it. Whipping the magical implement forward, the priest spat out a quick arrangement of syllables, casting a spell that, in truth, should have required more mana than he had left in him.

Rather than fail, the spell exploded outward, shaping a massive, hulking humanoid creature made of twisted magic and shadow that came to rest only feet from Gabrielle. She slammed her axe into it, but the beast bellowed back and lodged its fist in her stomach, sending her stumbling backward. That it hadn't blown her across the room was a testament to her determination, but at last the priest felt his familiar sense of confidence starting to return.

With his skeleton arm to power the wand, this fight was as good as won.

* * *

Eric awoke to a sharp pain in his face, one that somehow cut through the myriad of protests coming from the rest of his bones and organs. His eyes shot open to find Fritz's staring back at him with gorgeous, honey-colored irises that he might have appreciated more if not for the fact that her mouth was on his nose, teeth visibly breaking the skin.

"GHRMM!" Eric tried to yelp in surprise, but the elf had her hand stuck firmly over his mouth. As the sounds of nearby battle reached him, Eric understood why she was muffling the noise and gave a slight nod to show he wouldn't scream.

Moving slowly, as if she didn't quite trust him, Fritz pulled away her hand and opened her mouth, releasing Eric from both of her grips.

"Why did you bite me?" Eric quickly rubbed his nose even as he whispered fiercely at her.

"Oh, you know, heard it was the newest dwarven kink, and I just had to see for myself. Why do you *think* I did it? Gabrielle is fighting for all she's worth, and you're over here napping like the dead."

Eric could only imagine how bad things were; the priest had taken him out of the battle with a single shot. True, he wasn't the toughest member of the party, but it was still an impressive display. Taking a quick inventory of himself, Eric was a bit surprised to find that, amidst all the bruises and pains, nothing seemed to be broken. Had he caught sight of the empty glass vial tucked inside Fritz's sleeve, the mystery would have been easily solved; however, Eric did not catch the telltale twinkling, and as such, remained unaware of his rescue.

300

Scurrying to his feet, he picked up his short sword and nearly rushed toward the sounds of battle before thinking better of it. He was of limited use in a head-to-head fight, but his previous attempt had shown that the priest could be caught off guard. Charging to Gabrielle's side would provide little help; it might even make things harder for her. Better to trust in her to take care of herself and try to work his way through the room, hiding behind the strange, arcane devices to see if he could get another shot at the priest's back. This time, he wouldn't miss.

It was a good plan, and as Eric slunk through the room, he knew it was the right one. Still, it was hard to keep that in mind as he heard Gabrielle's fearsome screams and saw the shadow creature bobbing into view, so tall its horned head popped over even the tops of the oversized machines.

*   *   *

Talcia and Timuscor (and Mr. Peppers) found no priest with a skeletal arm, nor puzzle with a dark secret tucked away in its hidden solution. Instead, they came upon a room stuffed with various weapons, gems, and jewelry on display. Many boasted black bones in the center of their workings, but some merely appeared to be enchanted, at least as far as Talcia could discern. In the center of the room, written in runes that seemed to shift and mimic whatever language the reader was familiar with, was a single warning:

"On Penalty of Death: Take only what is needed."

"I get the feeling that we're not supposed to touch any of this, are we?" Timuscor said. Some of the swords carved from the dark bones drew his eye, tempting him to try his luck. Timuscor resisted, since he rather felt that any tomb with this much magical security was unlikely to cheap out on the room of cursed treasure.

Talcia made a quick motion with his hand, causing his eyes to glow, and looked around. "It's a pretty standard ward, though I've never seen one this powerful. Basically, if we were in actual danger and needed a weapon to defend ourselves or others, the curse would let us take anything required. But if we're here just stealing . . . well, the results depend on the mage who sets the trap, though it's generally never a good thing. I could probably disarm it, given enough time to study the room's layouts and enchantments. We'd be talking days, if not weeks, though, so we're probably better off just letting things be."

"I suppose we can at least stand guard here, lest that priest find this place and manage to arm himself." Timuscor turned back to the doorway, just in time to notice the boar rooting around in a small pile of jewelry. "Mr. Peppers! Leave that alone before you get yourself killed."

The boar immediately yanked its head out of the pile and trotted obediently over to Timuscor. Talcia watched the display with detached curiosity. He'd summoned many a creature before, and while they were made to be obedient by the magic, this was the first time he'd seen one take a shine to someone other than the summoner. It turned and stood next to Timuscor, coming up past the knight's knees, tusks pointed back toward the tunnel entrance. By Talcia's count, the spell should unwind itself soon. After seeing Mr. Peppers, though, he decided that perhaps he might do well to study summoned creatures more once he was back at the mages' guild.

Neither Timuscor nor Talcia, for the attention they paid Mr. Peppers, noticed that he'd left the pile with a small silver ring wedged firmly onto one of his many crooked teeth.

*   *   *

Thistle was drifting through a world made of light, all direction and sense of feeling suddenly meaningless. It was impossible to tell how long he spent there with nothing around him; time had faded back into the illusion it had always been. Thistle only knew that he was there for some while, and then he heard the voice.

"I never thought I'd meet another."

The light, formless and featureless and peaceful, began to fill with new colors, a world taking shape beneath Thistle's feet. Land came first, gray-and-brown dirt filling up with the sharp green of grass. It stretched out before him, turning dark as it climbed upward, becoming hills and then mountains. Above his head, a bright blue sky nearly blinded him, but then his eyes adjusted and Thistle understood where he was standing. He'd only seen it in paintings and heard of it through the mouths of travelers, but the craggy peaks of Baltmur were hard to mistake for any other kingdom.

A rattle filled Thistle's ears, but before he could turn to see the source, it stepped up next to him. The man from his visions, whom he'd seen only a few nights ago, stood by Thistle, staring at Baltmur with a curious expression—almost like pride and regret stoppered in a bottle and shaken until there was no telling where one ended and the other began.

"So, Grumble finally roped another one into taking up the mantle." He stared down at Thistle, a twinkle in his dark eyes and a surprisingly charming smile tucked into one corner of his mouth.

"What? Can't a gnome just decide that armor is the right look for him?" Thistle glanced down at himself, only to realize he still had the shriveled heart in his hand. It was somewhat embarrassing, though for the life of him, he couldn't figure out exactly why.

"It's possible, I suppose. But I know because you're here, holding that. So much of my body, nearly all of it really, was pillaged after my death, the hungry and ambitious trying to turn what I was into something they could wield. It took the minions who worshipped Grumble centuries to steal all of the pieces back. They built an entire tomb in secret, filling it with traps and seals to keep the curious away, even laying my cursed skull outside the entrance to sicken any non-worshippers who came too close. That, however, was never lost. It always remained in the hands of the loyal, until one came who could destroy it. Only a fellow paladin of Grumble could have met me here, could have held my heart without being burned by it."

Thistle looked the man up and down, noting his strong jaw and powerful features. "Sure we're talking about the same Grumble? Kobold, about eye-level with me, rules over the minions and henchmen of the world?"

"And slaves," the man added, meeting Thistle's gaze. "One need not be a gnome or goblin to be captured and sold as a child."

"Aye, I suppose they don't." Thistle turned away from him, eyes back on the outline of Baltmur, the kingdom in the mountains. "Seems to me you had a bit more magic than a mere paladin, though. From what I saw, anyway."

"Showed you that, did he? Bet he didn't even tell you what's really going on here. I remember having to work on nothing but visions; damn near drove me crazy more than once." The man pointed up to the tips of the mountains, where supposedly, there was a steep path that was the only way into Baltmur's depths. "Is this kingdom still home to many of the 'uncivilized' species of our world? Do the travelers tell of going there in hushed tones, like they're speaking of the dead, with grand stories of trolls, ogres, and other monsters running amok on the roads?"

"It's not exactly a favorite travel destination, no," Thistle admitted. "Shall I take the curiosity to mean that you have some sort of history there?"

"In a manner of speaking." He lowered his hand, but kept his eyes trained on the mountains. "I founded it. Carved through the mountains myself. It was meant to be a kingdom dedicated to Grumble, a place where the trod-upon of our world could be safe, free to live as they saw fit, not as the powerful forced them to."

Thistle tilted his head back and absorbed the information. He'd certainly heard many terrifying, fearful rumors about Baltmur, but in retrospect, that was always from travelers and adventurers. Never had Thistle ventured there to see it with his own two eyes. Perhaps what the stories told wasn't of a place that was openly hostile, merely one where different creatures were in power.

"Hold on; did you say you carved mountains? As in, whittled them as I would a piece of oak?"

"I thought you saw the fight," the man replied.

He had Thistle there; from the battle he'd witnessed, it was no small feat to believe that someone with so much power could form mountains to his liking. Still, none of it made sense—first and foremost being how he'd managed all this. Paladin powers were nothing to sneeze at, but the scale he was describing was far beyond what even the greatest paladin was capable of. Really, it was beyond anything a mortal should be able to do.

"Were . . . were you a god?"

"Not technically, no," the man admitted. "But I did manage to steal a piece of divinity from one. And boy was he pissed when he couldn't get it back, even after I died. Though the magic spread out to all parts of my body, the core of it, the part that would let him reclaim his power, was tucked away, somewhere neither he nor his cronies could ever touch. A place only someone I could trust would find it."

Perhaps on cue, the heart in Thistle's hands beat, reminding him it was still there.

"I see. Glossing over how you stole a piece of divinity from a god—though I'd very much like to get back to that later—I must assume that since only paladins of Grumble can touch your heart, he's not the one you stole it from."

"Of course not. I've been loyal to Grumble all my life. It's why he protected my heart, and no doubt why he led you here to put me to rest." The man touched his chest where his heart should have been and gazed at the organ in Thistle's hands. "As for who I stole it from, I'd have thought that was obvious. Or didn't you wonder why I hadn't introduced myself yet? No name to give."

Thistle's breath caught in his throat as the game board he was standing on became suddenly clear. This was why a priest of the god of shadows had been sent as soon as the skull was found. This was why he'd been ordered to break open the door, no matter how long it took. This was why he was desperate to accomplish the mission, no doubt under threat of lifetimes of torture should he fail. It was all, every bit of it, to get at the pulsing heart sitting in Thistle's hands.

"Kalzidar. You stole a piece of Kalzidar's divinity."

Chapter 36

"How is that even possible?"

"The thing about wicked gods—and people in general—is that they always tend to assume the worst of people." The man slowly lowered himself to the ground, resting cross-legged as he stared at the mountains. This had the interesting effect of putting him and Thistle almost at eye-level. "When someone starts amassing lots of creatures generally used for evil, assumptions are made about what he plans to do with his supposed army. Back when this happened, Grumble was a fairly new god and not getting much respect from the rest of the pantheon. I guess Kalzidar thought he could make me a better offer. After a little discussion with Grumble, he gave me the go ahead to try my hand at a bit of deception."

Thistle stared at the nameless man, who, he was just now realizing, possibly might have been the very first paladin Grumble ever had. "While I do find that fascinating, I think we both know that's not what I was asking."

"I know, but some secrets must follow me to the afterlife. Look at what they did to me. Turned my body into cursed artifacts, buried the history of my existence, denied me even the right of peaceful rest, of ascending to be with my god. Do you truly want to know how to steal divinity, my fellow paladin? Knowledge and temptation go hand in hand, as I'm sure you're well aware."

The curiosity burning in Thistle's chest demanded he press the issue, but decades of experience cooled the fire with memory and logic. How many would-be tyrants had he seen destroy themselves, and countless others, in the pursuit of a grand idea of power? How many people, filled with good intentions, had reached that goal only to have it turn them into something hideous? Perhaps there were exceptions, but Thistle's ego was not so grand that he assumed he'd be one of them.

He'd witnessed his darker parts emerge far too often to deny their existence.

"I suppose you make a good point," Thistle relented at last.

The man nodded appreciatively, as if he'd been waiting for this answer. "Seems Grumble has gotten smarter about choosing his paladins since I wore the mantle. Were I in your shoes, I doubt I'd have been able to resist trying to uncover such a secret."

"Aye, I'm the living physical incarnation of self-restraint and prudence. Or perhaps I simply wanted to skip to the issue at hand. You said I was here to do something with this." Thistle lightly jiggled the beating heart still clutched carefully in his hands.

"If you would be so kind, I'd like to ask you to destroy it." The man bowed his head, tilting his eyes until they were completely obscured by his brow and dangling dark hair. "Free my soul, let this pain come to an end, and—most importantly—annihilate the divinity residing in my body so that Kalzidar can never reclaim it and will be forever weakened."

"Something tells me this is going to require some sort of massive quest fraught with peril and constant danger," Thistle said.

"It did when it was begun, but you have come at the end of the journey. All I have been waiting for is a paladin of Grumble to take up the heart and bring it from the shadows into the sunlight. A simple task, if not for the fact that our kind are seen so rarely and that Kalzidar has hidden all rumor of this tomb's existence to keep others from questing for it, even as he himself desperately scoured the lands to find it. Only Grumble's will could have brought you here, so close to fulfilling the ritual and setting me free."

"He is a wily one indeed." Despite knowing he had been manipulated, Thistle found his own heart softening toward the kobold god. If this had all been about some pissing match, Thistle might have had harsh words the next time they met, as well as firm instructions as to

308

where Grumble could shove the paladinhood if he thought Thistle would be a willing pawn. But . . . to rescue one's servant, a man who needed help and had only his god to turn to, that was something Thistle could forgive. It was, after all, part and parcel with what he'd known would come with being a paladin: help the helpless, defend the defenseless, and fight for the common good no matter the personal cost. This, he supposed, fell within those parameters.

"So then, are there any special instructions I need to know when I get this into the sun?"

"A minor incantation, but most of the magic lies in the act of a brother paladin bringing it from the shadows into the light," the man said, raising his head and meeting Thistle's eyes. "But you need to be aware of another issue: my heart is what powers and supports this entire structure. The moment you take it out of the circle, everything will begin to collapse. You must make haste to leave this place as soon as possible, lest you be caught in the destruction."

Thistle let out a long, exasperated sigh. "That could be a problem. You see, I have friends in other parts of the catacombs. I won't leave them to die."

"Nor would I ask you to." The man creased his brow and visibly bit the inside of his cheek as he pondered the issue. "As the power source, my heart has some inherent connection to the rest of the catacombs. I believe I can teach you a few tricks to help your friends evacuate as well, if you're willing to learn them."

"Learning is quite possibly the only thing I do exceptionally well." Thistle dropped down into the grass, making sure to hold the heart out directly between him and its former owner. "Please, if it will help the others, I beg you to teach me."

The man reached his own hands out. Mimicking the grip Thistle had on the heart, he mimed as if he were holding one himself. Only when his hands were a perfect mirror did he begin, making a forceful pressing motion with his right thumb.

"First, you need to push the outermost valve like so . . ."

*   *   *

Rage was failing her. Furious as Gabrielle was, she was still unable to do more than tear off a few measly chunks of shadowy flesh from the malformed monster attacking her. It certainly didn't help that the priest would alternate between blasting at her with shots of that black lightning and healing his summoned warrior using some other sort of dark magic. In fact, it was only the creature's substantial bulk that shielded her from most of the priest's ranged attacks, as the hulking creature made shooting past it nearly impossible. While the priest no doubt could have reoriented himself, doing so might have let Gabrielle close the gap and attack him, and he seemed wisely set against such a possibility.

She swung hard, tearing away a slice of the monster's dark flesh, which fell to the ground and pooled like spilled ink, only to evaporate seconds later. It responded by charging, swing a meaty fist directly at her. Gabrielle managed to block with the hilt of the axe, but the blow still shoved her backward. By the time she recovered, her hard-won wound was healed, no doubt thanks to the priest standing behind the creature's back.

It was infuriating, yet fury seemed to do her no good. All of her anger was allowing her to survive against this thing, but beating it seemed impossible. As things stood, it was only a matter of time before she ran out of strength or the creature landed a lucky blow. She was going to lose. She was going to fail her friends. She wasn't strong enough to get the job done.

—I can make you stronger.—

Gabrielle was shocked by the voice in her head; however, she didn't betray it outwardly as she circled her opponent, searching for a weak spot. She had, after all, known this was a cursed axe when she bought it. Sudden voices hadn't been part of the selling pitch, but one had to expect these sorts of things when dealing with unknown magic.

310

"How?" She spat the word, no doubt making the priest think she was losing her mind and talking to herself. He could think her crazy as a town drunk for all she cared; all that mattered to her was whether or not the voice could keep its promise.

—**Magic. My magic. There is a toll, of course.**—

"Out with it, already." Gabrielle took a few steps back, preparing to charge. If this thing could really give her the strength she needed, then she was going to make use of it as soon as possible. If not, well, she still had to attack anyway. Might as well get into position.

—**Pain. Blood. Life. The only things worth taking.**—

Not exactly what she'd expected, but well within the lines. This was the axe that hurt to touch, after all. And there was no denying it had power. She'd cleaved through a magical shield with it already; perhaps it would be able to even the odds and let her take the bastard priest down for good.

"Give me every fucking thing you've got, and take whatever you want in return." With that, Gabrielle burst forward, heading right for the shadow creature's chest. In her hands, the axe went from merely burning to feeling as though she were gripping a blade fresh from the forge. It took everything she had to hang on, to refuse to let the pain overwhelm her fury. As she neared the creature, Gabrielle raised the torturous weapon and readied a strike. One blow would determine whether the axe really could make a difference. One blow would determine whether she was still in the fight.

Her axe made a harsh, sizzling whistle as it tore through the air, cleaving through the arm the dark creature had tried to guard with as if it were true shadow. The weapon continued, burying itself in and passing through the creature's chest without so much as slowing down. For a moment, Gabrielle's momentum carried her so far forward that she slammed into its torso, nearly losing grip of her axe as it carved its way through the magical monster. Then, just when she'd feared it was a failure, that damned axe proved its worth.

The beast exploded in all directions, coating the room in the ink-like substance that quickly began evaporating almost as soon as it hit. A wave of it splashed across the priest, whose confident sneer vanished as quickly as his monster. He stared in unmasked terror as Gabrielle pulled herself up from the ground where she'd been knocked in the blast and set her murderous gaze directly on him. It was a moment she would have relished, if not for the fact that she took one step forward and nearly collapsed.

Blood was dripping from her arms and back, jagged slices taken from her flesh like she'd been worked over with a knife. The pain cut through her rage-cloaked mind, sending her staggering and nearly toppling to the ground. So, this was the toll her axe took for its power: agony given to others meant agony for her as well. Digging deep into her mind, Gabrielle tried to wall off everything around her. The injuries, the fear, the uncertainty, even the self-doubt . . . she sent it all away to be contemplated later. All that existed for her was the priest. Her target. The man who'd murdered her best friend and was trying to kill her too. She found the strength to right herself and finally turned her attention back to the man she wanted dead.

Unfortunately, in the time that Gabrielle had spent regaining control of her body, the priest had recovered his composure as well. He raised the wand, still gripped in his skeletal, magical arm, and smiled as he prepared to unleash whatever dark spell had entered his mind. All it would take was a few motions and a couple of words, and that would be the end of Gabrielle the barbarian. She was too far away to make the charge, and even standing was taking everything she had. Blocking or dodging were completely out of the question. Still, she refused to close her eyes as he began his incantation. Gabrielle would at least meet her death head-on like the warrior she was.

It was this determination that allowed her to see the silent figure slip out from behind one of the mechanisms still scattered throughout the room and steal up behind the priest. He might have noticed were he a touch less concerned with the dual actions of casting and gloating, but in his hurry to seize victory, he ignored the single telltale sound of a sword whistling through the air.

The priest was unable to ignore the next sound that filled the room, as it was of the skeletal arm, still clutching his wand, clattering onto the ground, a bit of his shoulder going along with it. Before the priest could react, before he even had the chance to feel the pain and scream, a boot appeared from behind him and kicked the arm across the stone floor, over to where Gabrielle was still processing the fact that she wasn't about to die.

A horrible, anguished scream hit her ears just as she was wrapping her head around the situation. The priest was staring death at Eric, who'd slipped back a few feet and had his short sword in a defensive position. Blood was spurting from the fresh wound, which was not closing up quite so easily as before.

"Again!" The priest stared at Eric in furious disbelief, as if he were unable to comprehend what had just happened. "You cut off my fucking arm again!"

"Technically, I don't think that one belonged to you," Eric shot back. From the corner of his eye, he winked at Gabrielle, and just like that, she understood the plan.

When the priest turned to deal with the taunting rogue, he momentarily made the mistake of forgetting about the barbarian to his back. Mustering every last bit of strength she had, Gabrielle hoisted the axe in her hands and charged. The hellish burning, like much of her rage, had died down at the appearance of Eric, but it still stung as she ran toward the distracted priest. That was fine by her. If the axe had popped into her head and told her it was demanding a leg for the next attack, she likely would have agreed to the cost. This man had killed an entire town full of people, nearly murdered Eric, and would have happily tortured her friends to death if given the chance. His time ended now.

As Gabrielle swung, the priest realized his mistake and began to turn, but unlike Eric, she wasn't merely stabbing him with a short sword.

His movement this time only meant that her axe came bursting out of the left side of his stomach rather than the right, where she'd been aiming. His whole body shuddered in an involuntary spasm, and the nameless priest slid forward, landing limply on the ground.

Gabrielle smiled, even as she began to fall forward. A pair of friendly hands caught her by the shoulders. Eric stood next to her, staring down at the body of the man who'd taken so many lives as they waited for signs of stirring. Neither was so inexperienced that they were going to turn their back on a mage until they were sure he was dead.

"Good shot," Eric said, nodding at the axe-shaped hole in the man's back.

"You swing a pretty mean sword yourself."

"Meh, second time today someone's cut his arm off. At this point, it's just imitation."

"Then consider me flattered," Gabrielle replied. "Also, consider me worn to sh—"

"Attention everyone currently in the catacombs: this is Thistle, your friend and fellow adventurer."

Eric and Gabrielle both turned their heads, scanning around the room to see where the voice was coming from. The answer, as it turned out, was from everywhere. It seemed to emanate from every inch of the stone surface.

"Though I don't quite have time to explain how, I've found what we were looking for, and the time has come for us to leave this place. Very quickly, in fact. As soon as I finish talking, the whole place is going to start coming down, so everyone please hurry toward the surface. I've turned off all the traps, so it should be a straight shot. Just run for all you're worth. Thank you, and good luck."

There was scarcely enough time for Eric and Gabrielle to exchange confused glances before they heard an unmistakable rumble

314

come from the floor below them. Neither knew exactly what Thistle had gotten them into, but it seemed he hadn't been messing around.

With no other real option, they turned toward the exit and began to run with all the strength they had left, falling into line a few steps behind Fritz, who'd bolted as soon as she was told to.

Chapter 37

Talcia, Timuscor, and Mr. Peppers (who was still around despite Talcia being almost positive the spell's time had run out) were not engaged in any life or death fight when Thistle's announcement blasted through the catacombs, and thus wasted no time in immediately racing back up the tunnel they'd come down. For a moment, they feared they would get lost as the multitude of pathways that intersected on the treasure room began branching off again. But then Timuscor noticed that only the torches in one tunnel were still lit, so they decided to hurry through that route. It stood to reason, after all, that if Thistle could somehow magically turn off the traps and start collapsing the entire structure around them, he could probably set the torches to act as guides without much trouble.

They barreled along, moving far faster than they'd dared on the trip down, egged on by the creaks, groans, and rumblings coming from deeper in the labyrinth. When they reached the room filled with trapped tiles, the first visible evidence of their predicament became clear.

All along the walls and floor, cracks were splintering through the pristinely decorated tiles, sending several tumbling to the ground, where they shattered into fragments, often starting more cracks with their impact. It was daunting enough to give the group pause, save for Mr. Peppers, who kept right on running like the building was coming down, which, of course, it was. Timuscor and Talcia followed the boar's plan, bolting through the room nearly as quickly as they had the first time.

It was on the far side that they heard the howl ripple through the air, a dark, foreboding wail that seemed to bubble up from the catacombs' depths. Their feet, already moving with ample motivation, managed to find a bit more speed as they fled for the relative safety of the exit.

*　　　*　　　*

Grumph was clearly in a bad mood as he sprinted through the crumbling stone building, carefully clutching Thistle to his chest, who, himself, was holding the still-beating heart as though it might shatter at the slightest glance. Watching Thistle touch the heart and then pass out, eyes white as a soft summer cloud, had been worrying enough. Hearing the gnome's plan once he finally snapped out of the trance had almost been enough to make Grumph wish they hadn't found the damned heart in the first place.

The half-orc leapt over a chunk of crumbled white stone, entering the room with the altar to Grumble set in its center, the first clue they'd had that things weren't quite as straightforward as they'd seemed. It was splintering into pieces as Grumph raced by it, the foremost corner gone as the altar started to tip forward. Soon it, like the rest of this place, would be nothing more than rubble: rubble . . . and several corpses if they didn't hurry and find their way out of there. Grumph surged back into the tunnels, wishing with all his heart that he'd demanded Dejy teach him a teleportation spell.

He was rounding a bend when he heard the same otherworldly wail as Talcia and Timuscor, a noise so horrific he actually slowed down so he could look at Thistle.

"Your thing?"

Thistle shook his head, wide eyes darting about as though a clue to the sound's source would be in immediate view. "No, I wasn't warned of any horrifying monsters tucked away or cursed, screaming banshees to watch out for."

"On our own, then." Grumph picked his speed back up, racing for all he was worth toward what he hoped was the entrance. A collapsing temple and heart containing stolen god-magic were more than enough on his plate; some unknown, ancient monster wailing from the depths was simply more than Grumph could accommodate.

He was a firm "one catastrophe at a time" kind of wizard.

As the sound of fleeing footsteps filled the room, the bloody, one-armed-once-more priest stirred from his prone position on the ground. This was no miraculous resurrection or sudden spell kicking in. They'd killed him, those adventuring bastards; there was no doubt in his mind about that. He'd seen death enough times, often as its dealer, to know when the inevitable moment had arrived. It would be soon, perhaps less than a minute or so, before the last vestiges of life drained from him like blood through cupped hands. A lifetime measured in seconds. Most would have laid their heads down, said a prayer, and tried to think happy thoughts. Most did not serve the god Kalzidar, or know of his punishments for those who failed to see his will done.

He could not succeed, that much was clear, but perhaps he could stop his opponents from winning as well. It wouldn't ameliorate Kalzidar's wrath entirely—nothing short of success did that—but it might buy him at least a touch of mercy. Besides, the priest was a spiteful man; it was part of why he'd sought the power Kalzidar offered in the first place. If he had to die, he would gladly sacrifice what precious little time was left if it meant revenge on his killers.

Flipping himself over—a strained, gruesome ordeal—the priest managed to lie on his back, staring up at the steadily cracking ceiling. He reached into the satchel at his side, filled to the brim with folded paper creations, and jammed his bloody hand in all the way to the bottom. Animating even one would take more mana than he had left, but a wily mage knew there was more than one way to wring magic from the world. Life had a magic of its own, and the force that was animating his dying body was no less powerful for the broken vessel housing it. Soon, it would dissipate when his body failed entirely—soon, but not quite yet.

Closing his eyes, reaching deep into his mind for the forbidden magic given to him by Kalzidar, the priest's arrogant grin returned to his lips one last time as he began to mutter the ancient arcane words. Pain beyond anything he could have imagined flooded his body as he literally began tearing himself to pieces, yet still he pressed on. This was the last thing he could do with his life, and he would either die trying or see it through. With every syllable, the torture increased exponentially, enough to have driven him mad if he weren't there already.

The last word was not so much said as it was screamed, a throat-tearing wail that rose up from the chamber where his corpse would rest to terrify all those hurriedly fleeing the falling catacombs. His work done, the priest's body slid lifeless to the ground, marked only by a soft thump as his head bounced off the stone.

Around him, however, life teemed as creature after creature poured from his satchel, growing in size as soon as they hit the open air. The room filled with the scraping of paper claws, the gnashing of paper teeth, and the clacking of paper claws. Fast as they left the bag where they'd been born, they poured into the tunnel, following the same line of torches as the others, following the only command that lived in their magically animated minds:

"*Kill them all.*"

*   *   *

Strange as it was to admit, Gabrielle was actually thankful that the axe's curse had taken its toll on her arms and back. If her legs hurt as bad as her upper body, there would be no hope of escaping before the catacombs came crashing down on them. As it was, running was a nearly hellish experience, as her cumulative wounds screamed through her brain, their presence no longer beaten back by battle-fog and fury. She made careful note of them, acknowledging they existed and requesting they kindly mute their protests until she and Eric were out of harm's more immediate way. Healing, likely both magical and mundane, would come later, at a time when she wasn't dodging small pieces of falling debris.

Eric, loyal as he was, stayed by her side as she mustered what was currently counting as a sprint. He was faster than she—always had been, in fact—but he refused to abandon her, even if it meant he would end up being crushed too. Gabrielle would have chided him, urged him to run ahead and save himself, but she didn't have the free breath to waste, not with her ribs groaning in protest. And it would be a waste, because Eric would no more abandon her than she would him, or Thistle, or any of the others. They were in this mess together, and only through relying on each other had they managed to survive so far.

Fritz, to her credit, was keeping pace well, though she seemed to keep turning periodically to look at what was going on back in the direction they'd come. It was possible her elven ears were picking up on happenings their human ones were missing, but since she said nothing, Gabrielle trusted it couldn't be that important. Or else it was, and Fritz was also too out of breath spare the words.

When the wail hit everyone's ears, they were only a few steps across the thin stone bridge, now mercifully unbothered by the swinging blades which had lodged themselves into the walls. None lost their balance at the horrendous sound, but Eric and Gabrielle exchanged a simple look that said it all: they'd forgotten to finish off the priest in their hurry to leave, and it was possible he'd had a final trick or two up his sleeve.

They hurried across the bridge, going faster than was either wise or prudent, yet, thanks to luck and training, they both made it to the other side unharmed. Eric was about to step into the tunnel that would lead them out of this deathtrap when a sound like pages rustling reached both their ears. Turning around, they witnessed a menagerie of paper beasts exploding into the room, pouring in one after the other, quickly filling up the platform that stood before the bridge.

"You have to be fucking kidding me." Gabrielle's eyes were wide as she took in the sight: dozens of animals and monsters, more numerous than she'd ever seen grouped together, all bursting out and staring at them with hollow, folded eyes.

"We should be running." Eric smacked Gabrielle's shoulder, causing her to wince but also kicking her into gear. He grabbed Fritz by the hand and began pulling the elf along, dragging both into the tunnel and urging them to move as fast they could.

Monsters or no, the paper beasts would still have to cross the bridge to get to them, and hopefully that would buy enough time to at least warn the others. As they ran forward, following the torches and desperately hoping that each turn would be the one that brought them back to the main entrance, their ears were assaulted by the constant sounds of rustling paper. It was so bad they almost didn't notice the rumbling and cracks of the crumbling catacombs.

Almost.

*   *   *

Thistle and Grumph were the first to make it back to the main entranceway, but they'd scarcely been there for more than a few seconds, scanning around to see if the others were there, when Talcia, Timuscor, and a pig Thistle didn't recognize barreled out of their doorway. The trio was moving so fast they nearly slammed into Grumph, who quickly spun to the side, taking the chance to set Thistle down before any of the others could see he'd been getting carried.

"Why are you holding a heart?" Talcia demanded as soon as he got a good look at Thistle and Grumph.

"Long story, but it's causing this place to collapse. We have to get it into the sunlight. Well, I do: has to be a paladin of Grumble, you see. As I said, it's a bit of a long story." Thistle checked both men to see that they were uninjured, and then his curiosity, so well-restrained with his fellow paladin, got the better of him. "What's with the pig?"

"Mr. Peppers," Timuscor corrected.

"It's a summon that I used to help find traps," Talcia said. "Though, at this point, I feel like it should have long ago dissipated."

"Perhaps all the magic in this place is sustaining it. You have no idea what kind of power is concentrated in these walls." Thistle turned away from the two men and their pig, searching for the rogue, barbarian, and trader that completed his group of friends. When he found no trace of them, the gnome's face began to fall. "I'd expected at least Eric to beat us here."

"He probably stayed with the other two," Timuscor suggested.

"Or whatever made that horrible screech caught up to them, and they're dealing with it," Talcia added. "Either way, we need to get clear of this place."

Thistle glanced down at the beating heart in his hand. He had a duty to fulfill and a promise made to a brother paladin to keep, but leaving the others to whatever fate had befallen them . . . Thistle didn't know if that was in him. Luckily, this was not the day he would be tested on the issue, as the sound of footsteps began to echo from the final doorway. Unfortunately, behind those footsteps was a tsunami of strange scurrying sounds.

"Paper monsters!" Eric yelled, bolting out of the doorway with the elf in hand and Gabrielle only a few steps behind.

Thistle suppressed a gasp when he saw the bloody, sliced up woman, as well as some very unpaladin-like thoughts about what he'd like to do to whomever had inflicted such wounds. Concern was brushed away by pragmatism, however, as Eric's words and the cavalcade of sound behind him fit together and explained their predicament.

"How many?" Grumph asked, already turned around and running for the exit.

"Hundreds, at least," Gabrielle called back. She, Eric, and Fritz had never stopped running, making a line straight for the crack in the massive door. The others took the cue, and the race to escape resumed once more.

"'Hundreds, *at least*'?" Thistle turned back over his shoulder, waiting to see the first folded creature emerge from the tunnel's depths.

"We didn't really have time to get a good look." Eric reached the exit ahead of all the others, and then whirled Fritz, whose wrist he was still gripping, forward and into the narrow exit ahead of himself. "But if I were to guess, I'd say there's as many coming as pieces of gold in a dragon's hoard."

"Right then, so we're running," Talcia agreed. He quickly followed Fritz through the exit, squeezing as best he could into the narrow gap. Though Gabrielle tried to resist, she was more or less shoved through next, as no one else was willing to leave her in danger given how injured she was.

Her once-more-blonde head had just disappeared into the crevice when the sounds of movement reached a crescendo and out burst the first of what appeared to be countless paper monsters. Grumph, however, had been waiting for this, and no sooner did the paper ogres and trolls appear than he released the spell he'd readied, dousing the paper creations in a blast of magical fire. They screamed as their bodies burned and sizzled, folding backward and momentarily blocking the doorway.

"Don't suppose you can do more of those, can you?" Eric asked.

Grumph merely shook his head. "No mana left."

"You bought us some time, old friend, and that might just be enough. Now go; you need the most time getting through there." Thistle nodded to the crack, and Grumph complied. He'd barely managed to recover enough mana for two small spells after the day's trials; it was best he left the floor to those who still had arrows in their quivers.

"Timuscor, you go next; then Eric and I will follow," Thistle continued. He happened to notice the pig grunting about under Timuscor's feet and added, "Mr. Peppers can leave when he wants, as I suspect he'll have no more trouble than I getting through there."

"With all due respect, I have to decline," Timuscor replied, staring at the smoldering remains of the monsters Grumph had slain. "You, Eric, and Mr. Peppers go ahead of me."

"We can get through a lot faster than you," Eric said. "I'm nimble, and Thistle's small, while you've got all that armor. It makes more sense for you get through first."

"Perhaps it would," Timuscor agreed. "But that's only if I intended to leave."

Chapter 38

Despite all the strange things Eric had borne witness to since leaving Maplebark, that moment in time would always stay with him as one of the more surreal: the sounds of slowly dying flames being fed by murderous paper monsters serving as the background to a knight—a pig at his side—staring down a paladin whose stature was closer to the pig's than the knight's, neither seeming willing to budge.

"Those things will swarm us in the open area of the mountain," Timuscor said. "If there's as many as Eric and Gabrielle say, we'll be overwhelmed long before we can reach the surface, and even if we do, there's no guarantee they'll stop. These things die easily, but their attacks can still wound. We can't face that many."

"So, what's your solution here?" Thistle demanded. "Stay and sacrifice yourself for no reason, hoping that sates them?"

"Don't be ridiculous." Timuscor drew his sword and gestured to the crack in the doorway. "I can hold that position. If I go a bit in, they'll only be able to face me one or two at a time. If I can stay there long enough, then this place will come down and bury them under hundreds of pounds of stone."

"Them . . . and you." Thistle looked toward the flickering light of the dying flames. There wasn't much time left; arguing would only get them all killed for nothing. "You're right, Timuscor. One of us has to stay and stop them. So let it be me. I'm the paladin; this is my duty."

"You already have a duty in your hands, one that you must see through." Timuscor nodded to the heart, still beating in Thistle's grip. "You did say it had to be a paladin of Grumble, and as we all know, I am not a paladin, not of any god."

"Then why are you trying to die like one?" Thistle spat the words, frustrated and furious because Timuscor was right at every turn. One of them did have to stay. It couldn't be him because of his damned duty. Timuscor was going to win—he was going to stay and die for the others, and there was nothing the wily gnome could do about it. Some problems could not be solved by wit, no matter how much of it one might possess.

"Because it is the one way I can be a paladin." Timuscor kneeled down, meeting Thistle's eyes on their own level. "I remember so little about my life before you all . . . only bits and pieces, like a half-formed dream . . . but that desire shines like a beacon through it all. I want to be a paladin. It's the only constant thing I've had in this world. But I don't possess the heart of a servant, and it seems no god is interested in a man willing to do good without bowing. I will never get to live as a paladin; that goal is forever beyond my reach. But I can give my life protecting those in need, protecting the people I care for."

Timuscor rose from the ground, turning to face the doorway as the last flickers of firelight began to fade. He lifted his shield and readied his sword, gaze unmoving from the doorway where his enemies would soon be bursting forth.

"A paladin's life may be beyond me, but I can have a paladin's death. No man, nor beast, nor even god has the right to keep that from me. So please, Thistle and Eric, I beg of you, please go through that door. Let me save you. Let me save everyone. Let me live my dream, even if only with my dying breath."

Thistle stared at the armored man, a being who had once been their enemy and was now laying down his life to protect them. There were no words he could think of to dissuade Timuscor, and in truth, he didn't know that it was his place to try. A person's path was ultimately theirs to choose, and Timuscor had made his decision.

Motioning Eric to go through the crack in the doorway, Thistle began to follow, but then turned back. He looked at the boar and made a slight "come here" gesture with his hand, only to be completely ignored. Mr. Peppers, it seemed, would at least be there to keep Timuscor company. As Eric moved toward the crevice and the sound of a fresh attack echoed from the tunnels, Thistle faced Timuscor's back and lowered his head.

"For what it's worth, I will always remember you as the bravest paladin I've ever met."

"It's worth more than you can imagine," Timuscor replied. He still faced away from the gnome, for that was his duty. He would hold the line while the others escaped. He would stop the threat, no matter the cost.

With nothing else to say, Thistle took his leave through the massive door's crack, slipping easily back to the outside world . . . or at least to a mountain that wasn't falling to pieces around him. Timuscor began backing up quickly, wedging himself deeply into the opening so that none of the paper monsters would be able to slip past.

Mr. Peppers stood near his feet and snorted, tusks at the ready as the second wave of monsters came barreling into view.

"I know you're not real, you know. I'm not crazy," Timuscor said to the boar, rather effectively undercutting his argument of not being insane. "But . . . I've always sort of felt half-real too. I know what it's like. Our kind have to stick together."

With a grunt, Mr. Peppers seemed to signal his agreement. Then the time for talking was done, as a paper bear lunged forward across the entranceway, sharp, folded claws swiping directly for Timuscor's throat.

*   *   *

"We're it," Thistle said, following Eric back into the mountain's cavern.

"What do you mean, you're it? Where's Timuscor?" Gabrielle demanded.

"Doing one of the bravest things I've ever seen, and it'll all be for nothing if we don't get out of here," Thistle said, barely keeping himself from snapping at the poor barbarian. "I've got a feeling this mountain won't be a safe place once a giant tomb in its center collapses."

"Thistle's right, we have to go." Eric stood in front of Gabrielle, blocking her from trying to charge back through the entrance. "You can hit us all you want later on, but right now, just trust that this is the only way to give our friend's choice meaning."

For a moment, it seemed that Gabrielle might go for her axe. Her hand raised, reached halfway back, and then fell onto Eric's shoulder. "When you tell me the full story, I'd better damn well agree with you, or there will be hell to pay."

"Deal." Eric looked around, noting that Fritz and Talcia were whispering to themselves. "Something wrong?"

"No, nothing at all," Fritz replied. "We were just wondering how long it would take for you to notice that Ferdy and the undead are gone."

Eric blinked in surprise, and everyone quickly did a scan of the cavern. Sure enough: no glowing green spells, no animated corpses, no surly sorcerer, none of it. He could vaguely make out footprints moving through the dirt, but there was no way of telling when those had been made.

"Maybe they left?" Eric suggested.

Dumb an idea as it was, there was no chance to mock him for it, as a loud snapping and groaning sound filled the cavern. Thistle, it seemed, had been right about the structural integrity of where they were standing, and the race to freedom wasn't quite over yet. A large section of the walkway began to splinter, and that was all the prodding they needed to get back into gear. With hurried steps and more than a few glances back to where their friend was ostensibly spending his final moments, the group ran up the walkway even as it started to crack and crumble, hurrying toward freedom.

*   *   *

Not yet.

Timuscor raised his shield, deflecting a paper scorpion's stinger and chopping off the tip of its tail. He barely dodged a blow from a paper tiger as it swung its fearsome claws and scraped the side of his armor. With a kick to the tiger's midsection, Timuscor knocked it off balance and sliced its flank with his sword. Near his feet, Mr. Peppers drove his tusks into a paper spider's legs, sending it reeling to the ground, where he stomped it into pieces.

Not yet.

A flurry of paper birds with beaks like razors swarmed Timuscor, pecking at his exposed face and trying to tear away his eyes. Sweeping his shield like a hammer, he smashed them into the wall, praying the cuts they'd opened wouldn't bleed into his eyes. A paper wolf lunged for his throat, and Timuscor met it with an overhanded slice, splitting it at the jaw and shredding all the way down its body. A paper cobra the size of a dog was right behind it; Timuscor beheaded the beast before its fangs could press against his armor.

Not yet.

Another bear slammed a paw into him with enough force that Timuscor might have been driven back, were he not already braced by the door. Ducking the next swipe, Timuscor stabbed upward, taking the bear just below its paper throat and cleaving it into mismatched thirds. He had a moment to right himself and take in the room as the next monster prepared to attack.

There were so many of them; the number seemed irrelevant at this point. They may as well be infinite, and he was just a lone man. Already, his muscles burned and blood pooled in various parts of his armor. They were chipping away at him, one fang and claw at a time. Easily as they went down, each made sure to take a piece of him with it. Timuscor was going to fall to them; he knew it with complete and utter certainty.

But not yet. He tightened his grip on the sword and met the charging paper unicorn below its horn, taking off the top of its head. Timuscor couldn't let himself die yet. Not until the ceiling came down, and these things were taken with him. Not until his friends were safe. Being a paladin didn't just mean dying as an act of sacrifice: it meant being willing to do whatever it took to see the job done, even if it cost a life. If he fell now, he fell as a man, a knight, and a failure.

Timuscor slammed his shield into a paper panther's face, spinning it about so he could cut through the torso. These things could have his life, if that was the price demanded, but they would only get it on his terms. No matter what it took, Timuscor would meet a paladin's end.

Just not yet.

*   *   *

There were many sunrises Thistle prized throughout his life. The one he'd watched with Madroria after the night she agreed to be his wife. The one he'd seen crest a snowy hill when they'd feared they would freeze to death before morning. The one that had risen on him and his small wagon when he'd set out to start yet another new life. But as he came more tumbling than running out of the hidden entrance to the mountain, Thistle's eyes fell upon the most beautiful sunrise he could ever recall bearing witness to.

It coated the sky with purples, blues, and reds, burning away the darkness for what seemed like the first time in weeks. He bolted down the steep landscape, heart still clutched firmly in his hands, racing toward where the mountain's shadow would end and the first rays of sunlight would hit the paladin's heart. Behind him, the others followed, all keeping a few paces back out of both respect and prudence. After all, while Thistle hadn't given anyone but Grumph the full story yet, they could recognize dangerous magic when they saw it.

Thistle was only steps away from stepping into the light when the cloud appeared, dark as a starless midnight, stretching over the sky and barring him from the precious sunlight that would put his miserable journey to an end.

"What . . . how . . . *Kalzidar.*"

It was, of course, impossible for a cloud to laugh, but Thistle got the distinct impression that this one was doing just that. The dark mass whirled through the air, spreading out in all directions, blotting out even the charcoal grays of the fading night sky with its dark curtain.

Thistle's hands tightened around the heart as he watched the cloud spread. Before, he would have only seen it as an inconvenience, trusting that not even a god could block the sun indefinitely. Now, with Timuscor either dead or dying as a result of this wicked divinity's servant, there was no patience in Thistle's heart. Instead, it burned with the righteous fury of one who has seen a wrong done and will stand for it no longer. It was not an unfamiliar emotion to Thistle, but it was one he hadn't felt—hadn't let himself feel—for a very long time.

"O Grumble, he who cares for the beaten, the powerless, and the downtrodden. He who lends his ears to those with silenced voices. God of they who toil tirelessly, protector of the ones that cower, watcher of the weak." Thistle raised his hands high overhead, the heart in them beating so fast it seemed like it might burn itself out. "O Grumble, god of the minions, as your paladin I call upon you and ask: *Are you really going take this shit?*"

Above Thistle's head, the cloud seemed to boil, rolling and twisting through the sky, almost like it was convulsing in pain. For his part, Thistle closed his eyes and tried to focus on what he was praying for. Sunshine, enough to bathe this whole damned kingdom in it. To burn away the shadows where Kalzidar hid, to tear back the darkness that had festered here for too long. Thistle wanted to stand in the sunlight again, even if only for a moment.

Since his eyes were closed, Thistle didn't see the beam of light that broke through the cloud, but he felt it warm his body. Without opening his eyes, Thistle rattled off the words he'd been given by his fellow paladin. They were gibberish to him, a prayer from a time long before Thistle's days. Yet, with every syllable, he felt the heart moving, expanding, growing so big it was all he could do to keep the thing in his hands.

Then the final word came, and Thistle opened his eyes. As the last of the prayer slid from his lips, the heart began to glow with a golden light. It was burning, beautiful, too magical to look away from, yet too painful to watch. The heart grew lighter and lighter until Thistle was holding more sunbeam than organ. Just as it seemed it could grow no brighter, the heart began to dissolve. Flecks of golden light fell from his hand like grains of sand, burning away into nothingness before they touched the ground.

A sound, not unlike a far-off, distant scream, seemed to come from the sky, and Thistle suspected he heard the slightest bit of kobold-like laughter tickling his ear. At last, it was done, his mission in Briarwillow finally complete.

Thistle lowered himself to the ground, ready to take a moment of rest. That was, of course, when he heard the explosions begin.

Chapter 39

When Timuscor heard the first blast, he mistook it for a sign that the catacombs were finally coming down in earnest. Then another followed, and another, and it began to occur to him that something about them seemed unnatural, even for a situation where he was in a collapsing tomb fighting paper monsters. Mr. Peppers, scratched and bloody but still in the fight, reacted to them like he'd been waiting all along for such sonorous explosions.

Turning away from the paper snake he'd gored with his tusks, Mr. Peppers faced Timuscor, stamped his hoof once, and charged. Unlike all the other attackers so far, Mr. Peppers was able to catch the knight off guard, as Timuscor hadn't been expecting a blow from the only ally he had. Mr. Peppers did not, however, try to gore his friend by using those sharp tusks that had felled so many paper opponents.

Instead, Mr. Peppers used his tongue to free the ring he'd wedged on a crooked tooth, revealing a bright green gemstone that had faced the inside of his mouth. Twisting the trinket around carefully, Mr. Peppers slammed into Timuscor's leg, gemstone first. The two tumbled backward from the force, a fact that sent Timuscor's brain reeling since he'd been sure the door would stop their momentum.

When they finally landed—heavily at that—Timuscor quickly scrambled to his feet, lest the paper monsters should overtake them. So focused was he on incoming attacks that Timuscor failed to notice that there were no monsters. Or catacombs, for that matter. He was standing in the sunshine, a bit bright for so early, as explosions rang through the air. Turning in place, he found himself staring at his friends, who had their backs to him as they stared at the mountain, big chunks of which were collapsing inward, sending billows of dust into the air.

"But . . . I was supposed to die."

Mr. Peppers came up next to his legs, silver ring with a now-cracked gem still stuck in his mouth. Timuscor stared down at the boar

333

that, technically, wasn't still supposed to be there, and then scratched it carefully behind the ears.

"Good boy. I think." While he didn't understand precisely what had happened, Timuscor lived in a world of magic, monsters, and the unnatural. The occasional unexplained event was simply part of life, and it seemed Timuscor wasn't quite done living yet.

"If everyone's watching that thing, waiting for me to come out, I'm afraid you're facing the wrong direction!" Timuscor's voice echoed across the open plain, easily reaching the others, all of whom spun around at the sound, half-ready for another fight or more divine trickery. After they stared at him for a moment, everyone rushed forward, gripping the knight in embraces so fierce he feared he might accidently lose his life after all.

As deaths went, though, being smothered by the people he loved wouldn't be such a bad one.

*　　　*　　　*

"Wimberly's bomb . . ." —Russell threw the dice out in plain view, results intended for all to see— "succeeds! The blast sends the last of the wizards tumbling to the ground, leaving him prone until his next turn."

"That would be a lot cooler if his turn wasn't next," Cheri grumbled. Chalara had taken a beating in the battle and was down to only a few points of mana, which meant she was stuck on the sidelines while her friends cleaned things up. The fight was going their way—Timanuel scoring a critical hit and crippling the first of the trio of wizards at the start had been a huge boon in their favor—but she'd been playing SS&S for too long to count a battle as done until the bodies were beheaded.

"It is his turn indeed, but getting up still takes an action," Russell said. He glanced down at the module for guidance on the final wizard's plan. Wimberly's arcane bomb had knocked the poor guy down to only a few health points, and this was likely to be his last round of combat. The module usually had instructions for moments like these: final words or taunts, occasionally actions they would take when knowing their end was at hand. For this wizard, Russell had to flip through the pages to a section of the fight table, and what he found there gave him pause.

"Does he get up, or try to cast from the ground?" Tim asked. His turn followed the wizard's, and as a paladin, it didn't feel right attacking a downed opponent. At the same time, those wizards had tried to kill the party already. He'd feel a lot better about the whole thing if the wizard died on his feet, at least.

"He, um, he teleports." Russell stared at the instructions, checking them and double checking them to make sure it was right. Somewhere in his binder, he'd copied down this page, but it was clustered up with the appendix, nowhere near the juicy bits Russell had made certain to keep on hand. "According to this, he activates a ring of teleportation he'd been saving, allowing him to teleport freely."

"Horsecrap, he just now uses the thing?" Cheri found herself simultaneously annoyed and impressed. Chicken shit as it was for the last boss to duck out, she had to admit it was a good way to string quests together. "Let me guess, now we have to chase him to the ends of the earth to finish this once and for all."

"I'd actually be up for that," Bert said.

"If there are forests," Alexis added.

"Well, you definitely don't have to go chasing after him," Russell told them. "The wizard reappears at the other end of the room, standing over a small chest with arcane runes running up and down it. Before your eyes, he pulls out a dagger and presses it into his torso, coating the blade with his heart's blood."

"Holy shit, are you kidding me?" Cheri leaned forward, waffling between looking at the figurines on the map and her brother, who seemed to have gone a shade or two paler than minutes before.

"I wish. He pulls the blade out, presses it to the chest at his feet, and then looks up at you all and says: '*Better sealed from the world than in the hands of your kind.*' Then he touches his hand to the bloody dagger, and a blinding flash fills the air. When you can all see again, the wizard is slumped over dead, and a new set of blood-red runes are woven around the entire chest."

"What the hell was that?" Tim asked. He was the only other one to have seen things go awry once before, but he seemed more concerned with Russell than the game.

"Let me check it out." Cheri tossed her die onto the table, fingers crossed for a high number. "That's a twenty-two for my Arcane check."

"You . . . you know what it is," Russell said, slowly regaining his composure. "It's a blood seal, one of the highest forms of magic. The wizard gave his life to make that chest impossible to open—at least, impossible without a powerful archmage to undo the spell."

"Must be something really powerful in there," Bert speculated. "Do we have a clue what's inside?"

"Since your party will be looting the tower's top chamber anyway, I'll go ahead and give you this." Russell peered down at the writing in the book and swallowed, reminding himself that it was just words on paper. What he was seeing was a coincidence, nothing more. "The wizards have various notes scattered about their lab about a magical artifact they'd recently discovered. While they were taking pains to study it without triggering its latent magic, they speculated that it might have a myriad of different properties, most prominent of which was the power to connect their realm to other worlds."

"Oooh, dimension hopping. Now that's a good hook." Cheri nodded approvingly. "But I guess first we have to get the thing open."

"Wimberly will immediately begin investigating the chest from every angle, searching for physical flaws to exploit," Bert declared.

Russell nodded and motioned for him to roll, but the GM's eyes quickly found their way to Tim's. An artifact in the game that could impact other worlds . . . it was a long stretch to assume that was what had caused the events of their previous game. But both had watched Tim's die spin itself into dust with no explanation. Both knew that there was more to this than logic could readily explain.

For now, all they could do was keep playing. Once the session was over, however, Russell planned to pore through his notes and see if the book matched up with what he'd taken down. If it did, then he could relax, knowing that he was letting one unexplained incident get the better of him. If it didn't, though . . . well, Russell didn't actually have a plan for that contingency. Should that happen, he would officially have to decide whether to push it all aside and pretend it never happened or take another step forward and embrace theories that would technically mark him as insane.

At this point, he really didn't know which path he would choose.

*　　　*　　　*

"You're sure he's back in town?" Fritz, quite possibly for the first time since Gabrielle and Grumph had met her, seemed anxious as they rode through the farmlands toward the town of Briarwillow. This was doubly surprising since the "he" in question was Ferdy, a man they'd never seen muster a single cordial word for the elven trader.

"I cast a Finding spell, and that's what it told me," Talcia reiterated. "Plus, his horse was gone."

"Along with hundreds of undead." Eric's head kept moving as he rode, scanning the area lest an army of undead villagers burst out from hiding and overwhelm them. He didn't imagine his warning would make much difference in that sort of situation, but there was always the chance of escape if nothing else.

"Should we be worried about that? I mean the undead, obviously, but also the fact that we were all exposed to that cursed skull

337

back in the mountain." Gabrielle, despite the concerns she was voicing, felt far better than she had only an hour prior. Thistle had used the last of his daily healing to patch the worst of her wounds, and while she would still need rest and more healing, it was a world of improvement from where she had been.

"I think we'll be fine," Thistle assured her. "As it was explained to me, destroying the heart also destroyed every other piece of his body and the magic therein. A curse with no magic is simply ill-will, and it shall take more than that to bring all of us down."

"Well, that's one thing in our favor, at least." Eric noticed movement coming from up the road and held up his hand to halt the others.

It was a lone figure atop a horse, riding toward them slowly. Eric could feel the others tense; daggers were drawn and spells prepared. A whoop from Fritz broke the heavy worry in the air, as she leaned forward in her saddle and pointed to the oncoming figure.

"It's Ferdy!"

Sure enough, within minutes the young sorcerer could clearly be made out, and he waved at them as he approached, signaling his friendliness just in case they hadn't realized who he was. Soon, he'd covered the ground between them, and Ferdy slowed his horse to a halt, staring at the bloody, burned, and dust-covered party with curiosity and perhaps a tinge of admiration.

"You know, I was absolutely certain I was going to have the more interesting story to tell when you all emerged, but now I fear that may not be the case after all."

"It seems only fair that you at least get to go first, especially since we're all wondering what happened to you and your hundred or so undead opponents," Thistle replied.

Ferdy looked away, the most sheepish expression any of the adventurers had seen him make since their respective meetings, and then

338

turned his horse around and headed back toward town. "Let's ride and talk. Some of this will be easier to accept if you see it for yourself."

The others, not having any real option, and having planned on heading in that direction anyway, complied with his request and began to move forward once more. They rode for nearly five minutes before Ferdy spoke, and when he did, it was with a sense of humility that seemed utterly foreign in his proud voice.

"I overestimated myself. I thought that with Talcia helping me get started, I'd have the mana and focus to keep that many undead at bay. Sometime after you all left, though, it became clear I was wrong. My magic began to fail, and eventually, a cluster of undead broke free of their binding. At that point, I was sure I had reached the end of my journey. As they rose from the ground and began to approach me, I expected to be ripped limb from limb or eaten outright—perhaps even made into an undead myself. The last thing I anticipated, however, was what they actually did."

Ferdy slowed his pace just a touch, making sure everyone was in earshot for the next portion of his story. In the distance, Eric could make out the beginnings of Briarwillow and what seemed like movement between the town's buildings.

"They asked me, very politely at that, to let their friends and family up from the ground. No threats, no undead moaning, just a straightforward request. I honestly think they were far more afraid of me than I was of them; they kept talking, and then darting backward, like they expected me to hex them. Since it was going to happen soon anyway, I decided to take a chance and comply. I released the spell. The rest of the town rose from the ground . . . and proceeded to ask me for directions on how to get back to Briarwillow."

"Wait, so they came back to life?" Gabrielle asked.

"Oh no, they were still very much corpses. Magically animated undead through and through," Ferdy told her. "But it seems that without anyone holding the skull and ordering them about, their own minds returned. They were quiet, nice, farming folk, and they insisted on leaving the mountain and getting back home. I think they were afraid of the place, honestly. Since my job was to watch over the undead, I made a judgment call and followed them back."

"Interesting," Thistle said. "And they were still up and moving when last you saw them? They didn't suddenly drop into corpses an hour or so ago?"

"I've been with them until one of the men I asked to watch for you gave me the signal that you'd been spotted," Ferdy replied. "Why on earth would they simply stop moving?"

"The skull that commanded and cursed them was destroyed, so I assumed they would return to being, well, normal dead." Thistle turned the facts over in his head, trying to figure out what their continued existence could mean.

"Though I'm not a necromancer, I do know a little something about their magic," Talcia butted in. "While the skull might have made these people sick and been used as a totem for control, we don't know if it was used as the source of magic for the undead change or whether it was merely the impetus. If I cast a spell from my staff, for example, the spell doesn't end if you break the staff. If, however, I enchant my staff to glow, that will be destroyed with the staff's physical form."

"Great, so now we have a whole town of undead to deal with." Gabrielle started to reach for her axe, but then halted her hand. Perhaps the time for battle would come, but she didn't fancy gripping that weapon until the need was truly upon them. Having tasted such strength and paid the price for it, Gabrielle found herself with a sudden appreciation for restraint.

"You really don't; that's what I'm trying to tell you." Ferdy pointed up the road to where the buildings of Briarwillow were in plain view. "Listen, just come with me and see. Showing you will do what words never could."

340

With that, the group began to ride faster, hurrying down the road until they began to pass the outskirts of Briarwillow. What met their eyes was something that, even with Ferdy's warning, none of them could have ever imagined.

It was just like the first day the adventurers had come to Briarwillow. The streets were flooded with activity: booths were being set up, the smell of food just beginning to cook filled the air, and on top of it all, the citizens of the town darted about in a flurry of motion. They were preparing for another festival, and from the looks on everyone's faces, they seemed downright enthusiastic. It should have been a quant, heartwarming scene to walk into after the hard battle they'd fought.

Except, of course, for the teensy little problem that every one of those excited faces wore the telltale pallor of the undead.

They rode slowly through the streets, taking in the sights around them with a mix of relief and apprehension. The idea of not having to fight an entire town was deeply appealing, certainly, but none of them were quite certain this constituted a good ending. After all, Briarwillow was a moderately well-known outpost on the kingdom's roads, and when word spread that the plague had lifted, it would be filled with travelers once again. An entire town of undead, however, was not the sort of thing a proper kingdom tolerated.

It was Grumph who summed it up, twisting in his saddle to look at Thistle, whose own eyes seemed half-vacant as he took in the sprawling scene before him. "What now?" Grumph rumbled, capturing their complex sentiments as only he could.

Thistle looked up at his old friend, then at the others who had followed him bravely into the darkness of the mountain, and finally at the townsfolk that were flitting about, being sure to steer clear of the scary adventurers atop their horses.

"Personally, I am going to see if the woman with the meat pies will be setting up a booth. I don't know about the rest of you, but I after the night we've had, I am simply famished."

Epilogue

"Knock knock, little brother." Cheri stood in Russell's doorway, carefully observing the way he was staring at a piece of notebook paper clutched carefully in his slightly shaking hand. Russell was sitting on his bed, surrounded by a sea of papers and the module book, gazing into the scrap of writing like it contained all the secrets of the universe. "Thought I'd come check on you; after the game, you seemed a bit anxious."

"Smudged." Russell lifted his head to face her and pointed to the center of the page in his hand. "It's smudged. Like I spilled a drop of water on it, and it made the ink smear. I took down so many notes from this module, I worked so hard to make sure I wasn't going crazy, and now the one thing that would make it clear is, itself . . . smudged." Russell began to laugh softly to himself. "I swear to God, if I were playing in a game and the GM pulled this, I'd probably think it was brilliant. Never letting me know for sure, leaving me in a state of uncertainty."

"Okay, that's enough of all this." Cheri strode forward into the room, yanking the page out of her brother's hand and promptly tearing it in half. Russell tried to take it back from her, but a lifetime of noogies and horseplay had long ago established Cheri as the alpha sibling. She pushed Russell back and ripped up the page again and again until it was nothing more than confetti.

"Why . . . why did you do that?"

"Because it was a smudge. It was nothing, but if I'd let you, you'd have spent days obsessing over it, trying to see something that wasn't there." With a clap of her hands, Cheri cleared the scraps of paper from her fingers, then reached forward and plucked the module book from Russell's bed. He hurled himself forward, clearly ready to go to the mat over that item, but Cheri merely flipped it open and scanned to the back.

"You want to go down this road, that's fine. My summer was going to be boring anyway. But we're not going to be passive little bitches about this. Your note idea was a good one, and it seems like you think you found a lead doing it. That lead is gone, though, so it's time to stop sitting around, waiting for the truth to find you like an NPC. You think something strange is afoot? Go after it like an adventurer."

"A lovely speech," Russell replied. "But without an actual plan, it's just words."

"How about a little faith in your big sister?" Cheri flipped the book around and stuffed it back into Russell's hands, her finger resting on a single line near the very bottom of a paragraph of fine print. "Every quest starts with a call to action and usually a single clue. Here's yours: *Swords, Spells, & Stealth* might be the ones who publish these modules, but Broken Bridge is the company that's been writing them. If something screwy is going on, then they might know something about it."

Russell stared down at the small line of text, barely visible in its small font and black-on-black background. It was like they'd gone out of their way to bury the name of the creation company, the exact opposite of what most such places demanded. How had he never noticed that before? It was one more mystery on the growing pile, but at least this thread could be pulled. For the first time in a very long while, Russell didn't feel like he was stuck in a situation. Now, at last, there was a chance to start taking matters into his own hands.

"Thank you." He looked up from the book to find Cheri still staring at him, concern evident on her face. "For this. For . . . for not assuming I'm crazy."

"Oh, I think you're crazy as *hell*," Cheri replied. "But crazy is a lot more fun than sane, if you ask me." She turned and headed for the door, but stopped on her way out. "You know, if you're reeeeeeeally feeling grateful, you could always tell me what's in that chest we found. The whole party is dying with curiosity."

"Would if I could, but the module doesn't say," Russell replied. "Evidently, there's no one in the area it covers who can break a blood seal, though it does seem to hint that there might be a character in later expansions."

"Fucking corporations; ain't that always the way." Cheri shook her head and let out a resigned sigh. "Well, buy the damn expansion as soon as it comes out. I'm sort of enjoying this group you put together. Also, I'll deny it in front of the others, but you've shaped up to be a pretty good GM. At least, not the worst I've ever played under."

With that, Cheri was gone, leaving Russell to contemplate whether he was more unnerved by the possibility that he was losing his mind or that his sister had actually said something nice to him.

*   *   *

"Talcia almost has the teleportation spell ready." Ferdy leaned through the doorway of the inn's dining area, currently filled only with the adventurers, Fritz, the boar at Timuscor's feet, and a single undead cook who was stirring wonderful-smelling soup in a massive pot.

"Thanks; be a doll and let him know I'm on my way," Fritz replied. Ferdy took the time to give her a dark look, and then complied with the request, heading back to the open area outside town where the elder mage was completing the ritual.

It hadn't come as much surprise that those of the magical ilk didn't want to hang around in a town of the undead, so when Talcia said he was going to open a gate back to Cadence Hollow, no one tried to convince him to do otherwise.

"Now, you two take care of yourselves," Fritz said, rising from the table and locking eyes with Grumph and Gabrielle. "No unnecessary risks, no crazy bandit fights in the forest if they can be avoided, none of that. I'm counting on hearing some great stories from the two of you next time we meet, and that can't happen if you up and die on me."

Gabrielle got up from her chair, leaving a half-eaten pile of bear meat on her plate, and embraced Fritz in a powerful hug. "No dying for you either. What if we need to buy one of those fancy carts? Who else but you will give us a fair price?"

"Well . . . not that fair." Fritz returned the barbarian's hug, though she took great care not to touch the axe strapped to her back. As they broke apart, Grumph stepped in, offering the elf his massive hand. She accepted and the two shook, a sight that would have sent the less tolerant from both their races into absolute fits.

"Be careful," Grumph said, doing his best not to accidently crush the woman's slender hand.

"Keep taking care of this lot. I don't know how they survived for three days without you, but I doubt it will happen again." Fritz ended their handshake with a quick wink. By the time she turned, Eric was there, hand also sticking out, though he looked more awkward than Grumph had.

"Oh, so you were fine grabbing my arm in the deadly catacombs, but now you get all shy," Fritz quipped.

"That . . . was just me making sure everyone was keeping up," Eric replied. Though he'd given it no thought in the heat of the moment, it was an awfully familiar way to hold someone he'd barely met.

Fritz, thankfully, seemed to have little care for formality. She grabbed Eric's hand, and then pulled him forward, catching the normally nimble man by surprise and wrapping him in a hug.

"Thanks for making sure I was safe," Fritz said. She leaned deeper into the hug and whispered her next words into his ear so softly that only Eric could hear them. "You're kind of cute, though. Get a little confidence, and you might not have to play the hero to get me in your arms again."

Then they were parted, Fritz with a sly expression on her face and Eric suddenly turning so red it looked like Fritz had hexed him.

Which, in a way, she had. After all, not every magic requires spellcasting.

Timuscor was waiting to say goodbye next, Mr. Peppers still standing by his feet. No one had yet been able to figure out why the boar was still present long after the spell had ended, and after Talcia was convinced not to dismiss it, the group collectively decided to just chalk it up as a weird aftereffect from being around so much potent magic. Mr. Peppers grunted by Fritz's feet as she and Timuscor shook hands—no sudden hug or teasing words for him—and just like that, the elven traveler had reached the final adventurer.

"If I may, I would like to walk you out to the teleportation site myself," Thistle said. "One can never be too careful, after all."

"Why thank you, brave paladin. I gladly accept your offer." Fritz pushed open the wooden door, allowing Thistle to step into the bright afternoon sun. All around them, the festival was building to a full swing, every member of the town thankful to have control over their bodies once more, even if said bodies didn't work in exactly the way they remembered.

"Do you think these people will be all right?" Fritz asked, watching as a cluster of undead men carried a load of lumber across the street.

"Honestly, I have no idea," Thistle admitted. "But they aren't evil, and they aren't hurting anyone, so it's not my place to tell them their way of life is wrong. The world, I fear, will not be quite so accepting, though."

"Talcia has promised to explain the happenings to the Table of Mages, who will in turn speak to the leaders of Cadence Hollow. Perhaps with a bit of determination and persistence, we can convince them to lend the town aid, or at least not treat it as a hostile entity." Fritz began heading up the cobblestone road, walking lightly as they made their way toward the site of Talcia's ritual. "And what of you and yours, my brave paladin? What quest will you next venture on?"

"I can't say I have much of a quest in mind," Thistle admitted. "But this experience did ignite some curiosity in me. If my friends are willing, I think we may head farther north, make our way in the direction of the lone road into Baltmur. After learning of its origins, I find myself with a desire to see the kingdom firsthand."

"It's supposed to be dangerous," Fritz cautioned.

"And Briarwillow was supposed to be peaceful," Thistle countered. "Danger, whether we like it or not, comes with the life that we have chosen."

"Ah, the mighty adventurers, journeying across the lands. Yet, in all my travels, I can't say I've ever met any others quite like you five." Fritz looked down at Thistle, an unmistakable twinkle in her eye. "Why do you suppose that is?"

"I will happily answer that question, my fine trader, if you can tell me why it is I'm certain I know you, and yet have no memory of your face."

For the first time since Thistle or any of the others had met her, Fritz appeared visibly taken aback. Her eyes narrowed, and for an instant, the playful mask of the traveling elf slipped away. In that moment, Thistle could see the true mind at work, and he found himself unexpectedly intimidated.

"You, brave paladin, have either led a very interesting life or possess a will harder than iron."

"Likely the former over the latter," Thistle replied. "Shall we let it rest there, then? I mean you no ill will, and in fact would be happy to count you as a friend, if you would have me."

A smile bloomed on Fritz's face, and, with that, she was back to her usual self. Like glimpsing a crocodile swimming in a lake, though, the vanished threat didn't change what one knew was there. Still, as she stuck out her hand, Thistle accepted the gesture, for he'd meant his

347

words. Fritz was someone he would like to have as an ally, especially if his other option was an enemy.

"We are friends, Thistle. You and I, and all the others as well. Friends who trust one another and would never needlessly speak behind the other's back."

"That is a cornerstone of friendship," Thistle agreed.

Their hands parted, and they began walking once more. Soon, Talcia and Ferdy were in view, the elder of the two waving his staff about as he finished the last of his incantations. As the air around him began to flicker—a hole in space opening up in the soft dirt of a barren corn field—Fritz glanced at Thistle one last time.

"A word of caution to a friend: Even for a paladin, making enemies of gods is a dangerous game. Do not assume Kalzidar will take your slight lightly. Always keep your guard up, always be at the ready. What you have, your odd little family, is more precious than you can possibly know. There is no shortage of people and monsters in this world that would take it from you."

"Aye, that's a lesson I've already learned once." Thistle tilted his head back in the direction of the inn, where the others were likely slurping down warm bowls of delicious soup, the afternoon heat be damned. "I'll give everything I have to keep them safe."

"Then it seems, Thistle the paladin, that you are a good friend to have." Fritz stepped away from the gnome, walking over to Talcia and Ferdy, the latter of which greeted her with a glare. They turned and gave one last wave before stepping into the glowing doorway. Moments later, it vanished, leaving only the corn field, and Fritz's warning, behind.

Thistle began his walk through the village of the undead, back to the inn where his party was waiting.

About the Author

Drew Hayes is an author from Texas who has now found time and gumption to publish a few books. He graduated from Texas Tech with a B.A. in English, because evidently he's not familiar with what the term "employable" means. Drew has been called one of the most profound, prolific, and talented authors of his generation, but a table full of drunks will say almost anything when offered a round of free shots. Drew feels kind of like a D-bag writing about himself in the third person like this. He does appreciate that you're still reading, though.

Drew would like to sit down and have a beer with you. Or a cocktail. He's not here to judge your preferences. Drew is terrible at being serious, and has no real idea what a snippet biography is meant to convey anyway. Drew thinks you are awesome just the way you are. That part, he meant. You can reach Drew with questions or movie offers at NovelistDrew@gmail.com Drew is off to go high-five random people, because who doesn't love a good high-five? No one, that's who.

Read or purchase more of his work at his site: DrewHayesNovels.com

Made in the USA
Las Vegas, NV
26 January 2022